RHETT C BRUNO
TITAN'S RISE

TITAN'S RISE

©2019 RHETT C. BRUNO

Published by Aethon Books LLC.

Cover Art by: Jasper Schreurs

Cover Design, Print and eBook formatting and cover design by Steve Beaulieu.

CHILDREN OF TITAN

- Book 0: **The Collector**
- Book 1: **Titanborn**
- Book 2: **Titan's Son**
- Book 3: **Titan's Rise**
- Book 4: **Titan's Fury**

**Pick up the whole
series.**

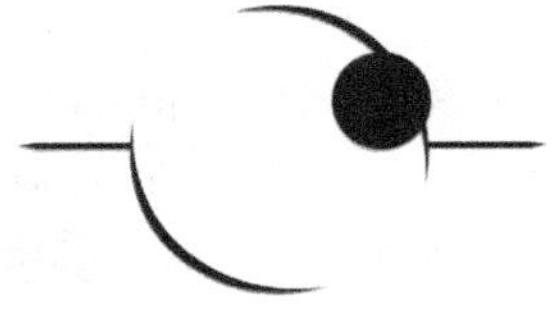

PROLOGUE

Luxarn Pervenio, CEO of the solar-system-wide entity known as Pervenio Corporation, stared at the pixels of light projecting from his wooden desk on Pervenio Station, orbiting just outside of Saturn's A ring. He leaned toward the holographic screen, the smell of rare oak greeting his nostrils. On it played a recording of Kale Trass, the newly emerged leader of the Children of Titan—an offworld, Ringer terrorist cell obsessed with retaking Titan no matter the cost.

On the screen, Kale said heartlessly, "From ice to ashes" before he exposed former Pervenio Corp Director James Sodervall to the icy surface of Titan. Luxarn had known the grumpy old wretch since he was but a boy. His father's right-hand man when they arrived on Titan, and then his. Now, Luxarn stared at the tiny shards of ice Sodervall had been reduced to after Kale Trass had shattered his frozen body.

Monsters, he thought. *Radicals, all of them!*

Kale had yanked on the thread and caused the entire operation around Saturn to begin unraveling like a fraying rope. Nearly half a century of the hard work Luxarn had undergone assimilating their peoples, undone. By now, the entire solar system had likely viewed the recording. The United Sol Federation's Assembly back on Earth would say Luxarn lost control. His rivals would smell blood in the water and come for his holdings—Venta Co, Red Wing Company, and whatever else sprang up.

"Sir, we've lost the Sector C hangars," someone addressed him urgently. "All public docks are under siege... There's... there's too many of them." Luxarn glanced up to see the commander of his security forces on Pervenio Station panting in his doorway. A door set on hold-open for the first time in... he couldn't remember how long.

"Where did we go wrong, Commander?" Luxarn asked calmly without averting his gaze from the ghastly footage. "The stars are so near. Don't they understand? If we squabble amongst each other like the humans of old, it'll all be lost."

"I... sir." The commander took a moment to gather himself. "There are more ships on their way, stolen from the surface of Titan. Orbital defenses are failing. They hit us there first. Somehow they knew the station's entire layout."

Luxarn released a weak chuckle. "Half these halls were built by Ringer hands."

The commander took a few steps further into the office. "Sir, we have to get you off the station before we're overrun."

Luxarn stood without a word. He turned and laid his hands against the cold viewport spanning the wall behind his desk. Beyond it, two sparking halves of a destroyed gas-harvesting vessel drifted aimlessly through the icy rocks of Saturn's rings. Another transport hurtled toward the station, its impulse drive flaring blue as it failed.

"I gave him away at birth," Luxarn said, "but wouldn't it be fitting now if we shared the same grave?"

"Sir, I don't know who you're talking about," the commander said.

"No, you don't. And I suppose that's my greatest failing."

"Sir, please. We'll wipe all the valuable data before they can get their hands on it, and we'll thwart this rebellion, but you need to get to safety. Pervenio Corp needs you. Earth needs you."

Luxarn breathed in the view of Saturn's star-and-moon-speckled archipelago one last time. His haven of resources was meant to usher in a new golden age of humanity. When the Meteorite struck Earth three centuries before and nearly wiped out his species, he wondered if his ancestors who poked their heads up from his family's fallout shelter ever could've imagined standing on a space station under siege from a group of angry offworlders halfway across the solar system.

Progress... It was something Kale and his horde of Ringers would never understand because their ancestors fled Earth, looking for greener pastures. For three hundred years, they lived in their little paradise on Titan—until Luxarn's family arrived, answering the call of the stars and the expansion necessary to ensure humanity was never sent to the brink of extinction again.

"Lead away," Luxarn sighed. He followed the commander. Kale's pale, hard gaze watched him from the holographic screen on his desk all the way out.

"Your new ship is nearly prepped," the commander said. "The Ringers won't be able to catch you, no matter how hard they try."

In the adjoined private hangar, a prototype starship sat perched atop an active fuel line. Constructed to be Luxarn's personal craft, it boasted a prototype impulse drive that was the fastest of its size in all of Sol. The ship was new it didn't even have a name yet, but Luxarn had always found disaster to be the impetus for advancement.

A host of corporate VIPs waited outside the closed loading ramp for boarding. All the brilliant minds and sycophants who helped the unstoppable Pervenio machine chug along. Luxarn scanned the hangar but didn't find what he was looking for.

"Where are the bodies?" he asked. "I requested they make the trip with me."

The commander paused from issuing orders to a unit of officers and turned back to Luxarn. "Excuse me, sir?"

"The bodies of my collectors retrieved from the surface of Titan before Kale blew it all to hell!" Luxarn roared. The commander winced and swallowed the lump in his throat. Malcolm and Zhaff had located the Children of Titan hideout under a Ringer quarantine but were murdered shortly before Kale detonated a nuclear engine core on top of the place, taking nearly half of Luxarn's armed forces with it.

"They've been transported directly to the corporate med block for treatment. Didn't anyone inform you? One is in a coma, but the doctors say without life support, he'll die immediately. The older survived exposure. They got to him just in time."

Luxarn grabbed the commander by his chest plate. "Malcolm Graves is alive?"

"Barely. Lost a leg to the cold, but that still makes him luckier than his freak partner."

Luxarn's hands curled into fists. That freak partner happened to be Luxarn's illegitimate son, Zhaff. Any other time, he would've had the commander spaced for spouting off like that, but he didn't know. Nobody knew the truth except for Malcolm.

"His *Cogent* partner," Luxarn corrected.

"Yes, sir... Sorry, sir."

"Take me to them immediately."

"Sir, there is no time. You must leave now. I'll have them dispatched on a medical transport as soon as the survivor is stabilized."

"I'm not going anywhere without—"

The far entry to the hangar exploded. The deafening blast sent Luxarn staggering, and a bullet slashed across the throat of a nearby security officer, spattering red onto Luxarn's face.

"They're here!" someone hollered. A horde of white-marble-faced offworld devils appeared like foaming waves through a broken dam. Pervenio officers charged ahead to return fire. All the VIPs ducked for cover, banging on the prototype ship's sealed ramp to be let inside.

"We're not done fueling!" an engineer shouted before a bullet knocked him off his feet. As Luxarn watched the chaos erupt, he couldn't help but see the irony. Surrounded by a wealth of all the fuel humanity could want for on Saturn, they lacked it at the most crucial moment.

"Stall them!" the commander ordered one officer. "Wipe Mr. Pervenio's office!" he directed another. He then took Luxarn by the arm and ran him in the opposite direction of the fray, leaving the VIPs behind. "This hangar is compromised, sir. We need to get you to another ship!"

Luxarn tore free and straightened his shirt. "Prepare a medical evac immediately and have the bodies of the collectors on them."

"Sir, those vessels aren't shielded or outfitted with sleep pods. You'll be vulnerable."

"Which is exactly why they won't bother targeting it."

"There are more capable transports in the reserve hangar. With Director Sodervall gone, I'm in charge of your safety while on the Ring."

"He's dead, and last I checked, I'm still the CEO of this corporation. Take me to them now. And consider this your promotion. Ring Director..." He paused to read the commander's tag. "...Lawrence. When I'm gone, the defense of our holdings here will be in your hands. I hope you prove more capable than your predecessor."

A promotion like that usually had Luxarn's subordinates beaming, but the commander's face filled with dread. He'd clearly expected to join Luxarn in fleeing the compromised station.

"I'm... I'm honored, sir," he forced out. "I won't let you down."

"Start by doing what you're told," Luxarn said.

The newly appointed director contacted the medical center over his com-link as they ran down the corporate wing's spacious passage. Luxarn stopped at the first turn and glanced back. As he watched the Ringer mob swarm his upper-level employees and tear them to pieces, he made himself a single promise.

Kale Trass and his Ringers would pay for everything they'd taken from him. His son, the Ring, trillions of credits. His father showed them mercy after the Great Reunion brought plague to their world... Never again.

ONE

KALE TRASS

Months had passed since the revolution started. Lack of sleep had all the days of unrest throughout Titan and the rest of the Ring beginning to blend together. I stood alone on my ship, holding on to the walls as she plunged through the upper atmosphere of Saturn. Wind tore across the hull and made her rattle, but there was no turning back now. The last bastion of Pervenio Corporation's forces on the Ring waited only a few thousand kilometers away.

I felt like I should be smiling. We'd come so far in so little time, but I knew we were just getting started. The people we were up against would never stop resisting us, and so our fight would never end.

I sighed and raised my hand-terminal to my ear. Then I listened, as I did before every battle with the Earthers and on every restless night, to the last private conversation recorded on Pervenio Station between its former owner, Luxarn Pervenio, and Director Sodervall. The renowned Luxarn Pervenio secretly monitored everyone there, no matter what their rank. Even the wealthiest person in the Sol system needed to ensure he had a leg up on everyone and everything. Manipulation, strong-arming—that was the Earther way, and it was what had allowed him to wrest control of Titan and the Ring from my people until I, Kale Trass, took it back.

"What is it, Sodervall?" Luxarn said on the recording. "I only have time for good news."

"It's Agents Zhaff and Graves, sir," Director Sodervall responded, the former Voice of the Ring on local news feeds. He'd been well accustomed to making composed speeches in the face of catastrophe, but his voice was shaky. "We made contact. They located a Children of Titan hideout burrowed underneath the Darien Quarantine where we believe the stolen supplies from Earth were taken. Zha—"

"Excellent! I trust that proper preparations are being made?"

"Of course. Sir, listen to me. Agent Zhaff was found shot outside."

There was a pause. "Is he all right?"

"I'm waiting for another update, but... it was in the head, sir."

A longer period of silence passed until, finally, Luxarn said, "And Graves?"

"We're still thawing him, but it doesn't look good." Sodervall swallowed audibly. "Sir, what do you want me to do?"

"My father should have let these inbred Ringers die off when we had the chance!" he growled. As if Luxarn's father, who organized the Great Reunion between our peoples, could knowingly control the plague that crippled us.

Before the Meteorite struck Earth more than three centuries ago, the first settlers of Titan had fled on an ark designed by Darien Trass. For all those long years, they lived free of Earther greed, hopping the moons of Saturn like their own icy, archipelago paradise. Living in peace. But the people of Earth didn't die off entirely. They recovered and set their sights on the worlds beyond Earth, so they would never risk being wiped out again.

Fifty years ago, they made contact, and Luxarn and his father traveled millions of kilometers across the Sol system to reunite the Earthers and the Titanborn or, as they call us, Ringers. Centuries away from Earth had left our immune systems crippled. Countless Titanborn grew sick, allowing Pervenio Corp to step in. They brought their system of credits to control us, stuffed the sick into quarantine, and reaped Saturn of valuable gases.

"I agree, sir," Sodervall said. "They're a cancer to Sol. But it's too late now. I need to know what you want me to do."

"To do?" Even listening through a hand-terminal, the fury in his voice was enough to raise the hairs on my reedy arms. "I want the Children of Titan exterminated, director! I want this Kale Drayton delivered to me in cuffs! Evacuate every survivor from the *Piccolo* until one of them tells us the truth."

That simple order had condemned Cora and all my former crew-mates on the *Piccolo* gas harvester to death.

"I... I'll get right to it, sir," Sodervall said.

"You damn well better! I don't care what it takes, but you will restore order down there. Tear that quarantine to pieces if you have to."

There it was. Luxarn's final, terrible mistake. It dispersed his forces and allowed us to break into Pervenio Station, hijack the *Piccolo,* and overload its nuclear-thermal engine to incinerate thousands of his officers in the Darien Quarantine.

"Sir," Sodervall said. "I don't think that's—"

"Just do it, Sodervall! If you hadn't allowed things to get so dreadful down there, none of this would have happened. My s— Zhaff's blood is on your hands."

"Sir, are you okay?"

"I'm fine! Now find Kale Drayton and end this insurgency,

or by Earth, I'll find somebody who can, and you can join the skellies in an airlock."

"I'll handle it, sir."

The conversation ended there after a series of loud crashes, which I could only assume was Luxarn Pervenio throwing things in rage.

Presently, my fingers squeezed around my own terminal so hard it nearly snapped. I captured Director Sodervall soon after and had him frozen to death—punishment for murdering Cora and countless other crimes against Ringers. But it was Luxarn who'd held his leash. I'd blamed the wrong man.

Every time I listened to the recording, I felt a sickening concoction of rage and delectation over what followed. Luxarn and all those who served him had taken everything from us, but it was his arrogance that brought his whole organization crashing down. I was publicly declared the heir to Darien Trass, and hearing it inspired my people to finally fight back against Pervenio Corp and all the other smaller Earther companies with holdings across the Ring.

None of what he demanded of Sodervall came to fruition, not even meeting me. Luxarn fled the Ring like a coward before we had the chance, but we would have our face to face one day. I swore it over and over in my head. He'd answer for all his family's atrocities against my people.

He'd answer for Cora...

"Kale." Rin interrupted my ruminations. Her hand fell upon my armored shoulder. "Kale, are you ready?"

I stowed my hand-terminal, lowered my helmet's visor, and turned without answering. A cohort of Titanborn fighters was arrayed in front of us in the cargo bay of my ship, the *Cora*. She was a prototype starship we'd stolen from Luxarn's private hangar on Pervenio Station, complete with the finest in contemporary impulse drive tech, reinforced iridium plating, and a full complement of anti-craft ordnance.

She was a one-man warship capable of fending off attacks from the worst manner of scrap pirates hiding throughout the asteroid belt... or helping take down the remnants of Luxarn's forces around the Ring. Like his personal recordings, the *Cora* was one of the many technical marvels earned during our takeover of Pervenio Station. Its name was my single addition.

I switched on my helmet's com-link. "I am now," I said.

"I was hoping you finally decided to listen to me and stay onboard," Rin replied, her voice now over coms.

I shot her a disapproving glance. Her visor obscured her face, half of it a mess of mangled flesh and sinew from an explosion when she led a mutiny against an Earther ship captain long before I met her. The scars made her appear like something from a nightmare, though the sight barely affected me anymore. Ever since our revolution started, she was by my side almost every second—plotting, fighting, figuring out what was best for the Ring. It was tough to find any Titanborn who'd lost more at the hands of the Earthers than her, and her coarse disposition made sure everyone around her always knew it.

"Director Lawrence ran security at Pervenio Station," I said. "How many of us do you think he spaced there?"

Lawrence currently led the last remnants of the Pervenio security forces stationed around the Ring. According to reports, at least a hundred of them were on board a luxury cruiser, ready to make their final stand. We would've sent the ship spiraling down into the crushing depths of Saturn if they hadn't managed to take a few vital Titanborn hostages before commandeering the vessel. But now we were going to get them back.

"I know," Rin replied. "But I'm not the one responsible for our people."

"No, you're not."

"We can handle this mission easy. If you were to get hurt..."

"Gareth will protect me." I nodded toward my towering guardian, standing at the back of the other Titanborn fighters waiting for us. Like Rin, he too had been with me since the start of the revolution.

He grunted his agreement as he walked over. He didn't say a word because he couldn't. He could only converse through sign language. The Earthers had stolen his tongue long before we ever met.

"Something just smells wrong about this, Kale," Rin said. "They're desperate, and I know what that's like. Nobody will judge if you stay behind. You can spend some more time in the cockpit with that ambassador you're so fond of. Whatever she is to you these days."

I ignored her last comment. "They took your half-sister, Rin. Isn't Rylah important to the cause?"

"I know who they have!" she snapped.

I turned my head so I could glare directly at her. Out of my periphery, I noticed the Titanborn fighters watching us. They couldn't hear what we were saying since we were on a private line, but the look Rin and I exchanged had them visibly concerned.

Rin drew a deep breath. "My apologies, Lord Trass," she said. "As your aunt, it's my job to protect you whenever I can. Gareth and I will take care of the Pervenio mongrels and bring Rylah back. You can trust us."

"You're starting to sound like my mother," I said.

"Fine, then come," Rin groaned. "Just don't ever tell me that."

"Are you two ever going to get along?"

"*Do you have a time machine?*" Gareth signed to me.

"She kept you from your father and your birthright," Rin stated, unamused. "She's lucky she's your mother."

"And you're lucky you're my aunt," I countered. "I'm tired of hearing about it. We're here now anyway, so let's end this together."

"As you command." She turned to face straight ahead and, after a few seconds of quiet, said, "You took your g-stim, right?"

"You're doing it again, Rin."

She grumbled something under her breath. I shifted coms to our unit-wide channel.

"The Pervenio mudstompers out there have taken one of our own!" I shouted. "A member of my family! Let us show them what it means to be Titanborn!"

"Missiles launched," voiced Aria over the com-link, right on schedule.

She was my ambassador to Earth, and the woman currently flying the *Cora*. I didn't like placing her in the danger of combat, but with Rin needed to lead the assault of Director Lawrence's ship, she was the only experienced pilot who could handle an Earther vessel as advanced as the *Cora*.

"Should be me flying," Rin remarked.

"Please no," Gareth signed. *"I don't want to puke again."*

"You're welcome to stay," I said to her. She ignored me.

"Ships in position," Aria announced. "Prepare for dispatch."

In unison, the Titanborn soldiers accompanying us rotated to face away from the ship's exit ramp. Rin, Gareth, and I crossed their ranks to the very back, ensuring we'd be the first out the door when the time came.

"Today, we finally take back the Ring!" I yelled. Dozens of Titanborn fighters voiced their agreement. Gareth pounded on his chest plate.

"Oxygen on! Wings down!" I spread my arms, stretching the tensile nano-fabric strung between them and the sides of my suit. Everyone else did the same. "From ice to ashes!"

The echo of my soldiers repeating that phrase was one I'd

grown used to. I closed my eyes as the words rang throughout my helmet. I remembered my first time soaring across Saturn from the *Sunfire*, how my hands shook and my heart pounded. Now they were both still.

A rare period of calm took hold. No gunfire or explosions. Nobody asking me what to do. I pictured Cora's eyes, as blue as Neptune. Then the exit ramp fell open, and my body was yanked backward by the winds of Saturn. Even with a g-stim alleviating the stress of being under the intense gravity of the Ringed World, nothing could ever prepare me for that feeling. Especially considering I hadn't taken my stim despite Rin's prodding. My winged suit would keep me alive, and I wanted to feel everything.

My muscles were pulled in every direction. My stomach felt like it was in my throat. I opened my throbbing eyes and reveled in the pain. The tension racking my body was just the distraction I needed.

Saturn's ruddy atmosphere whipped across my visor as we pierced the sky at incredible speeds. Bolts of lightning coruscated in the distance, as long as a Departure Ark. The great gray blob of a Pervenio luxury cruiser named the *Ring Skipper* encompassed most of my view straight ahead. A handful of smaller Titanborn ships surrounded it—gas harvesters that we'd stolen back mostly. Hundreds of soldiers soared toward flaming breaches in the hull.

"Redirect two degrees west," Rin instructed over coms, her voice sounding a thousand kilometers away as the wind howled.

I lifted my left arm a smidge to alter my heading. The entire squadron turned with me, like a flock of gulls on ancient Earth. At least, everybody except for one. In the second row of our formation, one of my people must have raised his arm too much and got caught in a wind stream. His body plummeted uncontrollably toward the depths of Saturn until he was obscured by the thick clouds.

I looked away. Everything happened so fast my people didn't have much time to train. All the scattered cells of the Children of Titan emerged under my command after Director Sodervall's execution, but it wasn't enough to fight. Most of the soldiers were factory-workers or hydro-farmers. Like me, they were thrown into the cauldron of war without a second to breathe.

"Hold steady," Rin said, choosing to ignore what had happened.

The *Ring Skipper* neared. Bullets lashed out through one of the breaches in its upper hull as another Titanborn squadron entered. A few of those clinging to the rim were hit and tumbled out into the abyss. Pervenio wasn't going to go down easily.

"Level out over the hull," Rin said. "Velocities are synchronized. Come down slow around the breach. Beta squadron will clear the dining hall for us."

My immediate view became a wall of gray metal as we soared a few meters above the ship. The first squadron to engage our target breach pushed forward. I lowered gradually over the hull until my hands were close enough to grip the jagged edge. Magnetized gloves ensured I wouldn't slide away after I retracted my wings—a new improvement to our armor that allowed for boarding operations such as this.

"Alpha engaged," Rin said. "Prepare to drop in..."

I ignored her. I couldn't hear anything through my helmet except for roaring wind, but I could see the flashes of muzzles below. We were late to the fight. I pulled my body forward, my powered armor providing the strength to fight the storm, and plunged into the ship. The wooden floor cracked beneath my feet as I landed in the luxury cruiser's ostentatious dining room. The tables were fastened, so they hadn't been sucked out by pressure change, but most were broken or flipped, peppered with bullet holes.

A squadron of my men was already among them, firing at Pervenio resistance positioned behind the corner of every entrance into the room. I reached back, removed my pulse rifle, and took aim at a chunky Earther decked out in Pervenio regalia. He was getting too bold about poking around the corner, and the next time he did it, I'd have him squarely in my sights.

"Protect Lord Trass!" Rin screamed.

Before I could squeeze the trigger, the whole of my squadron landed around me, and I was lost in a sea of white armor. Rin grabbed me by the back of the neck and shoved me into a crouch. Through a forest of limbs, I saw Gareth charge the doorway. When the officer I was aiming at popped out, Gareth riddled him with holes.

"Are you trying to get yourself killed?" Rin yelled at me over our secure line.

I brushed her off and hurried to catch up with Gareth. With our unit's reinforcements, we were taking the dining room with relative ease. All the crystal chandeliers and the garish paintings hanging on the walls were in tatters along with the Pervenio defenses.

"They're holding our people on the command deck!" a Titanborn at the entry informed me.

I hopped on coms. "Forward squadrons advance!" I said. "I want none left alive."

Gareth entered the adjoining hall first, and I made sure I was second. Two Pervenio mudstompers fled some ways down. Blood sprayed the wooden trim on the walls as we unloaded into their backs. Then we bounded forward with both squadrons at our backs and Rin bellyaching into my ears.

With two full squadrons following me and two more simultaneously breaching the ship's ruptured cargo bay, Director

Lawrence didn't have enough men to secure the corridors. The blast door to the command deck was sealed shut, but my men immediately got to work bringing it down with fusion cutters.

"Form two lines at the entry," Rin stepped in front of me and ordered. "Everything they have left will be holed up in there."

Rows of soldiers positioned themselves before me. I went to shove them aside, but Rin pressed her palm firmly against my chest plate. "You've done enough," she said sharply over our private line.

A harsh response simmered on the tip of my tongue until Gareth too moved out from my side and directly in front of me. He gestured to a blackened mark on the edge of my torso where a stray bullet had glanced off my armor.

"You fought well," he signed. *"Rin will handle the rest."*

I regarded my soldiers. Some of them trembled as they aimed, watching the sparks slowly wrap the blast door like a blooming rose, but they all stood firm. For Titan and for me. I finally conceded and took a step back.

"Do not fire unless you have a clean shot," I ordered over the mass coms. "They're holding our people in there. Pervenic Corp's hold on the Ring ends today!"

Chants of affirmation rang in my ears. The fusion cutters stopped.

"Check ammo," Rin said. "Prepare for advance!"

The thick blast door toppled inward with an earsplitting crash. My people flooded the command deck under Rin's leadership, but not a shot was fired on either side. Gareth and I entered last.

The *Ring Skipper*'s command deck was a marvel of engineering. The curved portion of the semicircular space was entirely comprised of a viewport looking out upon the thunderous skies of Saturn. Its burnished steel structure was so thin it didn't seem like it could support anything. Three stories of catwalks wrapped it, loaded with navigation consoles and other terminals, though currently, every workstation was vacated.

Director Lawrence and his troops stood near the central console on the main level. About a dozen of them were left, and they had our Titanborn hostages on their knees, pulse rifles aimed at the back of their heads. Rylah was under the watch of the new director himself. In the short time I'd known Rin's half-sister, she'd always been perfectly manicured and flaunted her lithe physique in exquisite, skintight dresses. She'd grown up in the Lowers just as I had, but she wasn't afraid of using both her assets and her intelligence to help her become the foremost information broker in the Ring. Now her hair was disheveled, her dress ragged, and her face blemished by splotches of blood and fresh bruises.

My fists tightened, and I immediately wished I was out front with Rin. If the new Titan we were building were a corporation like Pervenio, Rylah would be our chief technology officer. She didn't share Trass's blood from Rin's father, but she had a brilliant mind. A knack for understanding how things worked that, alongside Aria, was crucial as my people adapted to the Pervenio technology we now owned.

"I'm glad you could make it!" Director Lawrence hollered across the room. The wicked smirk he wore told me he knew we had reached a stalemate.

"Rin…" Rylah rasped. "Get out of here!"

"Quiet!" Lawrence smacked her in the back of the head.

Rin stomped forward. "Let them go!" she demanded. "And I promise you a quick death, mudstomper."

Lawrence continued to sneer. "I'd prefer slowly. And you'll all join me!"

The ship lurched to the side so violently that all of us were thrown off balance. One of my people smashed into my side, sending me scrambling to find my footing. But the ship didn't recover, stuck in a steepening tilt. In the chaos, I saw a bullet from Rin's gun slice through Lawrence's forehead just before he could execute Rylah. The rest of the officers went down just as quickly, trying to take a handful of hostages with them rather than put up a real fight.

"Kal—Lord Trass, they blew the engines!" Aria yelled over the com-link. "Half of Charlie and Delta Squadrons were lost. The ship is in free fall!"

"It was a trap!" Rin screamed. "Gareth, get Kale out of here now! All ships, we need emergency retrieval."

Before I could respond, Gareth pulled me free of a body and rushed me toward the exit. "We aren't leaving them!" I threw him off and turned around. Rin had Rylah and made her way toward us, but with the ship plunging headfirst, we were all heading uphill.

"I've got her," Rin said. "Dammit, Kale, you need to go!"

I slid down the angled floor until I reached Rin and could help her carry her injured sister. "Not without all of you," I said. Gareth arrived soon after and grabbed another hostage lucky enough to avoid a bullet from his captor. Even in our powered suits, the inertia and mounting gravity made climbing back across the command deck a challenge.

"Aria, tell all ships to grab as many soldiers as they can through existing breaches," I ordered. "We have Rylah. You'll be recovering us last at the command deck."

"I won't be able to get under the bow of the ship now," she replied, the urgency in her tone unmistakable.

"Use a hole in the top of the dining hall, then. We'll meet you there."

"I'm not sure this ship can handle the pressure if the *Ring Skipper* goes down much farther."

"Get it done, outsider," Rin growled. "All I hear is how great a pilot you are. Prove it."

"It'll hold," I assured. "Everyone move, now!"

Hearing my commands inspired a few of my soldiers to fall back so they could push us along. One slipped and rolled down the command deck, shattering the viewport on his way out into the storm. Air rushed into the command deck, and we just barely made it into the corridor, where we could use the walls to brace ourselves. A handful more Titanborn weren't so lucky. The viewport's structure bent as if it were made of paper and was torn out into Saturn's atmosphere along with everything and everybody else remaining on the command deck.

My muscles seared as we pulled ourselves along the wall back toward the dining hall. Luckily, Rin and I had been stowaways on the *Ring Skipper* before and knew a faster way. Reports from the other squadrons filled my ears. The pressure exerted from diving so deep into Saturn's atmosphere forced one rescue ship to have to pull away and abandon soldiers.

"Velocity synchronized," Aria said. "Hull integrity is holding, but I don't know how long. Please hurry, Kale!"

"We're close," I strained to say. The pressure on my lungs was almost too much to bear. Every armored soldier around me ground their jaws in an effort to keep conscious. Rylah and the other few hostages we hauled along had already passed out. No human body was built to survive the real depths of Saturn but especially not a Ringer's outside of powered armor.

"Through...here," Rin groaned. We plowed through a swinging door into the ship's kitchen, a mass of at least twenty people using each other's bodies to fight gravity and inertia to move. Shiny utensils were scattered all over the floor. Light and wind pierced the many bullet holes dappling the chrome walls.

As we entered, a violent bout of turbulence sent all of us sliding. Plates and frozen food shattered. I was the first to hit the wall, and I used it to try and steady us. My arms felt like worn rubber bands. Just as I went to join back with the group, the heavy hatch of a walk-in freezer cracked open.

Children were crammed inside, at least a dozen of them of all varying ages. Most were already unconscious from the pressure, but the cries of those who weren't were drowned out by the racket. Only I noticed them. A girl no older than five stared at me near the entrance, her eyes bulging and bloodshot. They'd probably been brought on board by their Pervenio Corp fathers and mothers who decided that being sacrificed to kill me was better than living under the rule of Ringers.

Someone grabbed me by the shoulder. "C'mon, Kale!" Rin's voice rang in my ear. "We need to get you out of here now!"

I remained still, eyes locked with the girl's. Tears streamed down her grimy cheeks as well as all the others'. They were Earthers, all of them. The *Cora* was probably built well enough to hold for the few extra seconds longer it'd take us to gather them; to save all the potential future collectors, security officers, and corporate directors. All I needed to do was give the order, and my people would listen...

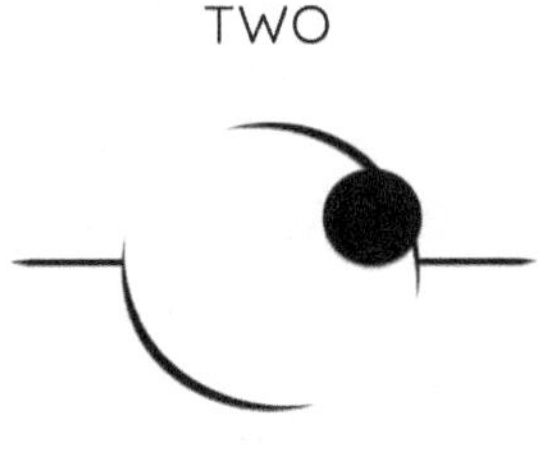

TWO

MALCOLM GRAVES

My eyes popped open. I lay back on a bed, poked all over with needles like a fleshy pincushion. No full respirator was stuffed my mouth, but tubes in my nostrils pumped me with oxygen. I think. Whatever it was, it had me lightheaded and remarkably calm, all things considered. My vision was improved too.

I studied my surroundings. I was in a medical room. The walls were polished white, and every piece of equipment shined like it was fresh out of the factory. All the highest quality stuff too. Holographic viewscreens monitored my bodily functions as a scanner slid back and forth along a thin rail above, projecting a tight grid of pinkish beams through me. An IV fed something clear into my veins, though it didn't seem to help with how insanely thirsty and hungry I felt.

There were no viewports, so I wasn't exactly sure where I was, but the color red answered a few of my questions. Pervenio Corp logos were everywhere, on everything—that branch wrapped in a crimson helix that I'd spent most of my life serving. So I wasn't in hell, but I was back in one of *their* facilities.

Whether it was as a prisoner awaiting interrogation for what had happened on Titan or purely as a patient, I wasn't sure.

What I did know was that my partner Zhaff was dead. He had been one of Luxarn Pervenio's Cogents, a group of elite special agents forged out of young men and women with a concoction of mental illnesses that left them unsuited for normal society. We hadn't worked together long, but he was a good kid and ten times the agent I ever was at his age.

Things got even better when I found out he was secretly Luxarn's troubled, illegitimate son. I was handpicked to show him the ropes of being a Pervenio Corp field agent, chasing down bounties and extinguishing rebellions throughout the solar system before they ever started. A dream assignment. One I didn't even realize I'd been waiting thirty years as a collector for until it was too late.

We were sent to Titan to uncover the truth behind a terrorist attack on Earth during the only holiday humans from that withering planet had left. M-Day, when we honored all the billions who'd died when a meteorite came crashing down three centuries ago. Only we stumbled upon something I'd never imagined. A rebel cell known as the Children of Titan wanted medicine to cure their beleaguered people, and my daughter, Aria, was helping them get it. Five years since we parted ways and never looked back, and that was the first time I'd seen the woman she'd grown into.

My sweet little Aria, working with radicals. Zhaff pinned her down and left me with a choice—take her in as a criminal or gun down my partner and set her free. I made the decision any father would. The last thing I could remember was both our pulse pistols going off. I hit him in the head, he hit me in the leg, and after lying on the surface of Titan freezing to death, my world went black, and I woke up in wherever the hell I was now.

One thing struck me: if Luxarn Pervenio blamed the person who was responsible for his son's death, it didn't seem likely I'd be kept on a soft mattress. If he blamed the Ringers or Aria... Her face flashed through my mind, teeming with apprehension as we bid our final goodbyes and I was left to die.

I tried to force the image away as I propped my head up to get a better look at the room. The entrance suddenly whooshed open and drew my focus. In walked a nurse. No, a doctor. Standoffish expression, graying hair tied back, white lab coat with a Pervenio emblem on the lapel—she was a seasoned vet.

"I'll have to ask you to please remain still this time, Mr. Graves," she said, voice as coarse as her face. "After your last excursion, some scans had to be re-administered."

Her gaze fell upon my hands, and as I tried to move them, I realized my wrists were restrained, ankles too. At least, one was. As much as I tried to wiggle the toes on the other, I couldn't feel anything.

"Right, sorry about that," I said, remembering my half-conscious adventure down the halls of wherever I was to a room filled with Zhaffs. Whatever drugs I was loaded up on clearly had me seeing things.

I coughed. My throat was also so dry, it was as if it was lined with cotton balls. I sounded like an eighty-year-old Ringer strolling under Earth's high G for the first time.

"I...where am I?" I asked.

"You are in an underground research facility of the Cogent Initiative beneath Sector A of the Undina Mining Facility," she said as she strolled over to my bed. She sat on a stool by the end, paying attention only to my medical readouts and not to me directly.

"Undina?" The irony that Luxarn's secret project to craft perfect agents was buried there made me chuckle, then cough again. "You've got to be kidding me. He was training them here?"

"I'm not kidding you, Mr. Graves. You nearly interrupted the research with your sloppiness back before M-day."

She referred to an assignment dealing with a miner's protest here I'd screwed up. My punishment was being paired with Zhaff to track the Children of Titan rather than working alone. At first, he was such an insufferable know-it-all, I actually *wanted* to put a bullet in his brain. But I rubbed off on him and he on me...before I offed him.

My features darkened. Her news also meant that the room full of Zhaffs wasn't a hallucination, but instead more people like him.

"I never thought I'd be back here," I whispered.

"Mr. Pervenio had you transported here specifically after you were found exposed to Titan. Most of you made it, but you're lucky to be alive."

"Most of me?"

She turned her attention to my legs and peeled up the blanket. My liver-spotted skin wrapped the one I could feel. The other was synthetic from the hip down, metal or more likely some kind of composite, fashioned to appear like a human leg without the skin. Plates formed each imagined muscle, tiny rifts between allowing for full range of movement. The foot was skeletal, sleek, and curved around the heel with independent toes featuring knobby, flexible, joints.

She prodded the ball of it with a blunt tool. The toes twitched automatically, or at least that was what I thought at first. An unusual, barely perceptible sensation affected the nerve endings on my hip where a scarred band of skin met the artificial limb. Like I was subconsciously controlling the motion. A reflex.

"Your leg was a mass of dead, frozen cells," she said. "Fortunately, that impeded the blood flow, and airships were able to get you indoors before the cold spread to your vital organs." She tapped another area of the foreign appendage. Again, I felt a faint pull as the entire top of it bent forward.

"It will take some time to grow accustomed to it as your nervous system acclimates to the new connections," she said. "Eventually, you'll think about moving it just like you used to, and it will happen. It will be like you never lost your leg. In fact, at your age, it should work better."

"Is every doctor in this place as sweet as you?"

"Don't flatter yourself, Mr. Graves. There are escaped survivors from the Ring in far worse condition than you. If not for our employer demanding your special treatment, I'd be tending to them."

"What the hell happened out there?" New leg. Survivors. I'd never woken up so confused in my life, and I'd endured too many drunken nights to count.

She grimaced, and for a moment, she no longer appeared like just a gruff old doctor. She seemed to be haunted. "Kale Trass happened."

"Who?" The name sounded familiar, but my head was so foggy I couldn't place it.

"Mr. Pervenio is on his way to apprise you of the situation as we speak."

I lost my train of thought when she ran her fingers around the top of both my new leg and my old one, as far up the inner thighs as she could go. It wasn't because of the sensation of her touching there either. It was because I could barely feel anything at all on either limb. I felt like one of Lucas Mannekin's perverse fake android creations. The thought made me shudder. Now that was a story for another time. Most twisted bastard I'd ever met, Lucas, and dealing with those types of men was my specialty.

"Now," she began, "it might be difficult to urinate on your own for a short while."

I reached desperately for my groin. I was wearing a loose-fitting robe, so making sure everything...important...was still in its proper place was simple enough.

"Relax," she said. "You're recovering nicely. There is no reason to believe that most of the sensation in your remaining lower extremities won't return. In time, you will be able to engage in all the reprehensible undertakings you collectors pride yourselves in. It just may not feel the same."

"May not?" I threw the blanket off me completely and spotted the catheter extending out from a flap in my robe. "That's supposed to cheer me up?"

"It's the best I can offer. Titan took its toll on your body, and at your age—"

"Would you stop bringing that up?"

Her lips formed a straight line; then she placed her hand on my upper chest and pressed me down. "I know you're confused and unsettled," she said, a failed attempt to sound caring. "Just try to remain still until Mr. Pervenio arrives." She gestured to the catheter. "And please don't rip that thing out again. I don't feel like scrubbing the floors, and he prefers a spotless room."

"Rip it out? Oh..." I realized I must've done that earlier when I'd stumbled out of the room and not even felt it. How could I not feel that?

As the doctor quietly checked more of my vitals, I started wishing Luxarn had left me on Titan to freeze. Things would've been a lot simpler. Instead, my employer, or former employer—I wasn't sure which yet—was on his way to see me. If he knew the truth about Zhaff, I was dead. If he didn't, then the army of Cogents I'd seen during my joy walk when I first woke up could likely pry it out of me. Reading people based on their reactions and acute facial twitches was one of their many skills. Either way, I was twenty-or-so-percent less of myself, impotent, and cuffed to a bed far away from the drink I so desperately needed.

"As I live and breathe," the familiar voice of my employer uttered. "Malcolm Graves, you really made it."

I looked up to see Luxarn Pervenio standing in the doorway, appearing as distinguished as ever. His finely tailored tunic bore the red and black of his corporate empire and hadn't a crease to be found. He was combed, manicured, shaved, and tidy, but none of that could steal my attention away from his face. Gone was his trademark confidence and voracity. The artificially stretched skin covering his skull finally showed creases, and for the first time, he looked every bit his age.

As I regarded his weary eyes, all I could see in them was Zhaff. Titan's icy sand wisped over the Cogent's crumpled body as his single green eye remained gaping. The gunshots rattled around inside my skull. I winced and turned away.

"Please, don't strain yourself," Luxarn said as he entered the room. My doctor hurried out without having to be told. "By Earth, you cannot imagine how good it is to see you awake again."

He sat on the end of my bed, giving me no choice but to regard him. His resemblance to Zhaff was so clear to me now, I don't know how I ever overlooked their relation. Some collector I was.

"It's..." I paused to gather my breath. He appeared an entire solar system away from happy, yet he didn't seem displeased with me. That meant either he didn't know the truth, or he was playing me. I had to be careful. "It's good to see you too, sir."

"They did fine work." He patted my artificial leg, which of course I couldn't feel, but the foot twitched. "Most cutting-edge piece of cybernetics in all of Sol. Dr. Aurora will have you back up in no time."

So he didn't know the truth. Luxarn was a businessman first

and foremost. He wouldn't waste however many millions of credits my new leg cost if he were going to space me. Only the best for his prized collector.

"That's good," I said. "I'm already getting tired of lying around."

"Of course you are," he said. "It's not in either of our natures."

I smirked and tried to sit up. The restraints impeded me. Luxarn noticed my struggle and freed my aching limbs. I yawned, stretched, and took the opportunity to tap my artificial leg and make sure I wasn't dreaming. The thing was a marvel—like I was wearing a spaceship on my bottom.

"What exactly happened down on Titan, sir?" I asked.

His features hardened. "I could ask you the same thing."

I swallowed the lump forming in my throat. What had happened was that I'd chosen my own flesh and blood over his. A hard choice, which I'd make a thousand times over, but not one a man like him would ever pardon. I needed a good lie, and I needed one fast if I didn't want him spacing me. I hadn't had much of a chance to think of one while I was out for... how long had it been? Undina orbited Earth and was a long ways from Titan.

"We took out a bunch of Ringers and got the stolen supplies out, but there were too many," I rattled off the top of my head. "The last thing I remember is one getting the jump on us." I took a deep breath. The last component of my self-preserving fib was coming, and it was the hardest part to get out. "Is Zhaff okay?"

I could tell Luxarn was forcing his lips not to tremble. Showing weakness wasn't his style. He reached into a pouch on his belt, removed the familiar Cogent eye-lens that allowed Zhaff to see on various light spectrums and enhanced ranges, and slapped it down on the side table right beside me. The center of the yellow-colored glass was gashed just wide enough for a bullet to pass through, the jagged edges stained with dried blood.

Again, my mind was stricken by Zhaff's impassive face. The sweaty hand I was using to prop up my body slipped. I squeezed one eye shut and angled the other toward the wall, hoping Luxarn might not notice how thrown I was.

"They took down my boy, Graves." The way his voice quavered sent a chill up my spine. "My son."

"By Earth..." I feigned shock. Another attempt to glance at Zhaff's lens yielded similar results. It was like I'd never killed someone before. "I didn't think that was possible."

"*You* were supposed to keep him safe."

Now it felt like he was playing me again. Trying to get me to admit it. That was probably the easiest way to go. I'd died once already anyway. Instead, a lifetime's worth of honed survival skills kicked in. I caressed the cold plating of my artificial leg and said, "I had a hard enough time doing that for myself."

"Relax, Graves. I don't blame you. I blame Director Sodervall for not providing an accurate assessment of the Children of Titan situation before I sent you and Zhaff down. Damn me for thinking he could handle it. Now Sodervall is dead too, executed in front of the whole damned solar system!" Luxarn exploded to his feet and slammed his fist on the nearest counter, causing the rack of syringes there to fall and clank across the glossy floor.

I waited a few seconds for him to relax. "Director Sodervall is dead?" I asked. My cantankerous old handler seemed like he would be around forever, grumbling about Ringer disregard for Pervenio decrees and how things used to be better. "Sir, how the hell long was I out?"

"Three months. We kept you under during transit and while we installed your new leg. And in that time, everything you accomplished has proven to be for nothing. I've nearly lost the entire Ring thanks to that madman."

"Sodervall's a dead madman now?"

Luxarn's brow furrowed. "I forgot. You don't know. After you and Zhaff discovered their hideout at the Darien Quarantine, I dispatched a sizable force to try and eliminate the Children of Titan once and for all. But they were expecting it. Kale Trass blew up—"

"Trass," I interrupted. "Why does everyone keep using that name?"

"You remember the Ringer boy Sodervall accused of being behind the Children of Titan raid on our gas harvester."

"Kale Draven? No...Drayton. I thought that was his name?"

"So did we. After the bastard escaped that poor excuse for a director's grasp, he commandeered that very same ship and crashed it into the Darien Quarantine. Countless officers died in the blast, and then Kale transmitted a public message claiming that he was a descendant of Darien Trass before executing Sodervall. We were completely unprepared. Kale drove the Ringers into a frenzy. They took over every colony block on Titan, imprisoned any citizen who didn't escape in time, and stole airships and weapons before turning their sights on Pervenio Station and the rest of the Ring."

Luxarn had to sit again to steady himself. I took the opportunity to lift my jaw, which had dropped involuntarily after hearing everything I'd missed. Darien Trass was the brilliant scientist who had dispatched an Ark full of humans before the Meteorite impacted Earth. The descendants of those lucky few lived on Titan for two hundred fifty years before Pervenio Corp orchestrated the Great Reunion between them and those who had survived back on Earth. His family line was supposed to have ended shortly after said reunion brought earthborn germs that left the Ringers reeling and Pervenio Corp in control of Saturn and all its moons. Apparently not.

"It was a massacre, Graves," Luxarn continued. "They attacked from within and without. Station defenses put up a fight, but after losing so many at the quarantine, we didn't last long. I got myself out along with your body, Zhaff's, and whatever else I could manage, but most of the Pervenio tech in the station was lost. Now it, along with thousands of captives, are in the hands of Kale Trass. The Ringers are calling the imposter a king, if you can believe that. Every other company with holdings on the Ring was either driven out or remains under constant duress."

It was all coming together. The Children of Titan were experts at sleight of hand, as Zhaff and I learned the hard way. They had bombed New London on Earth to cover for stealing medicine to mend their sick. Their attack on the gas harvester known as the *Piccolo* was used purposefully to get it onto Pervenio Station, where it could then be used as a weapon. Director Sodervall blamed this Kale character and bathed him in scrutiny so that his infamy would be built for him. All of it distracted us from what the Children of Titan really wanted...to lure Luxarn into invading an innocent Ringer quarantine and sparking a revolution united under a Trass.

"They were playing us at every turn," I muttered. Only I didn't say that I was the last piece of the puzzle. The one driven to kill Zhaff and inspire Luxarn's wrath. The sinking feeling in my chest begged me to come clean, but the survivalist kept fighting.

Luxarn squeezed his fists until his knuckles went as pale as an offworlder's; then he exhaled. "I thought I could tame the Ring," he said. "Blend our two people together so we could create the new epicenter of humanity Earth can no longer be. I gave them purpose."

"Some people can't ever be pleased, sir. They scrape and claw for more, and only once they have everything they thought they wanted do they realize they've lost everything else." It took me until the end of my rant to realize that I wasn't talking about Ringers at all. Luxarn didn't notice.

"Well, they will lose everything," he bristled. "I won't sit around while those animals take everything my family worked so hard to build." He knelt to pick up the rack of syringes he'd knocked over and carefully rearranged it exactly where it had been. "Nobody knows what the Ringers are capable of as well as you, Graves. As soon as we have you up again, we're going to end the rule of Kale Trass before it begins."

And there was the answer to all my questions. Why Luxarn kept me alive and had a leg constructed for me when I should've been dead. Corporate collectors don't get to retire. We work until our bodies give up on us or we're zipped up in a body bag.

"Sir, I..."

He hushed me. "I won't have any of that. They may have taken your leg, but you're still every bit the collector you've always been. We will reclaim the Ring no matter what it takes, and then, maybe, you can become the director there that Soder-vall failed to be. I've always taken notice of your knack for the business end of things."

"Thank you, sir. You know nobody enjoys a compliment like me; it's just..."

"Now," he tapped my artificial leg, signaling that as far as he was concerned, our conversation had concluded, "I've been told not to exhaust you. Rest, Graves. Our retribution is coming." He stepped out of the room, leaving a handful of possible responses on the tip of my tongue.

A short time ago, the promise of the credits due to a Pervenio Director would've been enough to have me drooling.

Sit on my ass, bark orders, and be richer than all the God-forsaken souls in Sol but for a few. It was a dream.

Presently, however, all I wanted to do was sit on my ass, empty my clouded brain, and sleep. I'd never felt so exhausted in my entire life. The most awkward thing about sacrificing yourself for someone is surviving it. Waking up and realizing you've got a second lease on life you never signed up for. If the Church of the Three Messiahs preachers back on Earth are right, and there is some all-powerful being out there watching us, judging us, I think we'd get along. He or she's got a twisted sense of humor.

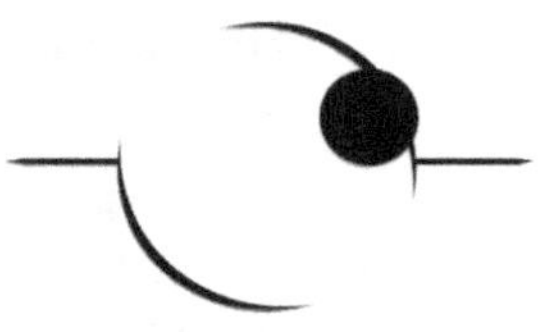

THREE

KALE

I STOOD BEFORE A VIEWPORT IN THE DARIEN UPPERS, staring out upon the pale, sandy surface of my homeworld that was so like my own skin. The dull glow of the sun barely pierced the thick veil of clouds from an impending storm. The Uppers were once again returned to the near-freezing temperatures my people embraced, but as far as Titan was from the sun, I could still feel the slightest tinge of its warmth through the transparency.

I had to close my eyes and breathe in the cold air to remind myself I wasn't dreaming. The din of my people's celebrations resounding throughout the city's massive enclosure didn't help break the illusion.

With the death of Director Lawrence, the Pervenio presence on the Ring was eradicated. Minus a few officials likely hiding out in small colonies on other moons belonging to other corporations, they now controlled nothing, not even a single room, within the orbit of Saturn.

So much had changed in the months since we had reclaimed Darien from our Earther oppressors, yet, in addition to the light and temperature, it still felt odd to stand in the

Uppers without continually checking over my shoulder for Pervenio security officers or making sure my sanitary mask was drawn tight enough over my mouth and nose. Some of my people still wore them. Even after we'd booted the Earthers and scrubbed every centimeter of the place, they couldn't break the habit.

I can't say I blamed them. The corners of my lips itched just at the thought of being exposed, but I had to set an example. We didn't have to be afraid anymore. Titan was ours again, just as Darien Trass had always intended. We could live at the top of Darien rather than submerged.

"Kale," someone whispered.

I thrust out my arm. My thin fingers grasped a shirt, and I turned to see my mother, Katrina Drayton. The name Trass came from my dead father's side. I don't know why I'd been so on edge. Gareth, my tongueless guardian, always stood by my side, fully armed and armored, although he was so quiet, sometimes I forgot he was there.

"Sorry," I muttered.

"I didn't mean to startle you," my mom replied softly. She tapped my hand to remind me to let go, then sat beside me. "Is everything all right?"

"Everything's fine."

She leaned closer. Her face was fuller and healthier than it had been in years, but that didn't mean we were finished. When she was sick before the rebellion, I'd visit her and remember the vibrant woman I'd known my whole life; now it was the opposite. She was a reminder of how far we'd come so fast, from prisoners to our immune systems to free men and women.

But there still was no missing the subtle lines of exhaustion plaguing the corners of her eyes. We all had them. Revolution wasn't easy, and even after taking Titan, Pervenio Station, and a handful of other vital facilities throughout the Ring, there was plenty more to be done.

"I know we don't have much time these days, but you can talk to me, you know," she said.

"Go and revel with the others, Mom. Pervenio is gone."

"And yet, here you stand alone. Everything might have changed, but you're still my son. You've been with me since you were smaller than a hand-terminal. I know when something is bothering you."

I exhaled. "We depart for Mars tomorrow. I'm too busy to celebrate and too tired of you telling me I shouldn't go. Or is there something else you came over here to talk about?"

Her lips pursed in frustration. "And why should you have to? What is the point of having an Earther ambassador if she can't handle things herself?"

"She's not an Earther," I snapped. She recoiled, but as I took a calming breath, she edged back closer. "They have to know we aren't afraid."

"After all of this, you don't think they know that?" She gestured toward the rest of the Uppers. It was difficult to ignore. Sure, we'd thoroughly decontaminated the place, but the scars of our revolution weren't something that could be cleaned. Gone was the luster. Walls were peppered with bullet holes, some torn to pieces. We'd never be able to find every shard of shattered glass from storefronts. Entire areas were discolored from blood stains.

The residential towers rising toward the lofty ceiling throughout the two-kilometer-long main level of the Uppers remained mostly empty after being plundered. Even though they were now accessible, my people still refused to inhabit them. Stores and markets were ravaged. Rejoicing Titanborn danced and drank upon their ruins. With the Earther credit system eliminated, nothing had yet taken its place. Everybody was equal on our new Titan. No credits to separate stature, no fences profiting off misfortune. It was a new way of life, yet I think Pervenio had kept us in the darkness so long it almost felt wrong to live in the light. It was going to take time.

"Until I stand in front of their leaders, they'll continue considering us some trivial rabble-rousers on one of their asteroid colonies," I said. "They'll think they can smooth over decades of abuse with a pile of credits or one well-placed collector with a bullet to my head."

"I know that. I... I'm only looking out for you, Kale."

"You don't need to anymore."

"I'm your mother," she said sternly. "I always will. I'm only afraid that with the entire solar system gunning for you, you're walking right into their hands."

"They won't risk their people's lives by touching me."

"And do you plan on holding those poor people here forever?"

"Poor? Who knows how many of them crushed one of us beneath their boot or withheld fair pay. I'll keep them here for as long as we need them."

"I..." She grimaced. "All I'm saying is maybe not all Earthers are as rational as you think. People died here, Kale. It impacted every one of their wallets and who knows how many clan-families. Any of them could—"

"Mom," I interrupted and stood. On top of everything, a growth spurt from after the *Piccolo* exploded had me towering over her and almost every other Ringer I knew. The way her expression darkened at that moment I think was her finally recognizing that I wasn't a boy any longer. "Stop worrying. I'll be fine."

She took my hands. "Then let me come with you."

"No. I need you here. Every colony block belongs to us, and I need you to help our people see that." She opened her mouth to reply, but I hushed her. "We can't stay in the Lowers' tunnels forever. After the celebration dies down, I want you working with Rylah on transitioning all daily food distribution periods to the Uppers to draw people up for good. Offer increased rations to those willing to take up residence in the Uppers of every colony block throughout Titan as well."

She considered saying something, then exhaled. "All right. I don't want another fight with you. Just promise me you'll be careful. Sometimes, I see this look in your eyes like you want them to kill you. It worries me, Kale."

"Your son will be fine, Katrina," Rin said as she approached from our side with a half-full glass of bright purple synthahol in hand. She wore a ratty white tunic, an orange circle of the Children of Titan painted proudly across her chest. Her sanitary mask wilted a bit to reveal the top half of the gruesome scars marring the right side of her face. She hadn't cracked a real smile since our crew mate Hayes gave his life to destroy the Darien Q-zone under my orders. We had that in common, I think.

"This is between my son and me," Mom grumbled.

"I think your son has proven he can handle himself." Rin leveled her glare at my mom and held it there as she scratched her wound a few times. Then she regarded me. "Come, Kale. You need to make some sort of appearance."

I nodded halfheartedly. "I have to go, Mom." I pulled her close to my chest and planted a kiss on her forehead. She forced a smile and replied with her usual, "I love you, Kale," but I was already turning halfway toward Rin and missed my opportunity to respond.

Rin took my arm and walked at a brisk pace. She was always eager to pry me away from my mom before she could drill my weary ears with criticism. They'd never been close. Rin blamed my mother for keeping me in the dark about who my father really was for most of my life. About who I was. A Trass.

"You did well out there, Kale," she said, surprising me with a compliment.

"Says the woman who didn't even want me coming along," I replied.

"I didn't want to send Hayes out to die either, but here we are. Doesn't mean he didn't do a hell of a job."

I wasn't sure how to respond. After a few drinks, Rin tended to harp on what had happened after we snuck onto Pervenio Station. Like Darien Trass, our late pilot Hayes gave his life to give us the Ring. It was a sacrifice nobody would ever forget, and the new colony Block Pervenio had begun building in the southern hemisphere now bore his name. He was a sharp pilot with an even sharper tongue. And no matter how often he teased Rin about meeting her sister, everyone knew it was an act and how he and Rin really felt about each other.

"Without Kale, we would have never had the chance to spring another one of Pervenio's traps," Gareth signed, rescuing me from a deepening silence.

Rin grunted in agreement. "The bastard must really be squirming now."

"Not enough," I added.

Rin raised her drink. "Fuck Pervenio!" she shouted. We neared the heart of the festivity now, and every one of my people within earshot elevated their drinks with her and chanted whatever came to their minds first. A few nearby then noticed I was with her and bowed their heads in reverence. Murmurs of "Lord Trass" filled the Uppers.

I tried to issue all of them an obligatory nod. It continued to be a bizarre sight to see tall, pallid Titanborn spread throughout a place meant for Earther commerce. Fighters and citizens alike. Militant members of the Children of Titan wore the orange circle, our swelling army who fought tirelessly to reclaim the Ring as well as maintain martial order during this tumultuous transition of power and economic standards.

Armor and pulse rifles were strewn all about, filling smashed market stands and counters. The coffee shop where I once convened with the Earther captain of the *Piccolo* to beg for my pathetic gas-harvesting job back was littered with bottles of synthahol. Advertisement viewscreens were set to flames at the base of the towering statue of my forebearer, Darien Trass, all while people danced around the vast atrium surrounding him.

It was a beautiful sight, but one I doubted I'd ever get used to.

Someone ran over and shoved a drink in my hand. "For you, Lord Trass," he slurred. Gareth promptly took him by the collar and tossed him back into the crowd. He then grabbed my arm and went to remove the drink, but I stopped him.

"Don't worry; I don't plan on drinking it," I said. Gareth nodded that he understood my meaning. When one of my people offered a gift, I was happy to accept it, but I didn't imbibe. There was too much to think about... too much to potentially forget.

Rin headed toward a group of combatants playing cards on top of an empty set of Pervenio armor.

"From ice to ashes, brothers," she said. They repeated the words in as exuberant a manner as they could force before nervously parting to allow her in. Not even synthahol could dull the edge she put others on, especially with her sanitary mask now hanging even further down so that the gruesome hole in her cheek was plainly visible.

She took my arm and pointed to a viewscreen hanging sideways from the wall. It was tuned to an Earther newsfeed.

"The fruits of our labor," she sneered.

The featured reporter on the screen said, "Terror at the

Ring. After a violent raid on the former Pervenio Corp Interplanetary Ship Factory on Phoebe at the hands of the Children of Titan, joint relief efforts on Enceladus are struggling to care for the new influx of displaced citizens. Many of the survivors fled the scene on the luxury cruiser *Ring Skipper* but lost their lives in what sources are calling an unprecedented massacre of noncombatants. The USF Assembly has refused to comment until all details are received, but CEO of Venta Co. and noted philanthropist Jamaru Venta had some strong words for our governing body as well as the rebels on Titan."

The entire message was crammed full of stock footage from other battles with Pervenio forces, considering there was nobody on board the *Ring Skipper* filming. Their word versus ours, and of course, I knew what the majority of Sol would believe. It wouldn't be that Director Lawrence had hired a freelance collector to capture Rylah, brought her to Phoebe, and put hundreds of civilians hiding out there in danger before they absconded with the *Ring Skipper* to lay their trap.

The sounds of people hushing each other filled the Uppers as the head of the corporate powerhouse Venta Co. appeared on the screen. Jamaru Venta wore thick, wide-rimmed glasses, something I'd never seen on an Earther before, considering their penchant for corrective surgeries, especially the rich ones. She also didn't appear to be wearing an ounce of makeup.

"The USF is failing us," she began. "This is why I have been staunchly behind organizing a summit with the self-proclaimed king of Titan, Kale Trass, to find out how we can amiably remedy this horrible situation. USF interference must be curtailed. It is their restrictions on an armed interplanetary fleet and weaponry that allowed this to escalate—"

"You hear that?" someone yelled, making it impossible to hear the rest of what she said. "They're calling him king now too."

"To King-Fucking-Trass!" shouted another. A bottle crashed into the viewscreen and knocked out the feed as cheers resonated throughout the Uppers. They were so loud, anyone caught unaware might've thought the enclosure broke.

Hundreds of eyes fell upon me, glittering with reverence and expectation, another thing I'd never grow accustomed to. I lifted my glass, and cheers again rained down from every direction. Their reaction still felt outlandish, but as I watched the jubilation intensify, I couldn't help the sense of pride swelling in me. If only I could tie Luxarn Pervenio down and have him watch us trash his prized jewel colony, Darien. There would be no greater torture for the man who thought he could make slaves of us all.

"Why don't you join us, Kale?" Rin said. She snatched up the cards and began dealing them herself, forcing a game to start. "Even a king needs to take a night off."

I laid my hand on her shoulder. "Maybe later. Have you seen Aria? I want to make sure everything is prepared."

Rin groaned. "Leave it to an outsider to make a landing on Mars into brain surgery. I saw her checking on Rylah down at the old Earther Bistro."

"Thank you." I turned to my guardian and held out my drink for him to take, low so that nobody would notice. "Why don't you join them, Gareth?" I asked. "I doubt Pervenio would try anything today."

"I'm fine."

"Please. You know Gareth doesn't drink," Rin remarked. "Trass knows why."

I nodded and went to continue on my way, but Rin tapped at my back to stop me. "Kale. You tell that bitch that if she tries anything, if she even looks at you the wrong way, I'll burn her pretty Earther face off."

I shook my head. "Sure thing, Rin."

She muttered something under her breath, then turned away from the others so that she could take a sip of her drink. She had to angle her head so that her unscarred cheek was facing downward and the colorful liquid wouldn't dribble through the hole on the other side. Everyone in the card game gawked, at least until she lifted her head and they pretended not to have noticed. She only drank or ate publicly on rare occasions. I assumed us departing for Mars in less than twenty-four hours was a huge part of it.

I left her there and followed Gareth. He parted the sea of celebrators for us to pass directly through. Leading was still new to me, but I'd learned early on the importance of making myself seen. Ever since we broadcasted the execution of Director Sodervall and declared my true name, it seemed to boost morale and keep my people focused. Luxarn's futile attempts at openly assassinating me with dried-up collectors and Cogent agents younger than me was just a part of the job.

"Lord Trass," a gray-bearded Titanborn in a fine Pervenio-designed tunic addressed me. Gareth leaped forward to pat him down, signed to me that the man was clear, then allowed him to pass. "I was hoping I might have the chance to speak with you while you're here."

I nodded for him to proceed.

He bowed his head. "I am Orson Fring. I've been assigned to manage the new factory on Phoebe and overseeing the construction of interplanetary ship engines and hulls."

"I know what it is."

"My apologies. Of course you do. I'm wondering if I could make a request."

"Administrator Rylah is back now. You can discuss any issues you have with her." I went to walk by, but he was persistent. He forced his way in front of us, earning a glower from Gareth.

"I'm afraid this is a matter in which only you can help. Please, Lord Trass."

I stopped. The trappings of leadership never took a day off, no matter how exhausted I was. Even while we celebrated victories over our Earther overseers, Titanborn from all corners of the Ring approached me with their difficulties. As if a Titan, united in race and purpose, could ever be worse than one where we survived under the constant fear of quarantine or shock batons, in self-made prisons made by the credits Earthers dangled on strings we couldn't reach.

"What is it?" I grumbled. Usually, I passed them along to Rylah or Rin if they didn't go through proper channels like everybody else, but the factory we took on Phoebe was now home to the Titanborn who were most experienced in Pervenio tech, engineering, and shipbuilding. They were required to ensure the vessels in our future fleet all went together without a hitch.

"Thank you." He bowed again. "The workers have expressed concerns that despite being pushed to our limits every day, they won't be adequately compensated. We understand the need to produce a defensive fleet to ensure our safety, but even under Pervenio, we—"

"Is the promise of increased food rations and shelter not sufficient?"

"It is. It's just... We were hoping you might be open to discussing something a bit more tangible."

Gareth rubbed his index finger and thumb together in front of the man's face.

"Credits," I spat. "Always credits. Relax, Manager Fring. Your workers have merely been conditioned by Pervenio to expect credits so they can buy their newest hand-terminal or suit, and for what?"

"I know, Lord Trass," Orson said. "But you have to understand—"

"There is nothing to understand. Tell your workers to be proud they hold such crucial positions in our revolution. As Titan flourishes, so will every Titanborn on the Ring. You have my word." He attempted to speak, but my glower stopped the words in the back of his throat. "We don't need credits anymore," I stated firmly. "We don't need anything Earth has to offer. Help me get our people to see that."

I shoved by him, causing him to bump into someone's drink and spill it all over himself. Gareth left the argument that erupted behind us and quickly caught up with me.

"Don't like the look of that one," he signed. *"He's been learning from them for too long, his best workers too. Like one of those Earth dogs begging for a treat before it stops barking."*

"He's harmless," I said. "They're just afraid that eventually things will go back to the way they were, and they'll be so deep in a hole they won't be able to climb out."

"They should be praising you for taking Pervenio Station and wiping away their debts. What I would've done to grow up not worrying about rent."

"Give them time, Gareth. All of this still feels like a dream."

"Better than a nightmare."

I turned left through the crowd, toward the Bistro, which once sold delectable pre-Meteorite cuisine. The sign outside was no longer legible. Rylah sat on one of the tables, a half-drained bottle of authentic Earther liquor next to her. She still appeared a bit frazzled, but that was multitudes better than when I last saw her. Upon noticing me, she immediately stood and approached. She had a slight hitch in her step from when a Pervenio collector had apparently shot her in the leg on the eve of our revolution. Being the most infamous information broker in the Ring made her susceptible to encounters of that sort.

"Please sit," I said.

The rest of her wounds from the *Ring Skipper* had her wincing with every move, so she gladly took my invitation. She stumbled once and banged her hip before plopping back up on the table.

"Lord Trass himself," she said, sweeping her arm in an exaggerated motion. "I didn't get a chance to thank you for what happened out there."

I gestured to her bad leg, where the scar from a collector's gunshot was the only blemish on her otherwise perfect body—a body which comprised all the best attributes from both pure Earthers and pure Titanborn. It made it easy for her to be in charge. Man or woman, people were nervous around her. I myself found her exceedingly flawless, like she was the product of some mad scientist's fantasies.

"You would have done the same for us," I said. "I was hoping to find Aria with you here."

"Not happy just seeing me?" she teased. My cheeks flushed a light shade of pink, which she seemed to enjoy. She took a swig from the bottle, scrunched her eyes as if the golden liquid burned her throat, and then took another. "You just missed her," she garbled. "I don't know what Rin has against that girl. One visit from our former doctor and I feel almost as good as new."

"Who doesn't Rin have something against?" Gareth signed.

"Why do you think I'm hiding in here?" Rylah replied.

"She's not too bad... when she drinks," I added.

Rylah chuckled. "Or when you do." She indulged in another sip, covering her mouth as she hiccupped after. The liquor on her breath was so pungent I had to stretch my nostrils. She was usually as composed as anyone I'd ever known, even more so than her sister. I couldn't imagine how much pain she had to be in to let loose like this in plain sight.

"If you want Aria, she said she was heading over to the

Hayes Memorial Hospital to check in on progress. Getting our people there up to speed."

"And after?"

"I'm not her babysitter." I leveled a glare her way, and she exhaled. "Said she planned to stay with the *Cora* all night and make sure everything was right for departure," Rylah said. "I've never seen anyone but an Earther so eager to get off Titan."

"Maybe too eager," Gareth interjected.

"Ignore them, Kale. She's just nervous. Organizing a meeting with the full USF Assembly is hard enough when you *aren't* enemy number one."

"I'm with Kale until the end, but it's still far from our home. She isn't Titanborn," Gareth signed.

"Slow those fingers down, would you?" Rylah blabbered.

I ignored her. "No, she's not," I said to Gareth, "but from what she's told me about where she grew up on Mars, it isn't far off from the Lowers."

"Unless she lied."

The thought had crossed my mind plenty of times. The Children of Titan had once referred to her as the Doctor before the revolution, when she helped steal medicine Pervenio Corp hoarded from Earth to cure our sick. Aria was the name by which she introduced herself to me, though. She was illegitimate and without a family name—half Earther and half offworlder—so there wasn't any record of her throughout Sol. Earthers tried to control everything, right down to breeding. For the betterment of the human race, they required all citizens to get approval before having children to ensure there was no risk of defect.

So Aria knew what it was like to be treated like dirt because of how and where she was born. Every day was a fight to survive until she'd found a gig smuggling for Venta Co. It was because of those connections I'd not only allowed her to help transform the unfinished Hayes Quarantine into a new medical facility open to all our people, but named her our ambassador to the USF and all their affiliated corporations. Or was it because her hybrid nature reminded me of Cora... I shook the thought out of my head.

"Not you too, now," I groused.

"You asked me to always be honest with you."

"I prefer when that honesty pits you against Rin, not with her."

"For what it's worth, I trust her," Rylah said. "We half-breed girls have to stick together. Besides, I've seen the way she looks at you. There's no treachery there, believe me. There was a time I made a living off the looks I gave men."

"It doesn't matter anyway," I said. "We need her." Rylah nodded her agreement, then raised the bottle for another swig, but I wrapped my hand around hers to stop her. "And I need you in charge while we're gone, Rylah." I took the bottle. "Focus on reparations, the Hayes Memorial Hospital, and developing a fleet at Phoebe using what we have, and we'll worry about the rest of the Ring beyond what Pervenio owned when we return. My mother is prepared to perform whatever outreach you need. If there's any trouble—"

"Kale." She stretched out her long, scarred leg and leaned back as if she hadn't a care in the world. "If anything goes wrong, you'll only be hundreds of millions of kilometers away. I'll be sure to consult with you, but nobody's going to make a move until the USF feels this out. Every eye in Sol will be on your visit to Mars. Enjoy it. I loved a man once who spent time there. Maybe you'll find someone too." Her mouth formed a mischievous grin after she uttered those last words.

I shook my head, partly out of exasperation, but mostly to hide the fact that my cheeks were again flushed. "I swear to Trass, I don't know how you and Rin are related."

"I'm pretty sure they're the ones lying about their fathers," Gareth signed.

Rylah slid forward on the table, ran the back of her mani-cured fingers up Gareth's arm and then around the back of his neck. I'll admit, even my perpetual frustration melted away as I watched him struggle with being so near to her. She pulled his head so close that her lips grazed his earlobe.

"Trust me, handsome, who would make up being related to her?" she whispered. When she was finished, she glanced up in my direction. "Life is too brief to spend every minute scowling. Why don't you head down to the docks and let the ambassador in on the celebration? Today, Pervenio finally got what was coming to them, even if they almost took me with them."

"Luxarn Pervenio could suffer for a thousand lifetimes, and he still wouldn't get all that he deserves," I said.

Rylah groaned in frustration. "Better yet, why don't you go and join my sister? You two are gluttons for misery. As for me." She lowered herself off the table and started limping toward the exit. On her way, she snagged her bottle back. "I'm going to go see if there's a Ringer out there drunk enough to pretend they don't know who I am before I have to keep your throne warm."

"Titanborn," I corrected.

"Right. Still getting used to that." She looked back, smiled warmly, and then left.

"I sure know why Hayes worshipped that woman," Gareth signed.

"He was all talk."

"Think she's in condition to look after things?"

"She better be," I stated. Gareth snorted in agreement.

"Docks?"

I considered it for a moment, then shook my head. "Take the night off, Gareth. That's an order."

He objected at first, but I shook him after a little convincing.

I decided that Aria could wait until the morning. I didn't want to distract her from her work, not when there was so much at stake. Instead, I snuck out through the Bistro's kitchen and used some of the vent lines I frequented in my heyday as a young pickpocket to get down to the Lowers alone. I traversed the narrow, subterranean passage all the way to Level B2, sticking to the shadows as I made my way to the old rocky hollow where my mother had raised me.

While I usually stayed in a luxurious room in an Uppers hotel meant for Luxarn Pervenio when he visited, I made sure that hollow always remained unoccupied. Celebrations of our liberation continued in the ice-rock tunnels of the Lowers, where the damage of revolution was less prevalent than above. They were all too busy to spot me, out of my armor and without my entourage.

I stole myself into the hollow, locked the hatch, and lay upon the hard mattress where I grew up. Where my responsibilities consisted of thinking up what I should steal next so that I could make life easier for my mother, or dreaming about how best to ask Cora out for a drink. I begged my mind to stop racing so that I might be able to get some sleep, but it never came. Instead, I lay there, staring at the barren ceiling and listening to that recording of Luxarn Pervenio and Director Sodervall on repeat. I listened to them discuss all the reasons Cora was so senselessly killed until my mind brought me back to the first day I ever met her...

———

"Drayton!" the voice of Captain Saunders thundered down the hall of Pervenio Station. I was mere seconds away from my assigned hangar when I heard him.

I picked up my pace and darted around the corner, where I

was greeted by his glower. Most Earthers tended to care about their appearance, but not him. A scraggly beard covered half his barrel-like chest.

He had a hand-terminal out so he could check off all the members of his crew. Clearly, I was last, since the moment he spotted me, he stowed the thing.

"You're late," he grumbled.

I took a moment to catch my breath. "I'm sorry, sir. It was my first time traveling. I didn't—"

"You Ringers and your excuses. My brother made me hire you for that pretty Ringer servant who's been cleaning his underwear for so long. You make him look bad, he'll do a lot worse than me."

"It won't happen again."

"Better not. Next time I'll dock you a day." He pointed toward a few other members of the crew loading up empty, transportable canisters to be filled with Saturn's most valuable gases. "Help them load up. I want to push off the moment Pervenio inspection is through."

He strolled away, barking orders at someone else while I set off into the hangar. The gas harvester *Piccolo* was moored in the center, and as I approached, I couldn't take my eyes off her. The ship wasn't anything special. An old rust-bucket mostly that probably dated to before the Great Reunion, but I'd never seen a ship so large up close.

It was the first time I'd ever stepped off Darien when I'd boarded the shuttle for Pervenio Station, passing through decontamination chamber after decontamination chamber, which Pervenio Corp said kept my kind safe from their diseases. Even so, I don't think I'd ever kept my sanitary mask and gloves pulled on as tightly as they were that day.

"Look, John," one of the Earther crewmen remarked as I approached the loading ramp. "Got some fresh meat."

"Extra pale, just how we like them," John answered.

He regarded me with the same shit-eating grin so many Earthers did when they came to the Lowers, thinking they could rip off some Ringers. I thought about snapping back, then noticed the baton hanging at his side. He and the two goons on either side of him were the ship's freelance security team. Pervenio Corp didn't waste good men on old, manned gas harvesters that could hardly make a profit compared to the new, fully automated ones.

"I don't want any trouble," I said. "I'm just here to work." I didn't mention that I'd promised my mother I'd be good and stay out of trouble for her sake. She'd gotten me out of trouble with her boss by offering to have me pay off my debts working for the *Piccolo*. Got me out from being under the thumb of the wrong kind of people too.

John cackled. A Ringer nudged me on his way by, pushing a cart stacked so absurdly high with supplies for our four-month stint on Saturn.

"Great," he grumbled. "Another one eager to lick the mudstomper's boots."

"Make sure to hurry back, Desmond," John called after the man. "Wouldn't want you to miss out on any work."

"Screw yourself."

I watched Desmond struggle to push his cart off the ramp. With so much weight piled on, it was a job more suited for an Earther, but his expression said all I needed to know. He wasn't going to let any mudstomper make him look weak.

John's burly arm wrapped the back of my neck, and he led me to another cart in need of loading.

"What's your name, kid?" he asked.

"Ka..." I sputtered over my own name. Growing up in the Lowers, you get used to feeling uncomfortable any time an Earther is close enough to grab your throat. "Kale Drayton."

"We have a tradition on board the *Piccolo*, Kale."

"Yeah?"

He glanced over at his cronies, suppressing a grin. "Yeah. The last Ringer who arrives for duty has to pick up the harvesting canisters."

John's buddies knocked a stack of cylindrical containers off their rack. They clanked along the metal floor, the sound filling the hangar. I felt my heart drop further and further with every impact until they stopped rolling.

"What in Earth's name is going on over there!" the captain shouted.

"Sorry, cap," John answered. "New guy's still getting up to speed. I'll sort him out." John then glanced up at me, that same grin smeared across his face. I stood two heads taller than him, but I'd never felt so small. "Whoops," he said. "We push off in thirty. You better get started."

My blood started to boil. My fingers dug into my palm as they curled into fists.

"What's wrong, boy?" he asked. "Your puny Ringers muscles too tired to do some lifting?"

"Kid looks like he wants to punch ya," one of his buddies said.

"Oh, please do it. I've been itching to snap a skelly's neck like a twig."

Anyone from the Lowers knew two things. Never trust an Earther, and never pick a fight with one unless you've got backup. Not a single one of the other Ringers on the crew came to my aid, even Desmond. A few gave us a passing glance, but nothing more.

I didn't care. I was young and stupid, and angry that I got caught stealing for the wrong man and forced to work on a rusty old ship. My arm tensed as I prepared to take my best shot—I'd only get one before I'd have to bolt—and then I saw something that paralyzed me.

A young woman strolled down the ramp of the ship. Hybrid by the look of her, with curves no Ringer should have and hair so blonde it looked silver. Maybe I'd just never seen a woman beyond the dim, flickering lights of the Lowers, but she was the most beautiful thing I'd ever seen.

"That's what I thought," John said. "Get to work, Ringer." He brushed by, he and his friends all cackling. They nudged some of the canisters with their feet on the way by to move them even further from the rack.

The woman stopped by the mess and knelt to help me. I was so taken aback by her, I let her lift the thing before I remembered to rush over and help her.

"I've got it," I said. I held out my arms, but the woman walked by and hauled the thing to the rack herself.

"They're jerks, but you'll get used to them," she said. All the tension in my muscles melted away as the sound of her soft, calming voice washed over me.

I'm not even sure my response was in English. She pretended not to notice.

"I'll get the rest. It's fine," I managed to utter. "My mess."

"First day?" she said.

I nodded.

"Sometimes, with them, it's best to just keep your mouth shut and your head down," she said. "You'll do fine."

She started ambling away toward the captain, when I blurted out, "What's your name?" My voice cracked halfway through. If my mother heard the way I cursed at myself inwardly for sounding so stupid, she'd have had a heart attack.

The woman turned back, her hair swishing over her slender shoulder. The tiniest inkling of a smile touched her thin lips. "Cora," she said. "I'm the navigator."

———

I wiped the tear from my cheek and tried to force myself to think about something else, anything else. That day seemed so meaningless at the time, but I'd been thinking back to the first time I met Cora more and more since she died. Not just seeing her for the first time, but what she'd said.

She truly believed we could ignore the way Earthers treated us, like one day they'd wake up and see the light. Beat them with kindness. She believed it because she was a better person than anyone left on Titan or Earth. It broke my heart every time I remembered the day she died to know how wrong she was.

I squeezed my eyelids shut and pressed my head into the pillow, desperately trying to sleep. After a few minutes of silence, my thumb found the key to set the recording of Luxarn's and Sodervall's fateful discussion to play again. As it did, I pulled up the only image I had of Cora—a grainy, overhead view from within the cell she was condemned to right before Director Sodervall spaced her simply because she wasn't one of them. Her face obscured by blood, tears, and messy hair; her arms and legs covered in bruises.

Because of them, that was all I had to remember her by. Nothing else.

FOUR

MALCOLM

Coming up on sixty years of living, I wasn't ever going to get used to my new leg. It wasn't the moving it part. That was relatively easy as long as I avoided strenuous situations. After a week in the depths of Undina, I was a relative pro at zipping around in straight lines. Dr. Aurora had me walking a few miles on a simulated Earth-G treadmill every day, pushing me like a drillmaster. That was followed by exhaustive physical therapy on my lower body to try and rekindle all the sensations I once enjoyed. The cantankerous old bat was utterly immune to my charms.

What really freaked me out about the limb was the voic every time I woke up. I found myself tapping the plated thigh just to make sure the leg was there, because other than a slight pinch on my hip when I willed any part of the artificial limb to move, I felt nothing. I'd even found that I couldn't look at the thing when I operated it. It made my skin crawl, like a neighbor I didn't like but was forced to tolerate had latched on to me, or like a partner, like Zhaff.

Whiskey would've helped a ton. My prison guard—doctor— didn't allow any. Not that there was any. I was in the clandestine training facility of the Cogent Initiative, where mentally troubled, illegitimate children with defects like Zhaff had were provided a chance to make a difference.

Mr. Pervenio insisted I stay until the doc gave me a clean bill of health, so I shared all my time with the Cogents. They weren't ones for conversation, so mostly I watched them train. Not that there was anything else to do. No bars, not even a viewscreen to watch a show or a newsfeed on. Their instructors claimed Mr. Pervenio didn't want them distracted by the turmoil in Sol, but instead to prepare their minds and bodies to end it.

So they trained. Every second they weren't sleeping. Martial arts, aptitude exams, physiognomy, psychology, weaponry—anything to sculpt them into perfect shadow agents. It put a whole lot into perspective about Zhaff, starting with making me feel like an idiot for ever thinking I could compete with him. Sure, I had instinct from thirty years on the job, but I'd be better off sitting in front of a screen telling them what to do than trying to keep up.

That seemed like the foremost responsibility of a director—like what Luxarn planned to make me. So, one day after giving up on my own exercise, I limped into the firing range. My new leg could go for an eternity, but the wrinkled one I had left over was weaker than ever after months being under for space travel and treatment. Painkillers dulled the soreness, but then I could hardly feel the pinch of moving the synth leg. There was no winning.

Varus, the youngest Cogent out of the three dozen or so in the facility, was honing his aim. Like Zhaff, he couldn't be much older than fifteen or sixteen, only he was squatter and built like a hovercar. Born on Earth by the looks of it. Like Zhaff had, I wondered what fresh horror he'd endured at the hands of kids who didn't understand him to wind up here.

His yellow eye lens was fixed down the sight of a pulse pistol. He kept his other exposed eye closed.

An instructor decked out in Pervenio gear leaned on the wall next to the shooting range console. He was older than the Cogent, though not by much. He couldn't even grow a beard, and it sure as hell didn't look like he'd ever seen a real firefight. He operated the controls like a tired dockworker, directing holographic targets in the shape of men to dart around the far side of the room like a flock of frenetic hummingbirds.

The Cogent fell into a perfect stance and fired calculated shots into the head of every target, whether they were close or far. One clip, two clips. A chart on the instructor's console provided the stats, and there wasn't a single miss. On the last round of the third clip, the instructor sent a target as far as possible down the long, rocky passage. Sixty meters easy. Varus lined it up a second longer than usual, fired, and plunked it right through the center of the forehead.

"Nice shot," I remarked.

He turned to me, and without a shred of emotion, said, "I was off by three centimeters." Then he returned to shooting.

I couldn't help but grin. He was all Zhaff, with none of the personality I'd squeezed out of him. I thought back to Zhaff on our first job, standing among the ruins of an ancient Earth city while a Ringer terrorist held me at gunpoint. He would've let the man kill me if it had meant a chance at taking him in alive like our mission entailed. By the end of our short time together, I'd like to think he would've seen the value in bending the rules to keep his partner alive.

Maybe I did have something to teach, or maybe I just missed the kid.

"Shut it off," I said to the instructor. He glared at me, but I didn't waver, and eventually, he did as I asked. He knew exactly who I was. A part of me felt like we'd met before—maybe he was a collector once who couldn't hack it—but my aging brain was getting fuzzy when it came to stray faces.

"What is it now, Graves?" he grumbled.

I ignored him and placed a hand on Varus's shoulder. The Cogent's head whipped around, his single exposed eye somehow equally inexpressive and intimidating.

"It isn't always as easy as pulling the trigger," I said to him.

"Is there another way to fire this pulse pistol?" he asked, voice as stale as Zhaff's was.

Again, I smirked. "No, what I mean is... Do you want to kill me?"

"I do not."

"Good." I patted him on the back and strolled out into the shooting aisle. I went about twenty meters and then turned toward him. "Instructor, position a target right behind me."

The instructor went to key the commands, then paused. His lip twisted. "Maybe I should ask Doct—"

"I'm fine. Just do it."

He didn't look happy but obliged. I noticed the cerulean glow of a holographic target on the back of my arm.

"Now, the target behind me has me hostage," I addressed Varus.

"He does not," Varus said.

"Pretend. He's your target, but he has a gun on me, and I'm upper-level Pervenio management." He opened his mouth to reply, but I stopped him. "I know. Just imagine it. You're left with two choices. He either escapes with a valuable hostage, or you risk taking the shot. What do you do?"

Varus eyed his instructor, who offered little more than a shrug. "I contact my primary handler and inquire how to proceed," he stated.

"There's no time. The man he has is your handler, and you're in a dead zone. Hell, imagine I'm Luxarn Pervenio himself. I see how well you shoot with nothing in the way, but can you make that shot? With everything on the line. Can you?"

"Yes," Varus said.

He raised his pulse pistol, and in that split second between him aiming and squeezing the trigger, my mind transported me back to Titan. Zhaff had my daughter in his clutches, so I pulled a gun on him. His weapon was up by the time my shot hit him but not quickly enough. His helmet snapped back before he crumpled to the ground in a heap of twisted limbs.

The vision caused me to reel, and Varus's shot struck my shoulder. I was lucky they were only using flathead training bullets, but the force was still enough to knock me back on my ass. His black-clad figure ran to me, yellow eye-lens glinting. I had to shake my head a few times to remind myself who it really was. Shave a boy's head, cover one eye, and make him pale from lack of sunlight—they all start to look the same.

"You moved into the path of the bullet," he stated categorically as he hauled me to my feet. "You are in need of medical assistance."

"I'm fine!" I shrugged him off and stumbled toward the wall. I leaned on it to gather myself and steady my breathing and heart rate. Thirty years on the job, never once had a gun pointed in my direction made me cower. *I* didn't have nightmares. Like any collector with the stomach to stay in the game, I placed all the traumatic, dreadful things I'd seen deep in my brain, buried beneath a well of liquor.

Damn, I needed a drink.

"Malcolm," someone whispered to me. I didn't answer. "Malcolm."

"What!" I snapped. I turned to see Dr. Aurora. Varus and the instructor were already back at the firing station, watching me. "Oh, Doc, it's you."

"Are you all right?"

I exhaled. "Yeah, I'm fine. Just needed a breather." I'm sure my expression betrayed my words, since her craggy brow furrowed. All her tests and prodding, I wonder if she knew what I'd only just discovered. That it didn't matter whether or not I even wanted to stay in my line of work for Mr. Pervenio—I was done. That a collector who can't escape the specters of his past always is.

"Mr. Pervenio is requesting to meet with you immediately," she said. She presented my worn duster as well as my beloved long-barreled F-3000 pulse pistol, collector issued. She'd joined me on more missions than I could remember.

"About?" I asked. I lifted the pistol and spun it around. It had a few new scrapes and blemishes from what had happened on Titan, but the old girl was in as good a shape as ever. I hadn't realized how much I'd missed her until she was back in my hand, like a long-lost friend.

"In my last report, I informed him you are back in satisfactory health. He would like to discuss the future of your employment."

"I can't wait," I droned.

Maybe Dr. Aurora was just eager to get rid of me and return to helping people who actually needed it. I took my belongings and followed her out, offering Varus a nod of encouragement on my way. I'm not sure he needed it. He didn't look in the least bit rattled. Zhaff never had either, even right before the moment I put him down like a rebel offworlder.

———

Dr. Aurora left me alone outside Mr. Pervenio's office in the deepest sanctum of the concealed facility. I straightened the creases of my worn duster and used the reflection in the shiny door to make sure all my effects were in order. Pistol hanging neatly, hair combed, beard trimmed. The doc even let me shave. There was nothing I could do about the new gray hairs on the top of my head or my deepened wrinkles, but at least I'd walk into my last meeting as a collector looking the part.

Nobody waited to greet me. There weren't even officers posted outside to keep Luxarn safe. The only noise came from a small white room behind me, in which the Cogent Varus was now restrained to a reclined chair. I could tell it was him by his stocky build. A VR visor was strapped over his eyes, and who knows what was playing on it because the usually staid young man squirmed from side to side.

"Welcome, Malcolm Graves," said a robotic voice. "Please, make yourself comfortable. Mr. Pervenio was delayed and will arrive shortly."

I turned, startled, to see the very same service bot Luxarn Pervenio had flaunted my first time meeting him floating out of his office to receive me. The bulbous orb of metal and limbs was bizarre as ever. Its single oculus lined up with my eyes, gave them a scan, and then it allowed me inside.

Apparently, Luxarn had found a purpose for his service bot prototypes that everyday drones couldn't really perform. Certified butler. I stepped in, and unlike the last time I entered his office, all the nerves of meeting with my employer had vanished. The bot didn't follow.

His office on Undina was a far cry from his authentic-wood-clad one with a view of Saturn on Pervenio Station. It was swankier than the Cogent living and training chambers, but more in the way of what you'd expect the manager of an asteroid mine to have. Which made sense, considering that to the outside world, that was all Undina really was. Even I hadn't known that buried deep in its crust was a training and research facility with the capability of installing the cybernetic marvel I now called my leg. It was no wonder Director Sodervall had been so irritated half-a-year back after I ravaged one of its mining sectors and risked exposing it to scrutiny.

I surveyed the room. A polished desk was centered in the back, with nothing on it but a console and Zhaff's cracked eye lens. Some scrapped service bots, which Luxarn had apparently been tinkering with, lay along the floor. A painting of a beach on pre-Meteorite Earth hung on the otherwise blank wall behind his desk. I headed straight for the cabinets sunken into one side, searching for some of that fine whiskey he had the last time we spoke. Nothing.

"What are we, in a Three Messiahs church?" I mumbled.

I rummaged through the last drawer, and right before my hand came up empty, the holographic viewscreen display of Luxarn's console caught my attention. One of the USF news feeds played on low volume, talking heads discussing the latest in Sol affairs.

"Pervenio Corp is dead," said a newswoman positioned in front of an all-too-perfect New London skyline shot. "The interplanetary giant we've known since the rebuilding of civilization is gone. Buried."

"How many corporations have we seen rise and fall?" a Pervenio Director named Barret Ulnor countered. I knew him by appearances, though he never handled offworld affairs. He ran the company's tree farming branch on Earth, and stood amidst one of the massive spaces before a wall of green leaves. From what I recalled, he was a buffoon—had to be to get stuck stationed on Earth.

"None with a CEO more bankable than Luxarn Pervenio," Barret went on. "We still retain innumerable ventures throughout Sol, including the service bot filming me right now. There's no reason to assume this is anything more than a hitch. A road bump."

"Sure, the promise of your new service bot is keeping you

afloat among the wealthy, but is pushing robotics on us really an answer? It's a sideshow. How can you expect anyone to put faith in your employer after what happened at the Ring? The deaths of thousands of privately contracted civilians at the hands of the Children of Titan. The subsequent imprisonment of refugees in inhumane conditions on the very station his family built to oversee the Ring. The precipitate loss of a majority fraction of the gas-harvesting industry."

The screen quickly cut to footage of firefights on Pervenio Station. Ringers armed with whatever they could find swarmed outmatched Pervenio officers. In the end, it froze on the image of Kale Trass with a pulse rifle in his hands. Behind him stood a woman with half her face burnt off. I recognized Kale from all the reports Director Sodervall issued when he was accused of raiding the *Piccolo*. The image was grainy, but there was no mistaking the look in his eyes. They exuded hate and rage I couldn't imagine feeling toward anything. Yet, behind all that, there was no denying the fact that he was still so young. Ruler of the Ring or not, he was a kid.

"Have you seen the price of a ticket to Mars?" Barret said as the feed cut back to him. "The operations on Jupiter aren't viable enough yet to sustain the expansion of our entire species at a decent price point. Even the recent buyout by Venta Co. of EuropaTek and Dynamo Shipworks won't boost yield to reach half of what was harvested just last year."

"People are going to have to get used to losing certain luxuries," said the newswoman. "I think we're all failing to recognize that we're in the midst of a full-scale offworld revolution. Nothing like we've seen before."

"Revolution," he scoffed.

"That's funny? Did you laugh when you watched the leaked recording of their captives?" The screen again shifted to display footage of the Pervenio Station Detention Center from the exterior. Each cell had glass facing out to space, like the Earther captives crammed within were on display at a zoo. Some were bloody, others crying, most both. Kale was turning the very prison lawbreaking Ringers once feared into a propaganda piece.

"Mr. Pervenio is working day and night to try and reach amenable terms with Kale Trass," Barret said. "Once they realize how much they're missing out on, they'll come crawling back like all the rest. There is no humanity stronger than a united one."

"With what resources? The Children of Titan have no interest in credits. Mr. Pervenio and all his directors may deny any losses, but rumors are, many experienced members of Pervenio's management have either been poached or resigned to spare themselves the embarrassment of staying on a sinking ship. I've been told that even you were overheard speaking with Jamaru Venta."

"Lies."

"All right. Then would you deny that Luxarn Pervenio pushed the Titanborn population—"

"Ringer," Barret corrected.

"Yes," the newswoman said adversely. "He pushed them by invading their quarantine without any discernible purpose. In my opinion, he should be tried for the deaths that occurred in the ongoing altercations. That isn't counting the thousands upon thousands still detained by the militant Children of Titan who now have access to weapons and technology he allowed to fall into their hands."

"Criminals who the USF must condemn and punish for their actions! It's either that or we might as well let this murderer Kale Trass stroll right into one of our cities for us to place a crown on his head. The first king of Titan. Is that what you want?"

"I didn't say that."

"It's all true, you know," Luxarn said. The feed suddenly switched off. I'd unconsciously taken a seat at his desk to watch and leaped up so fast the chair slid all the way to the back wall. Luxarn didn't seem to notice or care as he ambled in.

"What's that, sir?" I asked.

"What they're saying. It's all true. Worse probably. Most of my other collectors have abandoned us for greener pastures too. The new directors in charge of what properties I still retain are green or worthless, like Barret Ulnor. Most of them haven't managed more than a dock. They can hardly handle the upcoming, limited release of our service bots." The spherical bot floated in behind him, and he tapped it on the side, causing it to sway in its flight path, bang into the wall, and shut down. "These things were supposed to rekindle human interest in robotics. What a joke."

"They pour a mean drink as far as I can remember." It was a subtle nudge to try and get him to offer up some of the good stuff again, but it went right over his head.

"Yes. Kale forces me to issue an early release to try and boost revenue, and now we're shipping tin balls that can do little more than bartend a half-empty room or answer a door."

"And fly."

Luxarn chuckled exasperatedly. "It's all unraveling, thanks to that monster Kale."

"I'm sure that reporter is exaggerating. There isn't any shame in still being one of the richest men in Sol, sir."

"Spoken like a true collector." He sat on the edge of his desk. "It was my father's dream to usher humanity into our deserved future. To reach as far as we can until there isn't a star left we haven't seen. It's all going to change now. We can't spread when we aren't safe, and every offworld colony is going to be looking over their shoulders for the next Kale Trass."

"We'll figure it out. We always do. If we can survive the apocalypse, we can survive some pissed off Ringer throwing a tantrum. He'll realize they can't survive alone."

"They did before." Luxarn stood, approached the stark wall behind me, and spread his arm across it. I could picture him back on Pervenio Station, marveling out his viewport at all he'd built. Now he regarded little more than rust, metal, and a painting of what we could never have again.

"They say Kale has organized a formal meeting with the USF on Mars," Luxarn said. "I have a feeling he's going to demand that Titan be granted sovereignty, and considering all the hostages he has on Pervenio Station, ready to be spaced at the flick of a switch, the Assembly will have no choice but to settle. Even now he uses them to shield against retribution."

"Then maybe it's time they put an end to hostilities. Let Kale have whatever it is he wants and negotiate. There's nothing they could possibly do with all the resources they're in control of except trade them."

"I will not negotiate with him!" he growled. "They're locking our people up like rats while we squabble. People I was meant to protect. Maybe there's a Ringer under him that can be dealt with, but Kale has to be eliminated. I don't care what the Assembly thinks. He'll never let them go free."

"You kill him, and they might never get that chance." Cutting the head off snakes was my specialty for a long time, but the reporter was right about one thing. This wasn't some mere riot. I'd gotten enough sense of that in my last visit to Titan even before the shit hit the fan.

"If he kills them, nothing will keep the USF and all its corporations from bombing Titan out of existence. Kale has to go, Graves. It's the only way."

I glanced at Zhaff's eye lens. It still pained me to see it. In the reflection, I pictured him, a frosty, bloodied husk because of me. His death had to at least be a part of the rage fueling Luxarn's lust for vengeance. I considered for a moment that maybe if I told Luxarn the truth, he'd put aside his vendetta and focus on a real solution. Then I remembered how he'd kept Zhaff's true identity hidden for all those years while he forged him into a weapon. He might've loved him in his own way, but it had always been about Pervenio Corp. Company first, how I used to be.

I sighed. "Well, sir, it pains me to say you're going to have to do it without me."

His body whipped around to face me, and his plastic-surgery-enhanced façade didn't appear angered, but instead fearful. "That's nonsense. Dr. Aurora informed me that you're finally healthy. You're ready to finish what you and my son started and end the Children of Titan once and for all."

"My body is fine, thanks to you, but I'd rather get out before I embarrass myself any further or lose any more limbs. I let myself be goaded right into their hideout and..." Again I noticed Zhaff's eye lens out of the corner of my eye. My throat went dry. "And got Zhaff killed."

Luxarn's brow furrowed. After a few long seconds of silence, he said, "Let me show you something."

"Sir, I—"

"I won't take no for an answer."

He beckoned me out of the door, and I followed begrudgingly. Mostly, probably, because though I told myself my mind was made up, his Corp had a knack for convincing me to stick around.

He led me a short distance down the hall, to a door sealed by both a retina scan and vocal confirmation. That kind of security never meant anything good, but as we entered, I realized it was another treatment room like the one I'd woken up in. Doctor Aurora stood on the opposite side, only there was no bed. A cylindrical chamber rose in the center, filled with a greenish goo. A body floated within.

"Leave us," Luxarn ordered.

Doctor Aurora didn't seem pleased—though she never did—as she nodded and headed out, eyes poring over data readouts on her hand-terminal. Much of the same information covered the dozens of viewscreens mounted around the white room. Far more than it took to monitor me and my new leg.

Luxarn said nothing, so I invited myself in further to get a better look at the chamber. The liquid inside was thick, so I got right up to the glass to see the face of whoever it was suspended within. That was when my heart dropped clear through my gut. I stumbled back, and if I didn't have an artificial leg keeping me up, my knees would have given out.

I'd know the man inside anywhere. Zhaff Fucking Pervenio. I'd seen him in so many waking dreams since coming to, I could never mistake that face. He was stripped completely bare, countless circuits and tubes poking his sallow flesh. A portion of his torso and his entire left arm were replaced by the same material as my leg—synthetic. The half of his face he once wore his eye-lens over was reconstructed as well. But none of that was what drew my attention most. A respirator covered his mouth and plunged down his throat, and his chest rose subtly, in and out.

"I thought..." I swallowed back the sudden urge to vomit at the sight of my partner, now a Frankenstein patchwork of flesh and muscle. I squeezed my eyelids tight and checked again to make sure I wasn't seeing things. I clutched my chest, as if that could keep my heart from racing. Breathing suddenly became difficult, the air feeling hot and thick, while a shiver simultaneously ran up my spine, thanks to memories of being shot on Titan.

"I thought he was dead," I managed to say after a few strained breaths.

"Who told you that?"

"You did... or..." I wasn't often left speechless, but it happened from time to time. Like when previously thought dead partners pop up in a tube. Or when Ringers blow their own brains out for no damn reason.

"His eye-lens saved him. The bullet broke it, and the shards plugged the hole to prevent the change in pressure from killing him instantly. The cold of Titan still did major damage, but the bullet passed through non-critical parts of his brain. Or so they tell me."

Luxarn sounded frustrated, as if Zhaff should have been expected to survive a pulse-pistol round to the face. I summoned the courage to approach again and laid my hand over the glass, only to find it was quaking. Like it was my first day on the job seeing a body.

Zhaff's face looked so peaceful in there. He always appeared emotionless, but this was different—like he had no worries. Still, I kept expecting his remaining eye to snap open the moment I got too near, even though I knew that eye was blinded when he was younger.

"He's been in a coma since we recovered him," Luxarn said. "Doctor Aurora and dozens of doctors and scientists say he'll never wake. That the life support is all that's keeping him alive. She thinks it's time to pull the plug and 'set him free.' But while we've wasted decades developing vaccines for Ringers, other companies have made huge leaps in medicine. From cybernetics like your leg to curing certain cancers to—"

"I don't know, sir," I said, my voice robbed of all its timbre by shock. "Maybe Doctor Aurora is right." I wasn't sure if it was the self-preservationist in me speaking, who knew if Zhaff ever woke with his memory intact, I was as good as dead, or if it was the me who'd grown to care for him. Either way, I'd witnessed my share of mad scientists who thought they could play god and it never turned out well.

"I refuse to give up on my son until he's truly gone. And neither should you." Luxarn took me by the shoulders, forcing me, finally, to look away from the kid. "We can avenge what was done to him."

I peered back at the sleeping, barely recognizable cyborg floating in the tube. A nightmare if I'd ever seen one. "I believe I am." I backed away from Luxarn. "I'm sorry, sir, but I'm done with all of this."

Anger gripped Luxarn once more, though I wasn't affected like I once would've been. The impossibly powerful man I knew who gazed out upon space as if he were ready to devour it all was clearly gone. Now he hid away like a mad hermit while the Ring was pilfered, clinging on to half-dead corpses out of guilt. I knew the feeling well enough from a lifetime of failing Aria to know that's what this was.

"You would walk away from the chance to be a director?" he growled.

"Dying puts things into perspective. I'm tired of all the fighting. I spent a lifetime running from a vacation, but right about now, all I want to do is nothing."

"I know you're upset about what happened down there, but we can fix this, just like I can fix him. No matter how many credits it takes. Don't throw this away. You're the last man in this damn corporation I know I can trust, Graves."

I never thought I'd be in a world where I would pity Luxarn Pervenio, but if I was indeed the last man he could trust, then Pervenio Corp was doomed. Trust *me*? A collector well past his prime who'd only physically met him a few months ago, and who'd already betrayed him by putting his bastard son in a coma so I could help an illegitimate daughter I'd kept secret her whole life. That wasn't a world I knew how to operate in.

"I wish things could be different, sir, I really do," I said. "I've given my life to this company, and it's been a privilege, but it's time to check out." I removed the pulse pistol from my belt and slapped it down on a worktable beside Zhaff's tube.

Luxarn's eyes widened, as if he'd had zero doubt he was going to convince me to stay. A man like him would never get used to people saying no.

"You think you can just walk away?" he questioned. "You failed your last assignment, Graves. You were after stolen supplies, and they all got away."

"They did, but I remember a conversation about an extended job located the Children of Titan's hideout. Which *we* did."

Nothing got under my skin quite like bungling a job and getting called out for it. My wounded pride couldn't handle it. Though I couldn't say that we'd retrieved the supplies, but I made sure we failed. I pictured Aria fleeing with the stolen medical provisions. I remembered expecting what they took to be new weapon tech or a bomb. Instead, it was only meant to help heal the sick.

"You will watch your tone, Graves," Luxarn said. "Part of the job, part of the reward, then. And don't think you'll get any portion of my son's!"

"Keep the credits." Words I never thought I'd say to Luxarn Pervenio before turning my back to him. I needed to get out of the room before his anger and seeing Zhaff how he was caused me to say anything that would sour decades of loyal service. He kept using Zhaff like it'd convince me. If he cared about my old partner—his son—he wouldn't have sent him to battle terrorists as a teenager.

"That doesn't come anywhere close to what it cost to give you back your leg. You'll be paying it off the rest of your life."

That finally got me to stop in the exit and bite my lip. I grabbed my hunk of synthetics, turned, and lifted the knee toward him. "Do you want it back, then?" I said.

A wave of emotions passed across Mr. Pervenio's face. Finally, he settled on what looked like remorse. "Keep the leg," he conceded. "For research. What you have in your account won't cover it all, but consider the rest recompense for thirty good years of service. You deserve that at least, after all that you've done."

"Thank you, sir." I went to turn again, but he stopped me once more.

"If you really won't take my offer, at least consider this."

"What?"

"I'll provide transport to wherever you want to go. Do whatever it is with retirement you think you need, but keep an open mind. When you realize the mess Kale has made of our Sol, my offer remains." He tossed me my pulse pistol. It was a terrible throw, and I had to scramble to catch it, but it reached me. "If you see him in the meantime, put a bullet in him for Zhaff. I'll make you so rich you can crawl into a bottle for the rest of your life."

I studied the gun. Every dent was a faded memory. Every scratch a tussle. Whether or not I wanted to fire it again, I felt naked without it. I grinned slightly. "All right, sir. That sounds fair enough to me."

He nodded. "Pervenio Corporation thanks you for your service, Mr. Graves."

Something brash fought its way to the tip of my tongue before I caught a glimpse of Zhaff's floating body again and felt my throat tighten. "It's been fun," I said. "And, sir, maybe it's time for you to move on too. Set him free, or whatever. Wherever the dead go, it's got to be a hell of a lot more pleasant than here."

My words left him speechless as I walked away from the only job I'd known since I was a young man in a worthless clan-family who hadn't seen anything beyond New London. The door shut behind me, and I gasped for air as if I'd been drowning. I had to lean on the wall just to catch my breath.

Where to go now? Maybe I could try to find Aria again like I'd always planned to after retiring, though I kind of preferred our leaving things on good terms. I couldn't be there to play hero every time she got in trouble working with terrorists. She made her own choices, and I'd taught her well enough to be sure as hell she wasn't a captive. She'd either done the smart thing like I'd taught her to and run or had convinced her people I was the enemy and was back on Titan taking care of those injured in the revolution. Helping people always came so natural to her.

Either way, she'd be safer on her own. Nobody outside of Titan except me knew her role in sparking the revolution, and people didn't hunt down innocent doctors. Plus, if I did find her, I'd probably wind up screwing up again and someone else who didn't deserve it would die.

Yeah, she was a lot better off without me.

So, there I stood, an ex-Pervenio collector with a second lease on life who'd just turned down a chance at being a director. No future assignments. No handler. Nothing to do at all. I suppose it was finally time for that drink I owed myself.

FIVE

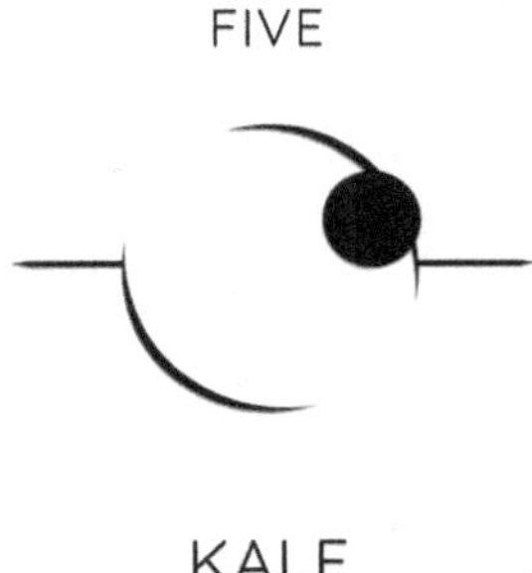

KALE

I won't say I was scared as I watched the ruddy, light-speckled orb of Mars grow beyond the viewport of the *Cora*. Anxious maybe, though I'd become an expert at keeping myself level enough to always appear composed. It was, however, my first time visiting a world beyond the Ring. Sure, I'd stepped onto many of the moons and stations orbiting Saturn since our revolution started, some as a soldier, others to keep the peace, but never anywhere so close to Earth.

We were nearing the end of our month-and-a-half-long journey to Mars. Earther influence on the Red Planet remained strong as always. Venta Co. and Red Wing Co., the two most significant Earther corporations remaining after Pervenio's decline, called it their base of operations, though Venta was in the process of transitioning much of their operations to Europa. Still, the USF Assembly had the nerve to consider it neutral ground. They initially asked to hold our formal meeting on Earth, where gravity would crush us into submission, so at least on Mars, I'd be able to walk without my heart feeling ready to explode. G-stims could only counteract the effects of gravity stronger than Titan's so much, and I needed to remain vigilant.

I twirled one of those very g-stims between my fingers, the Pervenio logo engraved into the pack, a constant reminder of how they'd taken everything from us. The concoction of chems used in them was actually a Titanborn invention from before the Great Reunion, when our ancestors started harvesting the gases of Saturn, which were far more efficient sources of fuel than Titan's abundant methane lakes. That was just one small part of our forgotten history, revealed from data logs after we occupied Pervenio Station.

After the plague that claimed so many of my people half a century ago, Pervenio took over production of the g-stims like they had everything else. The logo remained proof of that. We'd driven them out now but were left with their highly advanced manufacturing plants and labs, and very few with the skills to do anything more than operating the machinery. Some of the elements required to develop their specific product lines also weren't prevalent on Titan, meaning our supply was limited. We needed to be careful wasting any until we were able to strip back the formula to what our ancestors used. Boosting gas-harvesting yields to gain leverage over Earth was crucial, and Titanborn couldn't operate the manned harvesters under Saturn's gravity without g-stims.

So much was crucial...

I tried to act brazen around my people, but I knew the kind of struggle that lay ahead. It was like Luxarn Pervenio had been prepared that in the event we took over, they'd still be able to make our lives a living hell. My people had to simultaneously fight and teach themselves an entirely new stratum of technical skills to make use of their equipment. Not to mention all the repairs necessary after the heaviest of the fighting. From factories to ships, Titanborn men and women had put most of it together when we were their slaves, but like Rylah once told me, "Knowing where the pieces go isn't knowing how it works."

I didn't even realize that I was crushing the g-stim pack out of vexation until it cracked in half—releasing its chems into the air. From my perspective, the pieces floating out of my grip swarmed about the looming Red Planet like a field of the meteors Earthers were so afraid of. I wondered if Earth looked similar to Mars after their infamous M-Day Meteorite hit, if it was wreathed by red flames racing across its once verdant surface.

"Have you been awake the entire time?" Ambassador Aria asked, her voice groggy. A month in a sleep pod and it was like her vocal chords had forgotten what it was supposed to sound like.

I quickly snatched broken g-stims out of the air and shoved them into the pouch on my belt rather than my mouth. I didn't want to be numb on one of their worlds. Mars's gravity wasn't excruciatingly higher than Titan's. Enough to notice, but tolerable. I had to feel everything.

"Couldn't stomach going under," I said without looking back at her. Our course was on autopilot, and any danger would rouse the crew, but after watching everyone load into their pods, I couldn't do it. Instead, I'd roamed the halls of the ship alone the entire time, with nothing but yeasty ration bars, stars, and my thoughts to keep me company.

"Mal—" She stopped herself. "My father never liked it much either. He said it was like sleeping in a coffin, but that it was better than months with no company but space. Too long with the blackness could drive a man mad, or something like that."

"Not me," I replied.

She deftly pulled her weightless body along the bars on the ceiling until she was hovering behind me. This may have been my first long-distance space trip, but she was an expert at zero g. Her hand fell gently upon my shoulder, and with it, a stream of auburn hair that somehow after so long in stasis still smelled fresh. That got me to glance up, and we froze momentarily as our gazes met. Her usually rosy cheeks were a light shade of green from sleep sickness. I'd heard her vomiting a few times right after waking, but decided not to draw any attention to it.

Neither of us held each other's stare for long. She instinctually bowed her head out of respect, causing the pendant on her necklace to fall out from her collar. It was an old Ark Ship figurine she said her father had given to her before he disappeared and she raised herself.

"You need to rest more, Kale," she said softly. "I know there's a lot to deal with, but I've seen how you lie awake every night."

She was right. I hadn't had proper rest in longer than I cared to remember, and that didn't change during the trip. But something about artificial sleep made me uneasy. If I went under that long, maybe I would risk losing some memory of what Cora looked like. How her infrequent smiles made the tip of her nose wrinkle. How her silvery hair shimmered under the right light...

"How would you possibly know what I need?" I growled.

She didn't back down. Instead, she drew herself around me, so I had no choice but to stare straight into her bright green eyes. She wasn't born on Earth, but she wasn't Titanborn either. Somewhere in between, same as any first-generation offworlder born on Mars. Her skin was exceedingly pale like mine, though rosy on her cheeks and dappled with freckles. Curly ginger hair tumbled over an ample chest like nobody born on Titan could ever boast.

Whether or not she was one of us, her beauty was unquestionable. The loose-fitting dress she wore didn't hide it. She could've easily been Cora's red-haired sister, and every time I beheld her, my mind was brought back to that moment on

Pervenio Station when we'd found Cora's empty cell shortly after she was spaced.

"I'm your doctor too, remember?" she said. "It isn't healthy pushing yourself like you do."

"After we're done here, I'll try. Will that make you happy?"

Her lips formed the beginnings of a smile. The tip of her freckled nose creased as they did, causing my heart to race. Before I could turn away, she took my hand and wrapped it around her waist, pulling herself close. "Don't do it for me," she whispered.

"Never stuff me into one of those fucking things again!" Rin barked from the cabin behind us. The sound of a few other Titanborn puking echoed along with her.

Aria released my hand and immediately put a few feet between us. I was grateful for the opportunity to breathe. Being around her was equally suffocating and intoxicating.

"Kale, are we there yet?" Rin questioned. "I can't take another second of zero-g." She floated into the command deck, bits of vomit stuck in the crags of the scars marring half of her face.

All I did in response was point through the viewport, where Mars filled almost the entirety of the view. I could now perceive the clusters of metal and bright lights indicating the many domed colonies dappling the planet surface. Thousands of Earthers and first-or-second-generation offworlders were crammed into each of them.

Rin shoved Aria aside and took her place at the central navigation console beside mine, in front of a curving field of screens, holo-displays, and switches. Everything was top of the line. It made the command deck of the *Piccolo* seem like something out of the dark ages. Rin started picking at keys as if testing each one for poison.

"You have to switch the auto-pilot course off first." Aria indicated a screen to their left.

"I know that," Rin said.

She struck the command with verve, like she knew it the whole time, and took control. The *Cora* shuddered a bit but quickly leveled out. Countless readouts and automated fail-safes ensured it was impossible to mess up flying too badly, short of piloting us straight into the side of Olympus Mons. Aria had spent much of the weeks before this voyage training my reluctant aunt, who refused to put our lives in the hands of an outsider unless it was absolutely necessary like in the Ring Skipper raid.

As I watched Aria provide Rin with subtle clues to prepare her for landing, I realized how hard it was to bear the sight of her in a navigator's chair as well, no matter how much I trusted her. Especially the *Cora*'s.

The ship shook again, this time from breaching Mars's thin atmosphere. Nobody seemed shocked by it. It was nothing like being bowled side to side by the stormy Titanian skies upon entry. Gravity pulled me tight against my seat, straining my lungs just a hair beyond their comfort level since I'd decided against injecting a g-stim.

"Unidentified vessel, you are intruding on the airspace of the USF and its affiliated corporations," an operator spoke through our coms. "Venta Co. security has been dispatched and will be forced to fire if you do not reply."

"What are they talking about, girl?" Rin asked.

"I... I don't know," Aria replied. "I submitted our transponder codes before we left."

"See, Kale? This is the kind of sloppiness we can expect with an outsider in charge."

"I swear, I sent them."

"I altered the codes," I said matter-of-factly. They gawked at me, but I leaned forward and gazed at the tremendous web of segmented domes stretching between and filling a collection of craters. "What's New Beijing like?" I asked Aria.

"Kale, what the hell were you thinking?" she questioned. "I know these people. They aren't bluffing."

"Watch your tone," Rin interjected.

The boom of two fighters breaking the speed of sound on either side of the *Cora* made my bones chatter. Their bows were visible through the corners of the viewport. The dual white and blue overlapped V company logo was imprinted on their flanks.

"What's the plan, Kale?" Rin said, struggling to keep her eyes straight ahead.

"What's it like?" I asked Aria again.

"I repeat, identify yourself, or we will fire," the Venta operator demanded.

Rin held our course and kept quiet. Aria's eyes darted from side to side nervously as she clutched the pendant hanging from her neck. "It's like anywhere else," she said. "Clean on the surface, dirty underneath." The fighters dropped behind us, and *Cora*'s advanced defensive matrix started beeping as they targeted us.

I couldn't tear my gaze away from New Beijing. Every dome comprising the city extended toward the light. Their glass enclosures were tinted from radiation shielding and the diamond pattern of structural beams holding it up, but everyone below got to look up and see a real sky. The vast interiors were brimming with ad-covered skyscrapers and vertical layers of narrow hanging walkways. They were organized similarly to how the old cities of Earth I'd seen on documentaries were, only clustered more densely.

I'd heard about the great Martian domes, but seeing them was something else entirely. Only Earthers would be audacious enough to treat Mars like it was their homeworld. Just slap a lid over their ridiculous tower cities like a glass jar and be done.

"Kale!" Aria shouted.

I switched on our end of the coms. "This is Kale Trass requesting entry into the New Beijing Spaceport," I said calmly, earning a collective gasp from Aria and the other stirred members of our crew who had gathered behind.

"M... Mr. Trass," the operator stuttered. "My apologies, we didn't realize the vessel belonged to you."

"We're having some trouble with our new transponder."

"There is—" He paused, likely to speak with a supervisor. "No problem. Our fighters will escort you into your designated hangar to ensure your safety."

And to make sure it's really you, I knew he wanted to add. That settled the debate that had raged in my head while I sat alone throughout the journey. Hearing only my voice and name offered no certainty it was really me, but they couldn't risk shooting us down or denying me entry. That meant they were starting to take us seriously enough to at least be cautious.

"It's not smart to coerce them like that," Aria scolded as the Venta Co. airships sped out in front of us. "Madame Venta isn't known for her temperance."

"I told you to watch your tone," Rin bristled.

"Quiet, both of you," I said. "I wanted to see how close the *Cora*'s stealth systems could get us before they noticed. In case we need to leave in a hurry."

Rin obeyed for a few seconds, and then couldn't help herself. "This better not be another trap, *ambassador*," she muttered to Aria as if I wouldn't hear her.

"If I wanted you dead, Rin, you'd have never left Titan," Aria remarked. She didn't wait for a response either. The moment the last word escaped her lips, she patted my aunt's tense shoulder and drew herself out of the room.

I snickered. Rin shot me a sidelong glare. "She's lucky I'm flying."

"None of us are lucky for that," I replied.

The *Cora* suddenly banked so hard around the crest of a bulbous, barren mountain that my stomach lurched. Judging by how smoothly the ships leading us made their approach to New Beijing, it wasn't an accident. Turbulence was as alien to Mars as we were.

"You shouldn't encourage offworlders to talk to us like that," Rin advised. "Kale, are you listening? I don't care who they are or what they've done in the past. Earth's authority this far into the solar system is strong."

Our ship leveled out and headed straight for an open portion of a smaller dome bulging from the side of New Beijing's main one. I unfastened my restraints and stood.

"How I missed your lectures while you were asleep," I muttered. As a fellow Trass and experienced combat leader, Rin answered to nobody but me. I valued her opinion more than anybody's, but Aria's position within our fledgling administration had been our first disagreement.

"I'm serious," she said. "You let one of them in close, they'll spread like a sickness. Just like last time."

"Well, this one got us a meeting with the USF Assembly. She's given as much as any of us for the cause. Besides, even you know we need her."

Rin rolled her shoulders. "For now."

"Just try and pretend you can stand them at least a little bit. I have a feeling this will be the only meeting we get. For now, they have to see we come in peace."

"You're right. I'll just keep my mouth shut and let the Earther... offworlder... whatever the hell she is, speak for me." She licked the corner of her lip, and I could see the side of her tongue wriggling through the crater in her cheek.

Her support was always welcome, but maybe keeping her mouth shut was a good idea for now. Diplomacy wasn't her specialty. Plus, I could remember how terrified I was the first time I laid eyes on Rin. Even in a sanitary mask, there was no way to completely hide the horrors of what Earthers had done to her.

And now we were about to arrive on a planet full of them.

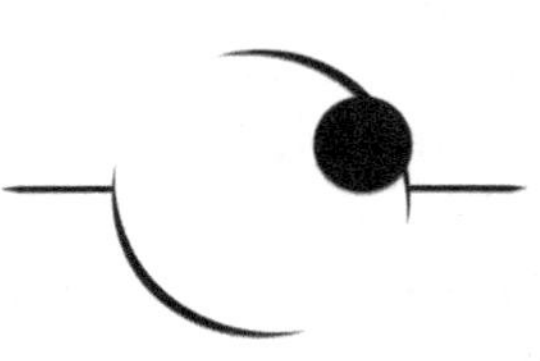

SIX

MALCOLM

Sol was filled with rotten and fuzzy memories. Everywhere I considered going in my retirement, I could think of a job that got ugly, a night that got out of hand, or a hotel where my daughter looked disappointed when I smuggled her in. I guess that's what happens when you get to be my age. No matter where you go, the past is lingering to haunt you.

So I searched for a place that was still a part of civilization where I could disappear easiest. I settled on New Beijing, Mars. Of all the shit memories I had, at least a handful of the good ones came from there. The expansionist propaganda rampant on Earth would drive me to put a gun in my mouth if I stayed there too long. Development around Jupiter was happening too rapidly to relax. I'd seen too many asteroid colonies busted open or wither when their wealth dried up to choose one of them. And the Ring... I'd rather board a Departure Ark out of the galaxy than go back there, even if it wasn't a war zone.

New Beijing it was.

The city both where my daughter was illegitimately born to a streetwalker and where I'd lost her. A city mostly free from that damn Pervenio logo I'd spent too much of my life honoring. News feeds all portrayed the grandeur of New Beijing with its vast domes, shiny towers, and cascading garden terraces. It was home to some of the wealthiest people, most elegant hotels, and best entertainment venues in Sol. Of course, that was all above surface level. The parts of New Beijing I knew best were where I'd once operated. In the shadows. I'd spent so long hunting offworlders that, ironically, they wound up being the people I felt most comfortable around.

Every city came with its own seedy underbelly, but few were on par with New Beijing's. Everything sandwiched between the main-level avenues and the expansive subway subterranean tram and sewer network were once covered by the city's original lower domes before they were radically extended. Rusty, amalgamated structures bridged the major walkways as more and more people were shoved down toward the planet's surface. They called the place Old Dome, and it boasted some of the best and grubbiest gambling dens, clubs, and street-walkers a person could buy.

Over-crowded, Venta-run, there was no better place for a retired old Pervenio collector like me to stay off the grid.

Too many years removing targets for Pervenio had left me with more enemies than I probably knew I had. And I couldn't be sure whether or not Luxarn would have me taken out just to be safe. As if I knew anything that really mattered. He put on a pleasant face when we parted ways, but men didn't get to be as rich as he was if they weren't good actors.

It didn't take me long on the Red Planet to find the hole I'd likely spend the rest of my life in. A little bar buried so far in Old Dome you could almost smell the rank of the sewers if you stepped outside. It shared a wall with one of the city's larger Redline Stations, the crisscrossing New Beijing subways. That meant constant rumbling within and a steady flow of homeless offworlders desperate for a place to sleep. Yeah, the Twilight Sun was my kind of dump.

They needed a new bouncer at their door, and since I'd apparently invested decades of collector service into a new leg I didn't ask for, I still needed credits despite retiring. The job made me wonder why I hadn't dragged my old bones into similar work sooner. There wasn't any glory in it and sure as hell no thrill, but I finally wasn't seeking any of that. In exchange for sitting at the door and making sure things stayed quiet in a place that usually had more tables than patrons, my new boss let me live in one of the apartments upstairs and drink as much as I liked. Enough to stop picturing poor Zhaff floating in that tube from time to time. It offset the garbage pay too.

The Twilight Sun tried to instill some old-world oriental charm with its bracketed faux-wood bar and the old ink paintings dotting the walls. They depicted ferocious beasts long extinct and serene landscapes the Meteorite ensured were now impossible, yet all of it was discolored or scratched. Even the sliding paper walls at the private booths were too torn to provide real seclusion, not that anyone was paying to use them. The owner hadn't put a credit into the place in years. Probably why he had to hire a gunman with no resume for the door. At least, not one I could elaborate on.

I raised the rim of a bottle to my mouth and leaned my head all the way back to coax out the last few drops of whiskey. I sighed. A lackluster month and a half had passed since I had taken the job, and all I'd accomplished was building my already impressive tolerance. From my seat by the front door, I had a great view of Wai, the only dancer the bar could afford to keep on the payroll. She was on the cracked stage behind the bar, wearing a skimpy leotard and a conical hat with blue beads falling from the brim to conceal her face.

She was a pretty young thing, with soft skin and almond-shaped eyes as deep brown as wet soil. A sewer girl just like Aria's mom. Too green for me, though, and too skinny. Her ribs protruded like the keys of a piano. All I could think about while watching her was ordering her a ration bar or three.

The night was so far gone only one patron was left watching her. The slovenly, gray-bearded man synced credits to the handterminal set upright by her nimble feet. He could hardly keep his swaying head up, and by then, she wasn't doing much more than wiggling her hips to eerie, atmospheric string music. When the song came to an end, the man reached out and stroked her calf.

My bottle dropped with a loud clank, and I stumbled toward her, using every table en route to steady myself. Intoxication limited my brain's ability to communicate with my artificial leg so that I could walk straight. That was what Doc Aurora had warned me about at least. I'm reasonably confident a full bottle of Martian whiskey would've had any man stumbling no matter what kind of legs he boasted.

"It's time to close," I said to the man.

He turned his head slowly, eyes lagging behind. "No, it ain't." He was slurring worse than I was. "I'm just getting started."

My hand fell toward my pulse pistol, the only friend I had left. He watched it, then started to chuckle.

"What're you gonna do? Shoot me over watchin' some sewer trash?" he asked.

"No. I'm going to shoot you so I can get some damn sleep." I grabbed him by the shirt and shoved him toward the door. Another good part about Old Dome. I was an Earther, and scrawny offworlders like him were easy to push around.

"Alright, alright," he said as he bumped a chair. He turned to say something else, hiccupped instead, and then continued on his winding path toward the door straight ahead.

"What the hell was that?" Wai said, visibly irritated. "He was still paying."

"Was he? Didn't realize." I slumped into his vacated seat and eyed his ale. It didn't look like he'd even taken a sip, so I took one for myself. Warm and metallic, like everything else on tap in the Twilight Sun.

"*Lǎo wán gù!*" she cursed in an ancient, oriental dialect still championed by the poor folk of New Beijing. "You weren't getting enough sleep over there?"

"Why are you even still here, Wai?"

"You know why. I guarantee your old Earther *pigu* hasn't ever had to sleep a night in the sewers."

I smirked. I remembered plenty of such nights, more than a few with Aria's mom or with Aria herself when I dragged her around on jobs.

"You could be dancing at one of the big corporate dens, you know," I said. "You're good enough. Got the looks. You'd make a hell of a lot more."

"And be asked to do a hell of a lot more." She twirled on the stage once before falling back into the couch across from me. She had a robe waiting in it, which she pulled over her body so that only her thin, pasty legs were showing.

"Can I have one more before we close? Synth, strong." She waved to the owner, who didn't have the money to hire a human bartender, let alone one of Pervenio's new service bots. Yan Ning was as old and ragged as I was. If I had to guess, I'd take him for an ex-security officer on some run-down asteroid mine. Without a nod or acknowledgment, he filled a glass with the most fluorescent yellow liquid you could imagine and carried it over to her.

"You're locking up, Haglin," he grumbled to me.

My brow furrowed; then I remembered. Sometimes I drank too much and forgot my fake name. I didn't care if anybody knew who I was, but something was appealing about disappearing where even Luxarn Pervenio couldn't find me. It made it easier to relax. Setting up a fake credit account and passable ID with a gun-carrying license wasn't too tough. I still had a few connections on Mars who owed a favor.

"Sure thing, boss." I saluted. I wondered if he had any idea how much of Sol I'd seen to know how ridiculous it was every time I called him that.

The room started to tremble as a subway train raced underground, kicking up dust and making the lights rattle. Yan Ning waited until it passed before placing Wai's colorful drink in front of her and heading out without a word. She took a long sip. Her lips scrunched as the awful-tasting synthahol went down, but after the initial shock, she sank back into the couch and made herself comfortable.

"I've known Yan Ning since I was a girl," Wai said. "I like it here. Everyone keeps their hands to themselves mostly or drinks so much that I can do it for them. And it's quiet."

I tipped my glass toward her. "We can agree on that."

One of her eyebrows lifted. "You really think a corps-den would hire me, though?"

"Sure."

"How much would you pay, *lǎo tóuzi?*"

"That's tough. Maybe the rest of this warm beer?"

"Earther pig!"

I smirked. Wai had a mouth on her. If I didn't know better, I might think I'd fathered another illegitimate daughter on Mars. I found myself staring as she raised her drink again. The way the dim lighting struck the sphere of ice inside it suddenly caused a glimmer of a yellow like Zhaff's eye lens to touch her eyes.

The glass slipped from my hand, and a healthy portion

spilled before I caught it. I coughed a few times, squeezed my eyelids tight, and when I reopened them, the yellow was gone.

"Okay, *lǎo tóuzi*, I think you've had enough to drink." She went to grab the glass, but I pulled back.

"I'm fine!" I objected then realized I'd snapped. "Sorry. Never come between an Earther and his drink."

She wasn't bothered by my tone. Instead, her gaze had wandered to my leg. The attempt at catching the glass had caused my pants leg to raise enough to spot my artificial ankle above a shoe I didn't need to wear.

"You weren't always a bouncer, were you?" she asked, wide-eyed.

I quickly fixed my clothing. "I don't know what you're talking about."

"Please. I may be from the sewers, but I'm not stupid. Nobody down here can afford *gāo kējì* like that, and the ones that can are running from something."

"Running," I snickered. "If only. What does it matter to you?"

"It doesn't, but you cost me credits tonight. I think I at least deserve to hear a good story to make up the time since you only pay in old beer."

I stood and chugged the rest of the ale. "I'll tell you what, when you find your way out of this shithole, I'll tell you."

She stuck out her hand and put on a wry grin. "Promise?"

I slapped my glass down and shook her hand. "Promise. Now I'm wide awake. You mind locking up?" She stared at me as if waiting for a better offer until, finally, I gave in. I reached into my pocket and pulled out the key card that got me into the tiny apartment upstairs. I tossed it to her. "You can stay in my place for the night if you do. I don't plan on turning in early."

"Oh, I definitely don't mind. As long as you don't mind

paying the Venta water bill on the longest shower I've ever taken."

"Fine, but no complaining next time I kick a drooling customer out if I don't like the way he looks." I started ambling toward the exit, able to maintain my balance better than normal. The yellow I'd seen in her eyes had me feeling a bit more sober.

"Oh, Haglin!" she shouted after me. "Make sure you get here on time tomorrow, or Yan will have a heart attack. It might be busy."

"What is it? M-Day again already?"

She exhaled. "Kale Trass and them Ringers are arriving, remember? Should draw crowds from all over Mars."

"Right." I glanced at the grainy viewscreen above the bar playing a live newsfeed. All anyone had been reporting for weeks was about how Kale Trass was meeting with the USF Assembly on Mars to discuss terms. I didn't know or care to watch much more. My involvement in Sol affairs was over with, especially when it came to Ringers. Giving my daughter the chance to get out from under their thumb at the cost of Zhaff's life was the last meaningful thing I'd ever do.

"Just be here!" she hollered.

I rolled my shoulders and continued out the door. The sun had long since set over Mars, not that much of its radiance reached Old Dome anyhow. Vibrant ads and signs all over dressed everything in their artificial light. Products and destinations, all favoring the rusty coloring of Mars' surface so that it was like I was stuck in perpetual dusk. It hid all the city's imperfections.

Not having a good night in Old Dome was a challenge. The Twilight Sun had closed, but the clubs never did. People propositioned me from every corner, selling their bodies, passes, drugs, or worse. Venta security watched it all from raised posts and with drones, but the only thing they really cared about was violence or illegal weaponry.

I headed onto Old Dome's main strip, aptly dubbed the Tongueway. There were many stories behind the name, but the most appropriate was that the place was a melting pot, crammed with so many dialects and people from different backgrounds that it was said there wasn't a secret that couldn't be found on the tongue of someone there.

The seemingly endless avenue stretched from one end of the New Beijing dome to the other. It was the only passage down in Old Dome wide enough for a vehicle to fit through, but so crammed with people, it took them hours to go a few blocks. Even hovercars couldn't go high without the risk of slamming into unplanned overhangs or lines strung between the structures, feeding who knows what system and lined with wet clothes, signs, or flags. Gangs, companies—people of all backgrounds staked a claim on the Tongueway.

At night, nobody cared about the stench. Drunkards pissed in the maze of alleys branching off, puked in the drains. Dried blood from spats or other nefarious dealings. The Lowers in Darien, Titan had similar doings, but the real difference was that nobody really wanted to be there. Citizens of Sol traveled from all over to get a taste of the Tongueway's temptations. So long as you kept out of the sewers, it was the best kind of filth.

"You lookin' for a good time, honey?" a woman asked me from the shadows behind a neon sign. I didn't get a chance to read the venue's name. I mustered the knowing grin of a man who belongs in the place and followed her up into a Venta-run exotic dance club. And, man, the dancers were exotic.

I'll hand it to Venta Co.; they could find a way to monetize anything. Every dancer who prowled the floor searching for deep pockets had something visibly wrong with them. Missing limb, extra limb, lack of pigmentation, deformed features—a who's who of physical abnormalities as if they plucked young boys and girls from a radiation farm.

You could find anything in Old Dome, but the key to getting rich was presenting something people didn't realize they wanted, like this place. Dim the lights, get a patron drunk, and invite them into the back, where he or she could hunt for the deformity under what little clothing the performers wore.

Presently, a male dancer with a body firmer than I'd ever seen was on stage, only he was missing both legs at the hip. He twirled around a pole, as gracefully as Wai or any other dancer. Made me feel like a dolt for not being able to walk a straight line just because I had an artificial leg.

After the woman who invited me in led me to the bar, I pulled an old move from my prime. Women loved hearing stories about my adventures as a collector. The best part was, they were mostly true, with an embellishment here and there. My captive audience leaned in closer as I spun a tale about a crazy job, like all girls do who are only interested in being paid. Who was I to complain about attention?

Right before the good part, I got distracted by a spotlight illuminating her face, where I discovered her disfiguration. The woman was a looker in every sense of the word. A tight dress hugged her lissome figure, and a glowing orange circlet wrapped her neck to purposely draw attention toward its low cut and her augmented breasts. But her nose, whether by force or birth defect, didn't exist.

"Haglin," the woman said. "You were saying?"

I quickly turned my attention to the stage and pretended I hadn't been staring.

"It's okay," she whispered, wrapping her fingers around my hand. They were cool from the condensation on the drink I'd bought her. "I don't mind if you stare."

I glanced up at the sinewy hole in the center of her face, and my mind temporarily transported me back to the Darien Quarantine Zone on Titan, where Zhaff and I traipsed through a hall filled with sick, desiccated Ringer bodies. Literally falling apart.

I blinked hard and forced a smile. "Why wouldn't I stare?" I said. "You're gorgeous."

"And you're sweet. How about I take you around back and show you what I do for sweet men?"

My leg stretched to stand before my mind could catch up. Eventually, it did, as I recalled that I could only feel the one leg... among other parts down there. I grabbed my glass of synthahol and downed what little was left. I couldn't afford the real stuff anymore.

"How about one more round?" I said. "I didn't get to finish my story."

"They're your credits, handsome," she said.

I slapped the counter to get the bartender's attention and held up two fingers. Then I skootched my stool forward.

"So, there I was," I began. "After fighting my way through at least forty rebels on Undina, Yev Tavar was about to plow into me with a rock hauler. I had two choices, dive out of the way and take my chances with the rest of his insurgents, or stand my ground and bet on my pistol." Two drinks slid over to us. "Thanks." I flashed my fake ID to sync credits and turned back to the woman.

"Where was I?" I said. "Right. So, here he comes, and I lift my pistol. This one, right here actually." I tapped my holster, and my escort had to place her hand on my side to keep me from toppling. I pretended I didn't realize. "I wait as long as I can—until I can see the whites of his eyes through the viewport—and then I pull the trigger."

"Did you hit him?" she asked. I'll give her this, she was

damn good at pretending to care. I guess a lifetime of half-ignoring repulsive men can be a good teacher.

"Did I hit him? I plunked him right in the chest. Had the bastard dead to rights too, only, after all the problems he'd given Pervenio, he wasn't going to go out without a fight. Do you... do you want to know what the mad offworlder tried next?"

"To pull your pants down?" a man sitting behind me interrupted. His buddy started cackling. One glance over my shoulder, and I made them for Venta collectors enjoying some time off. The man who spoke was clearly in charge and wore a duster in far better shape than my old one, but pulse pistols dangled from both their hips that weren't vestiges of a bygone age.

"How about you and your boyfriend keep your mouths shut?" I said.

They shoved off the bar and stood next to me. "We were trying, old man," the leader said, "but if I had to hear you bore the poor girl with one more bullshit story, my head was going to explode."

"Bullshit story? Don't you know who I am? I've been putting down insurgents since before either of you was wearing diapers."

"I didn't realize there were rebels in nursing homes."

His partner almost lost it laughing. I sprang to my feet too fast, and my artificial leg wasn't ready. I wobbled, caught my balance on the nearest table, and drew myself in front of them. They were tall, definitely not born on Earth, but still plenty strong enough to take me on in my inebriated state.

"Why don't we go, baby," my escort whispered into my ear.

"Yeah, go," the collector in the duster said. "Unless..." He turned to his partner and sneered. "Unless that's why you want to keep her here. You missing equipment like one of these mutants?" He went to poke me in the crotch, but I bobbed out of the way.

"Watch your mouth, boy." I grabbed my glass without thinking twice and smashed it into the side of his head. It shattered into countless pieces, but the one thing I was counting on was for him to go down. He didn't. The collector reeled but stayed upright, and his partner had me in a headlock before I could blink.

"You're going to wish you hadn't done that," the leader said. He picked a few shards out of his bloody hair and studied me from head to toe. "I don't usually like to beat old men, but now I'll have to make an exception."

"I'm sure," I said. "Why don't you tell your friend to let me go, and I'll teach you how to talk properly in front of a lady."

"What lady?" He grabbed my jaw and rotated my head toward the stool where my noseless escort had been. She was gone. "When you look like a prune, the only thing they're interested in is credits." His fist crashed into my gut so hard I collapsed onto the floor. He spat on me, and the two of them strutted away crowing.

"That's the problem with you young guns," I groaned as I rose to my knees. "No passion for the fight. Definitely not Pervenio men. Only Venta could train such pussies."

They stopped, and the leader sighed. "Now why did you have to go and keep running your mouth?" His fist crunched against my jaw and sent me sprawling. He knelt by my side, reached into my pocket, and removed my ID. He then flung it back at me. "We abandoned Luxarn's sinking ship months ago, Haglin Amissum. Funny thing is, all my time there, I've never heard of you in my life. Have you?" His partner shook his head.

"You—" A swift kick in the side shut me up and knocked me into a cluster of empty stools.

"Would you two knock it off?" the bartender ordered.

The lead collector flashed his Venta badge, making sure to flaunt his holstered pistol. "Why don't you shut the hell up!"

Not a soul protested. I remembered having that kind of influence, especially in Pervenio-owned venues. The collector tapped my cheek. "Where is the big bad Pervenio man now?" he said to me. "How many protestors was it you said you took on in that asteroid. Forty? What were they slapping you with? Picket signs?"

I licked the blood off my lip. "Makes me sick knowing that Sol is in the hands of brats like you."

"Do you really want to die tonight, old timer?"

"Maybe he is a washed-up old collector," the partner said. "That's a nice gun he's got. It'd look pretty in a trophy case."

"I'll be damned, you're right. A fine relic, just like him."

"Help me up, and I'll show you just what she's capable of," I snarled.

"Nah. I think you're going to hand it over, and then maybe, just maybe, I won't take you out back and leave your corpse in the alley. If you really were a collector, then you'd know that here on our turf, nobody would bat an eyelash." He seized my throat and squeezed. "How does that sound, Haglin Amissum."

I tried to respond, but his grip was too tight. At the same time, I felt his partner trying to figure out how to loosen my holster.

"What was that?" he chuckled. "I couldn't hear you."

"Malcolm... Graves..." I forced out.

"Who the hell is that?"

His partner was just about to free my gun, when my artificial leg stabbed out into his chest and sent him flying across the room into an occupied booth twenty meters away. The head collector's grip relaxed as he watched in shock, allowing me to draw my pistol and crack him across the skull with the handle. This time, he doubled over like a sack of plasticrete.

"Son of a bitch!" he screamed from the floor. Pistol in hand, he rolled over and fired one round over my shoulder. I kicked a stool at him. The metal legs struck with such force, they knocked his gun away. I didn't wait to hear his screams, not that I'd be able to over the panic his shot had caused throughout the club. I snatched up my ID and bolted out of the joint. Security had heard the gunshot and ran past me on my way out.

In seconds, I vanished into the perpetual Tongueway crowd. I was off the books at the Twilight Sun, so it'd take a fair bit of snooping if they wanted to track me down based on my fake name. I doubted two young, brash Venta collectors would go through the trouble, or be willing to admit they'd been taken down by a washed-up old man. I know I wouldn't have. But if they did come knocking, I'd be happy to greet them. It was the most thrilling thing that'd happened to me since retiring.

"Foundry salts, straight from Titan," a hawkish offworlder offered me from beneath the overhang of a casino on my way by, as if reading my thoughts. The bags under his eyes read so darkly against his pale skin, they might as well have been drawn on. His teeth were half rotted. He looked like Zhaff's sallow, half-dead body.

"I'll take it," I muttered, trying to force the image out. I synced whatever amount of credits he'd asked for, I couldn't say. One sniff of the stuff and the ache in my jaw from taking that collector's punch was gone.

I staggered into the casino, where slot machines dinged all around me like something out of a circus nightmare. I snorted and drank and gambled my way through the place, and then all along the Tongueway. Colors grew more vivid and dancers more beautiful. I braved a private booth with one, even though the feeling in my lower extremity still hadn't completely returned. It didn't matter while on foundry salts from Titan's Lower factories. Everything felt incredible, and I was compelled to keep moving before they grew frustrated by my impotence.

My world became a blur of activity, and I was merely a

ghost floating through it. Memories faded. History disappeared. I was living in the here and now; no worries, no ex-partners, no family, and no employer. Free.

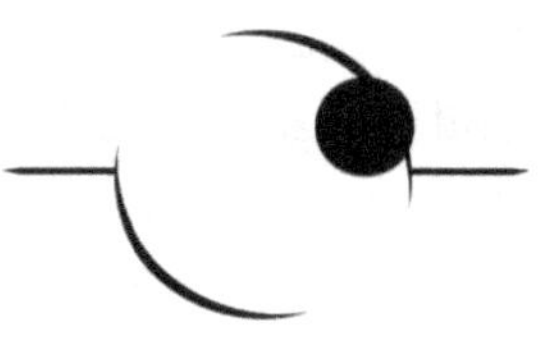

KALE

Our landing at Rin's hands went smoother than expected, though in a ship like the *Cora,* it was probably harder to screw it up. The crew began preparing for our exit in the cargo hold. Sixteen armed fighters, Ambassador Aria, and Rin. Roughly forty-five days in sleep pods on top of stronger gravity than they were accustomed to had them all looking exhausted.

While they worked, Gareth and I remained in my private quarters. When we stole the *Cora*, the room had been as garish as any Earther's I'd ever seen. I'd had it stripped to its bones. The wood trim was peeled off and the cushioned bed and couches removed, leaving behind nothing but hard metal corners and dull, unadorned surfaces.

"You are sure we can trust Aria with this?" Gareth signed as he helped me into my powered suit of armor. Blood had diminished its white color, and patches of the orange circle painted on the chestplate were fading. I made it a point not to have it refurbished.

"I thought we were done with this," I groused. I was growing tired of the constant questioning of Aria, even though I understood everyone's hesitance.

"We were, but now you won't have me watching your back."

"I'll have Rin and the others. You're not the only one who can shoot a gun, Gareth."

"No, but I'm the only one who can hit anything with one."

"I'll be sure not to tell my aunt you said that." He finished preparing my armor and took a step back. The lines of nervousness racking his face were plainly visible.

"I do trust Aria, though," I said. "We need someone who speaks their language now."

"But are you sure she speaks for us?" he signed. *"We're on Earther turf. Enough credits offered outside might be able to turn her."*

"They won't. If that's what she's after, all she'd have to do is ask. The Children of Titan had enough stored up in offworld accounts to make her as rich as Luxarn Pervenio."

"Fine. Just make sure you watch your back. Here, Aria is the least of your concerns."

"I know. Now stop worrying about me. I need you focused on your more important mission."

Gareth gestured to his clothing. Unlike me, he wore ordinary cloth rags with no printed orange circle or logo to speak of. He'd purposely dirtied his gaunt face to appear like a homeless, first-generation offworlder. Living under the high g of Saturn for so long had deepened the creases on his face enough that he almost looked like one. Most significant, however, was his lack of sanitary mask despite being on an Earther world.

"Good," I said. "Be as fast as possible. The fewer germs you pick up out there, the better."

"You won't even notice I'm gone."

He removed a loose portion of plating from the wall, revealing a circular duct that would comfortably fit a skinny Titanborn. It led out of a hidden hatch in the back of the ship. My favorite part about it was that we hadn't made the addition.

The great Luxarn Pervenio left a hole in his prized vessel so that even he could smuggle goods or people under the radar of the USF.

Gareth stopped in front of the opening. *"Tell Rin not to miss me too much,"* he signed.

"She'll be in touch with our location, but try to stay off your terminal if you can," I said. "We don't need anybody intercepting something without meaning to."

"You're not the only one who learned how to sneak around growing up in the Lowers."

I laid my hand on his shoulder. "Titan owes you for this. If I could go myself, you know I would."

He shook his head vigorously. *"You lead,"* he signed.

"Aria is with us. She'll be prepared if you come back with any infections. You have my word."

"I survived this long. Maybe my blood is as strong as a Trass's."

"You get him to us alive, and I'll tell the world you are one."

His eyes glinted as he bowed his head. *"From ice to ashes."*

"From ice to ashes."

We exchanged a nod, and then he disappeared into the guts of the ship to carry out a task equally as crucial as staking our claim to the Ring in front of the entire USF Assembly. The only difference was that only Rin and I knew about his.

I detached the helmet of my suit and placed it down. I didn't need a visor to hide my face, and the air of Mars's domes was breathable enough regardless of the Earther stench. Then I reached into my belt and removed an old companion. The moment my sanitary mask went on, it was like I'd never taken the thing off. I had to set an example that there was nothing to fear while on Titan, but I understood the urge to wear them, which my people couldn't break. The pressure as it tightened against the ridge of my nose, the way it muffled my voice... it just felt right. I was clean all over.

I made a few more adjustments to my armor before heading to the cargo bay. Rin and Aria waited by the exit ramp. My aunt wore armor similar to mine, and Aria was in another loose-fitting dress with an Earther flair—ornate around the collar and base, with an interweaving pattern of dark greens throughout. She had to look the part of non-militant diplomat.

"Where's Gareth?" Aria asked.

"I told him to stay with the ship," I replied. "I don't trust the *Cora* in anybody else's hands." The answer seemed to satisfy her, and my lie brought the edges of a smirk to the intact half of Rin's lips.

While the three of us were unarmed, the other Titanborn we brought along each had pulse rifles strapped to their armored backs. A few I recognized from battles around the Ring, but I didn't know any of them well, since Gareth and Rin were tasked with selecting them. I had to trust they'd be able to steady their eager trigger fingers for the time being. I had to trust Rin wouldn't provoke a fight. I had to trust Aria was as deft a negotiator as she seemed and wasn't being played right along with us.

I closed my eyes as the exit ramp unfolded. Sometimes I liked to picture the first time I ever stepped onto the *Piccolo* and saw the world beyond the Darien Lowers. My problems seemed so trivial back then. Nobody scrutinized every single little thing I said or did.

Then the ramp clanged as it fully extended, and I was greeted by the harsh reality of our situation. There were no trumpets or cheering crowds to embrace a visiting dignitary. Instead, the lofty hangar was filled by a battalion of Red Wing Company gunmen, decked out in crimson armor with sweeping helms that made them appear as though they were from a bygone era. They too stored rifles on their backs rather than in their hands as a gesture of peace. A smattering of Venta Co. men stood among them. Being that Venta essentially ran New Beijing under the umbrella of the USF, we'd all agreed on a privately-owned hangar to land in and a neutral party to monitor the summit.

Neutral... Just thinking that word made me feel idiotic. No matter what colors they wore, we were all at the mercy of Earthers once again.

"All right, everyone," Rin began, voice tempered by a sanitary mask of her own. "I want eyes all around us. Lord Trass isn't to be touched, do you hear me? I don't want any of these mudstompers even breathing on him." The legion of guards lined up on either side of us voiced their agreement. "From ice to ashes!"

The words reverberated through *Cora's* austere cargo hold as everyone repeated them, except for Aria. Instead, she took my arm. It was either that or nervousness for what was to come that made the hairs on the back of my neck stand on end. Probably both.

"Everything is going to work out," she assured.

"It better," Rin spat before I could reply. "You set it up."

"It will." Aria stood her ground like she always did, no matter how harsh I or any of my people ever were to her. She was as stubborn as she was brave.

"Too late to turn back now," I said. I pulled free of her and took the first step forward. Immediately, everyone followed. The eyes of all the Earther gunmen waiting on the burnished hangar floor below widened as they saw us.

"Greetings, Mr. Trass," said a man in an extravagantly patterned blue tunic as we emerged. "I am Director Yashikawa Venta." He extended a hand, and I glared at it. My gaze didn't falter, and after a brief moment, he noticed my sanitary mask and reeled it back. "Ah, yes. Forgive the mix-up during your entry. We aren't accustomed to this type of arrangement."

"Neither are we," I replied.

"Yes, well...I hope that's the last issue we experience. Captain Barnes and our Red Wing partners will help look after your ship and belongings." He nodded toward the most decorated Red Wing officer.

"A pleasure, Mr. Trass," Barnes said, bowing his head. A jagged scar on his jaw and military haircut left little doubt that he was a corporate-security lifer.

"Unfortunately, your people will be required to deposit their weapons before entering the USF Assembly Building," Director Yashikawa indicated. "Would you rather stow them here?"

I glanced at my guards. They were as tense as any of the Earther officers. "I think we'll hold on to them for now. Rin, leave two guards with our ship and belongings."

Rin pointed at two of my guards, and they promptly hurried back up *Cora's* ramp.

"As you wish." Director Yashikawa's eyes narrowed as he watched them, but he maintained his composure. The gray peppering his thin mustache was evidence of his experience. Aria had explained to me before we left how Venta Co. operated differently from the top down than Pervenio Corp. Where Luxarn appointed people based on merit, Madame Venta, their founder, built her corporation around her constantly growing clan-family. Every Earther born with the Venta name had a place in the organization, from her directors to the chefs in her office building's kitchen.

"We should get moving," Director Yashikawa insisted. "The Assembly is eager to meet with you so we can move beyond this and reestablish trade with the Ring that has been so beneficial to all of us."

"I'm sure that with your company's continued development around Jupiter, your employer is doing well enough," I said. "Let's get this over with."

I could tell by the way his features darkened that those words stung. I may have lived on Titan, but I kept careful track of Earther news feeds enough to know whose wallet was hurting and why. Darien Trass chose Saturn and its moons over Jupiter's three centuries ago for many reasons, and Venta was starting to find out why. Despite being the largest of all the solar system's gas giants, Jupiter simply didn't foster the condensed volume of rare resources that Saturn did.

Director Yashikawa put on a pleasant smile and beckoned us forward into the New Beijing Spaceport. It was vast, though still paled in comparison to Pervenio Station. Vibrant ads dotted the walls of every hallway and outside every hangar. Anything you might want could be found or bought on Mars. They spoke to everyone who passed, scanning their eyes to inform them what they might want for dinner, what to buy off Solnet, what shows were worth seeing. It reminded me of how the docks in Darien, Titan looked before our revolution shattered all the viewscreens.

"Do mudstompers build anything modest?" Rin muttered in my ear.

"You should see where I was born," Aria said.

"I'll pass."

Our arrival terminal was crammed with people from all walks of life. Tall and short, dirty and spotless. Some wore rags, others the poshest outfits imaginable, with heavy makeup in matching hues. Gareth would fit in fine as a homeless wretch.

Venta Co. security officers were everywhere, rifles out instead of shock batons. More patrolled a series of catwalks strung below the vaulted crystalline ceilings where images from more ads blinked. If I had to see one more about the new

Pervenio Corp service bot coming to Pervenio Solnet retailers soon, I feared I might snap.

My legs were sore by the time we emerged into the station's main concourse. Captain Barnes had our escorts fan out to maintain a wide perimeter. The front line pushed aside unarmed civilians with riot shields. If the people of Mars weren't expecting us before—which I highly doubted—they were now. The pure white of our armor and flesh contrasted with everything. Hateful glares and insults beset us from every direction, some spoken, others held up on holo-signs. My hands squeezed into fists when I spotted one that read: SEND THE DIRTY SKELLIES BACK HOME.

Half of my people drew their firearms and shouted back. Not all of us were as accustomed to Earther swearing as Rin and me, who'd served on mixed-race gas harvesters.

"Weapons down!" I barked. My people instantly obeyed.

"Thank you, Mr. Trass," Director Yashikawa said. "I do apologize. I can't believe our citizens would behave this way." He didn't deserve a response.

We continued our long slog across the concourse toward a landing pad. It was like plowing through two meters of snow with nothing but a shovel. The Red Wing men locked shields to hold back a swelling wave of protestors. Countless instigators were arrested by patrolling officers for throwing debris at us and our corporate escorts. Drones hovering overhead recorded us, their footage duplicated on news feeds wrapping the mezzanine level. Half of them zoomed in solely on my face.

SELF-PROCLAIMED KING OF TITAN KALE TRASS LANDS ON MARS. FOR PEACE OR WAR? some of the tickers read. THE BUTCHER OF THE RING IS GREETED BY WARRANTED PROTEST, said another. Just a few of the myriad titles they'd given me. King was my personal favorite, especially since I never once actually used the term like they always said I had. As if our revolution was so surprising and unwarranted that the only title its leader could bear had to derive from antiquity.

We reached a landing platform where the rich could navigate the overcrowded city in private hovercars and stay high above the rabble. Public transit through the city's Redline subway was out of the question for us. Again, the Red Wing officers gave a strong push to provide us passage. By then we were all covered in garbage, even Director Yashikawa, who seemed particularly disgusted. Men like him usually didn't have to even toss their own trash, let alone wear it.

The platform protruded into the open air of New Beijing's great dome, which extended high up and away from us and was jam-packed with glassy, ad-covered towers. We were about halfway up the skyline, looking out upon narrow streets below crammed with Earthers. All the plasticrete and metal surfaces bore a reddish tinge from being mined from Mars. Terraced gardens were everywhere, Earthborn plants literally dripping over the facades of buildings. The glass of the dome covering all of it was tinted blue, with its latticed structural members colored white like clouds, as if mimicking the sky of Earth.

A line of Red Wing airships waited above, engines humming. Protestors impeded their ability to land. Director Yashikawa leaned over to address Captain Barnes. "I want those things down immediately!" he demanded.

"You don't get to boss me around, Yashikawa," a stone-faced Captain Barnes replied.

Yashikawa drew a hand-terminal. "Do you want me to ask your board?"

The captain muttered something under his breath, then started issuing orders. One by one, his men shoved people out of the way; protestors and the wealthy alike, waiting for their rides. The three transport airships needed to land to carry all of us.

Nothing bigger would be able to squeeze between the city's tightly clustered towers, even toward their tops where they tapered.

"Repent, brothers!" someone shouted.

I spun and saw that the words had come from a withered, middle-aged Three Messiahs Preacher standing by the far railing, wearing a headscarf and with a long, scraggly beard. Layered robes and a white shawl with blue stripes covered his stout Earther body, and he held a hefty worn tome against his chest. His kind always had rosier skin than mine, but his cheeks were flushed so red they were like the surface of Mars. He appeared nauseated as well, even as he spouted his drivel.

"The Three Messiahs warn us of trespassing in the heavens!" he continued. "I beg you all, come home with me, lest we invite God's judgment once again."

"Would someone shut that nut up?" Director Yashikawa snapped. A few Red Wing officers tried to reach him, but a throng of civilians had quickly amassed in front of him.

"Every second you remain here reaching beyond the world meant for us is a sin!" The preacher paused to cover his mouth and cough, then went on. "And now you invite the demons from Titan closer to God's Earth. When our world was purged of sinners, the children of Trass fled His judgment. They are beyond salvation. All who harbor them shall feel the fist of Heaven!"

"Shut him up!" the director shouted.

Watching the officers push their way toward him was laughable. If there was one good thing about our presence on Mars, apparently, it was that it drew the fanatical Church of the Three Messiahs folk that Earther news feeds always complained about all the way to Mars to protest. It was our gracious host's turn to be derided.

I turned to see how Captain Barnes was progressing on

emptying the platform, and out of the corner of my vision, I spotted something that made my heart stop. Lying prone on top of the nearest airship was a Pervenio Cogent agent. Rylah knew about them and had even fended one off back on Titan before helping us infiltrate Pervenio Station.

A skintight uniform with some sort of active camouflage reflected this Cogent's surroundings so no sharpshooters or drones would spot him, but the lens over his eye that glinted yellow was clearly visible. He had his pulse pistol raised and was lining up a shot—at me.

I froze. The crazed preacher had drawn Rin just far enough away that there'd be no chance of her jumping in front of me to block the first shot. Death had come for me, with all of Sol watching. Another opportunity for Luxarn Pervenio to show the kind of man he really was while he hid.

I'm not sure how much time passed in that moment. A second or two, maybe less, but I closed my eyes, and for the first time in months, my tumultuous thoughts slowed down. I pictured Cora's beautiful face. I imagined myself free of war, like ashes on the winds of Titan alongside Cora for eternity.

At peace...

An explosion rang out. My instincts returned, and I grabbed Aria to shield her unarmored body just before we were launched across the platform. I rolled off her, ears ringing, vision filled with smoke and blurred figures. My body was numb, but I scrambled to my knees to try and make sense of the bedlam.

The airships banked noisily to the side to escape the blast. People screamed and moaned. Limbs of civilians thrashed from a pile around the preacher. Shreds of his robes and embers danced above his feet, which was all that remained of him.

Aria coughed beneath me, completely safe, thanks to my embrace. Rin wasn't as lucky. She lay a few feet away, unconscious but breathing. The few Titanborn nearest the preacher were far worse, though the crowd and the line of Red Wing offi-cers surrounding him had fortunately shielded most of my people from the brunt of the blast.

I disregarded all of it. Instead, I anxiously scanned the landing pad for the Cogent. I couldn't die yet. I couldn't join Cora's remains in the sky because her body had been lost to the vacuum. Thanks to Pervenio Corp, Luxarn Pervenio and his corporation had taken everything from me, but he wouldn't get my life. Anybody but him.

The shimmer of the Cogent's eye lens through the haze was impossible to miss. The blast forced him to topple off the airship, and he struggled to gather his bearings. I sprang up and drove my weary legs forward until I was running.

He got one shot off from a few meters away. It glanced off my shoulder plating but wasn't enough to slow me. I grabbed him by the jaw and, with my powered armor and reignited rage augmenting my muscles, snapped his neck like a twig.

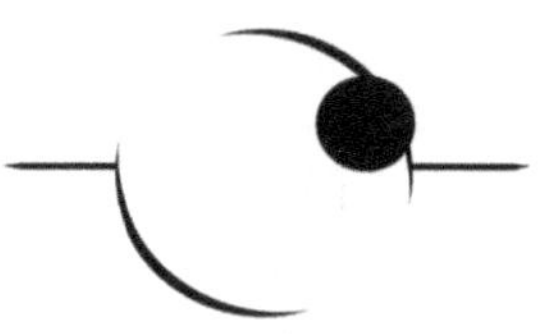

EIGHT

MALCOLM

"Haglin." Somebody shook my shoulders. "Haglin, wake up." Another shake came, promptly followed by a slap across my face. That got my eyes open.

A young woman's face hovered over me, silhouetted by a bright viewscreen overhead. All I could distinguish was the long, curly hair cascading down over her shoulders. "Aria?" I said softly. I reached out, brushed a lock of her hair, and then cupped my palm around her cheek.

"*Lǎo wán gù!*"

Again, my face was slapped, and the sting snapped my vision into focus. Wai hopped backward, her expression filled with disgust. I shook my head. A screen behind her advertised the new Pervenio service bot. TIRED OF BEING ALONE? it asked. THE PERVENIO SERVICE BOT IS THE FIRST MOBILE ROBOTIC HELPER WITH ADAPTIVE INTELLIGENCE TO LEARN WHAT YOU NEED BEFORE YOU NEED IT. PRE-ORDER YOUR MODEL TODAY. All I could focus on was the damn red-helix logo following me everywhere.

"Oh... Sorry, Wai," I said.

She fixed her hair and her shirt. I wasn't used to seeing her outside of her dancer's garb. A crummy parka covered her down to her knees, stained with grime and who knows what else from the sewers. I was glad I was too hungover to catch a whiff of it.

"Good dream, eh?" she asked. "Who's Aria? Some old fling from your secret life?"

My initial chuckle transitioned to a groan quickly. My head rang like someone had shoved a bell in my skull and kept bashing it. "Something like that," I groaned. "What time is it?"

"Time to get you cleaned up before Yan Ning has a heart attack."

She extended a hand. I took it and went to sit up, but pain wrenched my side and caused me to wince. I reached for a cluster of sore ribs, realizing that my knuckles were scraped and bloody. Had I been in a brawl? That's right; those uppity collectors who had the nerve not to recognize me.

I rolled over and realized we were in the garbage alley behind the Twilight Sun. I recognized it by the neon sign at the corner with half the letters unlit. My pants were soaking wet, and as much as I wanted to tell myself it was just beer, I knew the answer before I smelled it. I'd pissed myself. The sensation in my damaged lower body was strained enough while I was sober. Being loaded up as much as I was had apparently caused my bladder to lose control.

What a picture I must have painted. Former veteran collector for Pervenio Corp, and apparent confidant of Luxarn Pervenio himself, waking up in an alley covered in my own piss and blood.

Wai knelt and wrapped her arm around my shoulder. "C'mon, *lǎo tóuzi*. Let's get you up." She strained her weak offworlder muscles to help me, and eventually, I mustered the energy to beg my artificial leg to provide one final push. My other leg shook as I leaned against the wall and spit out whatever wretched taste the night had left in my mouth. My lip stung from a fresh cut.

"Your shower is already warmed up for you," she said. "C'mon, I'll help you."

"I can do it myself."

"Like hell you can." She wrapped her arm even further around me and guided me toward the rusty stairs leading up to my apartment. I'd never felt so hungover in my entire life. Every liver-spotted part of me wanted to fall off and be done with it. Find a new body to latch on to.

The stairs were brutal. I could tell my weight was crushing Wai, even though she did her best not to show it. At the top, we both had to lean on the railing to catch our breath.

"Why are you helping me, girl?" I panted.

"I have no idea." She shrugged then grinned impishly. "Because I like you, *lǎo tóuzi*. You're the first friend I've made up here who wasn't my boss or just there for a show."

"Friend." I sighed. I glanced over at her, unable to force myself to return a smile. I liked her too. She was strong, even if she didn't realize it. Anyone who grew up in the sewers and still managed to emerge with a shred of charm ought to be. She was better than the life she had at the Twilight Sun. A dancer for now, sure, but once her looks faded, the streets would call to her.

She deserved better than that. Better than me for a friend. Of the last two people I'd let get close to me, one was in a coma he'd never wake from by my hand, and the other was a daughter I'd chased so far away she joined up with terrorists.

Wai opened my door and went to help me again, but I brushed her off me, purposely throwing my Earther strength into the motion so she'd stagger.

"I can take it from here, dammit!" I growled.

"*Cào!*" she yelped. "Fine, *lǎo tóuzi*, I won't touch you."

She hurried in and flopped onto the patchwork of fabrics I

had for a couch. I followed her inside, slowly. The place was a dump. Tarnished finishes, furniture all beaten to death. Most of the tiles on the floor were cracked or missing. It was my first permanent home since growing up in a clan-family back on Earth, and it was all I had to show for a lifetime of hard labor. There wasn't even a single picture on the wall or memento on a table, like I'd materialized out of nowhere.

"Now I believe you owe me a story about who you really are," Wai said.

I leaned on the armrest right next to her, panting. "Trust me, girl. It's a sad tale. You don't want to hear it."

"You know I love a tearjerker."

"Not this one."

"Oh, *qǐng, lǎo tóuzi!*" She clasped my bloody knuckles. "I've known you long enough, Mr. Shénmi. Mysterious man. I won't tell a soul."

"Don't you have anything better to do than pester an old man?"

She put on a wicked grin. "Not a thing. At least tell me how you got that *gāo kējì* leg."

She leaned forward and started brushing the dirt off the pants leg on my artificial side. She didn't care that it was stained with urine, as if she were my live-in nurse. In fact, she didn't seem to care about anything. She treated my tiny piece-of-crap apartment like it was a palace. Like it was better than anything she could ever get outside the sewers. *Help her, Malcolm*, my brain told me. *Drive her far away from this place and from you.*

I pushed her hand away. "Do you really want to know who I am?" I asked. "I was a corporate collector, for too long. Made a living hunting down sewer rats like you who couldn't keep their hands to themselves."

She winced. She recovered quickly, but I could tell my

words hit her where it counted. "All right, *lǎo tóuzi*," she said. "I'm sorry I asked."

"No, you're not. Girls like you, they just can't help it. See a broken-down man like me and see just how far they can put him over without putting out."

Her pretty face contorted even more this time. "I... that's not true. You told me to stay here any time I wanted."

"Yeah. You think I did that just so that I could have the joy of you helping me up the stairs every night?"

She stood and skirted around me to get to my coffee table. She picked up a half-drunk glass of murky water from a night earlier and held it out for me. "I don't know what kind of poison *yàowù* you took last night, but maybe you should take a nap. You're acting loopy."

I smacked the glass into the wall. "You don't know a goddamn thing about me! I don't need the help of some two-bit sewer bitch who can barely dance!"

Her lower lip quivered. Tears started to well in the corners of her eyes. I didn't back down. I couldn't. The worst hangover I'd had in years helped my tone seem genuine. She attempted to respond, but I didn't give her the opportunity.

"Now, unless you're going to come in and help me shower, I don't understand why you're still here," I said. "Or did you think I was kind to you for another reason? Friends... down here, all you're worth is a dying man covered in piss, gir—"

A powerful slap across my face stopped me mid-word. She meant it, and despite her weak offworlder muscles, she made it sting. Tears rolled from her eyes, and she glowered at me for a few seconds before hurrying toward the exit without a word. I watched her the whole way.

She stopped for a moment in the opening, as if waiting for an apology. A sudden onset of nausea ensured I didn't do anything stupid like that. I liked her too much to let her waste her life clinging to a crummy gig all because she viewed the bouncer like a father she never had down in the sewers. She was better off driven far away.

She slammed the door. I leaned over the armrest and vomited the contents of a night I'd never remember all over my floor.

———

I was a half hour late for the Twilight Sun's opening. About the time I usually strolled in, and nobody seemed to care, but on the day Kale Trass was coming to Mars, Yan Ning pretended he did. He laid into me loud enough for all the kitchen and server staff to hear. I nodded without really listening, instead staring at the barren stage. Wai hadn't come in. She hadn't messaged sick or about an emergency either. I was glad. Maybe my little outburst was the final push she needed to seek out something better than the dump where I'd decided to hang up my gun.

"Haglin, are you listening to me?" Yan Ning shoved a fat, hairy finger into my chest, and he was an Earther, so I felt it.

"Yep," I lied.

"Good. And no drinking on the job today. I mean it."

"Sure thing, boss." I surveyed the room. A few patrons sat at the bar, eyes glued to the viewscreens. One couple sat at a corner booth eating what passed for lunch in the place. "I wouldn't want to scare off all of the customers."

Yan Ning's cheeks flushed a hot shade of red. "Just get to work. The Ringers are arriving soon, and people are coming from all over Mars. And where the hell is Wai!"

I shrugged then lumbered over to my post by the entrance. My headache had waned after a shower, but water in New Beijing was controlled by Venta Co., and they weren't generous with it. I only got a minute or two to wipe myself down and scrub out the tiny rifts in my artificial leg before it cut out. Wai's final gift to me. I could tell by how clean the inside of the stall was that she'd taken her time the night before.

There wasn't a doubt in my mind that I'd done the right thing by pushing her away, yet I couldn't seem to quiet the pangs of guilt pulling at my brain. The only thing that could cure me was a drink, so I snuck a flask out of my duster and kicked my legs up. I didn't even try to hide it.

Yan Ning was right. The Tongueway was bustling, though the Twilight Sun was everyone's last choice as always. I let in a few haggards who'd clearly had as rough a night as I had. I patted them down and scanned their IDs. Not that Yan Ning cared if I let in illegitimates, but we had to keep up appearances in case any Venta officers happened to check in.

"Malcolm Graves, I can't believe it!" someone exclaimed just as I was about to doze off.

A man in a Venta officer uniform altered his course toward me. At first, I worried that the collectors from the night before had decided to waste more time on me, but when he got close enough for my tired old eyes to distinguish him, I realized it was worse. I was glad I'd already thrown up that morning. It was Trevor Cross, a former rival Venta collector. Judging by his new uniform, his employers hadn't been overly kind to him since I ran into him my last time on Titan. He'd gotten in Zhaff's and my way while pursuing the Children of Titan, so I put a bullet in his leg. Should have aimed for his loud mouth instead.

"I heard two collectors down at the station grumbling about some crazy old coot named Malcolm who cheap-shotted them at the Mangled Mare," he said once he reached me, wearing that same damn pompous grin he always did.

"Those two had it coming." I lowered my feet and positioned myself in his way. Of all the shitholes in Sol, of course he had to stumble upon mine.

"Oh, I'm sure. They couldn't remember your real last name, but as soon as I searched your fake one, I couldn't believe my eyes. They wanted to come down here themselves, but I told them we had a history. Said I'd make things right."

"I hope you aren't expecting a thank you."

He snickered. "Never from you. I just had to see with my own eyes. I figured you'd finally died after bungling things on Titan."

"Maybe I'm remembering wrong, but you and Madame Venta had a hand in that, I think."

"Fucking Ringers, right?"

"Yep. Who would expect anybody to rebel after providing them with enough black market weapons to outfit an army? I see you've got a new job, though. I guess Venta put the blame on you too, huh?"

He ground his jaw but managed to maintain his composure. "I decided I was tired of getting shot in the leg by old men."

"I'm not going to lie; an officer's uniform suits you."

"Captain, actually."

"Sorry. I didn't realize I was in the presence of royalty." Someone else stepped up to the door to get inside. The bald man's rags were ripped all over, revealing his milk-white skin. He was a generational offworlder for sure, judging by how incredibly tall and lanky he was, but the deep, grime-caked wrinkles creasing his forehead were odd for someone from a low-g environment.

Trevor and I paused, waiting for him to say something. He didn't. All he did was stare at Trevor with eyes as dark as charcoal.

"You got an ID?" I asked. He shook his head. "What're you planning on doing without credits?"

He pointed over my shoulder at the viewscreens inside. Kale Trass and the other Ringers had apparently landed, but crowds and protesters in the spaceport were causing significant delays. I glanced back at the silent offworlder, studied him from head to toe, and then grinned.

"All right, head on in." I waved him forward and started to pat him down, struggling to reach his towering shoulders. All the while, he continued staring at Trevor.

"Really, Graves? An illegitimate right in front of me?" Trevor asked, gesturing to the Venta Co. insignia denoting his membership in their private security.

I finished up with the offworlder and lightly nudged him inside. "Shit, I forgot. Sorry about that, sir."

He sneered. "That's no problem; we're off duty. But you let rabble like that into your place, then I've got to see what's inside. C'mon, boys." He waved a crew of two other off-duty officers over and shoved by me. With their uniforms on, I couldn't do anything about it. I tolerated my new job too much. It kept me well imbibed. Trevor's eyes lit up as they beheld my new home in all its dingy glory.

"Welcome, officers!" Yan Ning greeted from behind the bar, as excited to see new customers as a kid on M-Day seeing a Departure Ark for the first time. "How can I help you?"

Trevor ignored him. "Oh, this is too good," he cackled. "The great Malcolm Graves, reduced to doorman for a bucket of shit."

My fingers started to itch. Yup. I should've gotten rid of him for good back on Titan.

"Don't even have a single dancer," one of his mates snickered.

"If this is what retirement is like, I hope I die young." Trevor laughed.

"Maybe I'll show you what I did to those two collectors last night," I said, seething.

"Please, old man. You don't have your little pet Cogent

around to protect you this time. What was his name? Zhaff, right? Heard he didn't get as lucky as you back on Titan."

I leaned in, inches away from his face. His men immediately crowded me, hands on their shock batons. "Don't you dare say his name."

Trevor grinned as he pushed me back. "You aren't worth wasting my time." He waved to Yan Ning. "How about a round of your best Martian vodka for everyone here. All five of them." He and his crew burst out in laughter as they took seats at the bar. Trevor plopped down right beside the grim, mute offworlder.

Yan Ning filled glasses and started shuffling them over to everybody at the bar. "What about one for the doorman?" Trevor asked. "Don't want him missing out."

"Sorry, sir," Yan Ning replied. "Staff doesn't drink on the job here."

"Staff? You do realize who that is, right?"

"I never ask." Yan Ning shrugged and finished handing out drinks. He placed the last in front of the mute offworlder, who glared at it as if it were toxic.

"What're you staring at, sewer trash?" Trevor barked at the stranger. "You gonna take this with us or what?"

The offworlder had remained utterly silent since sitting down, not even opening his mouth to breathe. He hadn't touched his drink either. In response to Trevor, he merely folded his arms in a conscious display of denial and turned his attention back toward the newsfeed.

"Too dumb to take a handout," Trevor grumbled. "How's about the keeper of this fine establishment joins us instead." He snatched the glass and slid it to Yan Ning so hard that he had no choice but to grab it or it'd spill everywhere.

"Sir, I insist—" Yan Ning said before being cut off.

"Take it. Days like this don't come around often." Trevor grabbed his own glass and raised it to signal a toast. "Old friends, new places. To Malcolm Graves!" he shouted, nodding toward the viewscreens, where every newsfeed depicted images of Kale Trass's face while also recording the ceaseless unrest at the spaceport. "Without him, none of what's happening today would be possible."

I stormed forward, grabbed Trevor by the collar, and pulled him from his seat. My fist was raised and ready to clock him. "Why don't we settle this again?" I growled. For a moment, fear twisted his smug façade, but then Yan Ning said something that brought the grin right back to his lips.

"Get your hands off of our guest, Haglin!" he ordered, using my fake name despite Trevor blurting out my real one. Either he wasn't paying attention or he knew better than to worry about the truth.

"Listen to him, *Haglin*," Trevor said. "You wouldn't want to spend your retirement behind bars."

I glared at him and his two companions. Their shit-eating grins matched his. A couple years back, I would've thrown the punch and known I could easily take down three shoddy Venta officers, but based on the night before, I wasn't even sure my battered body could knock Trevor out with one hit.

I dropped my fist and released him. The smirk he wore as I did renewed my sense of nausea. It didn't matter how many times I'd bested him in the past, letting him get the upper hand went against my nature. I might as well have changed my name for good because the weight Malcolm Graves used to carry was officially gone.

Trevor settled down in his seat and finally lifted his half-spilled drink to his lips. He took it, signaling everyone else in the bar with one to do the same. Then he slammed it down and cleared his throat. His smirk didn't fade for even a millisecond.

"Some things never change. New master's got you on an even tighter leash."

"Fuck it," I groaned. I reared my arm back to punch him, but just before my hand shot forward, the room shook. And not like it might from a passing train. It was the kind of violent tremor that occurs on board a spaceship while passing through Earth's dense atmosphere.

It caused me to stumble, and my hand smashed into the edge of the bar. The dated viewscreens went grainy or black, and light pendants throughout the bar swung. A layer of dust that hadn't been roused in years swirled about the Twilight Sun, drawing everyone into a frenzy of coughing.

"What the hell was that?" Trevor grated. His men had their weapons drawn as they struggled for a dust-free breath.

"Is everyone okay?" Yan Ning shouted.

"Get your damn screens working!" Trevor propped himself up on a stool and started slapping the nearest one. The image was now too fuzzy to see anything but blurs of motion.

The silent, illegitimate offworlder stood. His gangly fingers were wrapped so tight around the back of his stool that they went an impossible shade of white. For the first time since entering, he showed emotion—fear and rage all wreathed into an expression I knew too well but was too distracted to place just then.

Nobody had noticed my failed attempt at a punch, and after I steadied my artificial leg, which had yet to endure such a sudden motion, my experience as a collector took hold. I instinctually bolted out of the bar onto the Tongueway to see what was going on. People were in a panic, but other than loosened dust, there was nothing different about Old Dome.

Sirens echoed, and flashing red emergency lights filled the manmade crevices, offering a peek at the shimmering world of towers above. I didn't think. I made a break for the nearest

Redline station's stairs leading up to the city's upper level, fighting my way through a mob of frightened, wealthy Martians trying to force their way down.

At the surface, I saw the reflection of the New Beijing Spaceport in the glassy façade of a handful of towers. That was where everyone was running from. Smoke filled the air around one of its elevated landing platforms. Security hovercars and drones darted about as they tried to extinguish the spreading flames.

"This can't be happening again," I whispered to myself. A bombing of New London, Earth, carried out by Ringers, was the first and only case Zhaff and I ever got to work on.

I weaved my way down the sidewalk, having to duck under a few hovercars whose drivers were in too much of a panic to obey traffic laws. The plaza at the foot of the spaceport dome was even crazier. All those thousands I'd seen on the viewscreens protesting Kale Trass were now fleeing like a stampede of frightened animals.

Venta Co. and Red Wing officers had quickly established a perimeter. That was one benefit of living in a city off Earth. Private security groups were far better trained and more experienced.

"Sir, please step back while we evacuate," a Venta officer out front said to me.

I instinctually reached for my ID to show I was a collector and therefore above a lowly officer like him, and then suddenly, it all came back to me. I wasn't. The ability to run headfirst into peril with the promise of credits died the moment I denied Luxarn Pervenio. I was no longer any different than the mob fleeing.

My head sank. I'd have to wait for the news feeds to find out what happened just like everybody else. Smoke, withering flames, rubble—it was evidently the result of an explosion. But by who? Was this New London all over again? Was Kale Trass still up there? Had someone been stupid enough to make a move on him?

In my Pervenio days, I never had to wait long to find out the why behind crimes. Not that I ever let that affect my work. I did what was asked of me, kept my mouth shut, and got paid. But now that I was on the outside, it didn't mean I could turn off my innate curiosity over what made criminals tick.

I ducked around the crowd, trying to see if there was an unpatrolled area where I could sneak into the spaceport. I reached a break and got ready to plot my course, but that was when I saw what had parted the people nearby. A smoking piece of the spaceport's landing pad had blown free and crashed in the plaza. None of the medical teams had arrived yet, but a few officers were trying to clear the area of civilians.

I bounded toward one of the bodies crushed beneath the rubble. "Sir, you need to keep clear!" an officer shouted, giving chase. I ignored him.

A pair of skinny legs stuck out from a melted railing connected to a smoking chunk of plasticrete. I knew who they belonged to even before I rounded the corner to see her face.

"Sir!" The officer grabbed my shoulder. "I won't ask again."

"I know her!' I snarled. The look I shot at him must have sent a shiver up his spine because he backed off and gave me space. Wai's eyelids were stuck half open—and not the way someone's might go if they're caught dozing. Her torso was crushed like an empty tube of paste.

Dead.

A younger me wouldn't have been so rattled by it, but ever since Luxarn had partnered me up with Zhaff, I'd gone softer. Try as I did to drive the sweet young offworlder away from me and toward better things, she'd met the same fate as all the rest.

I glanced up at the smoldering portion of the platform from

which bloodcurdling screams echoed across the stale, dome-enclosed air. It felt like my body had been dipped in molten rock, I was so angry.

Someone made their last mistake planting a bomb up there. I wasn't a collector anymore, but I still had a gun. And this time, it was personal.

NINE

KALE

"Everyone in!" I boomed. I grabbed Rin and rushed her toward one of the airships forced to land on top of the debris. She was woozy, hardly able to walk a straight line, but she was going to live. I leaned her against the car so that I could catch my breath. Aria was already inside sorting the wounded.

The landing pad was chaos. Officers from Red Wing struggled to bring things to order. Shock batons crackled as they tried to scare people away from the scene. Pulse-rifles shot into the ground to further the same goal. The area nearest to where the preacher had been was a bloodbath. Martian citizens were in too many pieces to count the dead. Among our escorts, the Venta Co. officers had taken the biggest blow. Director Yashikawa was pinned upright with a length of railing sticking through the center of his chest. The only bodies I cared about, however, were the ones clad in white. Two of my guards lay dead, bodies broken and seared. They'd followed me to this foreign world, and now they'd never return home because of me.

"Mr. Trass!" Captain Barnes said as he clutched my arm. "That's too much weight for a single vehicle."

I seized him by the chest plate and pulled him close. "Is

this what you wanted, Captain?" I growled, then coughed. Even with my mask on, the taste of ash and smoke filled my mouth.

"I swear we had nothing to do with this. Many of my men are dead over there! Please, let us help keep you safe like we were hired to."

"I won't give you the chance to divide us."

"I will," Rin interjected. She attempted to stand on her own weight, failed, then closed her eyes and rubbed her temples. "There are drones everywhere, but they won't be able to see clearly enough to tell which one of us is you. We should scramble in plain sight and have every car take alternate routes in case of another attack."

"My thoughts exactly," the captain said.

"A lot of good Earther thoughts have done us!" She grimaced in pain from raising her voice. "It's up to you, Lord Trass. Or we can head straight back to the *Cora* and get off this rock."

"We aren't going back," I said. "Not yet. Captain, load each car and have your men transport our dead back to my ship. We came here together, and we'll be leaving that way."

"Absolutely, Mr. Trass." He started off toward his men, but I stopped him.

"If you try anything, I'll have every member of your clan-family across Sol hunted down."

"When Red Wing takes a contract, we do everything in our power to fulfill it. Now please, sir, let me do my job."

A thousand different insults bounced around in my head, but I decided just to let him go. If he was planning a hit on me, there was no reason to rile him further, and if he wasn't, no reason to give him cause to change his mind. A younger version of me wouldn't have shown such restraint, but I was slowly learning what it took to lead.

Rin moved to start giving orders, but it took only one step for her to grow faint and fall against the car again.

"Get inside and have Aria look at you," I said. "And when you get a chance, make sure Gareth knows we're all right. That's an order."

I could tell she wanted to protest, but for once, she couldn't muster the energy. After she was on board, I had my entire squadron of guards shuffle between cars. Fourteen of them were with us now, and since all of them wore sanitary masks, tricking any peeping Earthers would be easy. The most injured remained where they were in the car with Aria and Rin, and after I was sure every one of my people was safe, I prepared to join them.

Captain Barnes offered a resolute nod from across the pad, where medical personnel had now arrived. He specifically made sure my two fallen brethren were the first to be placed on gurneys. I swallowed my pride, returned the gesture, and right before I backed up onto the airship, noticed my would-be Cogent assassin on the ground. I hurried out and dragged the limp corpse onto the car. Everybody inside was too agitated to notice.

"I'm flying," Rin demanded to the anxious Red Wing officer seated at the controls.

"Not until I take a look at you," Aria replied.

"There's nothing to look at. I'm fine."

Just as she finished her sentence, her hand skated off the back of the pilot's chair, and she nearly fell. Aria didn't hesitate. She weaved her way across the cabin and shoved Rin into the nearest seat. Then she waved a light in front of her eyes.

"Definitely a concussion," Aria said. "You're not doing any piloting right now."

"You don't get to tell me what to do!" She went to stand, but Aria pushed her back down with ease.

"I do right now. If you don't trust him, I'll fly."

"No," I interrupted. All eyes snapped toward me. "They need their doctor right now. Take off," I addressed the Red Wing pilot. "Whatever route you had planned, take another."

The pilot swallowed hard, then turned to the controls. The airship's anti-grav engines promptly lifted us straight up before it zoomed toward New Beijing's forest of glass towers.

"Keep us in one piece, or you won't be," Rin threatened. While Aria continued examining her head, Rin stuck her arm into the cockpit, pulse pistol in hand, and aimed it at the pilot's side. I could see the sweat glistening on his cheek as he tried his best not to look.

I watched through the forward viewport as the other two airships in our escort diverged. I understood the strategy, though it pained me to know I might be sending more of my people to their slaughter. There could be more Cogents out there like the one who almost got me, prepared to take a chance on which car to hit. That was when I remembered I was holding a body.

I slid it into the center of the aisle. My people stared, their faces covered in ash and scrapes, eyes bright red from the smoke. Aria was about to pick shrapnel out of another injured Titan-born when she noticed the head by her boot and froze.

"Who is he?" Rin groaned. She looked like she was ready to throw up.

"He was about to shoot me before the explosion went off," I said. "A Cogent, I think. One of Luxarn's secret collectors that Rylah told us about."

"It is," Aria affirmed. "I saw one before the Darien Q-zone went up. He'd tracked me with that collector to our hideout underneath and killed dozens of us alone before I escaped."

"Before you *ran*," Rin amended.

"Rin," I said sternly.

"What?" she snapped. "Two people just tried to murder you, and you still think the outsider led us here to talk?"

"I would never!" Aria argued. Her hand slipped as she did, causing her patient to shriek in pain.

"You arranged this, didn't you?"

"Enough!" I bellowed. "Don't be blind, Rin. Luxarn might have sent the Cogent after me, but the bomber wasn't only aiming for us. A Venta director is probably dead. Red Wing men too. Who do you think Aria is working for if not one of them?"

"I don't know," Rin admitted. "Could be for her own pleasure. How much do we really know about *The Doctor* after all?"

"As much as I need to. She's the only one not wearing armor. She could've been killed more easily than any of us."

"Then tell me, Lord Trass. Who do you think did it?"

"Who cares? Luxarn would've had me dead without the bomber's interference. Whoever it was not only saved my life but helped us in more ways than one."

"I suppose one less Venta director can't hurt."

"Violence on Mars is too close to home," Aria said as she stretched a bandage tight around her patient's shoulder. "It will have the USF more eager for a resolution."

"Exactly," I replied. Aria's familiarity with Earther corporate politics was invaluable. Another reason to keep her around, which Rin just couldn't bring herself to see.

"Well, they better ask nicely for my gun," Rin muttered. She pressed her pistol harder against the pilot's ribs. The hovercar swerved slightly, but he hastily regained control.

The rest of our ride went in silence, save for the occasional moan from one of Aria's patients as she bound their injuries and prodded them with equipment. I stared out the viewport as the shimmering towers of New Beijing raced by along with myriad advertisements for companies and products. Countless Earther silhouettes passed behind the windows, filling offices and luxury apartments. Every single one of them was out for his or her own wallet. And the higher up they were, the more they had, just like it had been on Titan for most of my life.

Most of the air traffic in New Beijing was grounded after the attack, so Aria barely had time to finish her examinations before we touched down on the rooftop of the USF Assembly Building. It wasn't the tallest structure under the dome, but it was the most solid. The stark exterior walls were made from smooth, reddish stone mined from Mars's crust. A rigid pattern of tiny punched apertures gave it the appearance of an ancient fortress. The only thing that broke the solid wall was an amorphous glass volume protruding from the center like a womb, where the Assembly formally met. Where *we* would meet them.

I went to stand once the anti-grav engines shut off, but Rin barred me. She signaled to the guards, and they filed out of the craft first to ensure that this landing pad was safe. She swerved on her way to follow them, having to pause by the exit for a few seconds to gather herself due to her injuries.

"Is she always like this?" Aria whispered to me.

"Like what?" I said. Her lips twisted momentarily until I forced a meager grin. "She only wants what's best for us. If you knew everything she's been through, you'd understand."

"I know that." She sighed. Her hand grazed mine softly. I flinched, but her fingers threaded through mine before I had the chance to fully recoil. "I hope you know I had nothing to do with that."

"Trust me, if I thought otherwise, you wouldn't be here right now."

Her gaze drifted toward the floor. I guess it wasn't the vote of confidence she wanted, but with the yellow eye-lens of my would-be assassin glinting in the background, it was the best I could offer. She released my hand and started off toward the exit.

"Let's get this over with then," she said.

An apology found its way to the tip of my tongue as I stood to follow her, but it never went further.

"I know Madame Venta well," Aria said, back to business. "Too well. She's nothing like Luxarn Pervenio, even if you think they're all the same."

"You've warned me plenty of times, Aria."

"I just don't want you to be caught off-guard. She seems kind, like a loving mother. Spend too long with her, and you might even think she is. Don't trust a word she says."

"That won't be a problem. I already have an overbearing mother."

"I didn't know mine."

We emerged onto the USF Building roof, so there was no chance to respond. All three airships had made it safely. My people had formed a semicircle in front of us at Rin's command. This time, their weapons were armed. They faced a wall of Venta Co. security officers. One wrong move and I could tell by my aunt's demeanor nobody was walking away, sanitary mask on or not. She was right in the heart of it, and either she was feeling better or she was somehow managing to keep her stance firm despite her injuries. I wasn't surprised; Rin was most at home in a guns-drawn standoff like we'd had back on Pervenio Station, what seemed like an eternity ago.

"Mr. Trass," the middle-aged woman standing across from Rin announced. "I'm glad to see you're safe." I couldn't get a good look at her, but I knew instantly she was Madame Venta. She appeared on Earther news feeds plenty, especially now that she was trying to bury Pervenio Corp in the public eye. It was through her that this entire summit had been arranged.

"I'm sure you are," Rin said. Her gun went up higher as Madame Venta took a step closer. Every other weapon on the landing pad followed suit.

"Rin, everyone, lower your weapons," I said.

"Trapped on another landing pad, Kale," Rin said. "It doesn't feel right. Did you plan this too, Ambassador?"

I raised my arm in front of Aria to keep her quiet. "That isn't a request," I said. "We're guests here."

My guards did as commanded. Rin lingered in her battle stance a few seconds longer before finally giving in. I shot her a glower so firm, her head drooped in shame. Her insubordination in front of others was growing troublesome. My own people could handle it—they knew she was also a Trass—but while on Mars, every Earther needed to know that we Titanborn stood united, that I was in complete control.

My people parted for me, and I wound up face to face with the founder of Venta Co. Immediately, I noticed what Aria had been talking about. Unlike Luxarn Pervenio with his finely tailored outfits and surgically maintained face, up close, she had the appearance of any ordinary woman. Plain, wrinkly, garbed in a navy dress so conventional that Aria seemed like the unfathomably rich one.

"Excuse my aunt, Madame Venta," I said. "She suffered head trauma during the attack and isn't thinking straight."

"There is nothing to forgive." Her voice was sweet and gentle. Her almond-shaped eyes, though behind a thick pair of antique glasses, had a warmth to them that caught me so off guard I didn't even realize I was staring. She extended her hand, and I shook it without thinking. I was wearing gloves, so I'd been planning to do so as a display of good faith, but it usually took more for me to purposely touch a purebred Earther.

"What occurred at the spaceport is inexcusable," she said, her gaze fixed upon the Red Wing officers by our transports. "And it is what happens when you leave Red Wing Company in charge of security. You have my word, we will discover who was behind it and bring them to justice."

"Thank you," I replied. "May I offer my condolences for your clan-brother, Director Yashikawa."

"Don't. He too was in charge of your security." Though her words were harsh, they came out of her mouth with the softness of a mother reading a bedtime story.

"We told you, you should've put us in charge, Mother," the older of two young men standing behind her spoke up. Both of them looked like birds, with thin noses and permanent scowls. Brothers. I wasn't sure if she was actually their mother, but I suppose her being as famous and wealthy as she was made her mother to everyone in her clan-family.

"What did I tell you about interrupting while I'm conducting business?" she said.

"We're just saying," said the younger brother.

"So am I." She glanced back over her shoulder, and I couldn't see the look she shot at them, but both shut right up. By the time she turned back around, she wore a pleasant smile. "Excuse my sons. Karl and Fern are still learning when to keep their opinions to themselves."

I nodded, catching a glimpse of Rin in my peripheral vision. I never imagined me and Madame Venta agreeing on something, but it seemed there were some problems all leaders face, no matter the purity of their cause.

Madame Venta turned to Aria and raised her arms for an embrace. "Aria, my dear. It's wonderful to see you again. You look positively radiant."

Aria hesitated even longer than I had before giving in to the hug. "And you, Madame Venta," she said meekly.

"Please, I'm still Jamaru to you." She planted a kiss on Aria's cheek so close to her lips, I think the corners might have touched. Then she whispered something in her ear that drained the color from Aria's face. As she did, she lifted Aria's Ark Ship pendant and gave it a spin.

"Interesting piece," she said aloud as she backed away. "But you make anything look exquisite. I hope our cousins on Titan are treating you well?"

"They are, Mad— Jamaru. Of course." Aria had never been clear what the extent of their relationship was, but I'd never seen her so diffident in the face of anyone, even the first time she met Rin.

"I'm glad to hear it, dear." Madame Venta's attention swiveled back toward me with the aplomb of a woman who knew how to command a conference table. "Well, Mr. Trass, I don't want to waste any more of your time. In light of what has happened, the USF requests a postponement of your hearing."

I drew a deep breath. If Aria was cautious of her, then I knew there was good reason. Negotiation had never been my strong suit, even when I was running drugs for fences in the Darien Lowers trying to scrum up Earther credits. I needed to be careful. Not too severe and not too complaisant.

"If that is their decision," I began, "then I'm sorry, but unfortunately, we'll have to reconsider things."

"They have no intention of disrespecting you," Madame Venta insisted. "Nothing excessive. A few days to figure out who planned the bombing and ensure it doesn't happen again."

"Titan is in the midst of a considerable transition. I'm sure you understand what it's like developing settlements. We can't afford to waste even a single day. Rin." I gestured for her to return to the airship. As I turned away myself, Madame Venta's hand fell upon my arm. Now it was my turn to glower, and the one I shot at her finally sent a ripple of apprehension across her calm demeanor. Earthers should never touch Titanborn without consent. Luxarn Pervenio learned that the hard way when he invaded a quarantine.

"Please, Mr. Trass," she said. "You've come a long way. The

Assembly takes eons to arrange anything. Don't throw this chance away."

Now when I regarded her, all I saw was another Earther trying to get her way, with her hand on me as if she owned me. Aria was wrong. There was nothing to be afraid of. No matter how any of them conducted themselves, in the end, they were all after the same thing. Venta Co. put its neck out to arrange a meeting with the USF to discuss peace. That probably came with a handful of credits, promised contracts, and whatever else a mega-corporation might want. The only person with anything to lose was Madame Venta.

I held my silence, using my eyes to tell her I needed to hear more to be convinced.

Madame Venta leaned in close and lowered her voice. "We helped your organization when Pervenio squeezed too far. Sold you weapons. Materials."

"You didn't care that you were helping us, only that you were hurting them," Rin hissed. I allowed her that interjection.

"It's true," Madame Venta admitted. Without intending to, I returned to facing her fully. I'd expected her to defend herself. "I won't insult you with lies, but we came to an honest understanding with one of the men who led your insurgence before you."

"His father," Rin corrected. This time, I sent a sidelong glare her way so that she would back down.

"Yes, well, in any deal, there has to be a certain level of trust between parties. I'm asking you to trust me now. Re-opening free trade with the Ring benefits us all no matter who runs it. The USF knows this, and so do we."

"Would you mind giving us a moment to discuss this in private, Madame?" Aria asked.

"There's no need," I said. "If they know that, then they'll oblige. Tell them they can have the rest of the day to ensure the security of the hall. We will delay the meeting until tonight. That is my only offer."

Madame Venta ground her jaw, clearly fighting to retain her pleasant demeanor. "I will pass your terms along."

"Whether they accept or not, we leave for Titan tomorrow morning. Thank you, Madame Venta."

She bowed her head. "The pleasure is all mine, Mr. Trass. While you wait, my sons will escort you to your assigned floor of suites. You'll have to check in your weapons with the USF officers, and then you can head on up."

"In light of what's happened, I think we'll be keeping them on us. And I want our floor emptied of all USF officers in case they were behind what happened. Extra precaution seems like the smart decision for everybody right now, don't you agree?"

"I can only push the Assembly so far, Mr. Trass."

I leaned in to whisper in her ear this time. "I think we all know who is really in charge on Earth."

"I'll try my best," she said, biting her lip. "That's all I can promise."

"Perhaps I'll talk to them myself. I'm sure they'd love to know how weapons wound up on a Saturn gas harvester that was supposed to have disappeared. Or how a Martian nurse at a Venta Co. hospital somehow knew exactly where Pervenio was keeping medical supplies in New London. Aria tells a wonderful story about that one."

Madame Venta glared at Aria, then back at me. "Are you threatening me, Mr. Trass?"

"Not at all. *You* brought up your history working with my people. I merely assumed it was public knowledge."

"I should snap your twig body in two!" the elder of her two sons barked.

"Quiet, Karl!" Madame Venta shouted. "Mr. Trass was only trying to explain his brilliant idea." She expertly feigned a grin.

"We'll have your floor emptied immediately. I should have thought of that myself. In any case, I recommend that you and your people don't leave the premises. As Aria knows, New Beijing isn't all glitz and glamor."

"Of course," I said. "Who knows what would happen if the 'self-proclaimed King of Titan' were to be harmed here."

Her smile widened as she ignored my comment. She turned slightly and beckoned me toward the building entry. I could tell by the weight of her stance that I was under her skin. I guess she didn't expect a lowly "Ringer" like me to pay attention to the things she said on Earther news feeds.

"If everything is settled, we've had the finest Martian delicacies prepared for your arrival," she said. "Enjoy your day, Mr. Trass."

Aria was halfway through getting the word "thank" out when Madame Venta stormed away. I didn't get to see her expression but judging by the way the bottom of her dress whipped around to keep up with her, I could only imagine. Millions of people worked for Venta Co., and I knew that any of them who'd ever spoken to her like I had were probably floating through space without a suit.

"Right this way, Ri... Titanborns," Karl said. The other brother snickered. "That still what you people like being called?"

Rin drew herself so close to him that he couldn't miss the rippling edges of her scars peeking over the top of her sanitary mask. "Why don't you try the other word, and we'll find out," she said.

He nearly choked on his next breath. "Titanborn, of course. Just making sure. R—right this way."

I had two of my men retrieve the dead Cogent to bring with us, and then Rin, Aria, the guards, and I followed Madame Venta's sons in. The Venta officers had to wait on the landing pad while we strolled right in with weapons, armor, and a corpse. None of the USF officers posted in the upper lobby said a word either.

"That went relatively well," Aria whispered into my ear.

The corners of my lips curled into a grin—not forced like it had been countless times since we took Titan, but a genuine smile. Madame Venta surely had sway, but to me, it seemed like they were finally taking us seriously.

TEN

MALCOLM

I burst through the front door of the Twilight Sun. I'd kept my cool since discovering Wai's body, but inside, my blood boiled.

"There you are, Haglin!" Yan Ning shouted as he scurried out from behind the bar. The place was busier than I'd ever seen it, with at least half the tables filled and most of the bar. Every eye was fixed on the news feeds, which he'd somewhat managed to return to working order. "You've got some nerve running off at a time like this. I should—"

"Where the hell are they?" I growled, stunning him into silence.

"You... huh? Where's who?"

"Those Venta officers. Where'd they go?" Trevor and his cronies were nowhere to be seen.

"Probably to do their *jobs*." I peeked into a few booths just to make sure. Yan Ning followed me around. "Speaking of, I can't deal with any more slip-ups. I don't care who you are, this is your last warning."

I drew open the last booth. Two offworlders were busy humping inside; she in a dress and him with his drawers down. I startled them so bad they knocked heads and spilled two glasses of synthahol all over the floor. The two degenerates scurried past us and out the door. Calamity sure did bring out the best in people.

"Haglin, you hear that?" Yan Ning said.

I ignored him. I checked my holster to make sure everything was in the right place, then brushed by Yan Ning. He grabbed my arm a bit too aggressively and was lucky I didn't rip his hand off.

"Where the hell do you think you're going?" he questioned. "You're still on the clock."

"You know how many worthless sacks of meat like you I've stuffed in a cell on Mars? You touch me again, I'll make sure yours is on Pluto."

Nothing else needed to be said. He backed away, completely flabbergasted. All those weeks of ignoring what I might really be and the truth must have hit him like a hovercar. He returned to the bar so fast, he knocked over a few bottles.

"You can't stay upstairs if you don't work, Haglin," he shouted after me as I neared the exit. "You'll pay full rent!"

I reached into my pocket and removed the key card. I dropped it in the entry and continued on my way. I couldn't say where I'd spend the night, nor did I care. The search for information often brought me to corners darker than the Twilight Sun's, and I didn't plan to sleep until I found what I needed.

I had a refurbished hand-terminal, but with all my old Pervenio contacts lost, it was of little use to me. The news feeds wouldn't say anything substantial about what happened until the perpetrator was found and the truth could be spun in such a way that it appeased most parties. I had to do things the old-fashioned way. Since it was still daytime and many of the Old Dome workers in the city were out at the factories dotting Mars, I knew just where to start.

The worst part about a bombing in New Beijing was that Venta Security shut down the Redline. That meant crossing the Tongueway on foot. The crowds were smaller than usual as people hid in their homes, but every step was a reminder of the artificial limb I didn't want. One thing the doc never told me was that walking with one leg I couldn't feel meant the other felt everything. No matter how much I exercised it, which admittedly wasn't much, the muscles got sore fast. From my thigh to my foot. I couldn't even tell which side I was favoring anymore, but whatever I was doing, it was wrong.

It didn't matter. After I found the bastard responsible for pulverizing Wai into a puddle on the sidewalk, I could get back to retirement. There were dozens more hole-in-the-wall bars like the Twilight Sun waiting for a gun for hire in Old Dome.

I stopped outside of a Venta security outpost halfway down the Tongueway. They'd filled out a small shop connected to a Redline station. There were posts nearer to the Twilight Sun, but this one was special. For starters, I knew the captain, and it wasn't Trevor. If I found him, I knew I'd wind up doing something I'd regret.

A few drunks and strung-out offworlders were sprinkled around the lobby. Otherwise, it was empty. With Kale on Mars and the bombing, most officers would be heading to the security headquarters or USF Assembly Building. They had more important things to do than clean up sewer trash.

News feeds on viewscreens hanging from the ceiling played for nobody. I did my best to ignore them. The talking heads were at it again, speculating about who could be behind the attack to a backdrop of grainy footage taken by reporters who couldn't get close. I didn't want my instincts tainted by the musings of people saying what whoever paid their bills wanted them to say.

"Is Captain Harris in?" I asked the window attendant. She

was kicked back at her desk, boots up on the table and basically taking a nap while she watched something on her terminal's screen. Sounded more like an entertainment program than a newsfeed.

"Depends who's asking," she replied without looking up.

"Malcolm Graves. Tell him I've got a business proposition."

She hopped on the coms, voice as dreary as could be. You'd think the city was in perfect shape. Nothing more boring for a low-level security desk clerk like her than a crisis period.

"He's not interested," she said.

"Tell him I'd rather not hop on my hand-terminal and mention Mannekin to anyone," I replied.

"Don't you know what's going on out there? We're busy."

I glanced to my side. A salt sniffer coughed and decided to sprawl out across a line of empty seats. "It sure looks like it. Just tell him."

If a subordinate had rolled her eyes like she did while I was still a collector, I'd have had her ass shipped to an asteroid colony. I couldn't stand ineptitude. It slowed things down, and in my line of work, that was the difference between taking down a killer and him squeaking off a few extra shots.

"He said come in," she finally answered, only seconds before I considered taking my shiny new leg and shoving it through the door myself.

"Great," I said. "Thanks."

An officer at the entry confiscated my gun and then let me through. As a collector, even from a rival corporation, I once could flash my badge, and lowly officers wouldn't dare touch me. Now I stayed quiet and tried not to draw attention.

The outpost's bullpen wasn't big enough to fit more than a few desks. They were half empty, their officers off patrolling. Exposed water pipes rattled beneath the plasticrete ceiling. A few signs for what used to be a noodle shop still clung to the walls. Tiny outposts like this in the heart of Old Dome weren't used for more than ringing up miscreants like the ones inside. Minor offenders. Drug addicts. I guess Venta didn't think putting any credits toward looking appealing to those people was worth it.

That was one difference between Venta Co. and my old employer. Luxarn always ensured that anything visible to the public had a polished coat. A waste of credits at times, probably, but he was a perfectionist. He never wanted people to see the rust filling Sol, but instead, be constantly reminded of how far humanity had come despite the apocalypse.

"Graves," Captain Harris grumbled from inside his cramped office, as if I'd stirred him from a nap. Considering his legs were up on his desk and he was staring at the ceiling, I probably had. "I thought I was done with you."

He had a jaw like an anvil, but it didn't account for much. The rest of him was wrinkled and world-weary. Unkempt hair he'd never combed in his life. He was probably older than me and was happy never to advance any further than where he was. Typical Venta Co. rubbish.

"So did I." I plopped down in the seat across from him and made myself comfortable. There wasn't even a porthole inside the office, and a leaky pipe relentlessly dripped onto the edge of his desk, far too close to his console for comfort, like he cared.

"Sure, come right in," he said. "What is it, Graves? I heard about the trouble you caused the other night. Collectors? If you're here thinking I can get them off your back, you're even stupider than I thought."

"Oh, come on, Harris. Is that any way to greet an old friend?"

"I don't have time for your games today," he said.

"I need a favor."

"I thought we already made things even when I got you that ID you're carrying, no questions asked."

"Something came up," I said.

"Something always does." He kicked down his feet. "Let's hear it. I'm in the mood for a good laugh."

"I need access to the Venta reports about the bombing. Not the bullshit on the news feeds. The real intel."

"And I want to retire to a penthouse in New London. Unfortunately, Graves, I like my job. As far as I'm concerned, we're already square, so why don't you find another officer to screw over."

"But I like you."

"Too bad." He leaned back and closed his eyes. "I've got work to do."

"How about I put a call in to one of the reporters I know," I said. "I'm sure they'd love to find out about a security captain selling illegitimates to a mad scientist and keeping the credits." It happened almost a decade back when a deranged lunatic named Lucas Mannekin was trying to turn people into organic androids. I knew Harris was too lazy to ever find something on me to make us even, so I'd been using him to get what little bits of Venta Co. intel he knew ever since.

He bit his lip in frustration for a few seconds, then slammed his fist on his desk. "Do it, then. You think they're going to care anymore with what's going on out there? Fire one of their most experienced captains while Kale Trass and the Ringer circus are in town? Please, Graves, just leave and save yourself the humiliation."

"My humiliation?"

"Sure." He reached down, drew a pulse pistol, and aimed it at my chest. "You say a word, and I'll have my men bury you so deep in the sewers, even you won't be able to crawl out."

Now I was fuming. I had learned on Titan that you can only

push somebody so far, but I never expected any resistance from Harris. Mostly I was angry that I was foolish enough not to put up more of a ruckus before discarding my firearm. I was rusty.

"You're going to pull a gun on me?" I said.

"I did some digging around after I had that ID pulled for you. Turns out you aren't a collector anymore at all. And with all the shit Pervenio Corp's going through, I don't think they'd waste much effort helping a washed-up gun like you. So, how's about you get the hell out, and we pretend none of this ever happened." He stood and made his way to the door, keeping his sights trained on me the entire way.

"Do you really want to test that?" I asked.

"Test what?"

"That Mr. Pervenio won't care." I stood and glared straight into his eyes as I brought myself close enough that the barrel of his pistol pressed into my chest. "Go on, give it a try. You think I'm not still working for him because some leaks on the darknet might say so? With what's happening, we're not running things the same way. No more badges or titles. Undercover."

"You're full of shit." He tried to sound confident, but a slight twitch in the corner of his mouth told all. The seeds of doubt were planted.

I moved closer. His pistol dug into my sternum so hard it hurt. "Then pull the trigger and put us both out of our misery."

His jaw grated and his lips pursed while he considered his next move. Finally, he lowered his firearm and sighed. "Maybe there's a little something I can do to help you," he said as he returned to his seat.

Now that was the Captain Harris I knew. Never eager to go above and beyond. Always happy to take the path of least resistance. "I knew you were smart," I said. "All I need to know is who was behind the bombing."

"If I knew that, they'd be handing me a medal. The headquarters and collectors are still investigating." He started typing on his terminal with one hand. Whether he was intentionally going so slowly just to piss me off or was really that lazy, I wasn't sure.

"Surveillance feeds?"

"You think I get to see that? Only whatever footage the news managed to grab, which I'll tell you wasn't much. All drones that weren't synced to ours or the Red Wing headquarters were downed for safety concerns."

"Lot of good that did. Well, you give me what you do have, and there'll be some credits in it for you on the backend. Say, ten percent?" He perked up immediately. Of course, it was a lie, but the promise of being paid figured to be enough to keep him quiet for long enough to find another fake name.

"What kind of pie are we talking about?"

"One hundred thousand credits. Luxarn has interest in being first to bring in whoever was responsible for this morning. While everyone else is focused on securing the meeting, it shouldn't be too difficult."

"You won't be the only collector hunting."

"No, but I'll be the best one. So, Captain, what can you tell me?"

He keyed a few more commands and squinted at the screen. "I can tell you that whoever set off the bomb bungled it if they were aiming for Kale."

"So the boy king survived?"

"Not a scratch," he said. "Only two Ringers actually wound up dead. Most of the casualties were civilians and Red Wing men. Plus, there's a Venta director in the morgue."

"Director?"

"That's what it says."

"Anything else?" I asked.

"You want more, you're going to twist the arm of someone with higher access than me."

"I won't push my luck." I stood. "You've been a great help, Captain."

"Ten percent, Graves. If I find out you got the bastard and I don't see my credits, I'll be sure to tell those collectors exactly where to find you."

"You'll be rewarded as soon as I am."

His grin stretched from ear to ear. He said, "As usual, it's been a pleasure."

"Always. Now get that damn leak fixed," I grumbled before heading out of the room.

It wasn't exactly a lead, but the information opened plenty of possibilities. Who would purposely attack Red Wing, Venta, and the Ringers all together? My old employer was the obvious answer, but even in his flustered state, Luxarn wouldn't be so sloppy. If he wanted Kale dead, he'd make sure he went for him alone and not risk worsening relations with rival corporations, considering how dire things were for Pervenio Corp. So who could it be? Had the Children of Titan played their sleight-of-hand game again? Sacrifice two of their kind to draw our attention while they were up to something far worse?

I would have killed for access to the surveillance logs from the Venta and Red Wing drones, but that would take time I didn't have. Dedicated or not, there'd be collectors on the job with a hell of a lot more resources than I had. If I wanted to find Wai's killer and give whoever it was what they really deserved, I'd have to work fast.

———

It was the afternoon by the time my gun was finally returned to me, and I departed the Venta security post. Captain Harris's one last gift was having his officers dig through holding for the weapon at the speed of a slug caught in a snowstorm.

Things in Old Dome were starting to pick up. Not like usual, with so many citizens scared by the bombing, but that was the perfect time to find whoever I was after. Most of security remained in the upper city where people mattered, so all the gangs and streetwalkers had the run of things.

It was only when I stepped into the first cathouse on my list in the heart of the Tongueway that I realized I hadn't been so sober this late in the day since I left Luxarn Pervenio's office on Undina. That was why my human leg was so sore; there was nothing to dull the pain. I didn't mind. It kept me focused.

The average career of a streetwalker wasn't long, so most of my old informants were either already dead or lost in the slums. I spotted a dealer in an alley by a popular Red Wing casino who had somebody sneaking up to him for a fix every couple of minutes. A low-level slinger wouldn't know anything, but with that kind of traffic, he must have had access to the newest stuff—Titan's foundry salts. I could thank Kale for that treat. Ever since he took over the Ring, tons of Titan's chosen narcotic had found their way to Earther worlds like he was giving it away.

Addicts were only ever after a newer, better high, and the gangs of Old Dome were happy to oblige. It was a constantly shifting landscape of villainy. Corps shut them down, and they sprang up with new names and markings, but it was always the same scum. Hell, half the time I was convinced they were backed by corporate directors that only turned on the leaders when things got too hot.

The dealer's arms were festooned with tattoos, with a skull surrounded by Saturn's rings the most prominent. I was too out of touch with the Martian underworld to know any of the newest cliques, but I'd seen that symbol all over Old Dome. It didn't take me long to piece together that they were the new mob running things below where corporations cared to be seen.

I strolled up to him with my head low like I was trying not to be seen. My fist slammed into the dealer's stomach before he could ask me if I was interested in a hit. He gaped up at me from the ground, dumbfounded. Chapped nostrils, sunken eyes, and cheeks so shallow he looked like a skeleton—he was the kind of filth a collector rarely needed to deal with. They tended to take care of themselves.

"Are you fuckin' insane?" he snarled. "You know who you're messin' with? The Ringer Bones'll have your head."

"That what you lot are calling yourselves?"

"Wait. I remember you." His chapped lips parted as he grinned, revealing a mouthful of rotten teeth and shiny chrome fillings. "Sold to you just the other night."

"That explains a lot." Who could forget how awful my headache was when Wai found me all covered in piss.

"That was some high-end shit. No refunds."

I heaved him up by the collar so hard it choked him, and slammed his back against a dumpster.

"I'm not looking for a refund," I said.

His eyes were shifty, but they moved with intention. Every so often, he peeked over my shoulder, and I was glad to be sober enough to know what that meant. I whipped out my pistol and stuck it behind me, just in time for the barrel to impede some other Ringer Bones thug trying to peel me off his dealer.

"I suggest you run back the other way," I warned without looking. The footsteps of whoever it was fleeing promptly followed. That was the thing about having a Pervenio-issued pulse pistol like mine. I didn't need to flash a badge to prove who I was. If the Ringer Bones ever found out the truth, I'd have made another group of enemies, but I didn't care.

"Loyal group of friends you've got," I said as I tightened my grip on the dealer. "Maybe you should look for a new line of work."

"You ain't got no badge," he gurgled. "You're no collector."

"Nope." I turned my pistol on him and shoved it right up under his chin. "Free to kill whoever I want now."

"When the boss finds out about this, you're dead!"

"I have a feeling he won't be around long. They never are." I slammed him again. "The bombing, what do you know about it?"

"Upstairs?" he chortled. "We don't worry ourselves about them."

"Well, you better start. You're out here every day and night. Tell me what you've heard about it, or I'll make sure you've had your last hit." I reached into the pocket on his coat and tossed a tiny plastic bag filled with white powder into the nearest sewer grate. That got his attention.

"I don't know nothin'!" he cried, literal tears welling in his eyes as he stared at his drugs.

"You better give me something then."

"I swear! The boss questioned all of us already to see if any gang was behind it. Ain't nobody got a line on who done it."

I pushed the gun into him harder. The tears started running down his cheeks. "You're not helping yourself."

"I... uh... I heard some people laughin' about it. Yeah. That everyone up there got what was comin'."

"Who were they?"

"Nobodies! Some sewer trash on their way to pray at the Three Messiahs convent. People've been rumblin' all day about how those Ringers deserve worse. Whaddya you expect after what they done?"

I held my gun there for a few seconds longer, then grunted and dropped him. He pawed at his throat, bawling like he'd expected to die. If our little conversation accomplished one thing, at least it might illuminate the value of life. But as he rolled over and a few more baggies of foundry salts rolled out of his pocket, I realized how naïve a thought that was.

He scrambled to pick them up like a starving child for crumbs, then leaped at the sewer grate, ready to shove his whole arm through for more. A better man would've shot him just to put him out of his misery. I turned away to continue my quest for information without another word.

"You're a dead man!" he cried out as I fell into the crowd. "You hear that? Dead!"

I must have gone on to talk to hundreds of the worst degenerates New Beijing had to offer, in every shady corner of the Tongueway. Carrying myself like I was still a collector only got me so far, so I had to use what little was left in my credit account to get people talking. Guy, girl, it didn't matter. Most were too high to think of anything but grabbing me by the crotch, and none of them knew a thing. Even those who claimed they did just wound up spinning tales so ludicrous that they probably actually believed them. More than a few blamed it on a meteor, which somehow struck the spaceport without putting a hole into the New Beijing dome or anything.

None of it made much sense. By the time I neared the last few shitholes on my list, it was night, and my account was as drained as my withered old body. Pounding the streets was old-fashioned, but it usually yielded results after half a day. Whispers were the Tongueway's most lucrative trade. People talked, and those people talked. Rumors spread like venereal diseases through Old Dome, and those usually had a kernel of truth in them. Enough to get a lead. But there was nothing.

All I'd deduced was that the person responsible wasn't aiming for anyone specific unless they wanted to take out some second-rate Venta director. They hadn't bragged about it either. This was beginning to feel a lot less like the bombing in New

London. I understood sleight of hand, but the Ringers putting their leader that close to danger was senseless. Bombs could be unpredictable, even in the best-laid plans. A piece of debris could've done the same to him as it did to Wai.

I shuffled around a food cart selling some manner of minced meat raunchy enough to make me gag. I'd reached the steps of the Mangled Mare, and the noseless dancer I'd convened with the night before was outside trying to entice men. A mask covered her face, enough to hide her blemish at a distance, but up close, the cloth was transparent enough to see shadows of the ghastly surprise beneath.

She was one of the few things I remembered from my bender. Not much detail, but I hoped she might've enjoyed my company enough to spill something, anything, for free.

"Hey there, sweetheart," I said to her.

"Not you again," she groaned. Not the response I was hoping for.

She brushed by me and stroked the back of a well-off looking Martian woman strolling by. The woman took one peek at her and scurried away like it was her first time in Old Dome.

"Come on," I said. "I'm just looking for some information."

"No. You're trouble." She went to seduce another potential patron, but I wrenched my way in between them.

"You know that wasn't my fault."

She finally stopped to address me. "Oh, it wasn't? I've seen you stumbling around the Tongueway like a drunken fool every night for a month now. Always got a new cut on your knuckles."

"That was different."

"'Ey, Earther. I was talking to her." A scrawny offworlder grabbed my arm. Hoops in his ears hung so low, they stretched the lobe.

"Get in line." I shoved him, and since I was indeed an

Earther, he went flying onto his ass. He didn't dare interrupt again.

"The other girls warned me all you wanted to do was chew off our ears about your bullshit glory days," the dancer said. "I was fine giving you a chance then, but I bet this is the one club you haven't been kicked out of yet, isn't it, Haglin? I don't know what your deal is, but as soon as collectors get involved, I'm out."

I gawked at her. I hadn't been so clear-headed since I landed on Mars, so I had no idea if she was right. Haglin Amissum could have been kicked out of any number of places. I thought I'd made myself invisible on Mars, and now more people knew about me than even when I was a collector. I'd made enemies and embarrassed myself enough that a streetwalker from a curiosities club wouldn't even share another drink with me.

"Look," I said. "It hasn't been my finest month, but I'm getting desperate. A friend of mine lost her life, and all I want is to find out why."

Her demeanor softened. "A friend?"

"Yeah. Just a chat, that's all I need. Since collectors come through here, I'm hoping maybe you might've overheard something that could help."

"All right, a chat," she conceded. "But it isn't gonna be free."

I scratched my head. "That's the thing. My account's sort of... dried up right now."

"I knew you were trouble." She turned away, but this time, I took her shoulder and spun her around.

"I'll pay you whatever you want tomorrow. I'm good for it." I wasn't, but I didn't care about tomorrow. Today, I was desperate.

"Get your hands off me!" she shrieked.

The bouncers at the door heard her and pushed through the crowd to reach us. My pulse started racing, but it wasn't because of them. Her outburst had caught the attention of another interested party.

"By the damn Meteorite, that's him!" a man shouted from down the Tongueway. Brash look, clean duster, I was smart enough to remember that he was one of the collectors I'd affronted the night before. They were probably prowling the Tongueway looking for the same answers about the bombing I was. He grabbed his partner and pointed through the mob of heads at me, and then they bolted in my direction.

I booked it down the nearest alley, but they were right on my tail.

Stupid, I told myself. I should've stayed in the crowd, where they wouldn't risk firing off their pistols. Now the only other people in jeopardy were scattered homeless living in shipping cartons. Easy to cover up, especially for two Venta collectors.

"You're a dead man!" one hollered.

There was nobody to tell I-told-you-so when a gun went off, and the bullet blew through the wall to my right. Chunks of plasticrete bounced off my arm. I dug into the street with my artificial leg and made an otherwise impossibly short left-hand turn down another backstreet.

"Get the hell back here!" came another shout.

It bought me some time, but a peek over my shoulder, and I saw that they were hot on my heels again. The lead collector's muzzle flashed, and I ducked as a bullet zipped by and knocked the hinges off a dumpster. The haggard man sleeping inside it was lucky his head hadn't come off too.

I had to think fast. I could return fire, but with two of them already on me and my skills eroded, the most likely scenario was them turning me into a pincushion. And I couldn't slow down. Another shot rang out. This one glanced harmlessly off my artificial leg.

My leg! I spotted a service door coming up at the next bend.

It was locked but not for me. A bullet drilled into the adjoining wall as I lifted the hunk of synthetics hanging from my hips and kicked it open. I slammed it shut behind me, stomping on the handle to bend it far enough to jam the thing.

The tables inside were filled with gamblers and piles of foundry salts. The bartender shouted at me in the same old-tongue oriental slang Wai used sparsely. A busboy poked me with a broom while I tried to catch my breath. I hurried upstairs and then out the front, where I could get lost in the crowd. The collectors emerged from the backstreet a few seconds later. The partner limped while the leader spurred him along.

I ducked and flowed along the current of Martians until I was too far for them to spot me. Then I found a stool at the back side of the nearest bar, took a seat, and punched the metal edge of the counter so hard in frustration that the scrapes on my knuckles reopened. I'd failed Wai. Sunset was falling upon New Beijing's dome, and I had nothing. I knew from experience that, after a full day, crooks had an exponentially higher chance of disappearing. Or worse, those bastards at Venta or Red Wing or some other corps would find them first.

"Hey!" I hollered at the bartender who was too busy serving the younger crowd to come over on her own. I was prepared to order the strongest drink on the menu. I had at least enough credits left for that.

She waved back, and that was when I heard it. I'd managed to tune out news feeds all day, but this one caught my attention. A title of the speaker hit me so hard in the gut I knew it wasn't a coincidence.

"Herald Jeremiah," the reporter said, "you've been awfully critical of the USF and its affiliated corporations for inviting Kale Trass to New Beijing. As their private summit arrives, what is your opinion on the malicious attack that rocked the city earlier today?"

I shushed the stringy young offworlder next to me who was beaming like he didn't realize he was flirting with a working girl.

"First, thank you for having me on," the Herald replied. It was an audio-only connection, so all I had were his words to go by. I didn't know the man, but according to the ticker, he was the head of the Church of the Three Messiahs' convent in Old Dome.

"Of course," the reporter replied. "You've built quite a following down in Old Dome. With all the speculation coming through, I'm eager to hear the opinion of someone with an ear to the people of New Beijing."

"There is no justification for the taking of fellow human life; however, I cannot bring myself to either condemn or commend the actions of whoever was behind this."

The reporter's features tightened. "You're saying you have no opinion?"

"Quite the contrary. I'm saying that when it comes to infidels traveling too near our homeworld, the fate that befalls them is simply out of our hands."

"That is quite a statement, considering that an apostle from your church is reported to be one of the victims."

"And I have been praying for the soul of Apostle Grant since the moment I heard. However, we cannot fight the will of God. We invite this manner of tragedy upon ourselves when we reach beyond the realm of our Lord. He understood that, same as me."

Damned Three Messiahs preachers. Always speaking in riddles. Yet there was something about his tone regarding his fallen comrade, something that had me headed out of that bar before I could put in my order and toward their main convent at the southern end of the Tongueway. That foundry salt dealer had mentioned overhearing two people on their way to the convent discussing the attack. It didn't strike me as odd at the time, but I knew when to trust my gut feelings.

I had one about that Herald. I could feel it in my bones. Or maybe it was one last-ditch effort to make sense of things by a washed-up old collector trying to stay in the game past his expiration date.

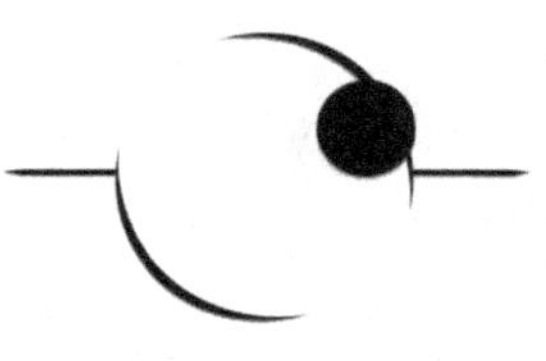

ELEVEN

KALE

"I WANT SOMEONE WATCHING EVERY ACCESS ONTO THIS level at all times," Rin ordered my guards once an elevator dropped us off on our assigned floor. "Every door, every window, every vent cover. If you need to sleep, too bad. Catch up on rest after we're back aboard the *Cora*."

"Yes, ma'am," they answered. They were exhausted. A cool shower would've been good for them, especially since the Assembly Building was kept balmy to accommodate its mostly Earther occupants. Someone had lowered the air-conditioning on our floor in a gesture of amity, but it still wasn't enough to keep my back from dripping sweat.

My people did as they were asked anyway. They knew what was at stake. I offered each one a nod of encouragement as they went by. The bloodier they were, the deeper I bent my neck. It was all I could do, considering I too was exhausted. Dealing with the Cogent, whose body was carried into one of the rooms, the explosion, more potent gravity than I was used to—it was a miracle I could keep my eyelids open. Skipping taking my g-stim may have been a mistake.

"Your room is in the center, Kale," Rin said. "Only one wall of windows. Keep the shades down." She pointed to a door halfway down the gracious, freshly polished hall. Potted plants lined it at precise intervals.

"Good," I replied.

"Yours is across the hall, outsider," she said to Aria. "I'll make sure someone is posted outside... listening."

"Thank you," Aria said.

"It isn't for you."

I placed my hand on the small of Aria's back to keep her from arguing, then led her to her door. "Are you okay, Aria?" I asked softly.

"I'm fine," she said. "What do you mean?"

"When you saw Madame Venta. I've never seen you like that."

"It's just been a long time. Organizing this over coms was one thing. Standing in front of her... Let's just say it wasn't easy rising through the ranks of Venta without getting my hands dirty."

"You don't need to explain that to me. You should get cleaned up though. You'll need to look like one of them."

"Is that the only reason?" she asked. The bags under her eyes belied the playfulness in her tone. "Come in with me, Kale. I'll help you relax. Trass knows we both need it."

"I wish I could."

She took my hand, either completely forgetting that Rin was stooped in our shadow or deciding not to care. "You can. You have to."

"If I stop focusing for one second—"

"You might actually enjoy life a little."

I exhaled. Constantly, I teetered on the precipice of snapping at her and knowing she was right. Her fingers cupped my gaunt cheek, cold despite the temperature, and she turned my head to face her. Her nails ran down my jaw and along my neck, sending a chill up my spine. My mind was instantly drawn back to the first time I shared her bed—a few nights after I'd executed Director Sodervall and declared Titan's independence.

She'd come to check on my health, and as soon as I gazed into her eyes, I could see, in that moment, she was as broken as I was. I didn't care why. I turned my mind off, let go, and felt her flesh against my flesh. Her lips against my lips. It didn't matter that she wasn't Titanborn or might've been carrying bacteria from her run-ins with Earthers. We got lost in each other, and those were the only few minutes of freedom from the prison of my thoughts that I'd enjoyed since stepping into Cora's evacuated prison cell on Pervenio Station.

It was only after, as she lay next to me, that I realized who she wasn't. Our nights spent together afterward were never as liberating and equally crushing. Time didn't fix it. Because, every day, I could tell that she was slowly and surely putting the pieces of herself back together again. And as much as she wanted me to join her, I couldn't.

"Kale," she said gently, breaking my train of thought.

"I'll rest when we're finished," I replied firmly.

"A wise man once told me to take advantage of every chance for sleep you get. You never know when you'll get another."

"Was that wise man in charge of ruling an entire people?"

She chuckled. "He probably liked to think he was." She rose onto her toes to whisper directly into my ear. "If you change your mind, I promise we don't have to talk." She planted a kiss on my sanitary mask, then sauntered into her room. I watched her the whole way, even after the door shut behind her.

"Is that why you trust her?" Rin asked from behind me, without even attempting to mask her disdain. "Pretty women like that know how to get what they want."

"It's not like that."

"A bastard offworlder who knows Madame Venta personally and winds up your ambassador. I know Rylah vouched for her from prior dealings when she was with Venta, but either she's got plans of her own or she's the luckiest girl in Sol. All I'm sure of is that the moment she gets whatever it is she wants from you, she'll drop you like a sickness. If she hasn't infected you first."

"We're careful. Besides, like you said, she's the Doctor."

Rin scoffed. "Only when it suits her."

I seized her arm. "What do you know about being with anybody, Rin? You think people don't get close to you because of your face?"

"This isn't the time, Kale." Her eyes darted from side to side, wary of the guards posted throughout the hall.

"You're right, it isn't." I released her, the augmented strength in my arms causing me to push her into the wall as I did. I'm not sure if it was on purpose or not. "I appreciate your advice, but when it comes to our ambassador, I'm tired of hearing it. I'm in control, Rin."

"I just don't want you to forget why we're here." She brushed her armor as if I'd somehow made it dirtier, then turned toward my room.

"You know me better than that."

"Fine." She gestured toward my door. "Shall we, then?"

I nodded, and we stepped through. Guards immediately positioned themselves outside. "Nobody gets in," Rin ordered them, then sealed the door behind us.

The suite's kitchen, packed with sparkling appliances, waited inside. The counter island on one side was covered end to end in food. Fruits, vegetables, juices; certain ones I'd never even seen before. A part of me was naïve enough to think they meant well, like someone from Titan should ever risk trying Earther food like this or the germs it might hold.

Admittedly, the intermingling of smells was intoxicating. As

I approached them for a closer look, my vision was drawn toward the open living space.

An enormous viewscreen was switched off, the windows were set to full tint, and every cushion on the elegant sofas was in place. A man in a tattered Venta uniform hung upside down from the ceiling between it all. His feet were strung up to an opulent crystal chandelier, blood dripping from a gash on his forehead.

"Is someone there?" he rasped as he struggled futilely to bend and reach his ankles. Even though he was a squat Earther, he wasn't strong enough to do it. "Thank Earth, you have to get me down! I didn't..." He trailed off as Rin rounded the corner. His stare transitioned from the orange circle on our chests to our tall faces. "Fuck."

Gareth stepped out of the bathroom, drying his hands on a towel. Blood circled the drain of the sink inside.

"Right on schedule," Rin said. "How the hell did you manage to get up here unseen? Actually, I don't want to know."

"These Earthers can't secure anything," Gareth signed.

"Tell us about it."

He hurried over and studied our faces. *"The explosion. I feared the worst."*

"Don't worry; we're fine," I said. I reached into a pouch on my belt, withdrew a folded sanitary mask and a pair of latex gloves, and handed it to him. He tore them out of my hand like a salt addict in need of a fix and threw them on.

"I don't know what this is about, but you'd better let me down!" his hanging captive shouted. "Do you know who I work for?"

We ignored him. Gareth drew an ID from his pocket and showed it to me and Rin. He was indeed the man we were after. Trevor Cross, a former collector who now worked a security detail for Venta Co.'s Chief Engineer, Basaam Venta. Basaam was in the midst of preparing their bid for designing the next Departure Ark, to be revealed at the year's upcoming M-Day celebrations. Any eligible company could present its plans there, with the USF Assembly choosing which one would receive the honor of designing a vessel to carry people across the stars. Venta Co. was supposedly the frontrunner, designing their ship in a factory on Europa.

"He was off duty when I found him," Gareth signed.

"Anybody see you?" I asked. His brow creased as if I'd offended him. "Sorry. I knew we could count on you. He's the key to everything."

"You didn't hurt him too bad yet, did you?" Rin said.

"I wouldn't dream of leaving you out."

We all approached Trevor. His eyes widened at the sight of three towering Titanborn, two bearing the Children of Titan emblem front and center. We'd come far since Rin released the video of them executing Earthers on my old gas harvester, the *Piccolo,* but that image was forever ingrained in the minds of Earthers. It was how they saw us, as heartless monsters, not freedom fighters. The orange circle signified that.

"I'm sure this is a misunderstanding," he said. "Just cut me loose, and we can talk... Wait, why do I know you?" I knelt in front of him so we were face to upside-down face. I didn't even need to lift my sanitary mask. I could tell before he mouthed the words that he'd figured out exactly who I was. I wasn't an everyday pickpocket in the Darien Lowers anymore who could hide in plain sight.

"Y....you're Kale Trass," he stuttered.

"Smarter than he looks," Rin said.

"Perfect! Now you're someone I can talk to. Not that beast who won't say a word."

"Collector," I said. "Tell me, Trevor Cross, how bad do you have to mess up to lose that title?"

"Collector? You've got it all wrong. I've always been a security officer."

"Sure."

He stretched his neck up as far as he could in one last effort to break free, then swung back. Gareth was there to steady him. He tightened the cuffs on Trevor's ankles until the Earther shrieked.

"Look, I don't know what you think I know!" he gasped. "But I swear I'm just a security officer now. How about you untie me so we can have a damn civil conversation?"

"I'll untie you after you help us," I said.

"Help you with what? I don't know what you possibly think I know!"

"I need you to tell me everything you know about Basaam Venta."

"What I know about him? Everybody knows him. He's some sort of ship-design genius Madame Venta adopted into her clan-family years ago. I didn't even know that was legal, but she managed it."

"Stop playing dumb, mudstomper!" Rin's fist pistoned into his gut. Without her armor on, her weak muscles probably wouldn't have been enough to bother him, but with it, all the veins on his neck bulged as he retched in pain.

"A former collector doesn't fall too far, does he," I said. "We've seen more than you'll ever know on Pervenio Station's unwiped servers. We know you were the collector who helped undermine Pervenio Corp on Titan, and we know you're now one of the captains in charge of Basaam's security."

He coughed. "Is that what this is about? I'm off duty. I couldn't tell you where he is even if I wanted to."

"We disagree." I nodded to Rin, who went off toward the kitchen. Gareth moved to the other side of Trevor, smacking him across the cheek with the back of his hand on his way.

"You fucking—!" Trevor screamed. "Why would I lie? You think I care about Venta after they took my collector's license? It's a job. We've all got to put credits on our table. You lived under Pervenio's thumb. You know how it is."

"All too well," I agreed. "The funny thing is, however, that according to our intel, you're one of the highest-ranking security officers working in Basaam's research lab on Europa. That you'd be the one with access to his itinerary, even while off duty."

"That's bullshit!"

"Are you calling my sister a liar?" Rin questioned.

I glanced over my shoulder, and she approached us, a carving knife from our catered feast in one hand and a cloth from one of the fruit baskets in the other. An apple was stuck to the end of the blade with a bite taken out of it. She had her sanitary mask drawn down, and chunks of fruit leaked through the grisly hole on the right side of her face as she chewed.

She tossed the apple to Gareth, and I stepped aside. Before Trevor could get a word out, she stuffed the cloth into his mouth. He squirmed and gagged as she used the blade to slice open the center of his shirt. Then she crouched in front of him. The way the light from the bathroom caught the sinewy hole in her cheek made it even more prominent than usual. Trevor's eyes bulged in horror.

"I'm so sick of you Earther liars," Rin bristled. She traced a long, shallow cut across his abdomen. He squealed into the rag. I let her draw another line with the knife before I yanked the cloth out.

"You skinny pieces of Ringer filth!" Trevor cried. "When I get out of here, I'm going to snap your necks!"

I shoved the cloth back in, and Rin carved another red line onto his chest. When he was done screaming, she swung his head toward her mouth and whispered, "You keep it up, you'll look like me by the time I'm done with you."

"At least that would be an improvement," Gareth signed.

"I'm going to remove the gag again, Trevor," I said calmly. "If you scream, Rin's going to whittle my name into your stomach. Do you understand?" Trevor nodded fretfully. "Good. Now we've heard that Basaam has been staying in New Beijing for the week before attending the summit tonight."

"That's not true," Trevor huffed after I freed the gag. "He's still at our facility on Europa, where you'll never be able to get him. Martelle Station is a damn fortress, not like Pervenio's."

"Are you really so eager to get back in Madame Venta's good graces that you'd die for her?" Rin raised the knife again.

"All right!" he yelped. "Fine! He's in New Beijing. With all the extra security needed at the Assembly compliments of you Ringers, he took an extended vacation. He's trying to grease palms with the Departure Ark committee just to ensure his design gets selected, even though it's a shoo-in. Thing's brilliant."

"Where is he staying?" I asked.

"I couldn't tell you. I run security at Europa specifically. Since he's not there, he gave me the month off. First vacation in too damn long." He chuckled. "You picked up the wrong officer."

Rin pressed the edge of the blade into his soft pink flesh, but I stopped her. "He's telling the truth."

"I swe—" His eyes brightened. "Yeah, I am. So just let me down, and we'll pretend this never happened, okay? I told you everything I know."

"Gareth, where is his hand-terminal?" I asked.

My mute guardian shuffled through a pile of belongings before pulling out the shiny device. It was top of the line. There was a time I would've killed to get my hands on one like that in the Darien markets. He tossed it to me.

"*Screen is locked,*" he signed. "*Thumbprint and password verification required.*"

"Didn't get a chance to ask for it?" Rin remarked. Gareth rolled his eyes.

I tapped the hand-terminal against the cut on Trevor's stomach. "As his chief of security on Europa's Martelle Station, I'm guessing you can access his travel itinerary if you wanted," I said. "Even while you're *off duty.*"

"I wouldn't know," Trevor replied.

"Listen, Trevor. I can spend the next few hours talking to my people on Titan and figuring out how to slice through, but if we can't do it before the summit, Basaam might already be on his way back to Europa. I can't have that. Like you said, it's a fortress."

"What a shame for you."

"How about you save me the trouble and tell me how to access your security logs. If you do me that favor, I'll let you leave here in one piece."

He snickered. "How about your deformed friend here sucks my cock through her cheek first. Then I'll tell you."

Rin lunged at him, but Gareth jumped in front of her to hold her back. I clutched Trevor by the jaw. "Say something like that again, and I'll let her slice it off. Don't be a fool. Don't throw your life away for them."

"I'm just trying to negotiate is all. 'Cause you see, King Trass, I know you mad Ringers are going to kill me no matter what I tell you. I might as well get something out of it, and I'm sure underneath all those scars, she's as ripe as any skelly whore."

I tore the knife out of Rin's hand and jammed it through his rib cage. It didn't strike anything vital, but I covered his mouth with one hand and twisted the blade. *Skelly.* I hated that term more than anything. All the years of Earther security officers and colleagues barking insults at me and my people raged through my mind like a Titanian storm. I felt the batons smashing my stomach; I saw my mom rotting away in a quarantine and Director Sodervall smirking before he spaced Cora for no good reason.

"Here's your choice," I growled as he writhed in pain. "You provide us access to your hand-terminal right now, and the worst-case scenario is I put a bullet in your brain and end this quickly. Maybe I'll even consider letting you walk out if it's easy enough to find what we're looking for. But if you don't, then I'm not going to kill you here. I'm going to drag you back to Titan with us first. I've been told about an old form of punishment from before the Great Reunion if a Titanborn killed another. They used to cut a tiny hatch in the side of a block enclosure, not big enough to fit more than a hand. They'd take the criminal's arm and shove it through the hatch until Titan's air froze it solid. Then, while he watched, they'd shatter it into a million pieces."

I could feel Trevor's head trembling through my glove. I knew he heard every word I was saying, but his gaze tracked Rin as she traced a circle around us like an ancient beast hunting wounded prey. Gareth stayed with her just in case she lost control.

"But I won't stop there," I continued. "No. One by one, I'll shatter every one of your limbs, keeping you alive until you're little more than a head on a stump. Then I'll stuff you in a glass box in the Darien Uppers for everyone to see. You'll starve there, slowly, like one of my people decaying in a quarantine." I removed my hand from his mouth and backed away. He was too traumatized to scream. He stared back and forth between Rin, Gareth, and me, blood trickling down his chest from the knife jutting out of his ribs.

"I know what I'd choose," I said. "Though perhaps you'd

rather die a hero for a company that couldn't care less about you."

"04172308," Trevor mumbled. "That's the password."

I typed it in, then wrenched his bound hand toward me so that I could get a clean thumbprint. The device *binged* that I had full access. I gawked at the screen for a few seconds. I expected a former collector to be harder to break. Their training was supposed to be unparalleled. Growing up on Darien, we were taught to fear them more than any other agent of the Earther corporatocracy.

"Th...there, you see?" he went on. "You're in. Just need the access codes on my ID, and you can access the security logs. Basaam's travel itinerary will be in there somewhere, I promise."

I handed Gareth the terminal. He started typing, then pointed to Trevor's ID. *"Password is his birthday,"* he signed, drawing a chuckle out of Rin and me.

"What is it?" Trevor asked. "I did like you said. Now, p... please, cut me down." He craned his neck to try and see the knife sticking out of him. "I swear, I won't tell anybody about this. I'll tell them I fell on it."

"You know, Kale, that limb-shattering idea wasn't half bad," Rin said. "You make that up yourself?"

"That old fence Dexter Howser told me the story as a threat once," I replied. "Always figured it was a myth."

"Maybe we can try it next time," Gareth added.

"Don't make me beg!" Trevor cried. "Please! I'll do whatever you ask. You need someone inside of Venta, right? Right? I can be that. Your informant. Anything you need. Screw 'em, right?"

"You think we'd trust another word that comes out of your mudstomper mouth?" Rin asked. "Swapping sides whenever it suits you. You people make me sick."

"I helped smuggle weapons and meds onto Titan for Venta,

you bitch!" he growled. "Helped you Ringers when you were still hiding from our big, bad germs."

"You helped yourself!" I spat. "You Earthers think you can trade your way out of anything." I picked up the rag and presented it to Rin. "I told him to watch his mouth, but he wouldn't listen. Do whatever you want with him."

"Nothing we can't clean up," Gareth signed.

I shrugged. "It's their floor."

"You lying, skelly bastards! I'll kill all of—" His screams were muffled by Rin squeezing the cloth into his mouth. She got to work carving the Pervenio logo into his chest, his muffled screams punctuated by sharp gasps.

I brushed off my bloody gloves, then turned and stood. The sight of Aria standing in the kitchen, aghast, stopped me in my tracks.

"It's their floor?" she repeated.

"I told them nobody gets in!" Rin barked.

"Aria..." I whispered.

She didn't say a word. She strolled across the room toward Trevor, avoiding eye contact with everybody. I went to grab her shoulder, but she brushed me away. She stopped in front of our captive, whose muffled pleas filled the air. Then she snatched Rin's pulse pistol out of her holster and, before any of us could stop her, put a bullet in Trevor's chest. Right through his heart, like it wasn't the first time she'd killed.

Rin leaped at her, and I was able to get between them just in time before she seized her by the throat.

"Who the hell do you think you are?" my aunt snarled.

"Rin, stop!" I struggled to hold her at bay since we were both wearing powered armor. Gareth stood still, at a loss as to who to help.

"I'll kill her too!"

"Are you both insane?" Aria shouted. "In here? Today? If

anybody heard him or saw him. If he escaped… we'd all be killed, and Titan would be right back to how it was. Leaderless."

"We aren't ever going back to that," Rin said, beginning to simmer down enough at least that I didn't have to expend all my energy blocking her.

"At least now I know why we really came here. I hope whatever you got out of him was worth it."

"Aria," I said. She dropped the pistol and started off toward the exit. "Aria, you don't understand! We're doing what we have to. You think they'll ever take us seriously through talking? We have to make them, no matter what it takes. I have to!"

She stopped. "Well, when you're done, I came to tell you that the USF agreed to your terms. I'm going to go prepare for that. Hopefully, I'll see you there tonight." Our gazes met for the briefest moment. For the first time in months, I glimpsed the broken woman she'd been when we first met, and then, just like that, she was gone.

Rin retrieved her gun. "Are you in control now, Kale?"

"*What do we do now?*" Gareth asked. "*She saw. If she talks—*"

"She won't," I said.

"That's all you've got to—"

"She won't!" I cut Rin off. "We stick to the plan. You help Gareth take Basaam Venta out of his room. Move him while everyone is distracted by the summit, and have him on the *Cora* before we arrive."

"Kale, we have to talk about this," Rin insisted. "Now she's shooting people?"

"Like you haven't done enough of that? How many people did you murder on the *Piccolo* just to get my attention?"

"That was war."

"So is this. She is our ambassador, Rin, whether you like it or not. I suggest you get control of your fighters, who can't seem to keep the door shut when you ask them to."

Rin opened her mouth to protest. Gareth quieted her by rubbing her shoulder.

"And clean up this mess!" I yelled.

She took a measured breath then bowed her head. "Right away, Lord Trass."

I stared at the door Aria departed through until the blood from Trevor's chest pooled far enough across the floor to submerge the soles of my boots. It was so fresh and the tile so polished that I could see my reflection in it. That same shattered young man who had lain with Aria for the first time all those months ago stared back.

TWELVE

MALCOLM

THE ORNATELY CARVED, FAUX-WOOD DOORS OF THE NEW Beijing Church of the Three Messiahs Convent were entirely out of place in the rundown heart of Old Dome. A fragrance was dispersed through its air recyclers that was much like Earth's out in the countryside, a transition so jarring compared to the reek of the Tongueway that I actually missed the latter.

The convent itself was brand new. Apparently, if the turmoil on Titan had been kind to any faction, it was the Church of the Three Messiahs. I suppose they appealed to transplanted Earthers who were maddened about all the death there. Those people blamed expanding beyond Earth for what had happened, and the Three Messiahs were there for them. They took in the poor and hapless on Mars who couldn't afford to return home and provided a temporary shelter while promising to arrange transportation and residency back on Earth.

A load of bullshit if you asked me.

Of all the grimy people assembling for a service, not one looked to be on the verge of moving anywhere. Lucky for them, there was plenty of room in the convent for more initiates. Don't ask me where all their credits came from to afford a lot this size in a city as jammed for space as New Beijing, but at least three Twilight Suns could fit inside.

"Peace be with you, son of God," an apostle by the entrance said. "Are you here for our daily sermon? We are about to begin." She wore the usual robes of her order, except unlike the men, her shawl covered her entire face and hair—everything except for her eyes.

"I'm here to speak with Herald Jeremiah," I replied, blowing past her.

"I'm sorry, he's about to read scripture."

"He can wait."

She laid her hand upon my shoulder and pointed toward the lofty vaulted ceiling running down the middle of the convent. Stairs by the entrance sank into Mars's crust so the roof could seem taller than anything else in Old Dome. The ceiling was painted blue, with pure white clouds mirroring the sky of pre-Meteorite Earth. Embedded in the center was an oculus with a screen in it that displayed imagery from a telescope seemingly placed on Mars's surface somewhere. The pale silhouette of Earth passed slowly across the blackness of space.

"It cannot," she said.

"Neither can I."

I brushed her off me and continued down the aisle. The dozens of worshippers stirred, positioning themselves on their knees across the floor so that they all kowtowed in the same direction. The presumed cardinal direction of Earth where the Meteorite struck, if I remembered my former dealings with the Church correctly.

"Sir, I must ask that you come back at another time," the apostle insisted. Her voice finally rose above a whisper, earning the attention of the congregation.

I ignored her and persisted on my trek toward the altar,

studying my surroundings out of habit. None of the wall decorations made any sense, but they were everywhere. It was like the designer had visited every spiritual ruin left on Earth and regurgitated pieces of all of them onto the polished walls. Restored paintings, which I imagine depicted scenes from their bulky text, surrounded me. Most focused on either a gruesome scene of a man nailed to a cross or various figures in the desert holding tomes and crude weaponry.

Pews of faux wood lined the central aisle, carved with strange patterns and geometries. They were empty now, as everyone who had been seated remained on their knees. Each of the columns separating the side aisles was wrapped in text. The languages were ancient, and even though I couldn't decipher them, there appeared to be numerous alphabets mixed together.

I'd visited similar convents on Earth when work took me there, but never one so opulent. The USF and its larger corporations like Pervenio preferred to keep their distance from religious sects like the Three Messiahs. The groups weren't usually violent, but doomsayers had a way of riling up the public. I only went in when they gave us no choice or decided to use their flock for smuggling. Some Heralds got off on that.

More apostles like the one following me roamed among the crowd, offering blessings before the daily prayer began, doing whatever it was they did to make the people feel whole, all while using hand-terminals to happily accept donations.

Herald Jeremiah stood by the reserved yet unsettling altar comprising the back of the convent. He wore the same outfit as all his brothers and sisters. In fact, the only thing that set him apart from them was a beard that fell all the way to his waist. Behind him towered a relief sculpture of Earth shielded by a giant hand as an onslaught of meteorites crashed into it. The altar itself was a modest stand made of real tree bark. I could tell by the scent. They must have paid a pretty penny to get it from a corporate tree farm on Earth, and it was engraved with all manner of figurative representations of the many ancient religions theirs was based on.

Jeremiah was busy leafing through the worn pages of the multi-thousand-page tome crammed with their teachings sitting on the altar when I stopped before him. I don't know why they didn't just upload it into a terminal. The worshippers nearest to us gasped as I stepped onto the raised dais, like I'd broken some unspoken law. I guess I did look out of place. Worn duster, gun strapped to my side, hair a mess from an entire day hounding the Tongueway and running from collectors.

"I said you should leave!" the apostle snapped, racing in front of me.

"Now, now, we don't deny any visitors here, sister," Herald Jeremiah said. He glanced up from his text.

"But, Your Holiness, he's going to interrupt your service."

"You lead it. Can you not sense it, sister? This man is in deep pain. He needs us now more than ever." The apostle grumbled under her breath but reluctantly moved aside. "Peace be with you, weary traveler," Jeremiah addressed me. "And welcome."

"I don't think I am," I replied.

Jeremiah's thin lips cracked a smile. "Just because you're stuck here doesn't mean you're forsaken by the world God created for us. He's calling you home, my son. All you need to do is listen."

"I was born there, and trust me, the only thing holy about the place is in between the legs of its women."

I was trying to get a rise out of him. Figure out what he was all about since his faith never made much sense to me. The nearby apostle covered her mouth in revulsion, but the Herald simply nodded for her to go on. She sighed before finally replacing him at the altar. She started yammering off gibberish from their massive tome for all the worshippers to hear.

Jeremiah took me to the side. "If you've come here to spread hate, I will not stop you," he said softly. "God teaches us to be tolerant of all peoples who have yet to embrace His grace."

"I don't hate, but I died once already, and I promise you I didn't see anything but black."

Jeremiah raised one open hand and gesticulated to the apocalyptic symbol of his order. "God comes to us in many forms. There was a time long ago when the Three Messiahs drove their followers apart because they didn't recognize the God they all spoke with was one and the same."

"Doesn't speak much for your idols."

"Perhaps God wanted them to witness all aspects of life to demonstrate the danger of separation."

"Or maybe He cares as little about you as He does for any of us. He was happy enough to ravage the planet He made with everyone on it after all." I joined him in front of the foreboding statue presiding over him. I suppose they got that one thing right. Fear does a hell of a job keeping people in line.

"Not everyone. The Meteorite was sent to purge and unite us after we strayed too far from the Lord's teachings. Some lost their way and their faith and fled Earth, but so long as man continues his foolish quest to settle the heavens, we risk judgment again."

"So then why are you people here? Mars is a long way from Earth."

"Depends on who is asking. I presume you didn't come here for a sermon. You don't seem like a man willing to open his mind and heart to the Almighty Father."

"You caught me."

Jeremiah wagged his finger. "Ah yes. I know a collector

when I see one. My guests don't deserve the kind of trouble your breed seems to bring everywhere you go."

"Well, lucky for you, I'm retired." I opened my duster and flashed the fake ID proving that I was telling the truth. The news piqued his interest. "Just a concerned citizen with some innocent questions. Is there somewhere private we can talk?"

"Why pretend to seek privacy from God when we can never have it?"

I took a measured breath. Spending too long with any Three Messiahs worshipper was infuriating. Interrogating one was like yelling at a wall that could only spit back anecdotes.

"This is a pretty big presence off Earth for your church," I said. "I've seen a post here and there on asteroids, but a full convent?"

"We are here to serve as a conduit for those who seek God's grace," Jeremiah said. "To offer them a means home through piousness. Not all the people on this world chose to leave behind God's holy world to live here. Why should they be punished?"

"Punished like all those who died during Kale Trass's rebellion, right?"

Jeremiah nodded sheepishly.

"It's funny, I spent all day wondering who benefits from a tragedy like that besides warmongers," I said. "But that bomb hit every party involved in the conflict. I was about ready to grab a bottle and give up searching until I realized I'd overlooked one group that seems to be feeding off this. An order that blames a meteorite wiping out most of the life on Earth on our failures as a species, and not cosmic misfortune."

"And what was your conclusion?"

"That you seemed awfully calm during your interview about a bombing that took out one of your own flock."

"I never question the will of God. It was... his time."

"Isn't that you, though? The voices of God, or whatever rubbish you Heralds claim. You see, I was a collector for a long, long time, so I know what an innocent man sounds like. When I heard you, I heard the voice of a man who wasn't fazed because he wasn't surprised." I drew my duster far enough to the side that my pistol was in plain sight. The people filling the convent continued their prayers, though a handful couldn't help but glance up at us. I'm guessing I didn't look as calm as I imagined.

"I'm going to ask you one time, and you damn well better tell me the truth," I said. "Decades dealing with fanatics like you, I'll know if you aren't. Do you know who was behind the bombing?"

Jeremiah's cheeks flushed, but he maintained his calm. In fact, his apostle seemed far more rattled. She paused in her readings to look back at us, eyes glued to the shine of my pistol. "Your Holiness, should I call security?" she whispered.

"It would only be a waste of time," the Herald replied. She bowed and returned to the text. "Venta Co. caused it," he said to me. "The moment they offered to host those heathen Ringers so close to Earth, the very haven of God that the deserter Darien Trass forsook at its gravest time of judgment."

I couldn't contain myself any longer. I snatched him by the robes and pulled him close. The soft murmur of prayers filling the convent silenced, and I could hear the brushing sound of all the kowtowing bodies shifting to face me.

"It wasn't only Ringers who died, Herald!" I barked.

"And every death weighs heavily on me, especially that of Apostle Grant. But God works in mysterious ways. I cannot presume to understand why He does what He does. I can merely offer my apologies for the actions of an apostle who has so clearly wounded you."

My hand slipped off him. I staggered backward. "What did you just say?"

Jeremiah looked to the floor. "Apostle Grant was a troubled man," he said, voice trembling. "His clan-family left him behind here so they could find work on thriving Titan when he was young. I took him in and guided him along God's path, but when much of his family was killed during Kale's rebellion... violence was his only solution. He lost his way. Felt that nobody was doing enough to free the survivors from Kale Trass's prisons. For the lives he took, I offer my deepest sympathies."

That was it? A full indictment of one of his own without me even having to issue a threat.

"Where is he?" I squeezed out of my suddenly parched throat.

Jeremiah's head sagged, eyes closing as if in mourning. "Dead."

"You're lying!" I ripped out my pulse pistol and aimed it right between his eyes. He didn't flinch. The rest of his flock screamed and took cover. His apostle had their tome clutched to her chest, arms quaking.

"Nobody panic or call anyone," he said. "Everything will be fine." He turned back to me. "It's the truth. And soon Venta collectors will come barging through my door after they thoroughly review surveillance, and I'll tell them the same. They will torture me as they have so many times before, but it won't change what happened. Good people often die thanks to the mistakes of the wicked. Venta Co. and Kale Trass, you and I— we'll all have to live with that. Just know that whoever you lost is in a better place now."

"Shut up!" I punched him across the nose. His head snapped backward, and blood squirted out all over his beard, but I held him up. "Who the fuck ordered it?"

"If you're seeking a corporeal boss or a corporate structure, you've come to the wrong place," he groaned. "Grant did what he thought he had to."

"He didn't do it alone!" I threw Jeremiah against his order's symbolic sculpture, one hand wrapping his throat and the other pressing my pistol against his forehead.

"I wish I could tell you I didn't try to stop him, but in this holy place, I will not lie. Ever since the revolution started, his thoughts grew darker, so I sent him away and instructed him to seek penance in his own way before returning. I know now I should have kept him close."

"You knew, and you still let him go?"

"I knew only his nature, not what he was planning. It is how God made him, and if I was meant to stop him, I would have. Everything happens for a reason, my son, even if God's plan is unclear to us at the time."

"You don't get to blame your imaginary friend!" I squeezed his throat harder.

"You're angry... I understand," he muttered. "Someone was taken from you, and you want retribution. Perhaps for some reason, you even need to blame yourself. Don't."

I punched Jeremiah across the jaw so hard, I wasn't strong enough to keep him from falling. I used the sculpture to maintain balance and aimed my gun at the top of his head.

"If vengeance is what you desire, then take it on me," he grated through bloodied teeth. "My guidance was not enough to help him, and now someone dear to you is dead. I will forgive you, and so will God."

My hand trembled. I felt like my eyes could shoot fire. The old Malcolm would've pulled the trigger and been done with it, but there were no credits on the line this time. It was in those brief seconds of hesitation that I realized killing him wouldn't accomplish a damn thing. I'd only be helping him.

The Church of the Three Messiahs was a corporation in a sense, whether they admitted it or not. There was nothing better for business than publicity. That was why Jeremiah was so pleased to find out I wasn't a collector. Somehow, he could tell I'd come to his convent to kill somebody, so he'd decided to tell the truth and sacrifice his life to me. And it wasn't like months ago when the Ringer I'd hunted on Earth blew his brains out right in front of me to preserve secrets. It was a purely mathematical decision.

If I killed Herald Jeremiah like this, it would look like an unprovoked hate crime that would embolden others to his cause. If I didn't, Venta Co. would find him, and he'd disappear. They'd lock him in a cell and listen to his yarn about the heartbroken apostle who blew himself up to destroy evil over and over, hoping there was something else to it when there wasn't.

The Herald could die a martyr or slowly in a cage. Either way, he was damned. For all his high claims and pretentiousness, he made the choice any shrewd businessman would when those were the only two options—exposure.

"I'm not your judgment, you piece of shit," I said. I released his throat and lowered my gun. He fell to his knees, gasping for air, but that wasn't what I was focused on. All I cared about was the shimmer of disappointment in his eyes that proved I was right.

"Fine... I knew," he squealed. "I knew what Apostle Grant was planning, and I let it happen. Is that what you want to hear?"

I kneeled beside him, keeping a watch out of the corner of my eye on the handful of apostles circling us. "I told you I can tell when a man's telling the truth, and you already spilled it," I said. "Now Venta's going to hear it too. I may not be able to kill the man who murdered Wai, but he can look up from your hell as his Herald suffers for the rest of his life."

"No!" He lunged forward and grabbed my hand. His finger tried to wriggle its way through the trigger of my pistol, and as I wrenched it away from him, my artificial leg shot forward into his arm. It was so strong that his forearm snapped in two before the bone was pulverized against the wall.

He howled in pain, his poised, assured expression completely shattering. I don't know why I was surprised. People like him always begged for their lives before the end, and begging for death wasn't much different when the alternative was so much worse.

I clutched his jaw and raised his face to mine. "When you do get to Heaven, Herald, tell God that Malcolm Graves says hello." I punched him one more time across the face, and he sprawled out across the bloody floor. Everything else was for Wai, but that last punch was for me.

"Peace be with you," I said to the young female apostle. Then I holstered my pistol and headed back toward the exit without another word. All his flock kept their distance. A few worshippers were on their hand terminals, finally deciding to ignore their Herald and call for security. Only as I left did his people run to him, cradling his head as he coughed up loose teeth.

I heaved open the convent's heavy manual doors and stepped outside. Night had fallen upon Mars, but with all the Tongueway's flashing signs, you wouldn't know it. One illuminated a pair of familiar Venta Co. collectors threading the crowd in my direction. I ducked and crept off to the side before quickly realizing they weren't coming for me. Between taking breaks to try and get even with me, they'd seemingly arrived at a possible answer about who was responsible for the bombing and were headed for the convent to question the Herald.

A chuckle escaped my lips. All those years racing Venta Co. for targets, and now I was letting them snag one free of charge.

What happened to me?

Shooting Zhaff to save my daughter. Quitting Pervenio Corp. I'd been so drunk since I got to New Beijing, it never really hit me until then that I really wasn't a collector anymore, and not only by title. It was like that whole essence of me had evaporated. How easy it would've been for me to turn the Herald in to those two hothead collectors and demand a reward, yet I couldn't care less.

It wouldn't bring Wai back. Despite my mad spree to try and justify her death, in reality, she'd been in the wrong place at the wrong time. I'd have to live with the fact that I was partially the reason she was there, but the Herald was right about one thing—we're barely in control. She could've wound up in that plaza, at that moment, no matter what I'd said to her. The victim of a senseless act of violence from a broken man, thanks to the revolution of a beleaguered people.

I was so sick of hypocrites and radicals. So sick of everyone. All the riffraff surrounding me, out for a night on the town to pretend their lives were all right or forget that they weren't. Happy to indulge in their vices until the sun illuminated the dome and they were part of the working class again. If I stayed on Mars, before long, I'd turn into one of them or maybe had been all along. The streetwalkers were the most honest people in the city. At least they didn't lie to themselves about what they were.

For the first time in my life, I didn't only feel lost because I had nothing to do. I didn't even feel like drinking. I simply felt... empty.

"First line of Departure Lottery tickets here!" someone shouted from behind a storefront. The U and the S of the USF blinked over his head, the other letter lost behind a wall of steam from an exhaust vent. "Best chance at winning a spot on the next Ark!"

USF stands like this one were the only place to get departure tickets. You couldn't do it over Solnet because they only wanted people winning who were willing to travel across the stars. Last year, Pervenio Corp sent forth the previous Departure Ark—a ship called the *Hermes*—and per the news feeds, Venta Co. was a lock to be selected in this year's M-Day celebrations to build a new Departure Ark to be dispatched from Earth in a little more than four years. Talk of a prototype engine invented by the genius Basaam Venta had people excited, so the line at the stand wrapped around the corner.

I stopped and stared at the representative behind the counter, proudly decked out in his USF uniform. In his hands was a chance at one-way tickets to a world far away. Maybe Venta had figured out a way to freeze the passengers so I'd actually survive if I won. Something new to see for an old man who'd seen everything Sol had to offer. The good and the much worse. For once, I finally understood why anyone would even want to win a Departure Lottery slot, and it had nothing to do with a prospect of expanding the dominion of the human race like the ads promoted.

Before I could overthink it, I stepped onto the end of the line. Sirens blared as a Venta security hovercar tried to force its way down the narrow avenue toward the convent, so I didn't have much of a choice anyway. Like it was meant to be.

I made it a few spots forward without running away, when from behind me, a familiar voice said a word I never thought I'd hear again.

"Dad?"

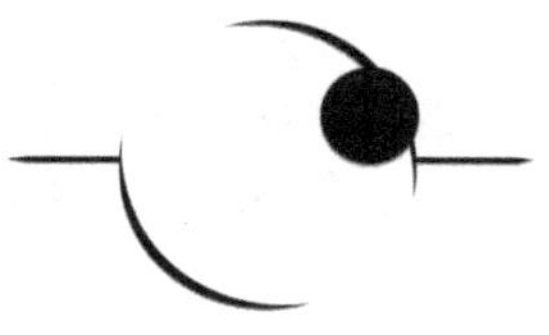

THIRTEEN

KALE

THE GREAT MAHOGANY DOORS OF THE NEW BEIJING USF Assembly Hall swung open. I offered Aria a nod before we entered, hoping she would return it. She wouldn't even look at me. She hadn't since we'd left our rooms. She was freshly showered, groomed, and wearing a loose, vibrant green dress reminiscent of a jungle. I hadn't even bothered to wash my face. Powered armor cradled my weary limbs, still stained with blood and grime from the explosion... and from Trevor.

Together, even though we couldn't be more different, we represented Titan. Rin and Gareth didn't accompany us. They'd been in touch sparingly since they left to grab Basaam, and I had to relinquish my hand-terminal and ear com-link before entering the hall. The only outside tech they allowed us to enter with was my own suit so I'd be comfortable. Everything had to be USF approved. My men weren't even permitted to wear theirs, but after the attack, my personal safety was apparently of the utmost concern.

The last thing Rin told me before they went dark was that they had located Chief Engineer Basaam's room and were preparing to take him. I would find the answer to whether they succeeded if I saw Basaam amongst the elite crowd invited to the hearing. Angry faces, teeming with such aversion that I couldn't help but feel uncomfortable as their glares fell upon us.

When they saw four of my people following behind us, their disdain gave way to shock. Maybe it was the sight of Titanborn out of their armor, so tall and stringy that we barely resembled the same species as those in the crowd who were born on Earth. Or maybe it was the fact that my guards carried with them the corpse of my would-be Cogent assassin.

USF officers wrapped the edge of the yawning horseshoe-shaped space. Theirs were the only weapons present, per custom. Inside the horseshoe, two rows of seats ran the length of the hall filled with representatives of the most powerful organizations of Sol's inner planets.

I recognized the major ones. A handful of Red Wing Company Board members and chairmen of other prominent corporations were at the front. Mining conglomerates, charities, environmental groups—anyone with a large enough stake in Sol to care about what happened around its furthest settled planet. I couldn't even imagine the accumulated wealth and influence I was sharing a room with. One well-placed bomb and the foundation of Earther society would be shaken to its core. After the landing-platform attack, however, getting even a hand-terminal within one hundred meters of the hall was impossible.

It wasn't enough to cut the heads off Earth's credit-generating, expansionist machine anyway. New ones would grow to take their places, like Venta Co. had after I crippled Pervenio Corp. They needed to fear us more than how one might a vagrant in a dark alley. We needed to be like the quarantines were for us—that ever-looming presence of dread placing every step and action into question.

"Mr. Trass, it is my pleasure to welcome you to New Beijing," said Talo Gavaren, the withered old man seated behind a tall wooden podium positioned in the center of the far end of the aisle. Talo was the appointed Voice of the Assembly —the elected governing body of the United Sol Federation that only citizens with home addresses on Earth could vote on. It didn't mean he had any more sway than the other forty-nine members, just that he disseminated their majority agreements to their constituents. Of course, I knew firsthand that true Earther power lay in the hands of corporate men and women like Madame Venta.

Behind him stretched a curving wall of glass with a view of the nighttime New Beijing skyline, blinking with building-sized ads and colorful lights. A curtain of security airships and drones zipping around just outside obscured most of it. On either side of Talo's podium, a lower desk curved away, with enough seats to fit all other forty-nine members of the USF Assembly. Most were occupied by delegates in green robes. The virtual presences of those who couldn't be there in person were projected above every empty seat.

"You have my deepest apologies for what occurred at the spaceport," Talo continued. "And we will do whatever it takes to make things..." He trailed off as he too noticed the body being carried behind me.

I stopped at the foot of the dais atop which his podium sat. The stage where powerless fools got to stake their claim for more to the powerless, while those truly in control watched from behind.

"Mr. Trass, what is the meaning of this?" Talo questioned. I didn't utter a word. I met his gaze and held it there. He, the man who was supposed to broker peace between our peoples, was as uninspiring as any Earther I'd ever seen. His sagging face was ripe with creases that seemed to grow deeper the longer I stared, and his wispy hair was as gray as the surface of Luna.

"Kale, say something," Aria whispered into my ear. "He has

to invite you up."

I glanced back over my shoulder. Madame Venta sat in the front row. Her sons Karl and Fern were on one side of her, and a gaggle of gorgeous young women was on the other. The closest held her hand and stroked her arm. Around them was a smattering of additional Venta directors and officials, but I didn't spot Basaam among them. That, in addition to the scowl plastered on Madame Venta's face, told me all I needed to know.

"Kale, don't," Aria warned.

I nodded to my people, and they presented the Cogent's body to me. I grabbed him by his limp neck. Even with my powered armor on, I couldn't bear the weight of a genuine Earther with one arm, so I dragged him out of their hands and rolled him onto the dais. Crusted dirt and blood stained the authentic wood floor as the body tumbled like a rag doll into the base of Talo's podium.

The collective gasp of the Assembly and all the other pretentious sycophants cluttering the room made me want to grin. I fought the impulse, holding my lips straight and my glare firm upon Talo.

"Mr. Trass!" he exclaimed.

"This is an outrage!" another Assembly member protested.

"We came here, Mr. Gavaren, under the promise that we would be safe," I said, mustering all the vim I could manage to project my voice through my sanitary mask.

"And we did everything we could to ensure that you were," Talo said. "I assure you, those responsible for the bombing will be found, and those who allowed it to happen will be reprimanded accordingly."

"If we weren't saddled by Venta regulations, it would have never happened!" a Red Wing Company director blurted out, her voice surprisingly robust considering how petite she was.

"Please, Galora. You second-rate mercs couldn't guard the

ass end of Old Russia without help," Madame Venta's son Karl countered from across the aisle.

As the Red Wing woman cursed, Talo banged a gavel on the podium. "Order!" he bellowed. "We aren't here to discuss the merits of Earth's many conglomerates. As far as I'm concerned, both of you failed." He leveled his stare at me, bushy eyebrows accentuating his already narrow eyes. "But that doesn't excuse you for tossing a body at our feet, Mr. Trass. I know you aren't from here, but that is not how we begin discussions. We have been more than accommodating since you arrived, conceding to all your demands. So, I ask you again, what is the meaning of this?"

"This assassin was sent to kill me upon my arrival at the spaceport," I said. "Had it not been for a terrorist bombing, he would have succeeded. That is two attempts on my life already, and I've been here less than a day. As a practical man, I have to assume this entire hearing was contrived to draw me close enough to kill."

"How dare you accuse us of that!" another Assembly member's voice echoed from all the way from the end of their crescent-shaped desk.

Talo raised his hand in objection. "That is not how we operate, Mr. Trass. The USF's sacred charge is ensuring the safety of *all* of humanity, not merely those remaining on Earth."

I gestured to the Cogent body. "If this is your example of safety, then it's no surprise your ancestors were almost wiped out."

Murmurs of outrage bubbled up all around me. I think I even heard Aria stifle a yelp. Talo grimaced, but he drew a deep breath to help retain his composure. "We all came from the same place," he said.

"Yet your ancestors weren't chosen by Darien Trass."

"We are not here to discuss the origins of our people." He

snapped his fingers toward a group of security officers behind the Assembly's desk. They rushed down the stairs to remove the body. "Our best agents are busy searching for who this cowardly attacker was and how he was able to slip past our drones."

"You know very well who it was." I tore the Cogent's cracked eye lens off his face and tossed it up to Talo. The USF banner draping down from the podium—bearing the USF emblem of eight small white dots along a line with a larger one in the center—rippled as it landed. "This isn't the first Cogent to take a shot at me, and it won't be the last."

Talo spun the eye lens around in his hand. Then he sighed and passed it along to the elderly Assembly member next to him. "We are all well aware of the grievances your ambassador has filed regarding Luxarn Pervenio. However, there is no evidence of any 'Cogent Initiative' or whatever you're calling these attackers. He has willingly disseminated all of his records."

"And yet, he isn't here. Not even a single representative."

"I wonder why, murderer!" someone from the back of the crowd hollered.

"You Ringers killed them all!" shouted another.

"Order!" Talo said, slamming his gavel. "This Assembly will not tolerate any more speaking out of turn! Mr. Pervenio sent his apologies for not attending and explained that Pervenio Corp has been extremely preoccupied with the limited release of its commercial line of service bots. After... what happened, the reshuffling of his company has left little time or resources to expend on hearings." He pointed to a floating spherical bot with a bulbous lens hovering in the back of the room. "Pervenio Corp is actively monitoring the contents of this summit and I'm sure will be happy to refute your claims afterward."

"I hope you checked that *thing* for explosives," I said. I recalled service bots from advertisements on Earther news feeds. The floating orbs and their many stringy appendages were a last-ditch effort for Luxarn Pervenio to recoup his losses after relinquishing his exclusive access to Saturn's valuable gases. I would've hated them if they didn't make it so obvious how much Luxarn was struggling. The releasing line could barely do more than respond to simple orders—"Get this. Move over there." They were a fun distraction, rather than the game-changing personal helpers Luxarn intended them to be.

"Is that a threat?" Talo said.

"Only against myself."

"Well, I can assure you that every inch of this hall has been swept, inside and out. You have never been safer."

"Then perhaps he's just too scared to face me himself."

Talo said nothing. His wrinkled lips pursed, his scowl matching the dozens of others aimed down at me from the Assembly. I could only imagine how many of them wished to hurl me out; those who had a hand dipped in Pervenio's pocket before his corporation went belly up and blamed me.

"I think you've made your point, Kale," Aria whispered in my ear, pleading with her vibrant green eyes for me to stop. She was right. There were many reasons why I was on Mars. They all required me to make it out of the Assembly Hall alive.

"Enough of this, Mr. Gavaren," I said. "My body and mind are worn after our long journey. Let's discuss why we're really all here."

"Let's," he replied.

I moved aside and allowed Aria to stand before the dais. She waited for Talo's invitation, then stepped up and bowed at the waist with the grace of a practiced dignitary.

"Sir, I speak as ambassador for the people of Titan," she said. "We've come here requesting that the USF Assembly recognize Titan and all its former properties throughout the Ring as their own sovereign state under the governance of Kale

Trass, descendant of Darien Trass. It is our opinion that his family's claim on Titan dates to before the Meteorite struck, making it more legitimate than any others."

"Darien Trass didn't murder anybody," the elder Assembly member beside Talo remarked. "You compare your leader to a man who saved people? All that makes him famous is that he dropped a ship on thousands and then publicly executed a Pervenio director. One of our people!"

"Enough, Lathra!" Talo demanded. "Everyone in this room is aware of history." He regarded Aria with a frown. "Ambassador, we deliberated endlessly while you traveled, but the truth of the matter is that much of what Lathra said is correct. We hesitate to meet your demands because we feel that they not only aren't in the interest of humanity as a whole but that they aren't in your interest either."

I was about stomp up onto the dais and scream at him. Aria reached back to stay me.

"The Ring is a valuable asset to our kind," Talo continued. "Darien Trass saw its worth centuries ago, and so do we now. While we respect your stance, there is no available DNA evidence proving this man is related to Darien. We also feel that leaving it solely in the hands of a young adult who has no experience running anything, presiding over a people who have a history of being highly susceptible to illness, would be irresponsible."

I couldn't hold my tongue any longer. "Illnesses your people brought over!" I barked.

"Let me finish," he replied sharply.

"Why waste my time?"

"Let him finish, Kale," Aria whispered.

I lowered my hands. They squeezed into fists.

Talo cleared his throat. "In an effort to cease hostilities, however, the United Sol Federation Assembly is prepared to grant you proprietary governorship over Titan on a demonstrative basis. You will have the privilege of directing the moon's affairs with limited interference, under the oversight of this elected body, which exists to harbor humanity's greater interests until we deem the results of this experiment suitable."

"And what of the other moon colonies and stations that were established by the Titanborn around Saturn before the Great Reunion?" Aria asked. "There are various ports and factories. Even a version of Pervenio Station was originally installed by Titanborn builders."

"As far as we are concerned, these properties have been seized illegally from a number of corporations and private companies that have established legal ownership since the calamity succeeding the Great Reunion. You may negotiate their future proprietorship with those bodies if you so desire, but we cannot condone such a policy of aggressive expansion."

"Aggressive expansion?" I said. "As far as I've seen, that's the only thing your kind does condone."

"Considering the damages caused by the fighting you incited throughout the Ring, we feel this is a fair compromise," Talo replied. "We are willing to sign a contract dictating these terms before you leave tonight. All you must do in return is agree to release all of the innocent civilians detained on Pervenio Station. We will negotiate the provision of ships for their transport in a way that does not hamper your colony as it adjusts to these new circumstances. In addition, you must surrender all private data and technology seized during the takeover of Pervenio Station. Consider it a demonstration of goodwill, to put all hostilities behind us and look forward to a brighter, more prosperous future."

"Is that all?"

"Those are our terms."

I had to fight to keep my entire body from quaking in anger.

I turned to Aria, and I could tell she knew what I was thinking. Her expression preached caution, but that was the last thing on my mind. Millions of kilometers of travel and their only solution was to strip everything of value from us—from gas-harvesting ports and ships to refineries and factory stations. Even ice hauling wasn't practical without controlling a facility closer to Saturn's rings than Titan. We'd be subsidiary, bound to their credits and desires. Eventually, we'd wind up having to rent out the residential blocks on Titan just to stay afloat, and everything would go right back to how it was.

Aria swallowed a lump in her throat then said, "I can discuss these terms with Mr. Trass privately, though I fear we're too far apart."

"Surely the Assembly is open to negotiation in a more private setting," the Red Wing Director named Galora insisted from her seat in the crowd. They were the only corporation we'd done any real business with since the revolution, so I wasn't surprised. It was a feeble effort at feigning support for us. She didn't even stand.

"We're willing to discuss further liberties as time progresses," Talo said. "And you have our assurance that proper care will be taken to ensure the health of Titan's populace. In that, you will have the full support of the USF and all its affiliated corporations. Our medical research and capabilities are yours."

"A kind gestu—" Aria began, but I cut her off by stomping up onto the dais myself, as far forward as I could go while maintaining eye contact with Talo.

"I don't understand why you think this is a discussion," I said harshly. He recoiled as if my words had physically struck him. I lowered my sanitary mask so he could see me in my entirety, unafraid. A dangerous move, but it had the desired effect. I could see the distress flood his features as he watched me.

"I came here to offer you *our* terms," I said, my voice now unimpeded. "Perhaps you weren't listening to my ambassador when she laid them out initially, so I'll tell you all in person."

I whipped around to face the crowd. If they appeared angry before, now they all looked like they wanted to shoot me. Red cheeks and raised brows characterized every face—everyone except Madame Venta. She remained staid, almost emotionless.

"Titan will not become another puppet of Earth!" I declared. "We are not a colony. We are the vision of Darien Trass. A better future on a new world. Our own world." I stuck my finger out at the Assembly, sweeping from one side to the other. "Until that happens, we will not stop harassing your colonies or your ships on the Ring, no matter whose supervision they fall under. We will not release our captives, and we will not open trade."

"Be reasonable, Mr. Trass," Talo said through clenched teeth.

"I believe I am. Soon, if your kind occupy the Ring, it will be under *our* supervision, not the other way around. If they want to land a ship or open a port, they will ask us for permission. If they want a speck of ice, they'll ask first. And until you agree to that, we'll harvest every ounce of gas on Saturn for ourselves. Until the planet has nothing left but its rings."

A few of the Assembly members blurted out in protest. I quickly silenced them by shouting, "I'm not finished! Last, you will deliver Luxarn Pervenio to my feet, wherever he is hiding. He will admit, to all of Sol, that the Ringer Plague brought about by the Great Reunion was no accident. That he and his father purposely dispersed germs to assume control over the Ring, knowing full well that after three centuries on Titan, my people hadn't the knowledge or experience in dealing with earthborn contagions."

"That is a blasphemous accusation!" someone behind me

yelled. The rest of what he said was drowned out by a torrent of opposition. The hammering of Talo's gavel went unheard as well. Not a soul remained sitting, whether they were in the crowd or the Assembly. All pleasantries were tossed aside. The USF officers even had to sprint down to the floor to keep objects from being flung at me, though I'm sure most of them wanted to join in.

"I think this discussion is over," I addressed Talo directly. He appeared as if he were about to have a stroke. "I look forward to the next one. Let's go, Aria."

She remained as still as a petrified tree, so I turned her gently. I walked her back down the aisle, now a narrow path through an incensed mob with my four guards surrounding us. It was different from when we landed in the spaceport. A sea of Earther dignitaries raged on either side of us, and there were no hired Red Wing officers or any weapons of our own to keep them at bay. The only thing that did was fear. Fear of what might happen to their people if they harmed me. Earther clan-families could be massive, and I guaranteed a few of their relatives were among those who weren't able to flee the Ring before we took over.

"You dare turn your back on us?" Talo hollered so loud his voice cracked. "Come back here, Mr. Trass!"

"I don't know if that was a good idea," Aria said to me softly, clinging tightly to my side.

"Now you finally see how they see us," I replied.

"They're never going to give in to all of that."

"Maybe not, but it'll make them see that we aren't a threat that can be solved by a pat on the head and a shipload of credits."

"We can't keep fighting forever."

"You don't have to worry about that. You did well getting us here, Aria. Earthers needed to put a voice to a conflict so far away. Now they know we won't bend. Whatever happens from here, they will start taking us seriously."

We reached the doors of the Assembly Hall. USF officers had to shove a wall of Earthers aside so we could pass, then slammed it shut behind us. The Red Wing men hired to oversee the event filled the antechamber, rifles up and ready for anything, while some held back a wave of reporters at the entrance. The room at our back sounded like the galley on the *Piccolo* during a brawl.

"Mr. Trass, your belongings," one of the Red Wing offered said to me. He handed me my hand-terminal and com-link, which I immediately shoved into my ear and switched on.

"That you, Kale?" Rin whispered through it.

"Kale... what are you really planning?" Aria asked, her voice trembling. Rin must have heard that because she was immediately comfortable enough to fill me in.

"We have him," she said, smart enough not to use Basaam Venta's name in case anybody was listening. "We had to dispense with some light security, but we weren't seen. Gareth has us on a concealed route back to the *Cora*. Smooth sailing from here. I'm switching off coms until we're on board."

"You can tell me, Kale," Aria implored. I was busy doing my best not to react to Rin's news. "I may not approve of your aunt's methods, but I do understand why you all might think violence is the answer."

I ran my hand across Aria's freckled cheek and looked her straight in the eyes. "I'm going to show them what they fear most. I promise you, the next time you discuss a treaty with Earth, it will be on our terms."

I could tell by her expression that the next logical question was on the tip of her tongue. She wanted to ask it, but I wasn't sure she wanted to hear the full answer. Aria believed that things could be handled fairly and with diplomacy—that was why I valued her so immensely as our ambassador. But she wasn't Titanborn. She couldn't understand, no matter how hard she tried. She didn't know what it was like to have an entire race look down upon yours like the dirt stuck to their boots. Even though she was an illegitimate offworlder who grew up ostracized and without a clan-family to call her own, she could still easily blend in with the rest of them.

Before either of us uttered another word, footsteps clacked across the antechamber. Madame Venta was approaching, wearing excessively high heels like she had made it a point that I would never be able to gaze so far down upon her again.

"You have quite a flair for dramatics, Mr. Trass," she said, her flamboyant entourage trailing closely behind her. "If I were you, I would have taken the deal."

"Anything to benefit you, right?" I replied.

"Their blessing is just a formality. Every corporation exists under that same pretense, and you don't seem naïve enough to think the USF makes any decision on their own."

"My ambassador has made me very aware of how your world works."

"Few have had such an intimate look." She ambled closer, until there was barely half a meter between us. The sweet tang of her perfume accosted my nostrils. Her very presence silenced Aria and left her staring.

"If you don't mind, Madame Venta, we have to go." I took Aria's hand and drew her around them, but both of Madame Venta's sons moved to impede us. My guards rushed in front of me. The Red Wing men watching over the room stirred.

"My Chief Engineer at Europa went missing earlier," Madame Venta said calmly. "He was supposed to be here. You wouldn't happen to have seen him anywhere, would you?"

"Losing track of your own people now?"

"He's not one to be late."

"Always prompt," Karl sneered.

"If I hear anything, I'll be sure to pass it along," I said. "Though I am an outsider here after all."

"So you are," Madame Venta said. "But she's not."

"She's been with me this entire time. I wish we could be of more help, but we really must go."

Again, I attempted to walk away. Madame Venta laid a hand on Aria's shoulder. It wasn't aggressive, but the way she did it made my blood boil. Like she owned her. "You should consider keeping better company, Aria," she whispered. Her fingers slid up Aria's collarbone toward her slender neck. Madame Venta stroked her once there tenderly; then she and her entire entourage marched in the other direction.

Aria released a breath as if she'd just been suffocating. We stopped outside of the elevator, currently being secured by Red Wing Company men.

"Ignore her, Aria. She'll earn the same fate as Luxarn soon enough." I took her wrist and stepped onto the lift, but she wriggled away.

"Kale, I... If you'll allow it, I'd like to go see an old friend from Old Dome before we leave," she said, standing just outside of the elevator doors with her thousand-meter stare still aimed toward where Madame Venta had been.

"It isn't safe."

"It is for me. It's like Rin always says, I'm not one of you."

"Aria, what's wrong?"

"It's..." She bit her lip, still unable to look at me. "I grew up here. There are people I haven't seen in a long time. Places I'd like to say goodbye to. I have a feeling this is the last time I'll ever be back."

"You said yourself how dangerous it could be here."

"I promise. I'll be back in our hangar before you leave. Please, Kale, for me?"

Something was obviously troubling her, and it was more than what she'd seen between me and Trevor Cross. More than being a part of our failed meeting with the Assembly. I remembered leaving my home for the first time and boarding a gas harvester; the feeling that I might never come back. Now she was the same. An outsider.

If anybody understood how much someone needs time for themselves, away from judgment or responsibility, it was me. And even though I knew both Rin and Gareth would warn me not to let her out of my sights on a world owned by Earth, I trusted her. Aria could have fled the moment she found us interrogating Trevor, but she didn't. She'd stuck by my side before the Assembly, and so I'd stand by hers.

"I understand," I said as I blocked the elevator doors and held her by her slight shoulders.

"Thank you." She leaned up on the balls of her feet and started to plant a kiss on my lips before realizing where we were and awkwardly shifting toward my cheek. It was too late. One of the relentless reporters at the building's entry had slipped a recording drone in and caught us from across the room.

"By Trass!" Aria murmured. "I'm so sorry."

I surveyed the antechamber. The drone zipped into the mob before anyone could stop it. Gone with a picture that'd earn thousands of credits. I thought I'd feel angry, but I didn't. After the summit, I couldn't care less what any Earther thought of me. If anything, my relationship with a non-Titanborn only proved we weren't as shallow as they were.

"Don't be," I said. "Just try to be as quick as you can and keep your terminal on just in case. I'll message you when we're preparing for takeoff." I addressed two of my guards. "Retrieve your weapons and stay with her. Keep her safe, or you'll feel Titan's air on your flesh."

"Yes, Lord Trass," they said.

"They'll just draw attention," Aria protested.

"They'll accompany you, or you won't go. Your face might be recognizable now after they air footage from this. Come upstairs and change into something plain." I turned to the guards. "And both of you change into unmarked clothing so you all blend in like poor offworlders."

Aria sighed and nodded meekly as she stepped onto the elevator. "All right, fine."

The elevator doors shut, and we shot up through the building. Our meeting with the USF was officially concluded, and it went exactly how I'd expected it to. Exactly how Aria hoped against reason it wouldn't. It was time to leave the stifling air and glittering towers of New Beijing behind, and thanks to Rin and Gareth, we wouldn't leave empty-handed.

The elevator reached our floor. I stopped outside of Aria's room. "Don't be long, okay?" I said. "We can't leave without you."

"Rin wouldn't mind," Aria replied, smirking.

"I don't know if I can handle her without you. I'll see you so —" Before I could finish, she leaned up on the balls of her feet so she could reach my lips and kissed me. I wasn't shy about returning the favor this time.

"We don't have time," I panted as our lips parted for a second.

"Stop. Your aunt's finally not watching."

Before I knew it, I was in her room, peeling off my armor. I couldn't stop it, and after a few seconds, didn't want to. Cora was timid the first and only night I'd had with her, but not Aria. I could barely breathe by the time she laid me on her bed. She grabbed my hand and ran it across her stomach, then around her narrow waist. That was the thing about Aria. We may have been around the same age, but whatever things Venta Co. had her do, she knew her way around a man. And she always took control, and in those few minutes of bliss, before the crushing weight of the world fell back upon me, I didn't have to be.

Sweat dripped from my brow when our lips finally parted, and I lay back. Exerting myself so in gravity stronger than Titan's had my chest heaving. She lay beside me, staring into my eyes.

"What was that for?" I asked.

"A thank you," she said, not nearly as winded as me. "I don't know why you really wanted to come to Mars, Kale, but thank you for letting me get you here."

I propped myself up against the headrest. "Next time it will be different. You'll see." She rolled over and laid her head upon my chest, and I ran my fingers through her hair. For a moment, under the lights, a strand of it looked silvery like Cora's had. I squeezed my eyes shut, and then it was red again.

"I'm sorry about what you walked in on earlier," I said. "It wasn't meant to go like that, but he gave us crucial information."

"You still should have told me."

I nodded in agreement. She was right. If I was going to preach to everybody about trusting her, I had to prove it myself. It was no different from how I lived in the Darien Uppers without a sanitary mask just to show my people it was safe.

"Whatever that business with the officer was, you're better than that," she said. "Maybe you don't see it, or Rin or Gareth, but I do. I have since the day we met." She ran her hand through my hair and stared straight into my eyes. "You're not the monster Earth paints you to be, and you never will be."

"Says the woman whose shot put him out of his misery without blinking." I watched the color flee her cheeks as she sank backward. "I... I'm sorry. I didn't mean—"

"It's okay. It's being around my old employer is all. Makes me feel a little crazy."

"That wasn't your first time shooting somebody, was it?"

She shook her head.

"You made the right move, Aria. We saw a bit about his history on Pervenio Station logs. Venta or not, he'd done plenty to hurt our people in the name of hurting Pervenio profits. Enough to deserve what he got, but he gave us what we needed. He earned a quick end."

I forced a smile then planted a kiss on her forehead. Anything to avoid staring into her eyes for too long. It was always the worst after we shared a bed—I'd see Cora in every little thing she did. No matter how much I begged my mind to stop and to focus on the incredible woman in front of me. The woman who'd sacrificed everything to help my people.

"You should really get going if we want to keep to schedule," I said.

She drew a deep breath then kissed me one last time. "You're right." She hopped off the bed and went to her luggage to pick out a plainer dress to wear. The windows in my room were always tinted, but hers weren't. Flashing vibrant lights from countless ads painted her glistening skin, emphasizing every one of her curves.

I couldn't help but stare as she dressed. She wrapped her father's Ark Ship pendant around her neck last, then straightened her outfit.

"Why do you help us?" I asked. I'm not sure why the questioned popped into my head then.

"Why do you let me?" she countered. She tightened her belt and made sure to show me that she had her hand-terminal on her. "I'll see you on the *Cora*?"

"If you run into any trouble."

"I'll call your aunt." She flashed me a smile, the kind that made her nose wrinkle in that particular way, then she headed out of the room.

I watched her until the door clicked shut, then dressed

myself and headed back to my own room. The youngest of the guards Rin and Gareth hand-picked was posted outside my door, holding a covered dinner-plate. He had fair skin, even for a Titanborn, and hair so unnaturally blonde, the lights gave it a shimmer. A scar ran down from his jaw to his collarbone, no doubt from our revolution.

"Lord Trass." He lowered his head in reverence. "Venta Co. had this sent up immediately following the summit. They wished to thank you for traveling such a long way."

I lifted the lid, and a smell I hadn't been privy to since Rin and I wound up serving Earthers dinner on a luxury cruiser greeted my nostrils. Freshly grilled meat.

"They said it was authentic, rare bovine meat from an animal farm on Earth," he explained.

I raised the slab, red juice dripping all over the floor. A common source of sustenance before the Meteorite hit, now a rare delicacy. Just another thing Earthers like Madame Venta could hold over us. Few animals had survived the apocalypse, and while there were a few farms on Mars, low gravity left their meat tough and almost inedible, the stuff sold to food stands in the darker parts of cities.

I lifted the meat to my mouth, but the guard stopped me. "Lord Trass, it's not healthy for us. My father snuck something like this from his Earther boss once and wound up in the Q-Zone a week later."

I ignored him and tore a piece off with my front teeth. They were accustomed to soft greens and condensed ration bars, never anything so chewy. The taste was rich with flavors I couldn't describe with any other word but *smoky*, as if someone had condensed the flaming halls of Pervenio Station after we stormed it into food.

I could understand why it was an Earther delicacy, unlike coffee or milk. They always had been proud to put their dominance on display, and what was more dominant than literally eating an animal? Slaughtering them. It was no different than stuffing my people into quarantines while they and their credits took over everything.

It was undoubtedly delicious, but nothing worth fighting over. None of their delights were. I slapped it back on the plate and replaced the lid.

"Toss it, and then thank our esteemed hosts," I said. "It's the last gift I'll ever take from them."

The young man bowed his head. "Right away, Lord Trass."

I entered the room and sealed the door behind me, leaving me alone with the garish display of other foods and finery on the counter meant to make us rethink our ways. The rest of the room was spotless, with no evidence that Trevor Cross had ever been hanging upside down, bleeding.

I leaned my hand-terminal on the counter, sat in front of the screen, and contacted Rylah back on Titan. It took a few minutes to reach her over Solnet since we were so far, but eventually, her face popped up on screen. The sounds of industry roared in the background. Metal clanking. Engines humming. Her soft face was covered in soot.

"Lord Trass, I wasn't expecting your call," she said. "Is the summit over?"

"It is, and nothing's changed, Rylah," I said.

"How's Aria? I tried to warn her that it would go like this."

"She's fine."

"I know you're lying. She really believed this summit might change things. She poured her soul into—"

"She's fine, Rylah," I interrupted. Sometimes she went out of her way to support Aria, I think because they were both born without an identifying race and struggled to fit in anywhere. Rin made it tough for our ambassador, and Rylah tried to ease the tension, but Aria could take care of herself well enough on her own.

"Listen to me," I said. "I need ship production on Phoebe accelerated. Bring on as many capable hands as you can find."

She hesitated for a moment before answering. "We'll need more than that. Workers are still asking when they'll receive some form of tangible payment for their overtime labor. Phoebe Station Production Manager Orson Fring has sparked some vocal protests over the lack of benefits."

"I told you to offer improved housing in Uppers throughout Titan and extra rations."

"Not all of them want to live up there where the air is fresh. I don't know what else to offer. And we won't have extra rations until we send all the Earther captives on the station back home. Let me provide the credits we've accumulated, for now."

"They don't need credits! We won't be trading with Earth for a long time. Lower the rations for the Earther captives, and make our people understand that Titan needs them. We need to be prepared to fight back once the USF decides to take their next inevitable step."

Rylah stifled a groan. "I'll do what I can without starving the poor Earthers to death, and I'll have your mother speak with Fring. She's the more convincing of the two of us."

"Good."

"You should contact her, you know. She's been asking about you constantly since the spaceport bombing."

"I'll talk to her when we're back. For now, I want everyone focused on building Titan a fleet Earth will respect. They won't hand us the Ring, Rylah. It's time for us to prepare to hold it by force. All of it, not only what Luxarn stole."

MALCOLM

"Dad?"

Just like that, everything changed. Only one person would call me that. Maybe whoever said the word wasn't talking to me. I didn't know Aria's voice well anymore. Seeing her one time in five years would do that. Maybe after what happened with Wai and a lack of sleep, I was hearing things.

I wanted more than anything to turn and look, but my feet felt like they were submerged in wet plasticrete. A gentle hand fell upon my shoulder as someone glided in front of me. I saw curly auburn hair first, then freckles dappling a rosy cheek, then Aria's eyes, green as the forests of Earth used to be.

"By Trass, you're alive!" she exclaimed. The sound of her excitement... now I was totally lost. Was it my aging mind playing a trick on me or my eyes growing fuzzy? After so many years wondering where she went off to, was it really possible that she would be the one to find me?

My tongue tripped over a few responses until the first one that slipped out was "Trass?"

"New habit, I guess." She paused to use her soft hand to angle my wrinkled face toward hers. I don't know why, but I couldn't get myself to look straight at her without the help. Hell, I could hardly breathe. "I can't believe it's you!" She threw her arms around me so tight I thought my head was going to pop. Now I knew I had to be dreaming. She hadn't hugged me like that since... I can't remember how long. Something poked into my chest, and as she drew back a bit, I saw the Ark Ship figurine I used to carry with me after we split ways. The narrow crack running down the middle where she'd once snapped it meant it had to be the same one.

"Dad," she said. "Are you all right?"

I stumbled out of her embrace and had to use a wall to keep myself upright. My heart was pounding; a sensation I thought I'd grown out of. Like I was in my first firefight or with a lady for the first time, or maybe having a heart attack. I squeezed my fist against my chest and struggled to steady my breathing.

"Dad."

"I'm fine," I said. "You surprised me is all."

"Surprised you? I thought you were dead!"

"So did I."

"How long have you been here? Why didn't you tell me?"

"I didn't realize we did that."

Her lips twisted. "Dad..."

"Sorry... I... I don't know what to say."

"You think I do? I never thought I'd see you in a Departure Lottery line."

The world suddenly snapped back into focus. This wasn't a dream.

I looked from side to side. The line had moved a few spots forward, and the people who'd gathered behind me were grumbling that I wasn't moving. I stepped away from them. M-Day Departure... What was wrong with me? For a moment, I was like all the fools around us, thinking I'd be one of the lucky thousands sent off to other solar systems that'd actually survive the journey and not just feel honored by a massive waste of time.

"Oh, I didn't even realize where I was," I said. "It's been a long day."

"Tell me about—"

"It's great to see you, Aria," I interrupted her accidentally.

"You too. Better circumstances than last time." She chuckled. The sound of it made my heart flutter. I couldn't imagine how many nights I'd lain awake trying to remember what her laugh sounded like before I took a drink to force myself down.

"I guess a good father would scold you for getting involved with people like that."

"A good father wouldn't have raised a daughter who would," she retorted.

"I deserve that one." I finally mustered the courage to place a hand on her shoulder and make sure one last time she wasn't a hallucination. It didn't pass through. Maybe I wasn't used to her adult stature, but she felt stronger than I recalled. "Really, though. I'm glad you got out."

Her brow furrowed as she took my hand. "You must not watch the news feeds at all anymore."

"I try not to."

She stepped aside to reveal two men standing in her shadow, holding pulse-rifles. At first glance, they looked like your average Old Dome gangbangers with their dirty faces, but while both were tall, one had features so stretched out and a body so stringy he could only be from once place—Titan. And their weapons. They were the same old Venta Co. model I'd found the Children of Titan using back on their homeworld. They were Ringers all right, and all that was missing was that damn orange circle painted on their chests.

My hand instinctually fell toward the grip of my pistol. I

wasn't about to be caught off guard by the Children of Titan again. They immediately shifted to aim in my direction.

"Kal—Lord Trass insisted they come along," she said, guiding my hand away from my gun. "He doesn't realize that I know this place better than anybody, thanks to you."

"You're working directly for Kale Trass now?"

"What, is Pervenio keeping you under a rock?" She pointed to a viewscreen above a bar in the shoddy restaurant nearby. On it, a news feed played footage from Kale Trass's meeting with the USF Assembly, which had apparently already taken place. It was a private summit, so all they could show was Kale and his accomplices leaving the New Beijing Assembly Building. The young king wore a scowl. A host of Ringer escorts were behind him, and the woman at his side wasn't the scarred one who always accompanied him in feeds. It wasn't a Ringer at all. It was Aria, her fire-red hair starkly contrasting the white worn by the others.

"They let a doctor in there?" I asked.

"No, Dad. I'm Titan's ambassador to the USF. You really didn't know?"

"No..." How the hell had I missed that? Ever since I'd woken up from my coma, I'd been telling myself that I'd helped her get out from under the thumb of the Children of Titan. But there she was, my daughter, side by side with the rebel who'd conquered the Ring.

"That bombing earlier," I rasped, my chest growing tight.

"Missed."

"It was damn well close enough! After what I did to get you out of there, you really went crawling back?"

"I guess I am your daughter."

"That isn't the point. Kale Trass is dangerous. You could have been crushed like Wai or worse."

"Wai? Would you listen to yourself, Dad? You never gave a

shit about what I did unless it had to do with one of your missions."

"I..." There I went again, pushing away like I always did. I took a deep breath to calm myself and steady my quaking hands. I was going to do my best not to make that mistake again.

"I always cared, Aria," I said.

She sighed. "Look. I don't want to argue with you. I'm so tired of it. Until now, I wasn't sure why I needed to come down here, but can't we just sit down and talk like old times? I could really use it."

"You're right, so could I. You name any place on the Tongueway, we'll go."

"I wish you wouldn't call it that."

"I didn't come up with the name. Come on, anywhere. Just keep those two Ringers off me."

She shot me an irritated look then said, "Twilight Sun?"

Of course she chose there. I honestly didn't remember until that moment that it was the bar I'd sent her to the last time we were on Mars together, intending to get close to a criminal named Elios Sevari. They fell in lust, and then he died because of me. Story of my life. I couldn't say why she'd ever want to go back, but now that I was truly observing her, I could tell she was distressed. And for once, it had nothing to do with me.

"After this morning, I'm probably not welcome there," I said.

"Oh, Dad, what did you do?"

"Long story... and it wasn't my fault." I heard sirens again and in my peripherals saw the entrance to the Three Messiahs convent. It swarmed with Venta Co. security interrogating the worshippers. "On second thought? How about we just head in there?" I gestured to a brightly lit bar across the street.

Aria smirked. "You'll never change."

I noticed that the bar was nestled above a strip joint. "It's not that. I just don't think these old legs can get much farther." I patted my artificial leg without thinking. She didn't notice the clank over the din of the noisy streets. That was going to be a fun story to tell her. Five years and one awful encounter on Titan in between... We had a lot to catch up on.

———

"What are you having?" I asked as we took a seat at the bar. The floor vibrated, and the bottles behind the bartender rattled from the pulsing music in the club below. My kind of place. At least, it would've been if not for the two hulking Titanborn guards standing behind us, sticking out like a sore thumb.

"I don't drink anymore," she said.

"And you call yourself my daughter." I waved to the bartender. "Two whiskeys, rocks."

"Dad."

"You don't drink it, I will." I took out my ID to hand over so the bartender could scan it and take the rest of what little was left in my credit account.

"Water too," Aria said as she blocked my hand and offered her ID instead. Per the USF, she was illegitimate, so I couldn't say who the thing belonged to until she told me willingly. Not that I could talk, considering my ID said Haglin Amissum.

"I have to use Titan's credits on something," Aria whispered to me.

I smirked. "Fine by me. Credits are tight these days."

"I can imagine. I'm sorry about what's happening to Pervenio, Dad. I know you care about the company. I swear, when I got involved in all of this, I didn't want it to affect you."

"It's not that. I retired." The bartender had given her a glass of water by the time I uttered the words, and she choked on her first sip.

"You're retired?"

I shrugged. "That's why I'm here."

"By Tra... Wow. I thought only you dying could cause that."

"Same." My first whiskey arrived, and I downed half of it in a single gulp. The swill burned all the way down, but man, did I need it.

"Well, after three decades, Pervenio must have offered you a nice severance?"

"Yep. A new leg."

She raised an eyebrow, so I lifted my pants leg. Her eyelids opened as far as they could go as she beheld the artificial limb beneath. She'd probably never seen tech like it in her life, considering I hadn't either. She reached out to touch it, then paused.

"It's fine," I said. She immediately grabbed the foot and started turning it gently so she could examine every side.

"It's amazing!" she exclaimed. "Is there sensation?"

I shook my head. "Very little. My reward for accidentally kicking off a revolution on Titan."

She dropped the limb. "Trust me, it was going to happen whether you got me out of there or not."

"None of you have any idea who the man I shot to save you was, do you?"

"One of Luxarn Pervenio's Cogents?"

What happened on Titan flashed through my head as it did so often when I was sober. I heard the bang of our pulse pistols going off, then the hole in Zhaff's face, which he'd somehow survived enough to become a curiosity in Luxarn's secret lab. I emptied the rest of my glass and picked up the other.

"That, yes," I said softly. "And a friend."

"You have friends now?" Her grin faded when she noticed I wasn't wearing one. She took my hand and gazed straight at me, the brilliant green eyes she got from her mother teeming with remorse. "I'm so sorry."

"Don't be. I would've done it the same way every time. I only wish you'd done the smart thing and kept running."

"I thought about it, Dad. I really did. But I couldn't leave my patients and all my work behind. I did take one bit of your advice, though."

"Yeah?"

"I got Elios' son out of there on a fleeing transport. He'll be better off placed in some clan-family after they scan through all the refugees."

"Then you're smarter than me. But I still wished you went with him. Being their doctor is a far cry from Kale Trass's ambassador to fucking Earth."

"You always taught me not to settle."

"There's a far cry from what my job was to helping a terror cell."

"Is there? We didn't talk for five years, Dad. I can handle myself. You have no idea the things I did to survive, to get in a position with Venta that I might be able to help the people of Titan. I spent a long time wanting to distance myself from you, but... it took seeing you that day to realize how similar we are."

There was a time I would have dreamed of hearing her utter those words. I'd spent so long trying to groom her into a collector after all. Now hearing them made my stomach turn over. "Trust me, we aren't. I was never good at helping people. Can't you go back to just healing them?"

"There's still time for both. I helped pull out the bullet you put in Rylah's leg that day."

"Rylah..." Now there was a name that could always get my blood pumping, of course until I remembered that the last time I saw her on Titan, she'd tried to have me killed. "You know, I figured she was part of the Children of Titan somehow. Don't know how she managed to lie to a Cogent, though, if anyone could, it's her. A bullet to the leg was generous."

"I'm not judging."

"How is she?"

"She regrets how you two left things." She could barely keep a straight face.

"Sure. I'm guessing she's the reason you're still alive?" Her one eyebrow lifted a smidge like it always did when she was confused, ever since she was a little girl. "C'mon, Aria. Those men in the Q-zone hideout weren't just shooting at me."

"I like to tell myself that they were trying to get me away from you, but I know how it looked. I risked letting a collector in, things went south, and our hideout was exposed. Rylah helped smooth things over, since she was the one who got me in contact with the Children of Titan in the first place, but Kale trusts me now. He's—" She hesitated, and I sensed there was more to her thought. I jumped in too soon and cut her off.

"Trust will never make you one of them."

"I know. And I know this all seems crazy, but this would be happening with or without me. I figure I might as well try keeping the transition as peaceful as I can, you know?"

"You'll have your hands full with this bunch."

"Nobody knows that better than me."

I tapped my artificial thigh. "I might."

We shared a smirk, then Aria's expression darkened. "Do you think there's any hope of things getting better?"

"Between us?" She shot me one of her infamous sidelong glares. I exhaled. "Do you want the honest answer or a father's answer?"

"I don't know. Both maybe?"

I took her by the hand, my thumb running over her knuckles. I wanted to memorize every camber so I would never forget her touch again. "I think that with you at their side, those

Ringers are a hell of a lot better off. But no. Things will never be how they were. We both know that. The moment I pulled that trigger on Titan, everything changed."

She nodded knowingly. "I could see how difficult it was for you, Dad. I don't know how I could possibly make it up to you."

I reached out and stroked the pendant hanging from her neck. "You never have to."

"To your fallen friend," she said, raising her glass. "May he watch over you forever from the winds of Titan. From ice to ashes."

"You really are one of them now, aren't you?"

"I blend in when I have to. I learned that from you."

I stared at her for a moment as she held her glass. Man, had she grown up. Stronger than me; more beautiful than her mother. And the way she was smiling—we hadn't gotten along this well in a decade. What happened on Titan changed something. The ease with which we could disagree on almost everything remained, but the fight was gone.

I lifted my second whiskey, the first already burning a hole in my stomach and leaving my head feeling less cluttered. "To Zhaff..." I paused. All his life, he was kept a secret. His almost-death too. With Aria beside me, the shooter and the reason for the shot, thanks to his father, it was the best funeral he'd ever get. "Pervenio," I finished.

The color drained from Aria's face. The same look I probably wore when Luxarn Pervenio told me the truth about his bastard son, the only member of a clan-family he didn't have. First, there was disbelief, and then, when my straight lips didn't falter, I could tell she knew it was the truth. That she finally understood the gravity of the gunshot that saved her life. The reason why Luxarn Pervenio was foolish enough to raid a quarantine zone for revenge and inspire Kale Trass's rebellion.

"To Zhaff," she said softly.

We tapped our glasses, and before I could toss mine back, blood splattered into it. Screams rattled the bar as patrons scattered. Aria's Titanborn guards had been standing behind us, and both had holes in their foreheads. I reached for my pistol, but alcohol slowed my movements. Before I could get it up, we were at the mercy of at least a dozen Venta Co. gunmen. The two in the middle were the collectors I'd become so friendly with, apparently called off their questioning of the Herald to find me. It didn't take thirty years of experience in their field to guess that someone at the convent tipped them off that a man by my description was involved.

"Hold your fire!" I blurted as I raised my hands. I tried to remain calm, but Aria was in their sights as well. I wasn't about to let my mistakes place her in harm's way for the umpteenth time. "I'll come in quietly."

"Dad?" Aria stuttered.

"Take her," the brash lead collector said. Officers stormed forward to seize Aria.

"What is this?!" she shouted.

"Let go of her!" I lunged for her, but the butt of a rifle slammed against my temple before I got far. My body collapsed on top of one of the armored Titanborn corpses. I saw stars. Aria's cries for help were drowned out by screeches. The collectors flashed their badges to pacify the patrons, and then they were gone. I don't know what hurt more, the blow to the face or the fact that they didn't even recognize me. Either the blood from Aria's guards obscured my face or they had more important things to worry about. Young guns. Always too eager for credits to pay attention to all the finer details.

I floundered along the floor. By the time I located my gun and spun around, they were all gone. I stumbled to the balcony overlooking the Tongueway. The people out there who'd somehow missed the excitement all surrounded me, asking if I was okay. I ignored them and searched the nighttime crowds. The head Venta collector in the duster was easy to spot across the street. They were on their way to a parked hovercar, Aria's body hanging limply over the partner's shoulder.

Even though I was in a fog, I didn't hesitate. I launched myself over the railing and bent my human leg so that only the synthetic one slammed on the street. I didn't tuck cleanly into a roll like my younger self might've, but I found my way to my feet and gave chase.

I wasn't going to lose her. Never again.

FIFTEEN

KALE

A Red Wing Company airship transported us to the New Beijing Spaceport in the dead of night. The upper portion of the city appeared lifeless minus the ads, but lights pulsed from clubs and other nightlife venues down in Old Dome below the main throughways. Like back in Darien where I grew up, the Earthers who designed the city kept the more dubious venues buried. Down there in what Aria referred to as Old Dome, New Beijing was a sleepless city.

That was where she still remained, and neither she nor the guards I'd sent with her had answered any messages since I let her venture there. She'd told me she'd grown up there, scrumming for food in the tremendous sewer lines and subway tunnels. I couldn't imagine what I was thinking letting her leave my side. She was far too important. If anybody recognized her...

"We're here," our pilot said, snapping me out of it.

I was overthinking things as usual. Aria could handle herself, I'd learned that well enough. If she could deal with Rin, she could deal with any strung-out offworlder in Old Dome looking for a quick payday. Nobody else would dare risk making so public a move.

My guards led me outside, where the Red Wing presence on our newly assigned landing pad was overwhelming. A quick peek into the concourse revealed that not a single civilian remained within the spaceport dome itself.

"There won't be any trouble this time, Mr. Trass," Captain Barnes from Red Wing security said as he met me outside the terminal. He bore only a few scratches on his already grizzled face as a result of the explosion.

"I hope not," I answered, a harsh edge creeping into my tone. We were halfway through the station when he decided to speak up again.

"The board extends its gravest apologies for what happened," he said. "There will be no more Venta interference from here on out. Remember, Mr. Trass, when the Red Wing Company security branch gets hired, we honor our agreements, no matter what."

"And what kind of offer would it take to get you to change your mind?"

Barnes looked appalled. "It would never happen, sir. We aren't like Venta dogs chasing after the highest bid. We were hired to keep you safe during your visit, and we failed. The board would like to offer recompense for the trauma our shortcomings caused you and your people as well as the two Titanborn lives claimed by the attack. They hope you will find the time to contact them and discuss what you might require to make your organization whole."

"I'm a very busy man these days."

"Please, sir. We pride ourselves on customer satisfaction and loyalty."

I exhaled. I'd had very few good experiences with his kind, but most of them still didn't refer to us as Titanborn. I hoped that meant something regarding his honesty. "Tell whoever is in charge that I'll be in contact when I can," I said.

"The board votes together on all matters of importance, but they will be eager to speak with you." We stopped outside the entrance to our private hangar, where the *Cora* waited patiently to carry us home. The captain stuck out a hand for me to shake, realized his mistake before I had a chance to react, and pulled it back. He bowed instead. "Thank you for your understanding, Mr. Trass."

"Keep this hangar under lockdown until we're gone. I don't want another soul within one hundred meters without consulting me."

"Of course."

Barnes allowed my escort and me in, then shut the gate behind us and started relaying orders to his men. Rin and the Titanborn we'd left with the *Cora* were finishing loading supplies. Two others lay on gurneys, wrapped in body bags, thanks to the bombing. None of my people were getting left behind. The ashes of the dead would be loosed upon the winds of Titan, where they were meant to be.

"I trust the meeting went as expected?" Rin shouted down from the entry ramp.

"As if you'd scripted it," I replied.

"Trass-damned mudstompers. Don't know when they're beat."

"Do you have him?"

"Even better."

Her sanitary mask lifted from a smirk beneath as she helped me up the ramp. Inside the cargo bay, three people with bags over their heads were on their knees in front of Gareth. Basaam Venta, the chubby man in the center, was clearly born of Earth, but the unfamiliar women on either side of him bore the slighter builds of offworlders.

"The one on the right is his clan-relative," Rin said.

"Caught them in his hotel room trying to legally conceive," Gareth signed. *"A bit of vacation romance."*

"And the other?" I asked.

"An illegitimate from the sewers. Apparently, she was along for the ride."

"Earthers…" Rin groaned.

I tore the bag off Basaam's head. Messy graying hair tumbled out over his shoulders. He and Madame Venta couldn't have been groomed more oppositely. His shaggy beard was a mess, his skin brown like caramel. The only thing they had in common was that, like her, ancient-style spectacles sat on the ridge of his nose, fogged by grime from his journey up.

I removed the sanitary mask strung tight over his mouth to muffle his cries. "What is the meaning of this?" he coughed. He fixed his glasses and glared at me, eyes magnified by the thick lenses. "Kale Trass? Does Madame Venta know about this? Your employees violated more codes of conduct than I can list. Do you—"

I placed a finger over his mouth. Words spewed forth from his lips so fast that his tongue could hardly keep up. Many considered him one of the brainiest men in Sol, and it showed.

"They aren't my employees," I said.

"Well, in any case, this is not proper business etiquette," he said. "I presume your meeting with the USF didn't go how you'd hoped. If you think taking me can convince Madame Venta to sway the opinion of the entire Assembly, you are in dire need of education."

"He's been blathering on like this since we grabbed him," Rin groaned.

"I'm being reasonable!" Basaam countered. "When she finds out you took me—"

"We'll be too far for her to do anything about it," I said.

"Your head of security is already dead, so I suggest you shut your mouth if you plan not to join him."

He swallowed hard and fiddled more with his glasses. "What do you want?" he asked finally.

"You're developing engine prototypes for your upcoming Departure Ark. Is that correct?"

"Yes. Fusion pulse engines, until I can think of a better name. They utilize supercritical fusion pulses of hydrogen-boron for propulsion, resulting in exponentially faster acceleration and top speeds that dwarf the best current ion-impulse drive tech. Nearly impossible to stabilize the plasma flow, but less reliance on our gas giant's rare assets."

"He didn't ask for a report," Rin bristled.

"Does it work?" I asked.

"Of course it does!" Basaam attested. "I invented it. We will be unveiling the prototype at this year's M-Day celebrations on Earth after we are undoubtedly chosen to design the Ark. This is all public knowledge, Mr. Trass, so if you kidnapped me simply to ask these questions, then I suggest you employ someone capable of utilizing Solnet."

"Place them in sleep pods," I said to Gareth. "We have what we came here for."

Gareth immediately grabbed both Basaam and his clan-relative by their collars. Another Titanborn took the unfortunate streetwalker who shared their bed, and together they dragged the three toward the ship's central corridor.

"Wait!" Basaam blurted. "What do you want with me? You release us, and I promise I can make it worth your while. Weapons tech. That's what you're after, right? For your war."

I raised a hand to halt Gareth. "Pervenio left us all the weapons we need," I said. "All I need are your fusion drives."

"Fusion pulse engines," he corrected, the word trailing off at the end as if he'd spoke purely out of impulse.

I bit my lip. "I need you to construct an operational version for me on Titan."

"B...but I can't," he stammered.

Rim seized him. "Why not?"

"The technology is still too volatile to be used on any vessel smaller than the Ark we're designing! You'd blow yourself to pieces. As a registered doctor, I cannot be party to that, no matter how poorly you treat me."

"It isn't your concern what we're using them for," I said.

"Regardless, I have none of my research. *She* broke my hand-terminal in my room, and even that isn't enough. Have you somehow transmitted my research from Martelle Station over Europa to Titan? Captured all my assistants. How do you expect me to build anything from scratch?"

My features darkened. "You'll find a way."

"In a few years, perhaps. But I've been working on this tech for almost a decade. Even my memory isn't that prodigious."

"That's too long," I said.

"You're lying," Rin snapped at Basaam.

"I'm not!" he answered. "Starting from scratch, in a new lab, with new technicians? I'll be lucky if I ever get it working."

"You'll do what we ask, or your friends here will have a difficult time enjoying their vacation."

"How dare you threaten them!" he yelled, spit dribbling down his beard. The shrill tone of his voice rendered his attempt at intimidation laughable.

"What is it with you Earthers?" Rin asked. "One woman isn't enough?"

Gareth playfully smacked Basaam in the back of the head, then signed, "*What. He's not your type, Rin?*"

"I wasn't born on Earth," Basaam said.

"Well, you're fat enough to have been," Rin said. The insult made him huff. "Lord Trass has given his orders. You all enjoy your sleep. Hopefully, after our long, long flight, you'll have a change of heart."

She waved Gareth to take him.

"You're asking the impossible! See reason, Mr. Trass!" Basaam and the two women kicked and squirmed, screaming at the top of their lungs for help until they disappeared around the corner. Rin turned to me and scratched her scarred jaw through her mask.

"The *Cora* is ready for departure when you are," she said. "Everything is loaded up."

"Not everything," I said.

"Oh, right. Where is our former doctor?"

"Coming. She had some affairs to see to before she leaves Mars behind for good."

"Well, she's late."

"She worked hard to organize all this, Rin. You weren't in there. To see everything unravel... her own people dismissing us like common protestors. I know you don't think she cares."

"But she's late. You realize who we have in our cabin, right, Kale? He's the most vital cog in Venta Co. right now besides his clan-sister. We got lucky the bombing distracted everyone enough to snatch him easy, but if Aria doesn't hurry, our luck will run out."

"Lord Trass," one of my guards interrupted us from the base of the cargo ramp.

"What!" I growled.

"Y... you need to come immediately."

My heated glare lingered on Rin a few seconds longer, then we followed him out into the hangar. Captain Barnes waited by the gate, holding a hand-terminal. The room's temperature was to his kind's preference, yet sweat matted his hair to his forehead.

"Mr. Trass," Barnes said anxiously. "May I?" He held out

the screen, refusing to cross the gate threshold without my permission.

"What is it?" I asked.

"It's Madame Venta, sir. She filed an urgent request to speak with you."

"About what?"

"Spit it out!" Rin hissed.

"Ask her yourself." Barnes handed me the device, then quickly retreated.

I took a moment to compose myself before rotating the screen to face me. Madame Venta's smug face was right in the center, hair pulled into a tight bun like she was about to tend a garden.

"Mr. Trass," she said, smiling. "Just when I thought we could be friends."

"We're preparing to leave, Madame, so make it quick."

"You kids have forgotten the value of a good conversation. One day I'll teach you how to play the game."

"Is that really why you called?"

"I know who you have." Her pleasant tone quickly eroded. "I don't know why, and I don't care, but I'm giving you one chance to hand him over. I'll consider it a rash act of impulse because of how the summit went, or because you fear his new engines may one day render Saturn's gases obsolete. We can continue on as we were."

I didn't provide Rin the luxury of a look, though I knew her expression was probably saying "I *told you so.*"

"I don't know who you're talking about," I addressed Madame Venta.

"I was hoping you wouldn't say that," she said.

Madame Venta handed the device to her son Fern, who cackled like a maniac as he crossed the room. He spun the camera around so that I could see a woman, shackled to a wall naked but for the pendant hanging from her neck. Not just a woman—Aria. The mop of auburn hair atop her head gave it away first, rumpled by her captors, then the pendant hanging from her neck. She wasn't bleeding or bruised, but she lurched when she saw me, her limber figure arching toward the camera as she struggled to pull herself free.

"Kale!" she screamed. "Don't listen to anything she says!" The rest of her words were muffled when Karl Venta slapped his hand over her mouth. She tried to bite it, but he cursed and slapped her before getting a tighter grip.

Madame Venta took the camera back. "You know, after I found out about Basaam, I found myself wondering how to possibly get to you when it seems you won't listen to anybody. Then I caught an early glimpse at a story cover featuring the little show you two put on outside the USF elevator, and it hit me."

"What's she talking about, Kale?" Rin asked.

I ignored her. "If you hurt her," I said, seething.

"I have a hard time damaging something so fair." She moved to Aria's side and ran the tip of her finger down her neck and over her breasts. Aria squirmed. "But sometimes, exceptions have to be made."

"Get your filthy hands off her!"

"Give me Basaam!" Madame Venta snarled. She grabbed Aria by the throat and shoved her face into the screen. "It is only out of respect for her former service to me that she still has all her fingers."

"I warned you, Kale," Rin whispered. "I told you we needed to leave."

"Let Aria go!" I demanded. "Or I swear to you—"

"That you'll what?" Madame Venta scoffed. "That you'll fucking what? You're in way over your head, boy. Give me Basaam, and she'll be returned in one piece. You have five minutes to decide; otherwise, I might start cutting things off." Madame Venta rubbed Aria's slightly swollen stomach, a bump still so subtle it was only visible while she was naked. "Or out."

The feed cut out just as Aria was able to squeeze a shriek through Karl's fingers. Without intending to, my strong grip cracked the screen of the device.

"You should have kept her by your side," Rin said crossly, but as my breathing started to hasten, her stance softened. She laid a hand on my shoulder. "I know you're close to her, but we can't risk everything for one offworlder. The *Cora* is faster than any ship they've got. We should leave now while Red Wing Company still backs us."

I couldn't get words out. I could hardly breathe.

"If you're right about her, she'd be happy to give herself for our cause," Rin continued. "Besides, that Earther bitch is all talk. They have history. She's one of the agents who Rylah first contacted for us years ago to set up supply exchanges with Venta Co. Madame Venta won't just kill her. She'll keep using her to get Basaam back until we don't need the fat slob anymore."

"She has my son!" I bellowed.

"What are you talking about?"

I clutched my chest, trying my best to steady my breathing. Rin wrapped her hand around my back to support me but was flung away as I punched the wall of the hangar as hard as I could. The bang nearly made Captain Barnes jump out of his armor, and Gareth immediately bounded down from the *Cora* to see what was wrong.

"My son..." I whispered. "Aria has him."

"What are you saying?" Rin clutched my face and stared deep into my eyes.

"Rin, listen to me. Aria is carrying him. The heir to Titan."

"Why... why didn't I..." She stumbled backward. I'd never

seen her appear so flabbergasted by anything. If Gareth hadn't arrived in time to brace her, she might have collapsed.

"It wasn't planned, but it's the truth," I said.

We'd found out shortly before the raid on Director Lawrence and the Luxury Cruiser. Being illegitimate meant she didn't get the Birth Control medications distributed to USF citizens without reproduction clearance.

I wasn't lying to Rin; her getting pregnant wasn't intended, but little with Aria ever was. I could still remember her face when she called me from the new Hayes Memorial Hospital to tell me about the tests she'd run on herself. It took me a few minutes to formulate words, but her—it was like her whole life had changed. Like the piece she'd been missing had come back to her.

In that moment, our occasionally nightly fling when both of us wanted to feel something became so much more. She started wanting to talk about things, and I did my best to open up—to see her, and not the woman Pervenio took from me. I wasn't sure if it'd been working until now that she was taken. All I could think about was getting her back, how she'd walked before the USF Assembly and stood up for us when so few would.

"You didn't tell me?" Rin asked.

"Would you have told you?" I replied.

She shook her head slowly.

"Now you know why I need to get her back," I said. "We'll find another way to get Basaam's tech or build something else. We've got the fuel."

She continued to stare blankly at me.

"Remember all that we went through just to save your sister?" I said, desperate to convince her.

"Stop." Rin dropped to one knee and lowered her head. "Just tell me what to do, Lord Trass."

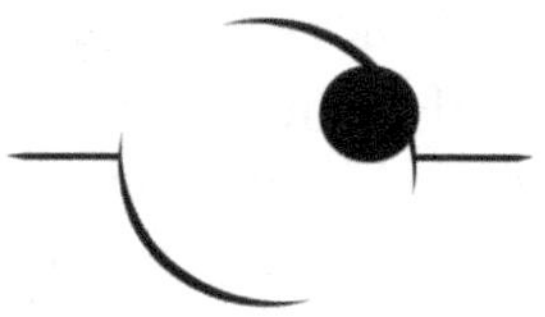

SIXTEEN

MALCOLM

Aria's captors hauled her through the main entrance of Venta Co.'s central office tower. Since it was located at the heart of New Beijing under the loftiest portion of the dome, it was the tallest structure. The tapering cylinder rose like a layered wedding cake with too many levels to count. A series of terraces wrapped every few floors, until the top one wasn't big enough to house more than a single office—Madame Jamaru Venta's office. Verdant green leaves and brilliant flowers draped over the railings of each terrace, the glass enclosure reflecting the flora all the way up. From the right angle, the entire tower seemed to be one giant plant with the blue, interlocked V's of their emblem beaming down from the highest point.

All my time as a collector, Venta was a shade behind Pervenio Corp in every facet. You wouldn't know it looking at their headquarters. Even Luxarn Pervenio wouldn't build something so ostentatious. The Hanging Gardens of New Beijing, that was what people called it, like it was some sort of world wonder.

I entered a quaint café nestled at the base of the dome-scraper across the street. The sweet aroma of leftover pastries filled my nostrils. The crust probably wasn't the real stuff, but my grumbling stomach hadn't ingested anything but alcohol for over twenty-four hours. I bought something stale with a layer of frosting to help it go down, and a strong coffee to keep me awake. A few other civilians around my age sat throughout the place, too old to follow the blinking lights and music toward the real nightlife below, but with too much on their minds to sleep. Living past your warranty does that to a man.

I parked my ass at one of the tables by the window and stared at Venta Tower. A smattering of lights glowed through windows here and there, employees hard at work in the middle of the night. Poor saps. The rest of the city's illumination derived from the countless ads festooning every other tower's enclosure. Venta's was the only one without them, as if the only thing they needed to publicize was how hard their employees worked.

I watched silently, sipping on coffee that could pass for melted rat shit and forcing down a pastry so manufactured even I could notice the fakeness. There were far better places to get a bite in New Beijing, but only for people who hadn't spent all their credits chasing a Three Messiah's Herald who wanted to be found.

Lights suddenly flashed on in Madame Venta's office up top, which meant my greatest fear was realized. That lady devil was personally involved with taking Aria. The talking heads on news feed behind the café's counter droned on about how poorly the summit between Kale and the USF had gone. No official details were released yet, but I had a roiling feeling in my gut that this was political.

Madame Venta had always been deliberate. Luxarn Pervenio could manipulate with the best of them, tugging strings from the shadows like a puppet master. She didn't play games or bluff, which meant that when she grabbed Titan's bastard ambassador off the street in public, she probably had her reasons.

"What the hell did you do, Kale?" I whispered to myself.

"Excuse me?" a fossil of a man asked from the table behind me.

I disregarded him and went to take another sip of coffee. I swallowed a small mouthful before I pictured the blood of Aria's guards staining my whiskey and lost my appetite. I'd been part of a number of corporate feuds, and that was an act of war as far as I was concerned. If Venta did something like that to Pervenio in its heyday, that was when collectors would start being sent out to take shots until everyone's lust for vengeance was satiated, and we could return to our uneasy economic alliances as if nothing had happened.

My real question was this: Was taking Aria meant to send a message to Kale for something he'd done or was she a trading chip? I couldn't stomach either option. Leaving Aria's life in the hands of a terrorist who fancied himself king wasn't in the cards. I'd seen his people shoot at her right after she saved one of their lives back on Titan. If it came to it, I was sure they'd leave her behind if it suited their needs in a heartbeat.

So I needed to get to her first, which meant I needed to break into a building as secure as the USF Assembly. A double layer of guard posts stood within the front entrance, filled with heavily armed officers. Security drones whizzed around each terrace, keeping 360-degree watch along with cameras. Not that I was in any condition to climb a tower anyway.

I sighed and glanced down at my pulse pistol. I could offer its service back to Luxarn in exchange for help, though I doubted he would risk angering Madame Venta for my daughter, who he didn't even know existed. As far as Sol was concerned, Aria was just another illegitimate offworlder. I spent a lot of energy keeping her a secret throughout my days as a collector so I wouldn't get slapped for infringing USF regulations. If I told Luxarn the truth now all these years later, I doubted he'd care, but he might find out she was there on Titan that day. That we were the reason for Zhaff's condition.

No, it was too risky. I had to go about this alone. Sneaking in wasn't possible, but I could bull-rush them. Take out the guards out front, grab one hostage, and hop straight onto the elevator before anyone knew what hit them. I had the element of surprise on my side.

I stood, closed my eyes, and downed the swill the shop called coffee. Then I stormed out the front door and straight for the Venta Tower front entrance. My whole body was exhausted, but it didn't matter. I didn't have to last much longer, and I had Luxarn's cybernetic gift to keep me upright.

The officers in the entry were too lost in conversation to notice me coming. Like anybody would. They might've been expecting reprisal from a Titanborn, but not from a wrinkled old wretch like me. They'd ask who I was once I was close enough, I'd tell them what I used to be, then they'd hesitate to contact Luxarn Pervenio for formality's sake, and I'd grab one. All I had to do was provide Aria a chance to run, and whatever happened to me, well, I'd died once already.

I lowered my hand until it grazed the handle of my pulse pistol. My trusty companion. The sensation again brought me flashbacks of when I'd shot Zhaff on Titan, his eye lens glinting right before his head snapped back. I hadn't fired it since. Hell, I wasn't sure if I still could. Maybe that was the reason I'd spared Herald Jeremiah. Not because it was the right decision, but because I lacked the gumption to make the wrong one anymore.

It didn't matter.

I unstrapped my holster and threaded my finger through the trigger guard. I'd pull it, even if it took two hands to apply the pressure. I had to.

Darkness suddenly fell over my eyes. Before I knew what hit me, my arms were wrenched behind my back, my gun stolen, and I was pulled forcefully to the side. I tried to gain a grip on the street using my artificial leg, but I was disoriented and being dragged backward had me at the wrong angle.

Dammit, Malcolm! That's rule number one on a job. Never be so tired that you can only focus straight ahead. Someone had come up right behind me and bagged my head. Not someone. Two voices chattered back and forth.

Just breathe, I told myself. Figure out who this is. Kidnapping wasn't Venta Co.'s MO. Double tap to the back of the head, that was what those two collectors would do to me if I wound up on their list. I glanced down to see the boots of my captors. They were worn and discolored, like they'd spent too much time wading through sewers.

Before I could analyze any more, I was thrown against a wall. The hood came off me, and all my questions were answered. Another one of my sloppy mistakes had come back to bite me in the ass.

"Yep. That's definitely the one," the same tattooed foundry salt dealer I'd harassed in the alley earlier yapped. His eyes twitched like he'd just taken a huge hit. He kicked me twice hard in the gut until my other captor pulled him off.

He removed Haglin Amissum's hand-terminal from my pocket and smashed it under his boot. "In case he's being followed," the man said.

"Smart. Let's off 'em, boss," crowed the dealer, though he wasn't looking at his friend.

We were in an empty stairwell leading down to one of the less-used Redline stations in New Beijing. Both of them held me at gunpoint. The last kind of scum you want aiming a gun at you, so hopped up that their quaking fingers could accidentally squeeze the trigger at any time.

"Now, now, boys. No need to be hasty." Those words came from a third, more restrained voice. It was cool and confident, but there was no denying the subtle tinge of madness clinging to the end of each word. He knelt in front of me.

"You've got to be kidding me," I groaned. This was the sorry lot that was going to keep me from my daughter? He looked like a clown. His frilly shirt was drawn open, with the mark of the Ringer Bones gang displayed prominently on the upper portion of his exposed chest. Bar piercings made his ears droop like wax from a hot candle. He even had white makeup smeared sloppily across his face to appear as pale as a Ringer, along with black eyeshadow.

"Thought you could hide from us, did you?" he said. He slapped me playfully across the face. That was when I recognized the lunacy he struggled to cage. His dark eyes stared right through me, like there was nothing there.

"You shoulda seen the way he came at me, boss," the dealer said.

"I hope you guys know who you're dealing with," I muttered.

The leader sprang to his feet and started pacing. He had my pistol in his hands and caressed the barrel. "A retired collector who couldn't stay clean." He cackled like a maniac. "I found out! I always find out. You're nothing anymore, Malcolm Graves." Of course he had connections. That was what allowed gangs like theirs to rise to the top.

"What're we gonna do with him?" the dealer asked.

"I haven't decided yet, but it sure will be fun."

"Well, you better think carefully," I said. "I wouldn't want the last thing you ever do to lack the flair of that outfit."

"Oh yes," he tittered. "So fun."

"You're the Ringer Boner crew, right?" I asked while I searched for a way out of this. I was unarmed, but I had my leg.

When he got close enough, I could kick him into one of his cronies and hope the other missed me before I was able to disarm him. It was a long shot, but these weren't trained collectors, just street bangers.

"Ringer Bones," the dealer spat.

"The more you talk, the more fun we're gonna have." The leader holstered my gun in his belt and drew an unnecessarily long dagger from the back of his belt. He grinned from ear to ear.

"Ah, right," I said. "And what're you calling yourself? The Prince of Bones or something? The older I get, the more idiotic the little play gangs like yours get."

My words didn't faze him. He spread his arms wide, as if he were performing for a crowd from a stage. What the hell had I gotten myself into?

"You can call me—"

His head popped like a water balloon filled with fruit juice. The dealer's buddy held his gun aimed at me while he searched from side to side to see where it came from. Then his body danced as it was riddled with holes. Terror gripped the drug-addled eyes of the dealer. His gun wavered in my direction, then he decided to drop it and run. He didn't get far. From the shadows, someone grabbed him, wrapped hands around his neck, and snapped it.

I froze as I saw who emerged from behind his crumpled body. It was a Cogent, yellow eye lens shimmering as it reflected the ads through the open door into the upper city. I poked the Ringer Bones leader's corpse to make sure this wasn't a figment of my imagination.

"Zhaff?" I said softly. I knew it was crazy; he'd never get out of that tube. It took me a few seconds to recognize Varus, the Earther Cogent who I'd challenged to shoot me back on Undina. Their field suits had seen an improvement since Zhaff.

The shadows clung to it to help conceal him, as if the fibers were fashioned to absorb their surroundings and reflect them.

He rushed over and heaved me to my feet with ease. Being a stout Earther made him considerably stronger than Zhaff was.

"Are you injured, Malcolm Graves?" he asked. His voice was as stale as my pastry in the café upstairs. It was like hearing an audio recording of my old partner. One day not drinking and, apparently, I'd fallen helplessly into a time trap.

"I'm fine," I said after a few seconds of gawking at him. I patted the dust off my clothing, then knelt to reclaim my pulse pistol. As soon as I grabbed it, Varus took my arm and pulled me toward the exit.

"We must leave immediately," he said.

I didn't fight him. A retired collector, an agent from a "nonexistent" initiative, if we were caught with three bodies, it would get ugly. Varus led me away from the Venta Tower and around a corner to an empty hovercar transit stop. I sat on the bench and stretched out my human leg.

"I had that completely under control, you know," I said.

He sat beside me. "From my vantage, it appeared these felons had you in a compromised position."

"No jokes with your kind. Now I remember."

"What did they desire from you?"

"My gun, I guess." I rolled my shoulders. "Anyway, thanks for the assist, Varus, but I have to ask, what the hell are you doing here? Luxarn keeping tabs on me?"

"It appears that you and I have come to the same conclusion," he replied. "Mr. Pervenio explained how proficient you are, so it is not a surprise. Did you forget to inform him that you reconsidered his proposition?"

"What proposition?"

"The elimination of Kale Trass."

"Elimination? What..." I paused. Had a plan for breaking

into the Venta headquarters come right to me? "Yeah. I decided to look into it. How'd you find me?"

"We have been watching you ever since the bombing subverted our best opportunity at Kale Trass."

"You were involved in that?"

"Another agent had him in his sights before an unanticipated explosion knocked him off balance and allowed Kale Trass to eliminate him."

"So why follow me?"

"Mr. Pervenio felt that with Kale Trass in New Beijing, you would be inclined to take him up on his offer. It appears, as usual, he was correct. After you discovered who was responsible for the bombing, I spotted you conversing with Titan's ambassador."

"I don't care for being tailed, Varus."

"Mr. Pervenio said you might say that. However, your deduction that using the ambassador would be the quickest way to expose Kale Trass was a brilliant tactic, Malcolm Graves. Based on recent intelligence, their relationship seems closer than expected, considering her origin."

I breathed a sigh of relief, which Varus either didn't notice or didn't care about. I always harbored a sneaking suspicion that Luxarn had always known about Aria and who she belonged to. Now that she was in the spotlight, it seemed only more likely that he'd find out. But if his Cogents thought I was using her to get to Kale, it meant he truly had no clue.

"Brilliant," I blustered. "At least until Venta took her first and those bangers got in my way." I nodded toward Venta Tower, slicing up high above the New Beijing skyline toward the dome. "The ambassador is up there now. If we want her, we're going to have to figure out a way to break in and fast." If anyone could get it done, it was a Cogent. I could use him to get her, then we'd disappear. Easy.

"That won't be necessary," a familiar voice said through a hand-terminal that Varus placed between us. The Cogent gestured for me to take it. I'm not sure why, but I hesitated for a moment, even though I already knew who it was addressing me. There was no getting used to talking directly to Luxarn Pervenio.

"Mr. Pervenio," I replied after finally gathering the nerve to lift the device. He appeared as haggard as when I'd left him, sitting before the stark backdrop of rock and metal within his Undina office. "I apologize. I had no idea you were listening."

"Can't be too cautious these days," he said. The corners of his lips lifted into a meager smile. "I knew you couldn't stay away, Graves. It's not in your nature."

"The Tongueway doesn't thrill like it used to," I joked.

"It's the job. The thrill of a challenge. Men like us, we can't keep away from it. The moment I found out Kale was traveling to Mars, I knew you'd wind up leading us to him. We're like addicts. Desperate for a fix."

I stretched my dry eyelids open as far as they could go. "It even comes with the hangover."

Mr. Pervenio chuckled. "I was worried all that wasted time would dull your wit."

"Only dying could do that, sir. So what's the move? Are your Cogents preparing to take the ambassador?"

"For the time being, we wait."

I bit my lip. "We can't use her if they have her."

"Thanks to your intuition, we knew to risk hacking Madame Venta's communications. She contacted Kale Trass, and they're in the process of planning a hostage exchange."

"Exchange?"

"Forgive me, I forgot that you have been operating out of the loop. It appears Venta Co. seized the ambassador in response to Kale Trass abducting Chief Engineer Basaam Venta."

"Why in the name of Earth would he do that?"

"His exact motives remain unclear, but if I had to guess, he's lashing out after what happened at the USF summit. As of this moment, none of this has been made public. Nobody saw Basaam get taken. Venta Co. has predictably refused Kale Trass' every demand, and you know how children get when they're told no."

"Fucking Ringers!" I slammed my fist on the bench.

I was right. Everything that was happening was Kale's fault. Aria could take care of herself, but last time I helped her, she made the mistake of sticking with the Ringers. She didn't like giving up—she got that from me—but I had to get her out for good this time. For her own sake. Even if she hated me for it, I could live with that. I'd done it for long enough.

"Where's the exchange going down?" I asked.

"She is sending her sons with the ambassador to Kale's private Red Wing Company hangar in the New Beijing Spaceport," Luxarn said. "I have permitted Varus and his unit to ambush them there, with no prejudice."

"You're sending them in weapons free with Venta Co. and Red Wing employees present?"

"Taking the life of Kale Trass here is the primary objective. We can cover it up until we're able to send a relief team to Pervenio Station, catch the Ringers off guard, and free his captives."

"When are you thinking of making your move?"

"We are preparing to infiltrate the spaceport presently," Varus said. "It is heavily defended."

"I advised Varus to contact you so that I may ask you personally to join them," Mr. Pervenio said. "Your presence will provide an experienced combatant who is familiar with Children of Titan tactics. The offer I made back on Undina remains unchanged. This is your chance to finish what you and Zhaff started, Graves."

I glanced back up at Venta Tower. Somewhere in its illuminated cap sat my daughter, probably thinking that Kale was making the trade because he viewed her as one of their own. Whatever the reason for his wanting Basaam Venta, I was sure about one thing: he wasn't saving Aria for her. Something she knew must have made her valuable, and now Kale was either flexing his muscles to see what he could get away with... or up to something worse. That was how the Children of Titan operated. A bombing to get you looking one way while their hands slipped into your pocket from the other.

What they didn't know was that they were strolling into a Cogent-led ambush. That only *I* could get Aria out alive.

"Keep your credits and your titles, sir," I said. Luxarn's jaw dropped. "A friend is dead because of the trail of suffering Kale Trass leaves in his wake. I'll help you take down Kale, and I'll do it this time for free."

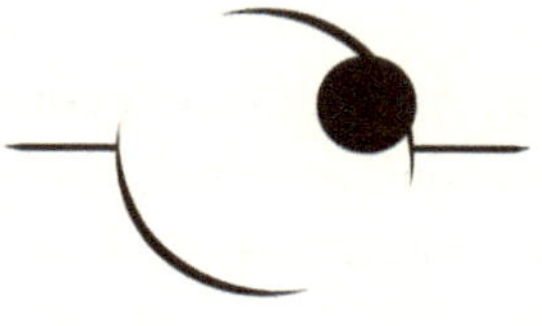

KALE

I sat alone in the *Cora's* cargo hold, pulse rifle lying across my lap. I removed the clip, checked it was full, then that all the weapon's pieces were in their proper places. Not that I knew how any of it really functioned, but it was comforting to know that it would shoot straight if I needed to use it.

Fingers snapped beside my ear, and my head whipped around to face the disturbance as if a bomb had gone off. I was relieved to find it was only Gareth trying to gain my attention. His eyes were uncharacteristically red, and I could hear his runny nose sniveling through his mask. It was from all the direct exposure to the inhabitants of Mars without any precautions. He'd loaded up on every bit of medication we had the moment we returned to the *Cora,* just in case.

"You look like someone I know," he signed to me, throwing a nod Rin's way. She was across the room giving orders to a handful of my guards, a perpetual scowl fixed to her marred face. I smirked and returned to attending to my rifle.

Gareth sat beside me and leaned forward so I could see his hands out of the corner of my eye. After months with him, I didn't need to focus all my attention anymore to read what he was saying.

"*I understand,*" he signed.

"Trust me, you don't," I said.

"*Caring about her does not make you weak. Love is pain.*"

I glanced back at his face. Concern softened his usually staid façade. "Rin told you everything, didn't she?"

He shook his head emphatically. "*Didn't need to.*"

"It's not..." I sighed. "What would you do, Gareth? Let her and my unborn child die because they aren't full Titanborn?"

"*I already have.*"

"What in Trass's name are you talking about?"

"*We can't ever give up on them, Kale. Even if we're unsure. Even if we don't understand.*"

My brow furrowed. I gestured toward Rin, but again, Gareth shook his head.

"*My late wife. She was so afraid of getting sick, she stopped leaving our hollow. I don't know how to sign the word for that. We fought so much over it, I never liked coming home. I called her crazy and irrational, she called me naive, and it went on. When we had a son, she never let him leave either.*"

"I didn't know you have a child."

"*Had.*" His hands began to quake gently. "*I was away, working security for a fence trying to broaden his reach to another block. I don't know how my boy got sick, but he did. When I returned, I found his limp body in our shower. She'd drowned him in the water, the only luxury we Titanborn could afford.*"

"Gareth, I—" He didn't allow me to finish.

"*I was so angry when I found our son, a child I barely ever saw, that I strangled her.*" His hands now shook so intensely he could barely use them to form words. "*She was sick. She needed help. And instead of finding it, I stayed away. I failed her. I failed my son.*"

My hand hovered over his leg. I wasn't sure whether to try and comfort him or give him space. Emotion wasn't something I'd known he could express, and the heartbreak in my fearless guardian's expression was almost too much to stomach.

"I had no idea," was what I managed to utter.

Gareth pointed at Rin. *"Neither does she,"* he signed. *"Don't ever give up on the people you care about, or you'll have nothing."*

"It was the Earthers, Gareth, not you. They put us in an impossible situation, and there's not one of us who turned out right. We had to survive."

"Maybe that's true, but they didn't wrap my hands around her neck. I can still feel her throat crunch. I tried to turn myself in for what I did, only Pervenio was too busy to care. One more pair of dead Ringers was just good business. So I ran as far as I could afford to and took the lowest post the Sunfire gas harvester had to offer. I met Rin and got caught up in a rebellion I couldn't care less about. If a Ringer like me could strangle his own help-less wife in cold blood, why should I care about the rest of us?

"I only followed Rin because if I hadn't done something to stay distracted, I would've spaced myself just to be free of the guilt. Until we found you. In the face of everything we put you through, all you wanted to do was try to save the people you cared about. Cora. The woman you loved. That was why I decided to follow you."

He patted me on the shoulder, and I swallowed the lump forming in my throat as I bobbed my head in approval. Then he rose to his feet and gazed down upon me from his towering vantage.

"We all have done terrible things," he signed. *"We don't need forgiveness. We don't need pity. All we can do is try to be better. You gave me a cause worth fighting for, Kale Trass. You helped me put the past behind me so I could try to do just that. I*

will follow you until the very end, and I will always understand."

There was no question he'd signed more to me at that moment than in all our prior conversations combined. I wasn't sure how his hands weren't exhausted and was equally unsure how to respond. Throughout all the chaos since I found myself at Rin's mercy on the *Piccolo*, I'd never had the time to think about why he, of all people, had been the first to truly throw his support behind me. He backed my move to rescue Cora from Director Sodervall's clutches when all the others thought it pointless.

Gareth turned to go help with preparations. I clicked my rifle's magazine into position and stood, but before I had the chance to say anything, Rin was in front of me. "They're here," she said, watching Gareth all the way out onto the *Cora*'s exit ramp. "What was that about?"

"Nothing," I said. "Let's go."

"The quicker we can get off this rock the better."

We followed Gareth out into the hangar, where the rest of my guards waited beneath the shadow of the *Cora* for Madame Venta's two hotheaded sons. Captain Barnes and the rest of his Red Wing unit stood guard at the hangar's entry. There was only one way in or out, and all that stood between us and them was some scattered empty containers and crates.

Rin nudged me. "You are aware this is probably a trap, right?" she said.

"Should we take bets?" Gareth signed.

"It was too easy getting them to agree to meet here. We'll have two Earther corps right on top of us. If they partner up, we won't be able to hold them off, even with that trick up your sleeve."

"It's simple," I said. "Madame Venta either needs Basaam

more than she thinks I need Aria, or somebody is leaving here in a body bag."

Gareth slapped his pulse rifle. *"Won't be us."*

"Sure as Saturn's Rings won't be," Rin said, her sanitary mask wriggling as she licked her scars beneath.

"We're here to get Aria back," I said. "That's all."

"I know. It's a shame letting Basaam go after all the work we did to get here, though."

"We've been over this. It's too risky for Aria going back on the deal. And like Basaam said, unless we steal his research, he's useless to our timetable."

"If he isn't lying."

"We'll find another way, Rin. We always do."

"Easier than breaking into the Pervenio Station prison for Cora and the others," Gareth signed.

Rin nodded. "Just a long way to travel to return empty-handed."

"Making Madame Venta and the USF sweat isn't nothing," I said. "Thanks to Aria, we've accomplished both."

"Those tubby mudstompers are always sweating." She snickered, and Gareth joined her. Then she wiped her own sweat-drenched brow. "Speaking of, I don't know how much longer I can stand being near these neutral engines."

I glanced from side to side. Altogether, twelve Titanborn were healthy enough to fight if it came to it, including me, Rin, and Gareth. Two of our dead lay in the cargo hold along with our bound hostages, two were captured alongside Aria, and another could no longer weather the injuries he suffered in the bombing and manned the *Cora*'s cockpit instead. Per my request, they had the engines primed, even though the hangar's outer airlock was closed and the room wasn't sealed off or pressurized. A heavily fineable offense, I was told, due to concerns over radioactive pollution. I hoped the *Cora*'s advanced tech was alien enough for both the Red Wing and Venta officers not to notice.

We all wore our weapons and armor, even the helmets. I wasn't going to take any chances. There was no reason to feign pleasantries during a prisoner exchange. My people were ready to do whatever I asked of them. Willing to die. Our revolution boasted no greater consequence. Instead of scraping and stealing from each other in the Lowers to survive, we stood shoulder to shoulder in the name of Titan and, like Gareth said, a cause worth fighting for.

Restless shadows gathered outside of the entry. Captain Barnes spoke with someone unseen.

"I want you watching for anything," Rin addressed our people. "If any of them even attempts to make a move on Lord Trass, end them."

I switched on the com-link in my ear. "Engines ready?"

"Yes, sir," one of the Titanborn in the cockpit replied. "On your command."

A wave of Venta blue flooded through the entry. Jamaru Venta's young sons strode out in front, swagger in their gait. Like nothing could touch them. At least three dozen security officers were with them, pulse rifles in hand. Just behind Karl, a slender woman was being prodded along with a bag over her head. I recognized her dress from earlier, though now it was stained with blood and ratty. One Titanborn body each was slung over the shoulders of the duster-wearing Venta collectors on either side of her.

My hands squeezed into fists.

"If they harmed your child," Rin said, fuming.

I didn't answer. Nobody else spoke a word until Karl, Fern, and their line of officers was no more than ten meters away from us. I could almost feel the air thicken with tension like fresh broth being stirred. We were outnumbered more than two to one, though we had the benefit of the *Cora*'s landing gear for coverage. Red Wing officers waited at the hangar entrance behind them as well. It was impossible to know if I could count on them for support. When it came down to honoring their agreement for "Ringers" or starting a corporate feud, I had a feeling I knew who they'd pick.

Madame Venta's sons stopped and regarded me, grins spreading across their rosy faces. They wore formal attire, as if this was any other meeting, and no weapons either. Their men would handle things for them. That was how it worked for corporate leaders—give an order and let their servants drop the hammer.

I leveled a glower in their direction but held my tongue. The silence had me starting to itch.

"I didn't think we'd get the pleasure of seeing each other again, Mr. Trass," Karl Venta said finally.

"Quite a pleasure," Fern remarked.

"On with it," I said sharply. "We don't need to drag this out."

Karl snapped his fingers. Two officers stepped forward and dropped the corpses of the Titanborn guards I'd sent down to Old Dome with Aria. Each had a hole in his head. More men dead because of me.

"You son of a bitch!" Rin yelled. She lurched at them, but I held her back. I could hear Gareth's rifle rattling against his armor on the other side of me.

"Forgive the state of your men," Karl said, still grinning.

"Madame Venta promised they'd be returned to us," I said.

"And they are. Unfortunately, they died long before we made this arrangement, but now you can return their bodies to Titan to do whatever it is you people do with your dead. Call it recompense for all of the unnecessary trouble you've cost us after we were gracious enough to arrange that summit."

"Screw this, Kale," Rin bristled. I raised a hand to quiet her.

"You admit to murdering two of my people and expect me to ignore it?" I said.

Karl rolled his eyes. "And you're innocent? There were Venta properties on the Ring too. You Ringers think you can take whatever you like. Something goes wrong, you just slap a band-aid on it and say sorry. You're like children throwing a tantrum."

"Big bad Pervenio was so mean," Fern mocked.

"Watch your mouth!" Rin hissed. "Mommy isn't here to watch over you now, is she?"

He glanced back toward his platoon of officers. They may as well have been foaming at the mouths. "No," he said. "No, she's not."

"If you want the blood of thousands on your hands, then by all means, go back on her word," I said. Karl's lips straightened, but he didn't reply. "Like I thought."

"Where's Basaam?" barked Fern.

"Waiting for you to take that hood off and prove that's the ambassador," I said.

Karl stepped back and took his sweet time wrapping his hand around Aria's lower back. She winced. "What, you didn't memorize every one of her curves?" he asked. "I know my mother did."

"Get your filthy hands off of her!" Rin shouted.

"Touch her like that again, and you'll get exactly what you want," I said, deepening my tone as much as I could. "Except my men have been instructed to aim at your and your brother's heads first. No matter what happens, you won't make it out alive."

The notion that Basaam was less important to them than I'd suspected was beginning to creep into my thoughts. Karl was obviously trying to provoke us into breaking the ceasefire and acting as the villains Sol so desperately wanted us to be. I quickly surveyed the room to see if there were any hidden cameras I'd missed that might bear witness if that happened. A security feed was posted above the entry watching over the hangar, though it had a Red Wing logo on the side. Was this their trap all along?

Karl grumbled something under his breath, then finally removed Aria's hood. Her hair was disheveled, like wildfire. Black circles wreathed her eyes all the way around. She didn't appear wounded, though. Once her eyes adjusted to the light, she fixed them firmly on the floor, tears welling in the corners.

"There," Karl said. "Quite the catch, this one. From nameless sewer rat to our mother's ripe whore, to yours."

"The only whore here is you, mudstomper!" Rin shouted. "Selling your souls for whatever you fancy until you tire of it."

Even Gareth signed an insult.

If not for the circumstances, I would've been pleased to hear my aunt finally treating Aria like one of our own; however, I knew it was only because of what she held in her belly. But Madame Venta's whore? Was that how Aria earned the clout to be supported by Venta Co. in her efforts to cure my people? I couldn't stop thinking about what else we didn't know about her, even though I knew I had to focus.

"Well, Trass," Karl said, regaining my full attention. Now wasn't the time to let doubts nest in my head and fester. "If you do tire of her, I'm sure Mother would pay a pretty credit to get her back. Sewer trash never goes rotten. And they're wild, friend. Like rabid dogs."

"We'll take her how she is," I affirmed.

"Your loss." He clutched Aria by the arm and tugged her forward. "Send down Basaam, and the whore is yours."

Aria finally mustered the courage to look up at me, and I saw in her eyes a torrent of rage and shame. For a moment, all my reservations about her withered away like ashes to a breeze. I knew I was making the right decision helping her. Earth would pay for all it had done to my people, but for now, I needed Aria back. No Earther corps was going to take anything I cared about from me ever again.

I waved back toward the *Cora*'s cargo bay. Two Titanborn immediately ran in and returned with our three captives. I'd removed their hoods earlier to save the time, but scraps of cloth were shoved into each of their mouths to silence the grating racket of their protests.

"As soon as she walks, they walk," I said.

Rin tapped her rifle and aimed at Basaam. "I see anything off, the first slug goes through his profitable brain."

"Basaam!" Karl yelled. "Clan-brother. Are you injured?" Basaam gawked at Rin, then shook his head fervently. "Got anything strapped to you? Earth knows these Ringers love their bombs." Again, Basaam shook his head. "All right, Trass. You're lucky my mother was feeling generous today. You've held up your end. Here she comes."

An explosion suddenly rocked the wall of the hangar to our right, causing anyone on that side of the room to stagger. Basaam's streetwalking girlfriend dashed forward in a panic, and just as she passed by me, a bullet splattered her brains. One of my people panicked and returned fire, shredding Karl Venta's kneecap. Gareth tackled me off the ramp. Rin lunged, grabbed Basaam and his clan-sister, and flung them back onto the *Cora* before they could escape.

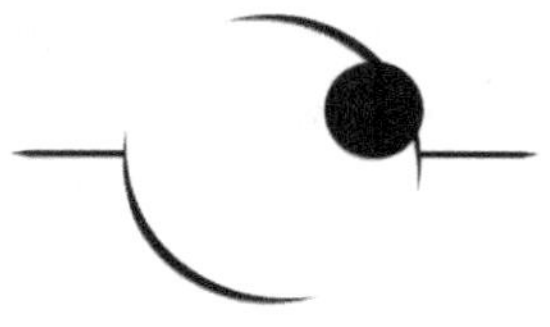

EIGHTEEN

MALCOLM

Varus led me to the rest of his unit. He had a squadron of six Cogents, burrowed away in the New Beijing Redline. It wasn't difficult getting into the cramped tunnels, with city security looking for worse offenders than squatters. We slipped in through an exhaust vent in an Old Dome alley.

Rusty barrels filled with fires illuminated the congested tube, surrounded by the poor and the depraved under hung tarps. Most didn't even notice our peculiar group going by, too strung out on synthahol or foundry salts or whatever other new synthetics were all the rage. Redline cars rumbled by, shattering bottles that had rolled onto the tracks. I even heard the faint and distant cries of some piece of sewer trash who was too drunk to stay against the outer walls and keep out of their way.

"We are beneath the spaceport now," Varus said as we reached a point where the single tunnel branched into three larger ones. We left the bonfires of the homeless behind, and I would've traded anything on me for a pair of spotters. It was pitch black.

I leaned against the wall to catch my breath. The effects of coffee and the adrenaline from being kidnapped were beginning to wear off. My human leg felt the ache of exhaustion, and my eyelids felt like they had ten-pound weights strapped to the lashes.

"This service passage leads directly beneath the main terminal," Varus said. "It is locked, but we should be able to break through." Varus's eye lens projected a beam of light to help me see. He slid aside an unconscious bearded man and knelt in front of a sealed hatch so thick it looked like it was designed for a spaceship. He held a hand-terminal up to the hatch's control panel, which bore an operation screen so fuzzy I couldn't read anything on it. I wasn't even sure it still worked.

I didn't have the time or patience to wait. I nudged Varus out of the way and kicked the hinge as hard as I could with my artificial leg. It caved, and a few more kicks busted it enough for the hatch to pop out. I was left gasping for breath.

"A much more efficient use of time," Varus acknowledged. He and the other Cogents grabbed the edge of a half-meter-thick slab of metal and yanked until it open wide enough for them to squeeze through.

Varus waved me along, and I paused. During my first days working with Zhaff, I had to endure constant questioning of my methods and his rattling off superfluous data. I had no idea what Luxarn told this group of Cogents, but they were so deferential, it made me uncomfortable. Almost reverential. Couldn't they stare at my face with their shiny, yellow eye lenses and see all the lies I was holding in? That I'd put the best of them into a coma from which he was never likely to wake.

"Are you coming, Malcolm Graves?" Varus said. "Time is of the essence."

I shook the thoughts out of my head and dragged my human leg along. He was right. This arrangement was only temporary. Extract Aria, and then Luxarn could do whatever he wanted with his Cogents. Kill Kale Trass, take back Titan—I couldn't give two shits so long as she was safe. Yet, couldn't I do that best as one of his directors rather than skulking through the shadows? If I was going to spend the rest of my life sitting around, why not be behind a real wooden desk?

"Malcolm Graves?"

My mind drifted in and out. I slapped myself across the face a few times to gain focus. My fingers wrapped the first step of the ladder, and I climbed. One step up the cramped passage and I knew where we were. An elevator shaft. Judging by the layer of grime wrapping every rung, nobody had bothered cleaning the place in decades either.

Mars was funny that way. It had been settled so suddenly and aggressively by corporations that layers of infrastructure wound up buried as the domes went up, one taller and wider than the next. Whatever skyscraper we were in transformed into a massive pier supporting the current spaceport.

Varus glanced down to check on me, and the light from his eye lens sliced through the blackness to provide more answers. An elevator car hung crookedly from a cluster of wilting cables, the Pervenio logo stamped on the side.

I chuckled, then coughed as I inhaled a mouthful of dust. It was almost like Luxarn had been planning this forever. That was how he knew about a route only someone who'd spent a lifetime mapping the warren of tunnels and sewers beneath New Beijing would be aware of. His father had it constructed even before his company abandoned Mars for the greener pastures around Saturn. All of Earth had thought the Pervenios were mad, going so far away and toward a people on Titan who hadn't yet responded to any communications.

"One hundred more meters," Varus informed me.

"Not ninety-nine?" I joked.

"Ninety-nine now."

My smirk was concealed by the darkness. It seemed

Cogents still hadn't been trained to comprehend sarcasm. I remembered all those times Zhaff had taken one of my jokes too literally. His eye lens would stare at me, gears churning behind the glass, brain trying to make sense of whatever idiom I'd spouted.

My hand slipped as I went to grab the next rung. My human foot came loose with it, too sore to fight the inertia of my swing. If not for my artificial leg, I would've taken a plummet that even Mars's weak gravity wouldn't have made possible to survive, but it jammed between two rungs and allowed me to regain my bearings. A rusty bolt clattered down the shaft.

"Please hurry, Mr. Graves," Varus called down.

"You don't worry about me," I panted.

My exhaustion was mounting, allowing any distraction to break my attention too easily. I decided it was best to watch my hands and feet. I concentrated on each step the little light afforded me. One hand up, second hand, push off with my fake leg. The other was too tired to do anything but maintain balance. If I had been climbing this high under Earth's gravity, I probably would've had a heart attack.

By the time Varus heaved me up through a service hatch at the top, I couldn't remember ever having been more beat in my life. Not even after months in a sleep pod traveling across the solar system. My entire body was drained, with my hands suffering from a bad case of the shakes.

I sat and squeezed my fists over and over to try and drive blood back into them. I should've exercised instead of spending my time on Mars shoving liquor down my gullet and napping. Maybe then I could have fought off the collectors who took Aria and avoided all of this.

"Focus, Malcolm," I whispered to myself, banging the back of my head lightly against a column. Varus placed his hand behind my neck to stop me. He pointed up. We were in a compact structural cavity crammed with thick columns and beams transferring weight down to the buried skyscraper. The Cogents all had to crouch to fit under the low ceiling.

"Thermals spot three officers in the hangar above," one of the Cogents whispered. "Communications signal indicates they belong to Red Wing Company."

"That's all Kale has with him?" I asked.

"They rent this entire wing," Varus said. "We are beneath the hangar adjacent to Kale Trass's."

"Mobile fusion cutter ready," said a female Cogent.

A small, gun-shaped device in her hand ignited, and she began to trace the white-hot tip across the ceiling. Sparks shot out as the structural alloy melted away. When the circle was complete, Varus positioned himself in the center and raised his hands against the loosened slab. Three others formed a circle around him, facing outward.

"Dislodging in three... two... one." Varus finished counting down, then his thick Earther legs stretched, and his biceps bulged. He freed the portion of the floor and propped it upward. The Cogents around him stood in sync, all together firing three calculated shots from silenced pulse pistols through the reveal. I didn't hear screams, only the gentle thud of three bodies collapsing in the hangar above.

"The path is clear, Malcolm Graves." Varus slid the slab aside, and he and the other Cogents leaped through the opening with ease. Their footsteps were as light as rats' scampering beneath the floorboards of Earth's shantytowns, no matter what world they appeared to have grown up on. I hauled myself through clumsily, arms shaking even harder as they supported my weight. I spilled out across the floor, the blinding lights on a faraway ceiling appearing to swirl about my vision as I rolled over. They were dizzying...

"I'm coming, Aria," I groaned.

I blinked away the brightness and forced myself to my feet. Lying down, even for a moment, was an awful idea considering how tired I was. I had to keep up with the Cogents. If they got in that hangar without me and started shooting... "No prejudice," were the specific words Luxarn used.

Varus and the others were already against the wall of Kale's hangar, attaching some manner of explosive to it. The bodies of the Red Wing officers were scattered about, and in the center of the hangar sat a lone ship. They had been unloading crates filled with unmarked bags of foundry salts. The drug originated in the old factories on Titan, and the bags weren't tagged because they weren't the byproduct of some corps trying to make an extra buck; it was poison given away by Kale Trass for nothing. Apparently, the self-proclaimed prideful and loyal Red Wing Company had taken the bait. Free credits explained their vested interest in keeping Kale Trass in power for as long as possible.

Good, I told myself. *Focus on the details, Malcolm. Stay awake.* There were some parts of being a collector I couldn't turn off. Seeing the world for what it really was happened to be one of them.

"Explosive prepared," Varus said, and it didn't take me long to realize he was addressing me specifically. Cogents had a way of fixing their eye lenses upon their target of conversation. "The thermal readings indicate the presence of at least fifty individuals."

"Can you tell which one is Kale?" I asked.

"Heat interference from their ship's engine is making it impossible to determine the exact number or specifics. Do you have a recommended attack strategy?"

"Isn't that what you people were trained to come up with?"

Varus leaned in, the shutters in his eye-lens gyrating as he fixated on me. "Yes, however, you have been involved in the execution of one hundred thirty-two violent criminals, as well as the arrest of an unspecified number of others. Your recommendation will be valued."

I swallowed hard as my fingers grazed the grip of my pulse pistol. I'd never counted before. One hundred thirty-two confirmed lives had been claimed by it over thirty years, and that wasn't including any collateral.

"Mr. Graves, the exchange is commencing," Varus interrupted my ruminations. "Your recommendation?"

"One hundred thirty-two," I muttered.

"Confirmed."

I couldn't remember the names of more than a handful. And of the faces... only the last one it punished. Zhaff's. Soon to be my one-hundred-thirty-third confirmed kill when Luxarn stomached pulling the plug. I could remember his face; it was right in front of me, every second of every day. I knew it so well that while everybody else would've claimed he always wore the exact same expressions as the six Cogents standing before me, I could point out all his quirks. The way his eyebrow twitched ever so slightly when I said something that didn't compute for him. The subtle tug at the corner of his lips when he learned how to tell a joke.

"What's one more, huh?" I said softly.

"One hundred thirty-three."

I released a somber chuckle. Zhaff would've responded the same way.

"My advice," I began, "is to shoot at Kale the way you shot at me back on Undina. Don't focus on anybody else. They'll be confused enough when we blow through. Get a clear shot, put one between Kale's eyes, and get out." Getting their attention away from Aria and Venta was my number one concern if I wanted an opening to grab her.

"Titanborn armor is dense. The proximity required for a confirmed fatal shot through his helmet is within ten meters."

"Well, you lot don't care about dying, do you?" He answered with silence, and that confounding blank stare Zhaff had been so proficient with.

While I waited for them, I removed the hand-terminal Varus had given me and allowed me to keep, since apparently, I was the leader of this mission. I pulled up Luxarn's information and drafted a message. The last interaction I ever planned to have with the man.

YOU'RE WELCOME, SIR.
    —MALCOLM

I took a deep breath and sent it, then grinned as I stowed the device. Simple, to the point, and ideally suited to our mostly impersonal relationship.

My wrinkled hand then slowly wrapped the grip of my pistol, the only true friend I'd ever known. My index finger slipped through the trigger guard as it had so many times before. Two-point-four pounds of pressure—that was the difference between life and death for the one hundred thirty-two poor souls who'd wound up on the wrong side of the barrel.

I drew it, ducked behind a nearby container, and covered my ears. It was time to help finish what Zhaff and I had started when we met back on Earth. Time to bring an end to the Children of Titan once and for all and avenge what the boy-king Kale had done to Pervenio Corp. That would make Luxarn and me even for the bullet I'd put in Zhaff. A life for a life, both times with my daughter's hanging in the balance.

"Blow it," I told Varus.

A second later, the contained blast peeled open a portion of the dense wall as if it were made of paper ribbons. My ears rang as I bounded through the breach alongside the Cogents. My gun was up, but I had no eye lens to help me see through the smoke. All I could distinguish was blurs of color and flashing muzzles.

I aimed from side to side as I pressed forward, panting, trying to keep up with my Cogent entourage. When I realized how futile that was, I lowered my pistol and rushed through the fog on my own path. The head of a Venta officer exploded as I took cover behind a shipping container. Another turned and spotted me, but I kicked him in the chest with the one part of my body that couldn't get tired. The force of my synthetic leg sent him flying, and once outside of cover, his body was ripped to shreds in the crossfire.

I peeked around the container.

Thirty years and I'd never seen employees of Earth's three biggest corporations open fire in the same room. Gunmen took cover wherever they could find it. The Red Wing officers by the gate seemed confused about who to shoot at, but that didn't stop most of them from doing so. The Venta Co. men unloaded in both directions, peppering fighters in white and red with bullets. And from the shadow of their ship, the Titanborn soldiers shot at anything that moved.

"Focus on the Cogents!" a woman taking cover somewhere near Kale shouted. He and the Titanborn soldiers who had survived the initial onslaught were tucked behind their ship's loading ramp.

"Aria!" I heard Kale roar after a few more seconds of fighting.

I followed the direction of his voice and located Aria. She'd made an attempt to escape that Venta collector I'd gotten friendly with the past two days. He tackled her out in the open. Nobody fired at them. The Cogents were wholly focused on eliminating Kale, and neither the Titanborn nor Venta officers wanted to risk killing one of their own.

The collector crawled on top of her and started pounding her face. My heart thumped so fast that my chest stung. I leaned around the corner and took aim. They were barely ten meters away—a shot I'd made plenty of times in my life—but all my attempts at focusing had my old eyes seeing two of him. I edged farther out of cover. Aria pushed back the collector's throat to slow his punches, groping with the other hand for the pulse pistol dangling from a fallen officer's hip.

Pull the trigger, Malcolm! I told myself. I had the vantage now, and I had him lined up in my sights. There was no chance I could miss. But I couldn't pull the trigger. My hand cramped. It felt freezing cold, like I was back on Titan aiming at Zhaff.

Blood suddenly spiraled out of the collector's back. I glanced down, wondering if I'd fired without realizing, but my fingers remained stuck. Aria grasped the nearby pistol as the collector lurched from that first shot, and buried two more slugs in his stomach. A female Titanborn promptly slid next to them, pulled Aria out from under the Earther, and emptied a pulse rifle clip into the Venta ranks as they ran in my direction.

I fell back behind the shipping container, winded. I smacked myself in the head to try and wake my hand up when the Titanborn woman and Aria dove around the same shipping container, backs against the side facing the Venta officers for some reason. They didn't notice me just around the corner. All I had to do was grab Aria, and we could book it out the way I'd come in before any of the Cogents knew the difference.

I peered around the container to see where my companions were. They were completely focused on Kale like I'd told them to be. The King of Titan used his men like a meat shield, or rather, they flocked to him as the Cogents tore into what remained of his people. Varus shot one through the chest, and another leaped in front of Kale. Bullets stung the loyal soul like a swarm of angry mutated hornets.

"Now, Kale!" the Titanborn woman with Aria screamed.

Kale's ship's impulse drive sparked, blooming with a blue light so bright my eyes immediately watered. The heat it expelled made the parts of my skin that were exposed start to blister. Varus and the Cogents paused. His lips were drawn into a pin-straight line, calm, even amid a firefight. The inner machinations of his eye lens whirled, the yellow glass reflecting the engine's star-like radiance.

"Zhaff!" I called out without thinking, my voice hoarse from lack of sleep.

He turned to face me, and then the impulse drives ignited. A tail of bluish plasma and distortion whipped across the center of the hangar. Varus and the Cogents were caught in the worst of it, the skin and muscle literally vaporized off their bones. Shock threw me to the ground just in time to avoid the same fate. I scrambled around the shipping container to the side Aria was on, jumped in front of her, and pinned our bodies so that only my synthetic leg was touching the boiling surface. It absorbed all the heat, and for the first time since it was installed, I felt the pain.

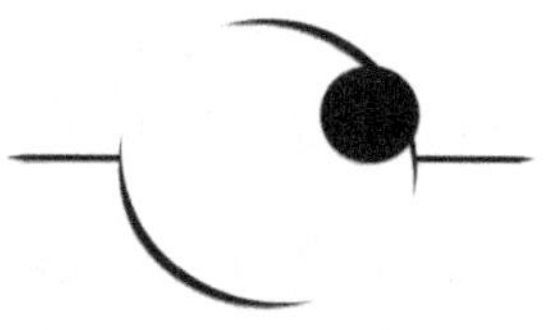

NINETEEN

KALE

"Focus on the Cogents!" Rin shouted.

I stuck my pulse rifle around the ramp of the *Cora* and fired blindly. Pervenio Corp Cogents bore down on our position from the right, with the Venta officers basically everywhere else. The only reason we weren't surrounded yet was because Captain Barnes kept his word, deciding shortly after the firefight commenced to try and keep us alive. I knew Aria was holed up somewhere out there because the last thing I saw before Gareth forced me to safety was Madame Venta's sons do the same to her.

One of my men leaned out from a landing support, but the Cogents popped him in the head. Their push was unremitting. One inch out of cover and their attention was already there, as if they could predict our movements.

"Basaam and his clan-sister are safely on board and in their sleep pods!" Rin hollered to me. "We can't survive this. Toast them now, Kale!"

"She's still out there!" I answered.

I peered around the ramp with one eye. Past a wall of Cogents marching at us like yellow-eyed cyclops all in black, I caught a quick glimpse of Aria. She now lay out in front of the fray, with a Venta collector hunched over and punching her.

"Aria!" I screamed at the top of my lungs. Gareth jerked me back to safety, bullets whizzing by my ear.

"Gareth, cover me!" Rin said. "I'll get her." The *Cora*'s ramp rumbled as she bounded down from the cargo bay into the firefight.

Gareth held me back with one hand while with the other giving the Cogents as much as they could handle. A bullet nipped him in his gun arm, sending his pulse rifle flying and knocking him off his feet. I grabbed him by the shoulders and helped him scramble back to shelter.

"My lord!" one of my guards yelled. "They're moving to flank us."

Off to my right, the Titanborn who'd spoken was peppered with holes as the Cogents got an angle on him. Soon they'd gain a favorable position on us as well. There was nowhere to run. Venta Co. had the other side of the *Cora* completely contained.

I tapped my armor, frantically searching for the switch to activate my helmet com-link to the *Cora*'s command deck. "Prepare to ignite engines," I stammered once I found it. "Full pow—" Bullets sparked on the floor less than a meter away.

My clip was low, but I managed to hit the shooter in the leg. Another yellow eye lens quickly appeared as my gun clicked empty. Gareth tried to pull himself in between us but was too slow. Another of my guards leaped in front of us instead, bullets pummeling him.

"Now!" Rin's voice echoed over the rattle of gunfire.

Gareth grabbed our savior's dancing corpse and used it as a shield while he fired upon the Cogents.

"Do it!" I barked over my com-link.

I drew Gareth back behind the ramp right as a dazzling tail of blue lashed across the hangar. The heat it emanated made my face feel like it was on fire, but together we watched. The Cogents were nearest, and their bodies vanished in the brightness. Venta men, Red Wing men... Anyone who wasn't behind dense enough cover was reduced to ashes. Even the surfaces of the shipping containers facing us melted like hot wax.

It only lasted for a few seconds, but by the time the engines cooled, groans supplanted the shooting. The remaining heat was grueling, even with my suit on. Gareth and I had to use each other to support our wobbling legs. I glanced over, noticing the blood oozing out of two bullet holes in his armor as he released the pitiful whimper his tongueless mouth allowed him to.

"Someone..." I smacked my lips. Despite my sealed visor, just opening my mouth made me feel like I was swallowing fire. "Someone help him!"

One of my men staggered over to us, but Gareth shoved him away. Gareth spat a glob of blood into the bottom of his helmet and pounded his fist on his abdomen. Red trickled through a gash in his armor there, the stream merging with the one already running down the length of his arm from a second hole in his left shoulder.

"*I'll be fine,*" he signed. "*They didn't go in deep. What are your orders?*"

I regarded him. His protruding brow constantly accentuated his grim demeanor; he appeared like the demons the Church of the Three Messiahs claimed we were. Blood and filth sullied his pale spartan features, coating the deep wrinkles a man from Titan's low g should never bear, thanks to working in Saturn's atmosphere. The two bullets he took were meant for me, and I knew that so long as he could walk, he'd keep fighting. My loyal guardian. The man who was the first to truly make me believe that I could lead anything.

I offered him a nod and turned to face the rest of the hangar. A broiling haze hung on the air, as if we were trapped on

Mercury. Distortion from the ion stream and a layer of radiation so copious my body would start devouring itself from the inside out if I didn't inject anti-rads soon. Even my suit wouldn't be enough to hold it at bay for too long, and all Aria had on was a dress. I needed to get her on board the *Cora* quickly.

"Kill Venta," I muttered to Gareth and the surviving Titanborn. "Then get our dead onto the ship. We're all going home."

They slogged through oppressive heat, stepping over shadows scorched into the floor... all that remained of the Cogents and anyone else exposed directly. Karl crawled from behind cover, his leg mangled beyond repair, body singed merely from touching anything in the ion stream's path.

"You Ringer filth," he moaned. Gareth raised his rifle with one arm and splattered the brains of Venta Co. royalty all over the burnished floor.

While he handled the other survivors, I went to search for Aria and Rin. My aunt had plotted ahead of time which container to get behind in the event Venta forced our hands. It was one we'd stuffed with spare parts to help resist the heat. The heat had still probably caused her and Aria to pass out. As I made my way toward it, Captain Barnes and a few Red Wing officers emerged from the opposite side of the hangar where the engine's blaze was weakest. The entry gate was welded shut to seal them in, the wall around it charred along with every security feed.

"Mr. Trass! Are you okay?" Barnes rasped.

Gareth glanced back at me, his eyes asking for permission to open fire. I shook my head, then lumbered toward the captain. Every step felt like I was wading through water. "You kept your word!" I hollered back to him.

"We always do." He winced as Gareth shot a Venta collector in the back who reached for a half-liquefied firearm. "What in Earth's name happened?"

"Luxarn Pervenio's last failed attempt on my life."

"Kale," someone whispered from the other side of the shipping container Rin was supposed to be behind.

I rushed around it to discover her and Aria there as expected, only they weren't alone. An Earther wearing a grimy duster hid behind my aunt with his pistol aimed at her head. His other hand wrapped tightly around Aria's arm. All three of their faces were flushed from the heat.

"It's a pleasure to finally make your acquaintance, Kale Drayton," the man said. The grit in his voice spoke of booze and a lifetime's worth of scuffles. He surely wasn't a Cogent. None of his clothing was marked with the Pervenio emblem. His face, mottled by furrows and faded scars, hid under the shadow of carelessly tousled gray hair. An unkempt salt-and-pepper beard wrapped his square jawline like he'd forgotten to shave for months.

I couldn't place why, but I recognized him from somewhere. Nobody outside of Darien would've known my mother's surname, Drayton, which I went by for most of my life. I figured maybe he was a former Pervenio officer I'd seen around the city growing up. He had the look of one. His hazel eyes were weary, like he'd already seen everything the world had to offer yet couldn't keep himself from seeking more.

"Just put a bullet in him," Rin gargled.

"Kale, listen to me," Aria implored. "He's not going to shoot anybody." That same rattled expression she wore around Madame Venta contorted her face.

"Listen to her," the old man said. "Nobody has to die."

"Then drop the weapon," I demanded. Gareth appeared by my side so fast it was like he'd teleported. The old man's eyes widened as he saw him.

"You're that illegitimate from the Twilight Sun, aren't you? Clever, kid. You've been planning this from the start, not because of the summit. Used that dumb fuck Trevor to get to Basaam, I'll bet."

I glanced at Gareth. He shrugged his shoulders. "How did you know that?" I asked.

"A hunch. Been doing this for a long time, Drayton."

"Stop calling me that."

"I suggest you listen to him," Captain Barnes said as he caught up with us. "You are under arrest for violating an official USF contract of suspended hostilities."

"Red Wing," the man scoffed. "Why don't you run along and let the adults handle this."

"Why you!" Barnes raised his gun, but I lowered the barrel. Gareth took my cue and forcefully shoved him aside so that he wouldn't intervene.

"What do you want?" I questioned.

"I want to back out of here alive," the old man said.

"Nobody is stopping you."

He smirked, and not like Madame Venta did when she wanted to act like she was in control. There was a blitheness to it, the kind of expression that said he hadn't been truly afraid of anything in a long time and he wasn't going to start now.

"I'll make this simple, Drayton—" he began.

"I said stop calling me that!" I interrupted.

"Ashamed of your mother? I can't say I blame you, kid. I was about your age when I left my clan-family and chose a name of my own. Nothing as fanciful as Trass, but, you know, different strokes."

"Stop stalling." I sidled forward, my fingers fidgeting around the trigger of my gun, desperate to put down another Earther who spoke at me like I was nothing. He took a healthy stride back, dragging Rin and Aria with him.

"Please," Aria urged me. "Stay calm."

"Just shoot him already," Rin croaked.

"I've got a feeling we've both seen enough of that today," the old man said. He coughed, causing his grip on Rin to loosen for a second. I took a hard step toward him, but he recovered and pressed the barrel of his pistol hard into her temple. Aria raised a hand to keep me back.

"Radiation. Every second you waste, your insides corrode a little more," I said. I gestured toward the whole of the hangar, still rife with contamination.

"It can't do a better job than whiskey."

I drew a deep, grating breath. "I'm going to ask again. What do you want?"

"Aria. She's walking out of here, straight to treatment and away from you. You can kill me if it makes you feel better, but she walks."

"In exchange for what?" Aria's brow furrowed at my query, though I couldn't tell if she was insulted or relieved. A chance to escape her responsibilities, what I wouldn't have given for that.

The old man motioned to Rin. "She lives."

"Rin would gladly give her life, and you'll be dead before she hits the floor," I said. "You can do better."

"I thought you people didn't like striking deals with Earthers?" Uncertainty momentarily rippled across his face. He was stalling... human after all.

"But you're different than the others, aren't you? You seem equally as tired of their rotten deals as I am."

"I can..." He searched the room, pausing on the molten remnants of a Cogent eye lens that had somehow remained intact enough to identify. "I was a Pervenio collector for three decades. That comes with certain skills. Certain privileges."

"He's lying, Kale," Rin said. "Just finish him. You have to get out of here."

Now his staunch demeanor was starting to make sense. This

was what the collectors of offworlder legend were supposed to be like. Not that rat Trevor Cross.

Gareth nudged me in the side. *"He's not lying,"* he signed. *"He and Trevor were arguing when I took him. His retirement came up."*

"And how does a retired collector help me?" I asked.

"How do you want it to?" he replied. "I know Luxarn Pervenio. How his mind works."

"Even where he hides?"

The Collector hesitated at first, then nodded ruefully. "I know where he shits. You let Aria go free of all this trouble, and my gun is yours. Anything you need." He stared at Aria with the same blend of sorrow and tenderness that my mother had when I used to visit her behind the divider of the Darien Quarantine. Of all the riddles of Aria's past, there was no denying one—this mysterious old man cared for her deeply.

"Don't do this for me, Dad!" Aria couldn't cover her mouth fast enough.

Hearing the title drew everyone's attention and provided Rin the opening she needed to break free. Her elbow smashed into the former collector's stomach. As he reeled, she twisted his arm until his pulse pistol popped out of his hand. Before any of us knew it, she had his own gun aimed back at him. She would've pulled the trigger too if Aria hadn't leaped between them.

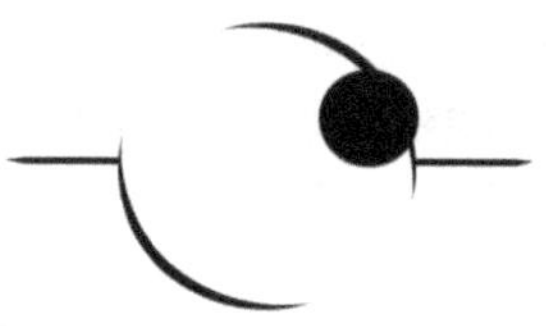

TWENTY

MALCOLM

I stood behind her, under the sights of yet another Titanborn who'd ripped a gun out of my hands. First on Earth when Zhaff was once forced to save me, then on Titan a number of times, now here. It was beginning to become a trend. If only I'd taken the time to nap instead of pointlessly gallivanting around Old Dome to try and find a good reason why Wai was dead when there was none. Then maybe I would've had my wits enough about me to get Aria out without starting a standoff with the adolescent king of Titan and his disfigured guard dog.

"A Pervenio collector?" the one Kale referred to as Rin said, her rage palpable. "You've been working with them the whole time!"

"I'm not!" Aria protested. "I swear I was going to tell you, Kale." She coughed once, then started to dry retch. I had to grab her to keep her upright. Kale and the other Titanborn wore airtight armor and helmets, but Aria and I weren't so fortunate. Radiation poisoning was a bitch. I recalled dealing with a bad bout of it, a decade ago back on an asteroid colony when a reactor overloaded. This was worse. It hurt all over just supporting Aria's weight, and she wasn't even born on Earth. My insides felt like they were fighting to squeeze through my pores.

"Working with me?" I released a weak chuckle. This was another fine mess I'd gotten her into. "I could hardly get her to talk to me." I looked past Rin and straight at Kale. He was in shock, his gun elevated but aimed at nothing. "Malcolm Graves. That's my name. Have you ever heard her use it? It's because I abandoned her on Mars, and I didn't look back. She was better off without me."

"Well, you're here now," Rin growled.

"A dying father come to rectify his sins, that's all," I said. "You think I wanted her working with you people? Under Luxarn Pervenio's lens? No, I came to get her out because Earth knows I'm the reason she went running into the arms of suicidal Ringers."

A bang at the entry reverberated across the hangar. The door was partially welded shut from their ship's impulse drive ignition, but it wouldn't hold long. "This property belongs to Madame Venta!" an officer outside shouted. "Open up, or we will be required to use force!"

"Venta Co. is here," a Red Wing captain, who Kale somehow had working for him, announced. "Mr. Trass, you must leave immediately."

"I'm aware," Kale said.

"We may still need Aria, but let me put a bullet in this Pervenio scum," Rin said.

Kale's dusky eyes darted between us and the continued banging at the gate.

"I know I should've told you," Aria pled. "From now on, I'll tell you everything. Just please, let him go. He's out of the business. He has nothing to do with any of this." Now she was the one trying to help me. Maybe we really were starting to get along better.

"Is this who you desperately needed to go see?" Kale questioned her. "Your illegitimate father? I don't care if he's out; he's still Pervenio."

"I swear, I didn't even know he was still alive until today."

"C'mon, Kale," Rin said. I could feel the familiar barrel of my pistol rustling through my hair. "It's time."

"Undina Mining facility," I said.

"What?" Kale said.

"That's where Luxarn Pervenio is holed up."

"Look how loyal the dog is," Rin spat.

I rolled my shoulders. It was tough being overly loyal to a man who drained my credit account out of spite after thirty years of doing whatever he asked, but that wasn't what made me say it. Undina was the closest asteroid to Earth in the system, pulled into its orbit for ease of mining years ago when Pervenio Corp was building a Departure Ark and still had influence. It also happened to house what was left of the Cogent Initiative. An attempt at breaking in to get to him was suicide. If I couldn't kill the boy-king and free Sol from all the trouble he was causing, then maybe he'd chase the man they held responsible for subjugating Titan and get himself killed for me.

"Now you know," I said. "Let us leave together. I promise, you won't ever see us again. Or better yet, take me if that'll make you feel better and let Aria go. The summit is over, so you can stop pretending to want peace. She'll disappear. She may be telling you the truth, but she's not one of you. Never will be."

"That's for damn certain," Rin added.

Sparks flew by the entry gate as the Venta Co. officers outside got to work cutting through. Kale averted his gaze from us and grabbed the Red Wing captain by the arm. I studied Rin as he did. If I wanted to make a move on her, now was the time to do it. Venta had them distracted, and Kale was clearly stalling to sort out his feelings.

"Captain, you said your board wished to remunerate us?" he asked.

"They do," the Red Wing man replied.

"Make contact, then. Venta Co. is conspiring with their old rivals to kill me. I fear we won't escape the planet's gravity well without support. Ask them to scramble fighters to ensure Madame Venta doesn't shoot us down. Do that, and we'll be even for all of this."

"Sir... that is a direct act of hostility. The board—"

"This is a third attempt on my life here! If your board denies us, I will see it as proof that your company is also involved, and all shipments will stop. Get it done, Captain."

The hole in the gate was nearly cut. After taking a few seconds to think things through, the captain wisely drew his hand-terminal to make the call while leading his remaining officers toward the entry.

"We can't waste any more time, Kale," Rin said harshly. "Our lives are in the hands of Earthers now, thanks to our lovely ambassador."

"Listen to her, kid," I said. "Just give the word, and we're out of your hair for good. Easy."

A deafening bang preceded the hangar gate falling inward. A line of Venta Co. officers appeared on the other side. The Red Wing captain and what little remained of his unit stood their ground and refused the orders to step aside. Kale's surviving guards swarmed us to form a semicircle in front of their leader. The Ringer from the Twilight Sun signed something to him, still upright despite an ample amount of blood dripping from his shoulder and stomach that nobody seemed to be concerned about.

Kale nodded. "Unfortunately for you, I still need her," he said to me, finally, his voice hoarse. "Rin, do—"

"Please!" Aria urged. "What would you do to have a second chance with the father who left you behind?"

Kale's stony curtain slipped fully from its hooks. For all his projected bravado, he appeared completely overwhelmed. Every bit the inexperienced young man playing leader that he was. Aria was smart enough to see it, appealing to one sentiment every son or daughter with an estranged parent could understand no matter what world they were born on. It only pained me knowing she'd learned that lesson from me.

"Take him with us onto the *Cora*, Rin," Kale decided. He clutched Aria's hand, his glare hardening again as he regarded her. "We can use him. For better or worse, he's family now."

Somehow, being referred to as family with the king of the Ringers wasn't the strangest thing about what he said. The *Cora?* I couldn't help but feel like the name of Kale's surprisingly advanced ship meant something to me.

"More Earther stowaways," Rin grumbled. She shoved my pistol against my spine and pushed me toward the ship. "Let's go, Collector. One wrong move and you'll spend your days on Titan drinking through a straw."

She smacked me in the back of the neck with my own gun before I could come up with a witty response and had me seeing stars. I stumbled forward, and when my vision cleared, I saw Aria with Kale and realized how badly I'd misinterpreted things. She wasn't purely an ambassador or a friend. Just like the last time Aria and I were on Mars together, some six or seven years back, I'd come between her and a lover. They exchanged an unmistakable look— the kind that could only be swapped between two people who'd shared a bed—before they and the rest of Kale's escort followed us.

Stupid old man, I cursed myself. I'd played my hand all

wrong in thinking Kale only needed my daughter to arrange this summit because she wasn't a Ringer. Even worse, I'd already handed him my best card by revealing where Luxarn was. Now I remembered why retiring seemed like the best plan for me back on Undina. Ever since Zhaff, I was covered in rust that I couldn't shake.

A gunshot echoed.

The Red Wing captain toppled over. The Venta Co. officers finally realized Kale was exposed. They mowed down the rest of the Red Wing men, and we were next. Kale's guards opened fire as they grabbed their king and rushed him into his ship.

"Move! Onto the *Cora!*" Rin barked.

Again, that name clung to my thoughts like a parasite and froze all my other functions, until Rin pushed me up the ramp as hard as she could. She then turned to help Kale and Aria up. Bullets clanged and hissed against the ship's hull, a few buzzing into the cargo bay, which was basically empty minus a line of Ringer bodies. I quickly counted at least five of them. Kale's surviving guards formed a wall at the entry while the ramp rose, returning fire as it sealed with a snap and hiss. One of the guards slumped to his knees face-first against it, a thick trail of blood snaking down the shiny surface. Dead.

"Everyone to the cockpit!" Kale ordered. "It's time to go."

The mute Ringer from the Twilight Sun signed something in my direction. His bleeding had stopped, but his breathing was beleaguered.

"No, Gareth," Kale said. "I want your eyes on him at all times."

Rin passed me off to him, and we all set off down the ship's winding corridors. It didn't take more than a few steps in to realize that I was in a former Pervenio vessel. The clean lines, sleek surfaces, and top-end materials were evidence enough of that. Aria was up ahead with Kale, and I struggled to catch a glimpse of her with Rin and the other Ringers in between.

"I'm flying," Rin said once we reached the spacious trapezoidal cockpit. An injured Ringer posted at the controls limped out of the way.

Flying ships had never been my specialty, but even after a lifetime around Pervenio equipment, that cockpit remained alien. Glittering holographic screens and informational readouts blinked from all over. The best of technology, along every wall and under the sweeping viewport. At first, I'd figured this was merely a stolen gas harvester, but it was clear Kale had taken something valuable to my former employer—a prototype ship the likes of which Sol had never seen.

Rin reached for one of the two navigation chairs nearest the viewport, but Kale towed her back. "Aria's flying."

"Her?" Rin said.

"Now isn't the time," Kale said, a harsh edge to his tone. "She's our best pilot."

"She's the whole reason we're in this mess."

"Would you two stop it already!" Aria snapped. She covered her mouth to suppress a racking fit of coughs, which must have been contagious because I did the same. The radiation sickness was getting worse.

"She's sick," Rin said. "She needs treatment, right now. You know why."

"If we don't make it off, it won't matter!" Aria said. "There are too many people on this ship I care about to let you fly. I'll last." Aria didn't bother waiting for Rin to move. She squeezed around her and into the chair.

"Fine," Rin grumbled. "I'll shoot."

She took the copilot seat next to Aria, and then I had the pleasure of seeing my daughter prepare for launch. Despite how nauseated she appeared, her hands flew across the controls, up and down, her chair swiveling from side to side. It was nothing I'd taught her. Just watching was exhausting.

The mute Ringer, Gareth, took me and shoved me into one of the chairs lining the back wall of the room. Quick movements rekindled my queasiness as my innards continued their war with each other. He sat beside me and pointed a pulse pistol at my ribcage. He wheezed even louder than I was. The penetrations in his suit left him compromised, and our old bodies were more susceptible to radiation poison than the others'. It was one type of sickness being born on Earth couldn't help with. I didn't utter a word.

He reached into my pocket and removed the hand-terminal Varus had given me. A Pervenio logo was stamped on the center of the screensaver. I'd been hoping that in the chaos they'd forget about it and I could send Luxarn our location the moment I got a chance. Gareth tapped Kale, handed it to him, and signed him something.

"Thank you, Gareth," Kale said. He stowed it and took his seat in the captain's chair, positioned behind and between Rin's and Aria's. "Aria, is everything ready?"

My daughter struck a few keys, then glanced back over her shoulder. Her cheeks were a subtle shade of green. She made eye contact with me and offered the slightest nod imaginable and a frail smile; something to tell me that I hadn't failed her. I would've returned the expression if my stomach wasn't so unsettled.

"All systems go," she said. She ran her hand across a holographic screen, and suddenly the back of both my chair and headrest went slack. Restraints popped out over my legs, chest, and forehead as the chair molded to the cambers of my body. It felt like the entire back half of me was submerged in warm goo. The same happened to everybody, only Gareth somehow continued to dig his pistol into my side.

"Open this place up, Rin," Kale commanded.

"*Cora*, armed," Rin said. "G-stims, everyone." While everybody but me injected a stim into their necks, Rin looked to Aria. "Pressure's going to give us a jolt. Think you can handle it?"

Aria ground her teeth, wearing a pained expression as she swallowed back what I assumed was bile. "Just shoot."

The *Cora*, I realized. Even my exhausted, poisoned mind couldn't forget that name because the girl it belonged to reminded me so much of Aria. It was the name of a young, mixed-blood Ringer woman I'd interrogated in relation to the attack on the gas harvester *Piccolo*, which claimed the lives of near twenty Earthers. Cora was a member of the crew during the attack, same as Kale, but when the latter disappeared, he was blamed for the attack by Director Sodervall. Cora refused to believe Kale had anything to do with it, thanks to some damn obvious feelings. Only, you didn't name ships after someone who was still alive.

What the hell had Director Sodervall done after I left her alive and headed for medical? The greatest revolution in the post-Meteorite era... could it all really be over a girl?

The ship lurched as missiles lanced out from beneath its wings. The wall of the hangar erupted in a plume of swirling smoke and flame that was swiftly extinguished by Mars's lack of oxygen. The rapid pressure change caused the ship to jolt, and then the impulse drives kicked in, and we shot forward through the breach.

If it weren't for my seat's malleable headrest, my neck would've snapped in two. Even still, the pressure exerted on my entire body was excruciating. It felt like the fattest Earther imaginable was sitting on my chest, driving his thumbs into my eyes harder and harder. The air grew thick, oxygen pumping in through the forward recyclers at elevated rates to keep the pilot and navigators conscious through the worst of it.

Mars's rusty sky filled the viewport. Anti-air fire flashed like lightning all around us as the Venta Co. defenses attempted to shoot us down. Aria whipped the *Cora* this way and that to avoid them. I could see the grimace pulling at her cheeks, even from my vantage behind her. No amateur would be able to focus under such strenuous conditions, but all Venta's attempts to stymie us sailed by harmlessly.

I sat in awe of my daughter. Her chest was restrained, but her arms masterfully worked the controls. The ship released flares and who knows what other evasive tech it was loaded with as she twirled. It wasn't even until a flock of blue-colored fighters appeared on the horizon that she even broke a sweat.

"Venta?" Kale asked.

"Seven, heading straight at us!" Aria replied. The end of her sentence trailed off as she dipped us hard to the left under the blast of an anti-air round. "Should I engage?"

"Let's see what this thing is capable of."

"My pleasure," Rin muttered. She worked her targeting array and unleashed a barrage of ordnance. Missiles, plasma torpedoes, high-caliber flak; enough to make Venta think twice. Aria held a straight course until the volley was released, then dropped into a spiral. I covered my mouth as the viewport spun.

The fighters fanned apart and returned fire. The *Cora* shuddered, missiles tearing into its shell. The screens and consoles in front of Aria chirped as readouts transmitted damage reports. As Aria leveled us out, one of the Ringers in the hold behind us puked so loudly, I could hear it over the clamor of exploding torpedoes outside.

"Three fighters down!" Aria shouted. "Ablative plating at 73 percent. No critical damage."

"They're looping back around," Rin said. "More fighters scrambling from the Little Peru Colony as well."

"We won't survive too many straight-on assaults like that."

"You going to take them all on, Trass?" I grated. "Take my daughter down with you?"

Gareth punched me in the rib with his pistol. I was surprised by how weak the blow felt, considering the powered armor he wore, although my whole body was so racked with pain that anything short of a bullet through the brain wouldn't faze me.

"We won't have to," Kale sneered.

"Intercepting coms with Madame Venta," Aria said. "We're being hooked in." She flicked a switch, and the message came through loud enough for everyone to hear.

"Madame Jamaru Venta, this is Galora Martinez, director of security for Red Wing Company on Mars. You are attacking a transport vehicle under our protection. If you do not retreat, we will be forced to engage."

"Oh, don't you fucking do this, Galora," Madame Venta responded. I'd only ever heard her speak over news feeds, but the ire in her tone was enough to give even me a shiver. "That vessel is harboring known criminals."

"Kale Trass and his followers have yet to be formally convicted of violating any colonial statutes. As inhabitants of greater Sol, they engaged in a contract with Red Wing Company to provide secure transit to and from Titan."

"I'm aware of the deal you made."

"Then you understand that the Red Wing Board has agreed it cannot allow you to infringe upon our agreement."

"Now isn't the time to flex your muscle, Galora. Are you really going to start a war with me over a band of terrorists?"

"We uphold all contracts to the best of our abilities."

"Do you know who they have on that ship? They abducted Basaam Venta. They killed my sons!"

"Basaam Venta remains a missing person with unconfirmed whereabouts. The only thing that we *can* confirm is that your employees stormed a private hangar chartered by us and caused the deaths of no less than seven Red Wing officers as well as an unknown number of Kale Trass's escort. You will be lucky to avoid USF sanctions."

Silence. Only the sounds of a ship's engine pushed to its limits, and the wheezing of the mute Ringer beside me met my ears. Mars' thin atmosphere gradually peeled away, like a giant was dropping a black canvas over us. The faint stars glittered like diamonds and grew brighter.

"When this lunatic kills more people," Madame Venta said, finally, "I want you and your damn board to remember that we could have ended it here." Her communications cut out.

"We have upheld our end of the agreement and will be expecting payment on schedule," Red Wing Director Galora addressed the *Cora*'s cockpit directly after a brief silence. "Red Wing hopes that despite unforeseen complications during your visit, our show of support will encourage you to continue the good faith export of certain goods exclusively to us. Our reach, however, extends only so far. May I suggest plotting a course to Titan that steers as far from Jupiter's orbit as possible. Safe journey, Kale Trass, and please, give your ambassador our best regards for instituting this contract."

"All Venta fighters are pulling back!" Aria said.

Aria turned down the throttle as we broke Mars's gravity well and were embraced by the oppressive blackness of space. The pressure exerted on every inch of my body waned, and for the first time since we took off, I felt like I could breathe again, at least until opening my mouth too wide almost made me heave.

Mars' moon Phobos hovered off to the right, speckled with lights and a host of Venta cruisers flocking the docking station on its surface. As agreed upon between Venta and Red Wing Company, none followed us or fired. Things really were out of whack with Pervenio Corp so weak. Luxarn, or rather the world-eating Luxarn I knew from before the Ring fell, would have never allowed himself to be played like Madame Venta was.

"Damn mudstompers can't get out of each other's way," Rin sneered.

"You do realize it was a mudstomper who just saved us," I said. I expected Gareth to try to quiet me with another forceful nudge, but none came.

"And where were they when we stood before the Assembly?" Kale retorted. "Barely a whimper of support."

"Gareth, keep him quiet," Rin ordered.

"You have a lot to learn about corporate politics, kid," I said. "Under-the-table drug trafficking doesn't net you public backing. It nets you credits."

Aria loosened her restraints and turned to join the argument, but the moment our gazes met, her eyes went wide in horror. The weight of Gareth's arm slumped into me, and his pistol drifted weightlessly across the cockpit. Blood followed it, leaking steadily in perfect scarlet droplets out of his mouth, shoulder, and stomach. The pressure of launch must have started the bleeding up again. His eyelids were three-quarters closed, slits of white in the reveals. If there was even the slightest pigment to the Ringer's skin, it was noticeably absent. I didn't need to be a doctor to know he was hanging on by a thread.

"Gareth!" Kale shouted, but he didn't move. He couldn't. I'd snatched Gareth's pistol out of the air and aimed it straight at the king of Titan's face.

A stroke of luck for once. I could end it all then, just like I'd helped get it started when I put Zhaff down. My hand wasn't even cramping this time. I was too sick for my compromised mind to hamper me. Kale Trass, or Drayton, or whatever he thought he was, had it coming. Not a soul on the *Cora*, even his allies, didn't know it.

But I didn't shoot.

Out of the corner of my eye, I noticed Aria's pleading face. I remembered when I'd killed the smuggler Elios Sevari to try and protect her—the first man she'd ever fallen in love with. I remembered all the times I'd let her down, and the last time I'd saved her by shooting my own partner and friend. Murdering Kale wouldn't free her from the life her bad choices led to. She wasn't one of them, and Rin would order our slaughter the moment I pulled the trigger. I could see that written all over her scarred face. Once the shooting started, nobody would get off the *Cora* alive.

So I made the only decision a father could. I coughed once, wiped my mouth, and then spared the boy king of Titan his warranted assassination. I released the gun and allowed his revolution to keep on churning.

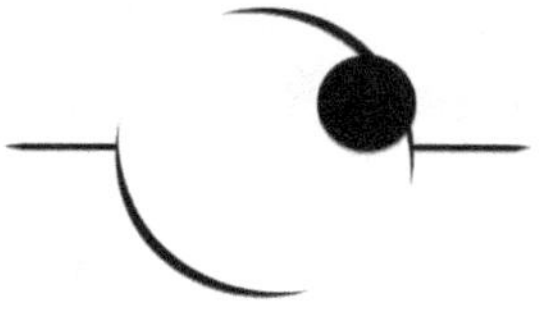

TWENTY-ONE

The moment Malcolm released the gun, I loosed my restraints, pushed off my chair, and zipped across the *Cora's* cockpit toward Gareth. I knew Malcolm wouldn't shoot, not with Aria there, but he'd wasted precious time.

"Earther scum!" Rin snarled as she shot forward and punched Malcolm across the face.

"Aria, he needs medical attention!" I said. Her gaze darted back and forth between the ship's controls and Gareth. "Now!"

Navigation could wait. So long as Venta upheld their end of things, drifting aimlessly through space posed no current threat. Aria unstrapped herself, glided over to us, and placed two fingers over Gareth's neck for a pulse.

"He's still alive," she panted. "We need to get him to the medical bay."

I nodded and grabbed the ceiling bars to help pull us along when I noticed Rin preparing to follow. "No. You have to stay and watch the collector."

"With all due respect, I'm no babysitter," Rin said.

"I'm happy to fly if you need a pilot," Malcolm muttered.

Rin grabbed Gareth's pistol and shoved it against Malcolm's cheek. "You sat there and let him bleed out!"

The old collector rolled his shoulders. "Seems like we all did."

Rin's hand quaked, and I was completely prepared for her to pull the trigger, when Aria intervened. "Would you shut up, Dad!" she snapped. "Just... just stay here and don't move."

Malcolm grabbed Aria's forearm, and they glowered into each other's eyes for a few seconds. Then he released her, exhaled, and allowed his head to sink back farther into his viscous headrest. He looked deathly ill. The radiation was ravaging his old body faster than his daughter's, but he didn't have a forming baby to worry about.

"Kale, let's go!" Aria shouted.

We drew Gareth's weightless body through the *Cora* as quickly as possible. It would've been easier with gravity. The only ships I'd served on in my life endured more of it within Saturn's atmosphere, not its absence. On our way, Rin ordered a few of the healthy Titanborn seated in the hall outside the cockpit to keep an eye on Malcolm and prepare the sleep pods with anti-rad infusion.

The medical bay was down through the ship's mostly vacant galley. A few of the burnished cabinets were stuffed with ration bars, though with everyone but me put under for the journey, there hadn't been much need for anything else.

We whipped around the corner into the med bay and laid Gareth down on the table in the center. Everything around me was white, like the halls of the Darien Q-zone before I razed the place to the ground and booted Luxarn Pervenio from the Ring.

"I need to stem the bleeding," Aria said as she rifled through the magnetically sealed cabinets searching for equipment. "Get his suit off him."

I fumbled along his back searching for the switch that loosened his red-stained armor, but I could hardly see straight. All the white was dizzying. Rin brushed me aside and unlatched him herself. Then she started removing his suit. His bloody shirt was stuck to the inner layer and had to be peeled away like a shell.

Zero-g made it difficult for her to gain leverage, and after a few seconds, I gathered my bearings enough to help. Gareth was injured badly. I knew right away I should have never let him keep pushing himself. Not that it would've mattered. Thanks to Aria and her suddenly appearing father, there would've been no time to treat him before taking off.

"Kale, move!"

Aria shoved me out of the way and cut his shirt down the center with a scalpel. His milk-white stomach was drenched with blood. The gaping hole in its center bubbled. A perfectly angled shot had apparently sliced clean through his armor and out the back.

Aria sprayed Pervenio Corp congealer over the wound. I'd learned a bit from watching her work. The stuff was as cold as the surface of Titan, enabling it to slow the flow of blood cells and cause them to clot.

"Is that it, Doctor?" Rin said.

"His heart's stopped," Aria said. "Hold him down." She ripped a defibrillator off a rack on the wall, touched the two pads together, then held them over his chest. His body arched toward the ceiling when she pressed them down once.

"He's not breathing!"

"Come on, Gareth!" She went to shock him again but lost her grip on the handles. She turned toward the sink right in time before vomiting. It bounced around the rim in zero-g, streaks of red in the bile. I wasn't sure if it was the extreme radiation, which was enough to penetrate my suit or the sight of another dead friend, but I joined her at the sink and vomited as well.

"Give me those!" Rin snatched up the defibrillators and continued jolting Gareth. The parts of him not held down all slowly lifted, limp like the arms of a puppet. By the third try, I couldn't watch anymore.

"He's dead," I rasped, holding out my arm.

"N... no..." Aria stuttered. She wiped her mouth and tried to return to Gareth's body. "We can still—"

"He's dead!" I smacked the defibrillators out of Rin's hands. "I don't need to be a damn doctor to know that!"

"I can... still save him," Aria whimpered.

"You've done enough, Ambassador." Rin lowered her face over Gareth's and pressed her lips against his forehead. I remained completely frozen, watching. "From ice to ashes, old friend," Rin whispered. She ran her fingers over Gareth's eyelids to close them.

Aria's hand suddenly slipped as she went to push off the wall again, and she knocked into the med table, startling us both. She released a bloodcurdling moan and held her stomach. I felt the pain in my gut too, like someone was lighting a bonfire in the pit of my stomach, but Aria had been totally exposed in the hangar.

"Kale," Rin said.

"Gareth," I finally managed to utter. I grasped his hand, and his long fingers rolled across my palm as if they were slabs of rubber left in the freezer too long. Rin pried me free.

"Kale. If we don't get Aria to a pod soon, I fear for your child's life. I'll plot our route home and update Rylah. Aria. Aria!" She slapped Aria's face lightly to keep her conscious. Her freckled cheeks were discolored, and her eyes rolled aimlessly between brief stints of focus and moaning. It was only then, as her hand rubbed across the barely perceptible bulge of her belly, that I remembered what she carried inside of it.

"I've got her," I gasped. I wrapped my arm under her shoulder.

"She knows?" Aria looked up at me and wheezed. Her eyes were bloodshot.

I nodded.

"We don't have long before it hits us too," Rin said. "Our suits were made to withstand many things, but nothing could block an impulse drive that close completely."

"I know," I said. "I feel it."

"The IVs in the sleep pods should all be set to pump us with every ounce of anti-rads that came with this thing."

"What about Gareth? We can't just leave him here like this."

"Oxygen to the ship will be off while we're all under. His body will be right here when we wake, unspoiled just like all the others. Now let's go."

"I don't want to sleep."

Rin took me by the jaw. "I know, Kale, but you have to this time. Pretend it's a long dream."

I bobbed my head. I didn't have the energy to fight her. Rin rushed by us on her way to the cockpit, and I took Aria around the waist so we could head to the sleep pods. She muttered incomprehensibly. I froze in the entry for a moment and stared back at the corpse of my guardian. Gareth always had a grim demeanor, like there was a foul taste in his mouth that he couldn't rid himself of. Until now. He looked almost... peaceful.

"Kale!" Rin called back to me. I finally tore my gaze away.

I swam down the corridors of the *Cora* with Aria in tow, through stale, frigid air that suddenly bore the heady stench of death. We drifted too hard and slammed into the controls for Aria's sleep pod. I righted myself and hovered in place to prepare the pod for her entry. My surviving guards were already busy loading themselves into theirs. Some were in worse condition than others. We knew releasing an ion stream at such close proximity was a risk, but whatever the *Cora* was packing in her prototype impulse drives was clearly worse than anticipated.

I fumbled with Aria's IV line as I raised her arm to stick it in. My fingers were getting numb. My stomach rolled. I lifted her weightless body to place her in the pod, and as I did, she leaned forward and pressed her lips against mine.

"I'm so sorry, Kale," she whispered. "I should have told you about him..."

I ignored her and tried to focus on getting everything hooked up properly. She was sick for two now. That was my main concern. She'd secretly enhanced her pod to provide nutrients for two before we left Titan, but nobody expected radiation sickness.

I lowered her into the gelatinous substance filling the pod and checked her IV and other connections.

"He didn't make it, did he?" Malcolm asked. He was being escorted by two of my guards. His lips went taut as he battled the same horrible pain that afflicted Aria. "Pressure from acceleration probably squished the blood out of him like a wet sponge."

"Be quiet, Dad," Aria said. She rolled her head from side to side and squeezed her eyes in agony.

"I want you to know exactly the type of man you're serving." He cleared his throat. "He'd rather run than slow down to save one of his own. Think about what he'll do with you if he has no other choice."

"Please... just stop."

"That's enough, Earther!" one of the guards barked. Malcolm was too debilitated to do anything about it as they stuffed him into a sleep pod, right next to the one in which Basaam Venta slept soundly. Two Earthers now on *my* ship.

"Kale..." Aria reached out and grazed my cheek. "I'm sorry..."

"If I hadn't let you leave, he'd still be alive," I said. "They all would be."

"We... we didn't know what she'd do..."

I folded her arms over her chest and signaled calming pharma to be injected into her veins and induce slumber. Then anti-rads would begin cleansing her system along with my unborn child's.

"You can't blame yourself for Gareth, Kale..." she uttered as she began to get drowsy. "You can't..."

I stared at her. Her leaf-green eyes glittered, that broken girl who'd eased my own anguish returning once more. That girl who had been there, right when she needed to be, and then conceived my child. And now she had her fingerprints all over everything that had gone wrong on Mars. The summit, a hostage negotiation, the Pervenio Cogents attacking under the lead of her estranged father—everything.

"I don't blame myself," I said, then pushed the pod's lid to seal her in.

Rin and Gareth were right. I really didn't know anything about her at all. And she sure as Trass wasn't one of us.

I turned, and one of my guards was immediately there to escort me. "Your pod is prepped, Lord Trass," he said. "I'll help you."

"I'll do it myself."

I headed straight for the open pod beside Malcolm's. My people were busy ensuring all of us got loaded in safely before worrying about him, even though he was in the worst shape. So I took it upon myself to hook him up, just as I'd done for his daughter. If what he told me about Luxarn Pervenio's hiding place was true, he would prove an asset.

"Every death is on you, Drayton," he grated. I stabbed his

arm with an IV needle as forcefully as I could. The veins on his irritated throat bulged as he released a half laugh, half chuckle. "That's what it means to be a leader. You don't get to blame the Earthers for your problems anymore."

"I could let you die, you know," I said. "Tell her the radiation ravaged your withering body before we could get you under."

"And I wouldn't blame you one bit. Just like you wouldn't have blamed me if I'd pulled the trigger."

"Only you didn't."

Malcolm groaned and leaned his head back into the pod. "I didn't."

I grabbed on to the edge and, hand over hand, pulled my weightless body up so that I could look down into it. The viscous substance formed around his body, the pod automatically stabbing a few more needles into the side of his neck.

"Do you know when I realized that I'd do anything to keep my people free?" I asked.

"Was it when you dropped a ship on thousands of officers?" Malcolm joked, then coughed. "Or no, before that. How about when you had the innocent Earther crew members of a gas harvester publicly executed and let all the Ringers on board, your own people, take the rap for it? Yeah, that must've been it."

I didn't let him get under my skin. Instead, I told him the truth. "One of your people took Rin's sister hostage, and we went to rescue her," I said. "A Pervenio man, like yourself. He set a trap, and as we were escaping it, I passed a room filled with children. Earther children. You see, he'd left them there to die because apparently, living under our rule wasn't worth living at all. So do you know what I did next?"

"I'll bet it's heroic."

"I left them there to die. I probably had time to save them, but I didn't. Future collectors, baton-wielding security officers, and corporate directors—I let them all be swallowed by Saturn. I still see their faces when I close my eyes, but I did what had to be done."

He didn't answer. He merely leveled his heated sickly gaze in my direction. I could tell how difficult it was for him to keep his eyes straight, but he managed.

"You're my collector now, Malcolm Graves," I said. I removed his hand-terminal from my pocket—Gareth's last heroic move, which ensured the collector wouldn't be able to contact his boss while we were all distracted. Then I pressed it against Malcolm's thumb, unlocking the screen.

"You're going to help me get to Luxarn Pervenio when the time is right," I said, shaking the device in front of his face, "and together, we'll show him and every Earther in Sol what it means to be afraid."

Even with all Malcolm's assumed training, his expression told all. I had him. I started to close the lid of his sleep pod until he whispered, "This is all about her, isn't it?"

I stopped. "Aria? She's lucky she's alive with all the secrets she kept from us. Her relations with Madame Venta, you—"

He shook his head. "No, Cora."

Hearing her name stunned me to silence.

"The girl you named this ship after," Malcolm said. "The girl who you left behind on the *Piccolo* while you ran off to play rebel. Who you left to die at the hands of a tired bigot like Sodervall. He may have flipped the switch, but you put her there."

"Don't," I said, seething.

"That's it. Cora's dead and you can't handle it because deep down you know the truth. That it's your fault."

"No."

He chuckled then coughed. "You put this crown upon your own head, Drayton. I hope you wear it proudly."

"No!" I slammed the lid and pushed off. Rin was there to catch me, apparently finished plotting our course in the cockpit. She rubbed my shoulders in a way that told me she hadn't heard what he'd said.

"It's time to sleep, Kale," she said.

Her sanitary mask was removed, making the clicking of her tongue against her marred cheek with every hard syllable more noticeable. She prodded me back toward my own pod and held my body against the rim.

"Get off of me!" I roared, throwing her aside and pulling my body toward the command deck, panting like a madman.

"What are you doing?" she asked as I hunched over the navigation and started keying commands.

"We're making one stop before we go home." I set the ship to slow a short distance away from Europa. Then I raised Malcolm's hand-terminal to my face. Luxarn Pervenio's personal contact information was already pulled up, with one cryptic message sent to him from Malcolm. I started drafting one of my own, forcing myself to focus as sickness made me see two of every key.

YOU'LL PAY FOR ALL THAT YOU'VE TAKEN FROM US, LUXARN. WHAT I DID TO SODERVALL WON'T EVEN COMPARE. I HAVE YOUR COLLECTOR, AND YOU'RE NEXT.

"Kale," Rin said, laying her hand on my shoulder. She leaned over me to get a look at where I'd set our coordinates. "You don't plan on—"

"I do," I said. Then I sent the message to the man who'd turned my home into his own personal bank. I wheezed a few times while staring at the screen, the adrenaline driving me slowly waning. After a few long seconds, Rin tore the device out of my hand. I couldn't fight her, even with my suit augmenting my strength. I tried to snap at her, but a fit of coughing made it impossible.

She switched it off, then pried open the back and removed the battery. "In case they try to use it to track us," she said, coughing as well. She stored it in her pocket. "Now let's get you loaded up before it's too late."

She helped me back to my pod since I could barely feel my limbs. One by one, she helped remove the sections of my armor. The pieces fell away from me into the depths of the *Cora,* and then I plunged backward into the pod.

"He won't have died for nothing," Rin said as she hooked me in. I didn't respond. I couldn't. My brutally scarred aunt continued prepping me for sleep as if she were my mother, until soothing pharma was flowing through my veins.

"I know you're worried about your child, but he's going to be fine," Rin assured me. "These anti-rads are strong, and it hasn't been long. I'll pull him out of that deceitful witch myself if I have to."

It took every ounce of what little energy I had remaining, but I reached up and closed the lid myself before she could manage another word. Silence enveloped me. I was finally alone.

I wasn't sure what would happen next. The inside of the pod felt like it was spinning, and everything seemed like a lucid dream. I hadn't wanted to be put under during our voyage to Mars because I was afraid I'd forget Cora, but at that moment, forgetting was all I wanted to do. I wanted to evaporate into the sky of Titan.

I told myself over and over that what Malcolm said was wrong. That he was only trying to get a rise out of me. Every death couldn't possibly be on me. I couldn't control everything.

And as I lied to myself, again and again, my world went dark...

EPILOGUE

Undina was an unassuming place. A metal-rich asteroid dragged into near-Earth orbit a few million kilometers beyond the moon by Pervenio Corp to help with the construction of the Departure Ark, Hermes. The pull Luxarn used to have for the USF to allow him to draw a celestial body so near to Earth considering the fear people still held of meteorites... Madame Jamaru Venta longed for it.

Yet the interior bore none of the sleek walls and smartly designed spaces indicative of Pervenio Corp. The moment Madame Venta landed in the hangar, she felt like she'd stepped into the deepest slum on Mars. The whole place was rundown, rusting. It stank of burned-out engine cores, and there was an overbearing metallic tinge to the air, like Luxarn's entire operation was bleeding out. A dockhand shuffled over, boiler suit rumpled and covered in grime, e-cig hanging out of his lips. Miners lounged about in the adjacent galley, nothing to do, disinterested. No drills or haulers echoed from the deep. In fact, for a mine that was still considered active, the cavernous halls were deathly quiet.

Jamaru spent a lifetime in rivalry with Luxarn Pervenio.

She held equal parts respect and hatred for the man but seeing his company plunge so far troubled even her. It wasn't pity—he'd done enough never to deserve that—but she knew how easily Venta could now wind up in the same place, dragged through the mud by some ill-fated offworlders who thought the universe owed them something.

Sol was truly changing.

A doctor met her by the opposite end of the hangar. The old hag had skin like wrinkled parchment and hair she didn't even bother to comb.

"This way," she croaked. She led Jamaru Venta and the armed collector guarding her to a lift. The doctor stuck out her arm to bar her. "Not him," she said, nodding at her escort.

"Excuse me?" Jamaru glared down at the doctor's arm. Nobody in her company would dare have the balls to touch her or to also ask her to enter a meeting in a mysterious place alone. She'd been under constant guard ever since Red Wing Company allowed that savage Ringer, Kale Trass, to escape. Ever since she found her favored clan-children in New Beijing, charred and brutalized at his hands.

"Mr. Pervenio would prefer to keep the contents of this facility undisclosed."

He's really lost it, Jamaru thought. She wanted to curse at the doctor and go back to her ship, but instead, a sigh came out. She'd come this far already. No need for company to make a deal with the devil.

"Wait with the ship," she ordered the collector.

"Madame," he replied. "You shouldn't go in alone."

"I've known Luxarn for decades. He wouldn't dare touch me."

She stepped into the lift, which took them deep into the bedrock of Undina. She could feel the gravity relax as they delved further away from the surface and the centripetal force of the asteroid's incited spin. Deeper than the mines. When the doors opened, she finally entered a place that looked like it belonged to the former wealthiest man in Sol.

Clean metallic walls with genuine wood trim, polished tile floors—the place was as well put together as anything she owned. An artist couldn't paint the picture of a more perfect research facility. There wasn't even a mote of dust in the air. One or two researchers strolled down an adjacent hall, but that was all.

"He's waiting for you inside," the doctor said when they reached the polished doors at the end of a long hall. She muttered something to a hovering service bot, and it sputtered a response, then the doors slid open with a snap and hiss.

Luxarn sat on the edge of his mahogany desk within, staring at the entry like a dog waiting for a meal. The desk was the only luxurious thing inside. Like the rest of the facility, the room had a lifeless, clinical quality.

"I didn't think you'd actually come," Luxarn Pervenio said, smiling from ear to ear. She'd known him for decades, and for the first time, his age was starting to show. Wrinkles formed around his mouth and piercing eyes.

"Who's stupid enough to turn down a meeting with Luxarn Pervenio?" she replied, smirking. She knew he had to be mentally frail after losing so much. Petting his ego like he was still king of Sol seemed the best way to make sure she wound up on the more profitable end of their bargain.

"Too many people these days, I fear." He crossed the room and stuck out a hand. She hesitated before shaking it. She couldn't count on just those fingers how many deals they'd shattered between each other in their quest to rule Sol. They were members of the first clan-families to begin settling the worlds beyond Earth after the Meteorite hit. The old guard. Rivalry like theirs hadn't existed since the warring countries that existed before it.

Now all that was unraveling, thanks to Kale, like thread from a broken spool.

"I'm sorry about what happened," Jamaru said, struggling to make it sound wholly genuine.

"No, you aren't." He smirked, then turned his back to her and started pacing the room.

"You see right through me, as always. Things were simpler when it was just us out here."

"Was it that fun living in my shadow?"

"I..." She bit back a scathing response and took a measured breath. "I know we've had our differences, Luxarn, but I'm here. Don't waste my time."

"Differences? You helped them take the Ring. You think I don't know about the weapons you snuck over? The intel? You handed Titan to that monster on a silver platter."

"You know you would've done exactly the same. Neither of us had any idea it'd put a madman in power. It was politics, pure and simple."

"That's the only reason you're still alive."

Jamaru Venta scoffed. "At least you haven't lost your sense of humor."

He grinned, then snapped his fingers at his service bot. "Bot, get us drinks." It immediately hovered across the room to a mostly empty cupboard without asking what they wanted. Like he'd trained it to know.

"I don't drink," Jamaru Venta said.

"You do today," Luxarn replied.

"Luxarn, it's madness out there. Everyone is after a slice of your pie. Red Wing Company made a power grab... *Red Wing*, for Earth's sake. The USF is clueless—"

"Relax, Jamaru. If you're serious about this alliance, then everything will be taken care of."

"You got my attention, Luxarn, but if you want any more than that, I'll need to see more than some old mine."

The bot poked two glasses of whiskey into his hands with its spindly arms, and he sauntered back over to her, a hop in his step. She'd honestly expected him to be more somber. That was why she'd bought into this idea in the first place. She could manipulate that.

"Kale Trass has taken too many things I care about," Luxarn said as he approached her. "Now he's threatened my life, personally. It's time to end it."

He presented the glass and didn't leave Jamaru much choice but to take it. She hated putting anything in her body that blunted her wit.

"PerVenta Corp," Luxarn ruminated. "Has a nice ring, doesn't it?"

She took one whiff of the vile liquid, which devoured the souls of weak men, and recoiled. "I'm not in the mood for your games," she said. "He killed my biological sons, Luxarn. Not clan-children. They came from my belly, and he torched them like kitchen meat. Now I'm not agreeing to a thing until you tell me what this plan of yours is."

"First, we show Red Wing what happens when you side against your own kind," Luxarn said.

"How?"

He put on a wicked grin, took a long sip of his drink, and then gestured to the door. Madame Venta turned to see a young offworlder standing in the doorway wearing the white armor of the Children of Titan, an orange circle printed on his chest. At first, she shuddered, thinking she'd been betrayed and sold out to the Ringers; then she noticed his vacant expression.

He looked like one of Luxarn's Cogent agents, only the eye lens covering this one's right eye wasn't only an apparatus; it was part of him. Shiny synthetics covered half his face, extending up over his skull so that hair only grew on one side, and down his neck toward his collarbone. The other side of his face was covered by sallow, veiny skin, with a calloused white human eye that didn't work. He was more machine than man, and as he faced blankly forward, Jamaru felt a very human chill run up her spine.

"Kale Trass may have taken your sons, but it's time for him to meet mine," Luxarn said as he wrapped his arm around the man's shoulders. "Thank you for that last bit of research that made this possible, Jamaru. Now Zhaff can finish what he started, and together, we will take back the Ring. Kale Trass will pay. For everything."

THANKS FOR READING!

To all you wonderful readers out there, I hope you enjoyed this book. Even if you didn't, please consider leaving an honest review wherever you prefer to leave your bookish thoughts online. Reviews are the lifeblood of newer authors like me, and they help more than you could possibly imagine.

And if you enjoyed this story about the growing rebellion on Titan, continue reading the rest of the *Children of Titan*! In Book 4, *Titan's Fury,* the tension between Titan and Earth comes to a head.

If you'd like to be updated about the series and its upcoming releases, as well as gain exclusive access to limited content, ARCs, and more, please subscribe to my monthly newsletter below.

Subscribe here: http://rhettbruno.com/newsletter

ABOUT THE AUTHOR

Rhett C Bruno is the USA Today Bestselling and Nebula Award Nominated Author of *The Circuit Saga* (Diversion Books, Podium Publishing), *Children of Titan* (Aethon Books, Audible Studios), and the *Buried Goddess Saga* (Aethon Books, Audible Studios); among other works.

He has been writing since before he can remember, scribbling down what he thought were epic stories when he was young to show to his friends and family. He currently works as a full-time author and publisher in Stamford, Connecticut, with his wife and their dog, Raven.

You can find out more about his work at www.rhettbruno.com

You can find out more about his work at www.rhettbruno.com

SPECIAL THANKS TO:

ADAWIA E. ASAD
BARDE PRESS
CALUM BEAULIEU
BEN
BECKY BEWERSDORF
BHAM
TANNER BLOTTER
ALFRED JOSEPH BOHNE IV
CHAD BOWDEN
ERREL BRAUDE
DAMIEN BROUSSARD
CATHERINE BULLINER
JUSTIN BURGESS
MATT BURNS
BERNIE CINKOSKE
MARTIN COOK
ALISTAIR DILWORTH
JAN DRAKE
BRET DULEY
RAY DUNN
ROB EDWARDS
RICHARD EYRES
MARK FERNANDEZ
CHARLES T FINCHER
SYLVIA FOIL
GAZELLE OF CAERBANNOG
DAVID GEARY
MICHEAL GREEN
BRIAN GRIFFIN

EDDIE HALLAHAN
JOSH HAYES
PAT HAYES
BILL HENDERSON
JEFF HOFFMAN
GODFREY HUEN
JOAN QUERALTÓ IBÁÑEZ
JONATHAN JOHNSON
MARCEL DE JONG
KABRINA
PETRI KANERVA
ROBERT KARALASH
VIKTOR KASPERSSON
TESLAN KIERINHAWK
ALEXANDER KIMBALL
JIM KOSMICKI
FRANKLIN KUZENSKI
MEENAZ LODHI
DAVID MACFARLANE
JAMIE MCFARLANE
HENRY MARIN
CRAIG MARTELLE
THOMAS MARTIN
ALAN D. MCDONALD
JAMES MCGLINCHEY
MICHAEL MCMURRAY
CHRISTIAN MEYER
SEBASTIAN MÜLLER
MARK NEWMAN
JULIAN NORTH

KYLE OATHOUT
LILY OMIDI
TROY OSGOOD
GEOFF PARKER
NICHOLAS (BUZ) PENNEY
JASON PENNOCK
THOMAS PETSCHAUER
JENNIFER PRIESTER
RHEL
JODY ROBERTS
JOHN BEAR ROSS
DONNA SANDERS
FABIAN SARAVIA
TERRY SCHOTT
SCOTT
ALLEN SIMMONS
KEVIN MICHAEL STEPHENS
MICHAEL J. SULLIVAN
PAUL SUMMERHAYES
JOHN TREADWELL
CHRISTOPHER J. VALIN
PHILIP VAN ITALLIE
JAAP VAN POELGEEST
FRANCK VAQUIER
VORTEX
DAVID WALTERS JR
MIKE A. WEBER
PAMELA WICKERT
JON WOODALL
BRUCE YOUNG